WHAT YOU WISH FOR

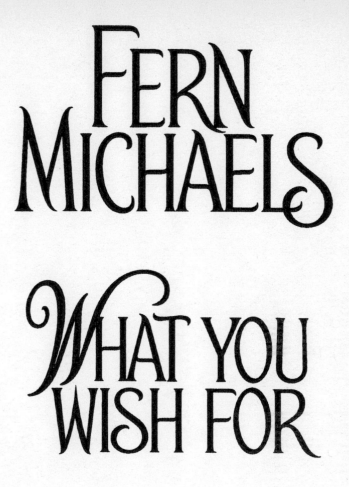

FERN MICHAELS

WHAT YOU WISH FOR

Kensington Books

KENSINGTON BOOKS are published by

Kensington Publishing Corp.
850 Third Avenue
New York, NY 10022

Kensington and the K logo Reg. U.S. Pat. & TM Off.

ISBN 1-57566-573-5

Printed in the United States of America

1

One by one, the million-dollar Tudor and Colonial houses in Whispering Willows twinkled to life as they announced the arrival of the Christmas season. Each elaborate display of multicolored lights and fragrant evergreens was testament to the annual Chamber of Commerce contest whose grand prize was a trip for two to Hawaii. The lone exception to the festive season was the unlighted house at 24565 Willow Lane.

Helen waited, her entire body trembling, for the door to open.

The terrier at her feet hugged her ankles, then started to whimper.

Helen let her gaze sweep through the rooms. As always, she was amazed at the costly furnishings, the custom draperies, the thick pile carpeting, the antiques, the art on the walls. Her life in a trailer park hadn't prepared her for this grandeur. None of the rich furnishings were to her taste, though. She preferred cozy and comfortable, but her husband Daniel lived to outdo his neighbors and coworkers with fine things. Among other things, her husband was a braggart.

Her image bounced off the foyer mirror—the image her husband would see when he opened the door. Maybe she should have slipped into a sack dress instead of the sweats. Surely those dark brown eyes full of terror weren't hers. Would the rich chestnut hair piled high on her head stay in its pins once Daniel entered the house? Who was this tall, shapely woman? A woman who was terrified of her husband, she answered herself. She wished she could lie down and go to sleep for a week. She wished she had the courage to run out into the night and never return. She wished she was a widow. She wished for so many things, but most of all she wished for peace and harmony. None of her wishes was within her grasp.

Helen tore her gaze away from the foyer mirror.

The car had careened into the driveway much too fast. The slam of the car door was too forceful, too loud. All indicators that Daniel Ward was in a rage. When Daniel was in one of his rages, she ended up bruised and bloody. An icy chill ran down Helen Ward's spine. The little dog whimpered.

"Go in your bed, Lucie. Hurry! Run, Lucie!" The little dog listened to the terror in her mistress's voice and scampered off, her pudgy rear end wobbling from side to side.

Her eyes full of fear, her shoulders stiff with apprehension, Helen struggled for a light tone when the front door burst open. "Hello, Daniel, did you have a good day?" She wondered if the terror showed on her face. Obviously it did, because Daniel's eyes narrowed to slits as he strode through the living room, stopping in the doorway to the dining room, where she was standing. He was so close she could smell his breath.

"I thought I told you to be ready when I got home. Christ Almighty, do you *ever* do anything you're told?"

"I am ready, Daniel. All I have to do is slip on my dress. It's linen, and I didn't want it to wrinkle," Helen said, her gaze never leaving her husband's face.

"Then why in the goddamn hell did you buy a linen dress? You're going to look like a fucking bag lady by the time we get to the party."

"Then I'll wear something different. It's not a problem, Daniel."

"Do I have to do all your thinking? Why can't you ever make a decent decision? You're supposed to wear something festive and sparkly to a Christmas party. Linen is not sparkly and festive. Linen is boring, just like you, Helen."

Maybe if she turned now and headed for the bedroom, he'd let it go. Maybe a lot of things. She wasn't going to move, and she knew it. How could she? Her feet were rooted to the floor.

Daniel stepped forward and then to the side, his feet scattering pine needles that had dropped from the Christmas tree. "What the fuck do you do all day, Helen? Why are these needles all over the floor? Look! They're all over the dining-room table, too. How goddamn hard is it to clean up pine needles?"

Helen's voice was a mere whisper. "The evergreens are dry. I did sprinkle water on the centerpiece. There's water in the tree stand. I cleaned it several times today. The tree and centerpiece are two weeks old," she murmured. She wasn't sure if her husband heard her defense or not. In the end, it wouldn't matter.

"Are you telling me I made a bad choice when I picked out the tree and the centerpiece?" His voice was so ugly, so hateful, Helen felt her insides start to shrivel.

Yes, yes, yes. "That's not what I said, Daniel. The trees are dry from the lack of rain this summer. The man at the tree stand told us that when we bought the tree. It's been on the news, too. The commentators are warning people to be careful of Christmas tree fires."

"I didn't hear the tree man say that, and I sure as hell didn't hear it on the news either. You're just one fucking excuse after another. Clean up this damn mess or we're going to be late."

To Daniel, cleaning up the mess meant dragging out the vacuum cleaner, brushing the needles into a neat little pile, then scooping them up with a dustpan followed by a thorough vacuuming. The centerpiece would require a clean tablecloth and then more needles would fall. The vacuum would have to be returned to the closet. More time, thirty minutes at best. Those thirty minutes would make them late for Arthur King's yearly Christmas party. She wanted to cry. Instead she bit down on her lower lip until she tasted her own blood. She had to get the vacuum cleaner and she had to get it *now*.

Don't look at his eyes. Just get the vacuum. Easy to say, not so easy to do. "I'll just be a minute, Daniel."

"A minute my ass. It's going to take you at least a half hour if you do it right. You still have to get dressed. You should have been dressed and waiting at the door. King hates it when anyone is late. He plans on some big announcements this evening. That means a promotion. How's it going to look when we arrive an hour late?"

Helen's shoulders slumped. There would be no party for her

tonight. *Just do it, Daniel, and get it over with. Beat me black-and-blue and then storm out of the house. Do it already*, her mind shrieked.

She took the first blow high on her cheekbone. The second punch sent her reeling backwards straight into the Christmas tree, toppling it sideways. She was aware of tinkling glass and a flurry of pine needles whipping past her face. She felt her own warm blood trickling down her cheek and neck. Stitches. God in heaven, what excuse would she give the ER people this time? She struggled to right herself, but the prickly, dry pine branches were everywhere. Suddenly she was yanked upright, her head jerking backward. A hard driving punch to her chest threw her into the tree a second time. She screamed before she lost her breath. "Stop! Please, Daniel, stop! Go to the party. I'll clean this up. Tell them I have the flu. Please, Daniel!"

"Damn right, you'll clean this up. I'm tired of lying for you. You ruin everything! You think you know everything. You're just like my mother and my sister, but they have brains. You're fucking stupid, Helen. There's not a brain in your head."

Gasping for breath, Helen struggled to extricate herself from the Christmas tree. She was on her knees when she saw Daniel raise his foot. She tried to roll away but the trunk of the huge evergreen and its branches held her prisoner as her husband's foot shot forward with 180 pounds of force. She screamed and screamed as hot flashing pain seared her body. She knew she was going to black out. She even welcomed the darkness she would slip into.

A furious flurry of movement startled her. Her one good eye fixed on the small terrier bent on coming to her aid. She saw Daniel's foot rise a second time, saw Lucie on the end of his shoe, and then Lucie was sailing through the air to land next to her head in the nest of evergreens. "You bastard! You miserable, stinking bastard," Helen shrieked. With every ounce of will left in her body, she rolled away from the tree to land next to the hearth, where she grappled for the fire tongs that had fallen over. Above her own screeching voice she could hear Lucie whimpering. "I'm coming, Lucie, I'm coming, baby."

The poker in her hand, she was on her knees, pain driving through her body as she struggled to get upright. The moment she saw Daniel start to raise his foot a third time she swung the poker with all her might. The instant Daniel doubled over, she swung a second time, down across his back. "How does it feel, you son of a bitch? How does this feel, Daniel?" Helen screamed as she jabbed the poker into the small of her husband's back. When she saw blood start to soak his jacket she lifted her leg and brought her foot down on her husband's head and ground the heel of her sneaker back and forth. "Wait a minute. You need to feel this, too." She raised her foot again and sent it crashing into his side, not once, not twice, but three times. "Now go to your damn party. You have yourself a fucking good time. You hear me, Daniel!" Helen raged. The pain in her body was so intense she reached out to hold on to the mantel.

A second later she had Lucie in her arms. She crooned to the little dog as she staggered out into the dark night. "I'm taking you to a vet, Lucie. I'll get you help. We're never going back there. I'll clean toilets in a dirty gas station before I go back there. You're going to be okay, baby. Just hang on. Please hang on, Lucie, you're all I have. It's going to be okay, Lucie. I promise. I promise, Lucie. I never make a promise I can't keep. Trust me, baby. I have to rest a minute. Just for a minute, Lucie. I have to get my bearings. I can't see very well. My eyes are swelling shut. It's going to be okay, Lucie. I promise. I promise, Lucie."

She was a deer caught in the headlights when a motorist screeched to a stop. Blinded by the light, Helen dropped to her knees. Her hold on the little dog was fierce.

"Lady, are you okay? What's wrong?" the driver shouted. "I didn't see you!"

It was a kind voice, a caring voice. "Help me. Please. Take me to the nearest vet. My dog needs attention. Can you do that?"

"Can you get in the car?" the caring voice asked.

"Yes. Please hurry. My dog needs a vet."

The good Samaritan's voice turned anxious. "There's a vet a few blocks away. I think his name is Davis. His office is in the back of his house. Is that okay?"

"I don't care if he works in a tent. It's fine. I appreciate this. I don't have any money to . . . pay you."

"I don't want any money. I don't even want to know what happened ... I don't mean that the way it sounds. What I meant was, I don't want to get involved."

"All I want is to get to a vet. You can drop me off, and you'll never see me again. Aren't we there yet?"

"We are now. I'll pull right into the driveway and ring the bell for you. I have to leave then. Let me help you. Jesus, lady, are you sure you're okay? You look worse than your dog. Take my arm. Do you want me to carry the dog?"

"I thought you didn't want to get involved. The answer is no. I'll hold my own dog. Thanks for the ride. Someday I hope I can return the favor."

"The light's on. A door's opening. Careful now. You need to see a doctor, lady."

"I will when I'm sure my dog is okay. Thanks again."

Tears rolled down Helen's cheeks as she walked into the sterile, antiseptic-smelling office. "Help my dog. Please. She's all I have. I know what I look like. Don't worry about me. I've been worse. You have to talk to her. She's scared. I just ran with her. Maybe I shouldn't have moved her. I didn't know what else to do. You can help her, can't you? I promised her she would be okay. I promised to take care of her forever and ever. I never break a promise. She's all I have. I'm all she has. Please, please, I beg you, help her."

"Young woman, sit! Do not move. That's an order! I will take care of this dog. It's what I do for a living. I'll patch you up when I'm finished with your pet. What's her name?" His voice while stern was not unkind.

"Lucie. She's all I have. I need you to understand that. She ... she likes it when you sing, 'Twinkle, twinkle, little star ...' " Helen's voice trailed off.

"I think I can handle that. Don't move, young woman. There's some brandy in a bottle over the sink. Take a couple of belts. You need it."

Helen took a minute to stare into a set of kind eyes. The perfect vet. White hair, pink cheeks, wire-rim glasses, warm smile, and wonderful hands. Hands that would make Lucie well. She nodded as she swigged from the brandy bottle.

And then she waited.

Time lost all meaning as Helen stared at the sterile-looking wall with its pictures of heartworms, fleas, and other parasites. She prayed for Lucie, cursed her husband, and then asked for forgiveness for her wicked thoughts.

Was Daniel dead? She hoped he was. Mean, ugly people like Daniel didn't die. They just lived on to torment other people. If Daniel died, she would be a murderer. She'd go to jail. Who would take care of Lucie? Would Dr. Gerald Davis take her in and love her the way she loved her? Maybe she should call the house to see if Daniel was alive or dead. If police answered the phone, then she'd know he was dead.

What was going to happen to her? If Daniel was still alive, would he file a police report? Would the authorities start looking for her? She didn't have a nickel to her name. Maybe she could go to a woman's shelter. Maybe this kindly vet would take her there. Then again, maybe he was like the good Samaritan who didn't want to get involved. What time was it? Somehow she'd lost her watch.

She heard his quiet tread. She looked up. How tall he was. Almost as tall as Daniel. She struggled to get up, but the vet put his hand on her shoulder, an indication that she should stay seated.

"Lucie is resting. You're right, she calmed right down when I started to . . . ah . . . sing to her. We'll know more in the next few hours. I won't lie to you. It's going to be touch-and-go."

"I want to see her."

"She's sleeping. She's stable."

"I don't care. I need to see her. She needs to feel my touch. Dogs can tell even when they're sleeping. I don't want her to think I deserted her. Please."

Helen limped behind the vet, her hand flying to her mouth when she saw her beloved little dog lying so still. She threw herself over the animal and started to babble. "Don't you die on me, Lucie. Do you hear me? You're all I have. I didn't bring you here to die. I brought you here to get better. It's me and you, Lucie. We're never going back there, not ever. Do you hear me? Not ever. I'm going to find someone to help us. First you have to get better. I promised to take care of you forever and ever. I never break a promise, Lucie. 'Twinkle, twinkle, little star, how I wonder where you are . . .'

"Now, she's sleeping. It's a good sleep. She needed to hear my voice, to know I'm here. I can tell by the way she's breathing. Look, Dr. Davis, see for yourself."

"Well, gosh darn, and to think I went to medical school all those years and never learned to sing to a dog. You're right. She is breathing easier. Come now, let me see what I can do to fix you up. Lucie is okay for now. We're just going to be in the next room. Take a couple of more pulls from that brandy bottle. You're going to need some stitches. I suspect you have a couple of cracked ribs, too. Who did this to you?"

"My husband." God, it was such a relief to say the words out loud.

"How long has he been doing this to you?"

"A long time. I wanted to leave. I tried, but he always found me and dragged me back. I have no money, nowhere to go. I . . . I didn't want anyone to know. I feel so . . . dirty, so pathetic. I tried . . . no matter what I did it wasn't good enough. He would always say he was sorry, he'd promise never to do it again. There's so much pressure on his job. He'd bring me gifts, be really nice to me for a while, and then he'd do it all over again. I called a shelter once, and he found out. He would come home and check the phone to see whom I called. It has that button on it. He said if I ever tried to do that again, he'd kill Lucie. Tonight was the last straw for me. He never hurt Lucie before. He's the one who gave her to me. When Lucie is well enough, can you take me to a shelter? I'll find a way to make it up to you. It might take me a while, but I will repay you."

"Lift up your shirt. I'm going to take some X rays. Young lady, you are in worse shape than your dog. Why didn't you ever report this to the police?"

"Fear is a terrible thing, Dr. Davis. I lived in fear, every day of my life. Just the thought of going to the police was more than I could bear. I'm a coward. I truly, truly believed he would kill me. Lucie made it all bearable. She loves me."

"Yes, I believe she does. Animals are amazing. They bring comfort, they love unconditionally, and they are loyal. Man's best friend. A woman's, too," the vet added hastily.

"She got me through some bad times. I can't tell you how much I love her."

"I think I have a pretty good idea. Now that we have you all patched up, I think it might be a good idea if I set up a cot here next to Lucie. I'm about ready to call it a night myself. Not as young as I used to be. I'll be retiring very soon. If you need me, just go through the door from the examining room and call me. I'll sleep with one eye and ear open."

"I don't know how to thank you, Dr. Davis."

"All the thanks I need is seeing you and Lucie getting better. Is there anything I can get you before I retire?"

"No. You don't have to get a cot. I can sleep in the chair. I'm going to have to leave in the morning. Daniel is going to be looking for me. He knows he hurt Lucie and knows I would take her to a vet."

"From what you've told me, I don't think he's going to come looking for you for a few days. I imagine he might be in the hospital himself. I can check that out in the morning. Call me if Lucie wakes up. I don't think she will, but she might."

Helen nodded as she waited for the vet to return with a folding cot, blankets, and pillow.

The moment the door closed, Helen opened the oversize kennel door and climbed in next to Lucie. Tears rolled down her cheeks. "Twinkle, twinkle, little star, how I . . ."

In his upstairs bedroom, Gerald Davis picked up the phone and punched in a set of numbers. "Izzie, Gerry. I need you to come over to the office first thing in the morning. I have someone I want you to meet. She needs you, Izzie, and her dog Lucie needs you. The morning will be time enough, I'm sure. I knew as soon as I mentioned Lucie you'd want to barrel right over here. Trust me. Five-thirty will be fine." The vet sighed. "You aren't going to sleep, are you? Fine, come now. Use the front door. Coffee? I was thinking more along the lines of a double shot of bourbon. I'll have it ready. I knew I could count on you. I'll see you in a bit."

*   *   *

She was one hundred pounds of pure energy as she sashayed into Gerald Davis's living room. "I hope no one saw me coming here at this hour of the night. It could damage your reputation, Gerry. Where is she?"

"For God's sake, Izzie, sit down and have a drink. The young lady and her dog are sleeping. There's nothing we can do till it gets light, and I'm not sure we can do anything then. I'm not even sure the little dog is going to make it. I think she will, but I'm not sure. I've never seen anything so sad in my life. Well, maybe once before. Okay, okay, let's go. Not a peep, Izzie. We look in the door, and that's it. Swear!"

"I swear. What took you so long in calling me?" the little woman squawked. Gerry ignored her as he tiptoed to the operating room.

"Lord have mercy," Isabel Tyger whispered as she wiped at a tear in her eye. She handed her tissue to Gerry, who gave his own eyes a quick swipe.

In the kitchen, Isabel, hands on hips, her voice shaking with rage, demanded to know who the woman was.

"I don't know. I didn't ask her name. I figured I was ahead of the game when she told me the dog's name. She said her husband beat her. This time she gave back as good as she got. All these years she never fought back. Never defended herself. Tonight the husband attacked her dog. That was her breaking point. Some good might come of this, Izzie. You'll take her to your shelter when she's well enough, won't you?"

"Yes. She won't leave the dog, you know that, don't you?"

"She can stay as long as necessary. I just want to make sure she has a place to go to. My fear is the husband might show up. He's likely to canvass all the vets in the area."

"If he shows up, you lie, Gerry. Where's the bourbon you promised me?"

"Make me a double, Izzie. It's going to be a long night, and we need a plan."

Isabel Tyger, wealthy philanthropist and lover of animals, poured generously.

"I called you because . . ."

"I know why you called me," the diminutive woman said. "Drink up!"

"No, Izzie, I need to tell you. She kept talking to the little dog, saying, I promised to take care of you for the rest of your life. I made a promise to you. She said it over and over. It took me back, Izzie. I remember you saying those exact same words, and there was nothing we could do. This is our chance now, yours, mine, and Artie's. Do you understand what I'm saying?"

"Yes, of course I do. I think you're right. Thank God that motorist brought her to you and not that yuppie vet two blocks over. You look tired, Gerry. Go to bed. I'll stay here with them. She's going to be one very sore lady come morning. Aren't you glad now I made you get that Jacuzzi? She's going to need it. She looks familiar to me. I've seen her someplace before."

"If you figure it out, don't wake me. Tell me in the morning. Thanks for coming over, Izzie."

"I guess it's payback time for all the times I woke you and Artie at four in the morning to come out to the ranch."

"Go easy on that bottle. I'm just going to take a catnap. Wake me if things go awry."

"All right, Gerry. Sleep well."

In the blink of an eye, Isabel slid off the chair and trotted into the clinic, where she gently eased herself to the floor. She stared at the sleeping woman and dog, her thoughts taking her back in time to a place and a time she hated. She stretched out her hand to smooth the hair back from the young woman's face, but her eyes were on the little dog. Tears rolled down her cheeks. She blinked them away.

Sometimes memories were a terrible thing.

2

"The sun is about to come up, Gerry. Shouldn't we be checking on your patients? Good Lord, I didn't realize how long a night could be."

"We just checked on them thirty minutes ago, Izzie," Gerald said, using the childhood nickname he'd favored for Isabel while they were growing up.

"You haven't called me Izzie for a while. Last night was the first time in a long time. The name always makes me smile for some reason. It makes me feel young again. But if I'm going to help this woman, you'd better call me something else in her presence. How about Billie?"

"Okay Izzie. Billie it is. And I know what you mean. I wish you would stop being such a recluse. You refuse to go out in public unless it's something catastrophic like tonight. You don't want to go to dinner or a movie when I do call or Artie calls. You'll always be Izzie to me just the way Arthur is Artie. We're old, Izzie, in case you haven't noticed. I've made up my mind to retire next year. I'll sell off the business, and we'll go fishing every day."

"Did you just realize we're getting old, Gerry? It's okay, my friend. All three of us made a difference. We didn't walk down the road taking up space or breathing other people's air just to get to this point in time. We've all contributed." Isabel's voice turned as flat as the vet's when she said, "They will remember us, won't they, Gerry?"

"Thousands of women will remember that you gave them a new lease on life with your shelters, Izzie. The high-tech world has named Artie 'Business Leader of the Year' five years running. I'm not sure about me."

"If there was ever a horse's patoot, you're it, Gerry! You've saved thousands and thousands of animals. You've made people happy, especially children. I remember the day you brought me forty animals and stood there with tears streaming down your cheeks. You marched right into the pound and stole those animals so they wouldn't be put to sleep. God knows that, Gerry. You're a savior."

"I couldn't have done it without you and Artie. I didn't have the money to feed them."

"You're getting maudlin, Gerry, and I refuse to be a party to self-pity. Now pull up your damn socks and let's check on your patients."

"You know who you remind me of, Izzie? That little woman, the doctor, what's her name? Dr. Ruth. You look just like her except you have red hair. You're sassy like her, too."

"I'm going to take that as a compliment. You're afraid, aren't you, Gerald?"

"Yes, Izzie, I am. Come along. Let's see what we can do. If they're still sleeping, we aren't waking them. Agreed?"

"All right, already. Let's get to it."

"Shhh," Gerald said, cracking the door to peer inside. "Listen."

"It's going to be light soon, Lucie. We made it through the night. I know you hurt. I'm going to call Dr. Davis in a minute. You are such a sweet girl. You have to get better. I'm not leaving you. Just let him try to kick me out of here. I won't let him. I'm going to stay with you until you can run like a rabbit. I'm going to get you a new ball. A bright red one. I might even have them put your name on it. They do that in those fancy dog boutiques. I don't care what it costs. When we're both better and I get a job, I'm going to get you the fanciest leash and collar I can find. You're going to look like a princess. I promised to take care of you. Dr. Davis is helping me to help you. I won't let you down. A promise is a promise. I need a sign, Lucie, just a little one. I hate him, Lucie. I hate him for what he did to you. 'Twinkle, twinkle, little star . . .' *Dr. Davisssss!*"

"I'm here. What's wrong?"

"It's Lucie. She licked my hand. That means she's going to be okay. That's what it means, doesn't it, Dr. Davis?"

"Absolutely, that's what it means," Isabel said happily. "It is, isn't it, Gerry?"

"Let's take a look. Do you think you could move over a little, young lady, so I can check my patient? I'm not asking you to get out. I'm just asking you to move. Ah, this is good, she's awake. Iz . . . Billie, get me some ice chips. We need to fix a new IV drip. We're looking good here, young lady. I'm referring to Lucie, not you," the vet said, addressing Helen.

"Is she going to be all right? I want you to tell me the truth, Dr. Davis. I am not moving. I'm staying right here."

"I told you last night you could stay as long as you like. I never say anything I don't mean. There's a world of difference since last night. Lucie isn't out of the woods yet, but I'd say her prognosis is getting better and better. I'm giving her a shot so she'll sleep, which is the best thing for her right now. When you feel it safe to leave for a few minutes, you might want to shower and brush your teeth. There's a Jacuzzi upstairs you might want to soak in for a while. I'd like to change your dressings and clean them up. Take your time. I'll be in the kitchen. By the way, I'd like you to meet a very good friend of mine. Billie, this is Jane Doe, and this is her dog Lucie.

"When you're ready to leave, Billie will take you to a shelter. For now, though, she's going to make us some breakfast. She makes wonderful waffles. Her coffee is just as good. Are you in pain?"

Helen looked into the vet's eyes and saw concern and compassion. Had she ever seen those two emotions? If so, when? She simply couldn't remember. "Yes. My name is Helen. Helen Ward."

"I like Jane Doe better," Izzie said. "Perhaps someday we can tell each other dog stories."

"I'd like that," Helen said.

"There's a small lavatory over there in the corner. When you're ready, we'll be in the kitchen. I don't start my office hours till eleven. If it will make you feel better, Billie will stay and help, and I'll give the girls the day off." Helen nodded gratefully.

In the kitchen, with the door closed, the vet turned to his old friend, and said, "Why do they stay, Izzie? Why do they let some s.o.b. do this to them?"

Isabel opened cabinets and banged doors. "Do you want the long version or the short version?"

"I don't want either one. I know why. I just said that to have something to say. She has bruises on top of old bruises. Scars, too. When she came in here last night, she said she'd been worse off. I had trouble with that statement. You saw her. What could be worse than how she looks now?"

"I know the name, Gerry. I think I've seen her someplace or at least her picture. She's a beautiful young woman. You're right. We are getting old. I can't remember things the way I used to."

"Let me ask you a question, Izzie. What do you think the chances are that this man will call the police or start to look for her? She said he would know she took the dog to a vet. Do abusers do that?"

"Of course they do. They want their punching bag back. They need someone safe who's afraid of them to take their anger out on. They're gutless scum, and, in my opinion, no amount of counseling helps. I've seen it too often. If she's willing, I'll take care of her."

"Only if the dog goes along. It's a package deal."

"I know that. I wouldn't have it any other way. Damnation, I know that name. I just hate it when I can't remember things."

"You have to shift into neutral, and when you least expect it, the answer pops up," the vet said.

"Smart-ass."

"Among other things. Are you going to Artie's Christmas party on Sunday? It will be his first solo party since Marie passed away. We have to go, Izzie. I think his company party was last night. Maybe it's tonight. See, I can't remember either."

"I hate those damn things. You sit around drinking too much wine, you eat too much, you gossip too much and end up talking about everyone. You take some tacky present out of a grab bag and go home. I'd rather stay home and watch reruns of *M*A*S*H*. I don't know why you even asked me that, since I never go. Are you going?"

"Can't. I have to cover for the Sanders's clinic since I had to attend that do-or-die Thanksgiving dinner of yours. He won't miss us. Artie will rag on us for a few days, and then he'll forget about it. He's done so well. Your shelters couldn't function without that program he designed." His voice turned sly. "We could stop in when the party is almost over. Just for a nightcap. I can use that confounded beeper if anyone needs me."

"God Almighty, that's it, Gerry. That's where I heard the name. Artie's top man is Daniel Ward. That's Daniel Ward's wife in there," Isabel said, jerking her head in the direction of the clinic door. "I've seen her pictures in ComStar's newsletters."

Gerald Davis sat down on the kitchen chair with a thump, his mouth hanging open. "Artie hires people like that?"

"Trust me when I tell you, Artie doesn't have a clue. Men like Daniel Ward are pros when it comes to covering up. Dear God, I was going to put her name in the system today. We can't do that now."

"Hold on, Izzie, you don't know for sure . . ."

"I do know for sure, Gerry. Artie has such high regard for Daniel Ward's capabilities he was considering having him take over when he retires. I'm telling you, he doesn't know, probably doesn't even suspect. If he did, his secretary Michelle would have told me. She works at the shelter three days a week. She's up on all this stuff."

"What are you going to do?"

"Make some discreet telephone calls," Isabel said.

"I think I'll take that pill now, Dr. Davis," Helen said, limping into the kitchen.

"Sit down, honey. I'm going to fix you some nice hot rum tea and some oatmeal. What in the world were you thinking of, Gerry, when you asked me to make waffles? Helen can't chew. You have some straws, don't you? Get her the pill, Gerry!"

Helen sat down gingerly. "Thank you." She felt tears welling in her good eye. When was the last time someone spoke so kindly, so compassionately to her? Never, that's when. She held out her hand for the two blue pills in Gerald Davis's hand.

"Gerry, you make breakfast. I'm going to take Helen upstairs and help her into the shower. Where can I find some clothes? Dry blood smells terrible. I think we can wash her hair, don't you?"

Gerald nodded. "I'll dress the wounds when you come down. Don't worry if the bandages get wet. Just let the water sluice over her. I'll sit with Lucie. I don't think any of us are in the mood for anything but coffee anyway."

Helen allowed herself to be led away, each step agony as she followed the little woman's spry steps.

She refused to meet Isabel's gaze as she stripped away her clothing. "No man will ever strike you again, my dear. You have my promise. I see your shame. You have to let that go. This is the first day of your new life. View it as such. In a day or so the Jacuzzi will work wonders for you. For now, step into the shower and let the water heal your body while I rummage for some clothing for you. Gerry's sister comes to stay for weeks at a time. She might have left some clothing behind."

Helen stepped under the soothing warm spray. How good it felt. She felt warm and safe. There was no one lurking outside the shower door to assault her. There was no one waiting downstairs to strike her senseless. The good Samaritan who had brought her and Lucie here last night had done her the biggest favor of her life. "Thank you, God," Helen said over and over.

Outside the door, Isabel wiped at her eyes. "I thank you, too.

"I found some clothes, Helen. Sweats. They're probably going to be a little big, but, personally, I like roomy clothes. We'll get you some new ones later today. I'll pat you dry, honey. We don't want to open any of your old cuts and bruises, not to mention your new ones. Stand still, and I'll slip this over your head. Can you pull on the underwear and pants? Good girl. Socks will do nicely. We aren't going to worry about shoes right now. Do you feel any better? Did the pills kick in?"

Helen nodded. "You're very kind. I am so grateful to Dr. Davis. What ... what if ... my husband ... I think I hurt him pretty badly. There was ... there was blood all over the place. He won't let that stop him. I know him. I know what he is capable of doing."

"Was capable. Those are the operative words. He can't hurt you anymore. You're safe now. Lucie is safe, too. Hold on to the railing and put both feet on each step. We have all day. Take your time."

Helen was exhausted by the time Isabel led her to the comfortable kitchen chair. "Tea or coffee?"

"Tea. Could you check on Lucie?"

Isabel was back in a moment. "She's sleeping. She's comfortable. Gerry was singing to her. I'm sure his voice isn't as soothing as yours, but his touch is gentle. Animals trust him. Lucie knows she's in good hands. I don't think it's a good idea for you to go back into her kennel. I think we might be able to fashion a bed for her at the far end of the clinic. Lucie isn't going to be doing much moving around, and you'll be more comfortable. I'm going to stay here today. I'll need some information from you before I can take you to the shelter. You will have to be honest with me."

"I'll tell you anything you want to know as long as you promise me my husband can't get to me and Lucie."

"I promise. For now, I want you to stop thinking of your husband as your husband. He is someone you used to know, someone who stole your life and then abused that life. He doesn't deserve the title of husband. Now, what is his name and where does he work? Do you know his social security number? I need to document everything where that man is concerned. No matter how insignificant a detail might seem, I want you to talk about it. Are we clear on this?"

"Yes, we're clear on everything."

"Good. Now, how old are you? Do you have children? Where exactly do you live?"

Helen blinked. She hated thinking about Daniel, and she detested talking about the man she'd married. "I'm 28. No, we don't have children. I secretly took the pill. I didn't want Daniel's children because I didn't know if he would abuse them or not. I kept the pills in my tampon box so Daniel wouldn't know I was taking them. We live . . . lived in Whispering Willows. Daniel insisted we move there because he said it was the place to live. There are several mortgages on the house now. Everything is on time payments. I wanted to get a job, but he said no."

"So typical," Isabel muttered.

Halfway through Helen's monologue, the phone rang. Isabel reached behind her to grab at the kitchen phone. "Davis Clinic."

She listened a moment before she said, "I just came in, let me put Dr. Davis on the phone." The color drained from Helen's face when she saw Isabel put her finger to her lips. Daniel.

Isabel opened the kitchen door that led into the clinic. "Dr. Davis, there's a gentleman on the phone who needs to speak to you." She mouthed the words, Helen's husband.

Helen struggled up from the chair she'd been sitting on to join Isabel in the doorway, her eyes wide with fear.

"Gerald Davis speaking. No, I haven't had any emergencies in over a week, Mr. Ward. As a matter of fact, I haven't taken on any new patients in over a year. You could try the Sanders Clinic. They're open twenty-four hours a day. Good-bye."

"How . . . how did he . . . sound?" Helen whispered.

"Normal. Said he was walking his dog and she ran into the road, got grazed, and then ran off into the night. He said he'd been searching all night for her."

"He'll come here. I know he will. I have to leave. You don't know my . . . you don't know this man."

"You can't leave, Helen," Isabel said. "Lucie can't be moved yet. You're safe. I'm going to sit at the desk all day. You are going to stay back here with Lucie. Gerald keeps the doors locked and the buzzer opens them. You have to trust us, Helen."

"I do trust you. It's *him* I don't trust. You don't know him like I do. You don't know what he's capable of doing to get what he wants."

Isabel wrapped her arm around Helen's shoulder. "It's true, I don't know the man, but I know thousands of men just like him. Those thousands of men have not gotten to one of the women in the shelter. In all the years we've been helping battered women, we only lost two. They elected to return to their husbands. One is now dead at her husband's hand, and the other one is still with her husband. She is still being battered."

"I'm going to sit with Lucie," Helen said. "If you need to know anything else, just ask me."

"I have enough for now. Take your tea with you. Gerry will help you make up a bed. It's going to be all right, Helen. You need to believe that," Isabel said gently.

"I want to believe you. I need to believe you. Why am I still afraid?"

"We're strangers. This is new to you. Your mind isn't ready to accept or believe there are people who truly care about you. It comes in time the way trust does. Go now, sing to Lucie."

When the door closed behind Helen, Gerry said, "Seems to me I remember you singing to that stray mutt you found when we were kids. You actually had him a whole year before your father found out."

"I couldn't have done it without you and Artie. God, how I loved that dog. You're right, I used to sing, 'You are my sunshine, my only sunshine' until my ears would ring with the words. He loved it. He'd bark and whine and howl."

Gerry laughed. "The best was when the three of us used to sing together. All off-key. As I recall, the dog loved it!"

"It was all so long ago, Gerry. Sometimes I can't believe I was ever young. My father . . ."

"We aren't going down that road today, Izzie. He's dead, let him rest in peace."

"He doesn't deserve peace. You're right. That road has too many potholes. It's almost ten o'clock. I'll sit out at the desk. Let me know if there's any change in Lucie. I'm going to get a head start on Helen's new life. I want to thank you, Gerry, for everything, especially for being my friend. Getting to this place in time wouldn't have been easy if it weren't for you and Artie."

"I hate maudlin women," Gerry said gruffly.

"Not as much as I hate maudlin men," Isabel said, tweaking his kneecap. "We're just a couple of old softies."

"You'll make it work for them, won't you, Izzie?"

"Of course, but she has to do her part. Talk to her today. She really needs to know someone cares. She trusts you, and that's half the battle as you well know."

"Do you want me to tell her about the sanctuary or do you just want me to talk about nothing?"

"Ordinary things at first, pave the way for the sanctuary. It will probably be your voice more than your words that will calm her down. She's scared out of her wits, and she has every right to be scared. People like Daniel Ward are like those monsters we used to think hid in our closets at night when we were kids. I'm calling Artie as soon as I get things squared away. I want that man off my project. I want new passwords installed immediately. It will tip him off, but I can't take the chance. I have to do it."

"Then do it. For whatever it's worth, you have my blessing."

"Thanks, Gerry."

"No. Thank *you*, Izzie."

3

Helen stared down at the green nylon bag that held her meager belongings. All compliments of a woman named Billie. In her life she'd never felt this alone, this vulnerable. Tears welled in her eyes. She did her best to blink them away.

"Are you having second thoughts, Helen?" the veterinarian asked.

"No, not really. I've always been afraid of the unknown. All I know is my past. My future is like a blank canvas. That frightens me. I've never been anywhere outside this state, outside this area really. I went straight from my mother's house to a small efficiency apartment. I worked at a boutique and the pay wasn't that great. I took night courses, graduated from college, and got a job with a graphics-design company. Daniel was the first man who showed any interest in me, and I fell for him. He was so unlike any of the men my mother brought home. He was all polished and handsome, and nine years older than I. The boys at school seemed immature and only wanted to score. My mother never cared about me, and her last man friend certainly didn't care about me. I knew it was just a matter of time before he homed in on me. That's why I moved out. My mother had a fit because she wanted me to pay her rent. Daniel made so many promises to me. He said he would take care of me for the rest of my life. For some reason hearing all those promises was important to me at that particular time. I tried to be a good wife, Dr. Davis. I know he's going to find me. Somehow, some way, he will. That frightens me more than anything."

"No, he will not find you. I want you to trust Billie and all the people at the shelter. They won't let it happen. I give you my word on that."

"How am I ever going to repay you, Dr. Davis?"

"You aren't. It's that simple. Seeing Lucie walk across the clinic floor was all the thanks I needed. Sometimes, young lady, when God is good to you, you have to give back. He has been very good to me. Someday you will do the same thing for someone. Kind of a trade-off. I'm going to miss you and our nightly game of checkers," the vet said gruffly. "Your spaghetti wasn't bad either. You realize you can never call me, don't you?"

The tears she'd been unable to hold in check rolled down Helen's cheeks. "I know."

"In many ways it's going to be like being in the Witness Protection Program. You and Lucie are going to be well taken care of. You'll rebuild your life, and someday you will meet someone worthy of your affection. Daniel Ward is never going to be able to hurt you again."

"Can I ask a question? I know you said questions are discouraged, but I want to know why, after that first day, Billie never came back. Is she your lady friend?"

Gerald Davis threw back his head and laughed. "I wish. Billie works tirelessly for the shelter. It's a job she takes very seriously. Names aren't important. The less you know, the better off you are. We're good friends. There were times when I thought . . . times when I would have liked to have it be more, but she discouraged it. Billie didn't have too good a time of it growing up. She is independent and wants to stay that way. It works for us. She's that rare person one calls friend. You know the kind you can call in the middle of the night the way I did when you arrived. She's the kind of person you would trust your kids, your animals, and your money with."

Helen nodded. "I would give anything to have a friend like that. I never really had a friend. Perhaps one day I will."

"If you had such a friend, I wonder if you would have confided in her. I wonder if having such a friend would have kept you in that house even after this last incident. Friendships can be very powerful and an incentive to stay in a bad relationship."

"I don't know, Dr. Davis. Lucie got me through it all. Sometimes I would talk to her for hours. I want to believe she understood.

For a little dog, she is extremely protective and loving. I couldn't have made it without her. You saved her life. I'll never forget that."

The vet's voice turned gruff again. "I really think she liked my singing. She didn't howl after the first few days. I hear the shelter's van. Are you sure you have everything?"

"Everything except Lucie. Are you sure it's okay for me to keep the carrier?"

"Absolutely. Don't let her get too active. She's feeling better, but I don't want her to overdo it. She needs another week at the most. Well, young lady, these past ten days are going into my memory book. Trust Billie and her friends, and you won't go wrong."

Helen didn't trust herself to speak. Instead she gave the vet a bone-crushing hug that he returned until Helen squealed. A second later she was out the door, the carrier in one hand and the nylon bag in the other. She didn't look back.

It was a long, comfortable ride with ordinary day-to-day conversation. The two women discussed the weather, Dr. Davis's busy practice, and Lucie's wonderful recovery. Knowing she was in capable hands, Helen relaxed.

It was the first day of the rest of her life. She offered up a silent prayer of thanks.

"One more block, and we're there," Izzie said an hour later.

"Will you be staying, Billie? You never said, do you work here?"

"No, I won't be staying. I suppose you could say I work here in a manner of speaking. That was a question, and you aren't supposed to ask questions. Until we get your papers finalized, you are guest Number Nine. Lucie is guest Number Nine-A. Our records will indicate that you arrived with someone. Once you are inside, everything will be explained to you. Lucie will love the walled-in garden. I wish we could have met under other circumstances. We will do our very best for you. We will expect nothing less from you. Good-bye and good luck. I'll wait here in the van until you get inside. Oh, one last thing. I thought this might be of interest to you. Read it at your leisure. It's the latest copy of *Silicon*

Alley. Good-bye, Lucie." Lucie yipped and whimpered as Helen lifted the carrier from the van.

It was a beautiful, sprawling, mission-style house in a quiet, private neighborhood. The scent of newly mown grass tantalized Helen's nostrils as she made her way up the colorful brick path leading to the front door. Before she had a chance to ring the bell, the door was opened by a tiny, smiling woman wearing a coronet of gray braids. "Welcome. Come, come. It's cool inside."

Helen turned to wave, but the dark blue van with the tinted windows was already headed back the way it came. "I'm Number Nine and . . . this is Number Nine-A."

"I know. We've been expecting you both. I'm Mona. Follow me, and I'll show you to your room. While you're here, you will be responsible for your room, and we take turns with the bathrooms. We also take turns cooking and cleaning up. When you're ready to join us, ring the bell at the top of the steps. Someone will fetch you to the garden. It's everyone's favorite spot. We're about to begin one of our group-therapy sessions. You can observe, or you can join in. Tomorrow you will be required to join the discussion. This is your room."

Helen stepped across the threshold. She had no idea what she was expecting, but this pretty room with its crisscross sheer curtains billowing in the late-afternoon breeze wasn't it. It was a feminine room right down to the ruffled organdy skirt on the small dressing table. She sighed with relief as she bent over to open the kennel door for Lucie. "She's trained. She won't pee on the carpet."

"I'm glad to hear that." Mona smiled. "There are four wings to the house, all extending around the back. The only way into the garden is from the house. It was a safety measure. Just ring the bell when you're ready."

The moment the door closed, Helen scooped up Lucie and then sat down on the bed. "This is our new home, at least for now. We don't have any choices, Lucie. I think it's going to work for us. You can sleep with me, but you can't jump up and down. I'll lift you. Mind me now. I always wanted a room like this with a frilly, flowered spread that matched a comfortable chair. Maybe I can read some books while I'm here. Ohhh, this carpet is so soft. We could even sleep on the floor if we wanted. And, look at this, we have our own personal fireplace nestled there in the corner. In case we get cold at night." She cupped the Yorkie's face in her hands. "I think we're going to be just fine."

Lucie nuzzled Helen's hand and then yipped softly.

As Helen rang the bell at the top of the stairs, thirty miles away in Santa Clara, thirty-seven-year-old Daniel Ward was painfully struggling with his cane on the long walk down the hall to Arthur King's offices. Each step was pure torture. His eyes murderous, he gritted his teeth. What the hell did the old goat want with him now? So what if he took ten days off. He never missed a day, never called in sick. Maybe he should quit this job and open up his own business. He could, if he wanted to. Give Arthur King a run for his money with his hands tied behind his back.

He'd taken great pains with his dress that day, knowing a meeting was imminent. The charcoal gray suit that was Silicon Valley's mode of dress was cashmere. His shoes were Brooks Brothers, his pristine white shirt was monogrammed and his two-hundred-dollar tie was classic. He knew he would meet with Arthur King's approval. One of Arthur's personal one-on-one meetings that either boded excitement or disaster. Daniel wasn't sure what to expect. He hadn't been made COO, that much he knew. Maybe King was going to bump him up to another prestigious position. King was great at creating unique titles and job demands. They were already draining his blood. What the hell more could he give them? First off, he would be chastised for missing the Christmas party. He'd rehearsed his prepared lies so many times he was starting to believe them himself. He was confident he could skate by on the lies and use his boyish charm.

Daniel stopped at the solid mahogany door leading to Arthur King's private offices. He sucked in his breath, then let it out in a soft *swoosh* before he opened the door. His knuckles turned white at the solid grip on the leather-topped cane.

"You wanted to see me, Arthur?" he asked pleasantly.

"Yes, Daniel. We missed you and Helen at the Christmas party. Come to think of it, we missed Helen at Thanksgiving, the Labor

Day picnic, and the Fourth of July party. Did you know the field office had a pool going on whether you or Helen would show at the Christmas party?" King asked lazily as he leaned back in his swivel chair.

"No, I didn't know that, Arthur. I didn't realize people paid so much attention to my personal life." The guy was looking older and older each time he saw him. Maybe he was finally going to announce his retirement.

"We're a family here at ComStar, Daniel. You know that. I can understand you not attending with your injury and all, but I rather thought Helen would come."

"She said she would feel out of place without me. Most people don't know this, but Helen is painfully shy. I didn't realize it was so important, Arthur. Since you elected not to make me COO, I can't see that it matters."

"I don't like sour grapes, Daniel. Wexler was the best man for the job. He has five years of seniority over you. Therefore, he was the logical choice. To show there are no hard feelings, I would like it if you and Helen would come to dinner this evening. I have some ideas I'd like to run by you *and* Helen."

Daniel felt his stomach muscles tighten into a knot. "I can make it, but Helen went to Los Angeles with a friend."

"When will she be back, Daniel?"

Daniel could feel perspiration start to soak his shirt collar at the back of his neck. "I guess when they're done shopping. She didn't give me a definite day. You know women when it comes to shopping."

"As a matter of fact, I do know a thing or two about women. I'm sure you know the hotel she's staying in. I suggest you call her and ask her to come back. We'll schedule dinner for tomorrow night. You look like you're having a problem with this, Daniel."

"I don't understand why you're making my wife's trip to Los Angeles sound so important. Helen wanted to take advantage of the after-Christmas sales. We didn't take a vacation last year. I promised her this trip. She just left. How can I call her back? What's so important about a social dinner?" Daniel asked, his voice turning desperate.

"Why don't you give me the phone number of the hotel, and I'll call her personally."

The knot in Daniel's stomach moved up to his chest. His hands felt clammy and cold. He struggled to maintain his composure. "Isn't this an invasion of my privacy, Arthur?"

The CEO leaned across his desk, his eyes narrow and icy cold. "Yes. Yes, it is, Daniel. I've heard some shocking things these past ten days, and I don't like what I heard. Prior to the recent stories I've been hearing, my secretary had hinted that possibly you were abusing your wife. Needless to say, I was shocked. This is a family business with family-oriented personnel. I will not tolerate such behavior. What I'm saying to you, Daniel, is this. Produce your wife, or I'll have to terminate your employment. And while you're at it, I'd like to hear about your injury in more detail. Falling over a chair on the deck doesn't warrant the kind of claims that showed up on your health-insurance forms."

Sweat trickled down the front and back of Daniel's starched shirt. "Is that why you froze me out of the Tyger account? I designed that program. Who told you those lies? Your secretary? She doesn't know me or my wife," he blustered.

"It's not important. What's important is, are those rumors true?"

"I've worked for you for fifteen years, Arthur. I gave you my blood, my sweat and yes, even my tears at times. Yes, you paid me, and you paid me well. This is not fair. I refuse to stand here and have you make accusations that are totally false. When Helen gets back, I will personally drive her over to your house for breakfast, lunch, and dinner. We can have a goddamn sleepover if you want. Until then, stay out of my private life, or you'll be looking down the wrong end of a lawsuit."

"What would you say if I told you I know exactly where Helen is? What if I told you I could pick up the phone and talk to her right now, this very minute?"

"I'd say you're lying. What you are implying is that I manhandled her, and now she is in Isabel Tyger's program. It doesn't work that way, and we both know it. Call her, Arthur. Right now."

Arthur King leaned back in his chair, his fingers making a steeple against his nose. He saw the fear in his employee's eyes and drove home his point. "That's true, Daniel. I can't call her, but Isabel can. I'm giving you twenty-four hours to bring your wife into this office. If you don't, your employment is terminated. If we can prove you physically abused your wife, a police report will be filed. You will leave here with no stock options, no severance. Your 401K will go with you. That's it. I'll see to it that you never work in this industry again."

"You can't do that!" His head was wet now. Soon his sweat would be dripping into his eyes.

Arthur shook his head sadly. "One or two more years, Daniel, and you could have stepped into my shoes. I'm retiring in the not-too-distant future. That was always my long-term plan for you. I'm sorry it didn't work out. I brought you along at a slow pace, taught you everything I know. I was looking forward to turning the reins over to you when I retire. We both know you aren't going to have Helen here by tomorrow, so why don't you clear out your office and leave now."

"This is a nightmare," Daniel mumbled.

"If you abused Helen, then yes, this is a nightmare. You need help, Daniel. I suggest counseling. Your insurance will be in effect for eighteen months. Take advantage of it. Give me your pass and your keys to the building."

Daniel licked at his dry lips. He unhooked the pass from his belt and tossed it on the table. The keys to the building slid across the shiny surface. "You haven't heard the last of this, Arthur. My attorney will be in touch."

"You have twenty-four hours, Daniel. Call me if Helen appears. I'll be more than happy to listen to anything she has to say."

"You aren't the only computer company in this valley, Arthur. I've been fighting off offers for the last five years. Kiss my ass, Mr. CEO," Daniel shouted in the open doorway.

They were all looking at him like they *knew*. Son of a fucking bitch!

Daniel slammed the door of his office so hard a paperweight slid across his desk onto the floor. He looked around. The best office in the building, better than Arthur's because it had three walls of windows. Fifteen years of mind-boggling devotion to

Arthur King and ComStar, and here he was kicked out on his ass and all because he'd pushed his wife around a little. No stock options, no severance. He could fight that. His 401K was healthy, with ComStar kicking in a buck for each five he put in. How the hell long would that last him with a two-thousand-dollar-a-month mortgage and that much again in a second and third mortgage, along with a thousand-dollar-a-month leased car? And the equity loan on the house, he couldn't forget that. The time payments on the baby grand, the in-ground pool payments, the furniture and carpet payments. That didn't count food, liquor, gas, or utilities and the maxed-out credit cards, all seven of them. Ten months, maybe a full year if he was frugal once he factored in the taxes and penalties.

Clear out his office. What the fuck was there to clear out? Nothing he wanted. Did Arthur really think he was going to take the sorry-assed rubber plant in the corner? Maybe he'd take the two bottles of scotch in the bottom drawer, but that was it. Hell yes, he'd have to take Helen's smiling picture. Anything to make Arthur King happy.

"Sayonara, ComStar," Daniel said as he offered up a sloppy salute in the direction of Arthur King's portrait hanging on his wall. He took a healthy pull from one of the scotch bottles before he dumped both into his briefcase.

"Fuck you, Arthur! This ain't over until I say it's over!"

4

Lucie in her arms, Helen followed a tall thin woman down the stairs and out to the garden. She saw everything at a glance—the women seated in comfortable garden chairs, three sparkling pitchers of ice tea on the table, bright-jacketed books, the colorful array of flowers and vines climbing the walls, the emerald green shrubbery and perfectly manicured borders of velvety grass. Someone had spent a lot of time creating this restful garden. She knew she would spend as much time there as allowed.

"Ladies, this is guest number Nine and guest number Nine-A. Going clockwise, this is Angela, Paula, Carol, Susan, Mary, Connie, Delphine, and Ardeth. We're equipped to handle twenty guests at any one time. Sometimes we have to crunch a little if an emergency arises. There are seven children in the west wing. I'm Mona. I live here permanently. If you ladies are comfortable, I think we can get started. If you feel you would like to join in, Nine, feel free."

Helen settled back into the comfortable cushions, Lucie cuddled in her lap. She listened to the women as they shared their experiences and wanted to cry for them and for herself as well. *How strange*, she thought, *they look so normal, so ordinary, and yet they're just like me.* With the realization, the tightness between her shoulder blades eased.

Two small birds perched on the highest part of the wall. Helen stared at them as she envied their freedom to fly away at a moment's notice. Like her, though, they had to watch for predators. *I was never a weak-kneed person until I met Daniel*, she thought. *I managed to raise myself, grow up, go to college, take care of myself—and destroy all my hard work in that one moment when I said, "I do."* She wondered if the others felt the same way. She asked.

The chorus of yeses rang in Helen's ears.

Helen started to cry when Ardeth, the last to speak, stood up with her glass of ice tea in her hand. "I want to toast all of us sitting here today. We're the lucky ones. I'm going to miss all of you when I leave tomorrow. I know I'll never see you again, and that's okay because even though our stay here is brief, all of you touched my life and my children's lives as well. I wish for you what I wish for myself: peace, sanity, and a healthy life free of fear."

Helen cleared her throat. "Good luck," she murmured. Lucie squirmed to be let down. Mona nodded. Helen watched her dog, her gaze intent. She was off her chair in a flash when the little dog ventured too far from her sight. Panic rivered through her as she ran to Lucie to scoop her into her arms.

"It's all right. She can't go anywhere. This is as new to her as it is to you. She has to sniff and find her way. We've had other animals here from time to time. She's picking up their scent," Mona said soothingly.

"I know. It's just that . . ."

"She's all you have left," the woman named Mary said. "Mona told us about you. You have us for a short while. It's my turn to cook tonight. Any suggestions?"

Helen surprised herself by saying, "Pepper steak."

"Pepper steak it is."

"It's my turn to clean the downstairs bathrooms," Alice said. "However, I will be on time for our book discussion at four."

Mona turned to Helen. "Our guests lead a very sheltered life for the sixty days they spend with us before being transferred. We try to keep up-to-date. Newspapers, books, the latest videos. We don't ignore the spiritual here either. Three days a week a minister, priest, and rabbi come to talk to us. At night we have a candlelight service here in the garden before retiring. Come if you like. It's not mandatory. There are two other points I want to touch on. Strange as this may sound, we discourage friendships. There's no way you can maintain a friendship when you leave here, so it is best all around. The second thing I want to mention is our self-defense course. Trained professionals come here on a voluntary basis. We expect you to cooperate. The course could save your life. Our rules are carved in stone. I know you know all this, Number Nine, but it bears repeating. No one answers the door but me. You are not permitted to make phone calls or answer the phone. We do not discuss our previous lives or share events of the past, only those things that brought you here. If you break any of the rules, you could endanger our other guests. If that happens, you will be asked to leave. It's that simple."

"I understand," Helen said quietly.

"In all the years we've been in operation, we've only lost two guests. I'll take it as a personal affront if we lose another," Mona said briskly.

"Mona, tell Number Nine whose picture is in the foyer," one of the women said.

Mona's face was grim when she spoke. "Sheila was Number Eight when she came to us in the month of August nine years ago. She adapted well, liked our program, and did everything she was supposed to do, but she felt guilty and truly believed in her marriage vows of until death do us part. She . . . left in the middle of the night and went back to her husband. Two months later she was dead. Her husband beat her so badly they could only identify her through her dental records. The man was a high-powered attorney in Los Angeles. He's in prison now. She left four children who are in foster care today. If you go back, there will be a next time just the way there was a next time for Sheila."

A lump the size of a golf ball settled in Helen's throat. She struggled to speak. "Are we allowed off the premises?" Helen asked.

As one, the answer was a resounding, "No!"

"At first it seems like you're in prison," Angela said quietly. "Once you learn to let it all go, it gets better. You'll learn to think in terms of safety and a life with no fear. You won't be waiting for what comes next. You won't worry that the kitchen or bathroom is spotless or that you forgot to take out the trash. You won't have to fear that hour of the day we all dread when *he* walks through the door and you can tell by the look in his eyes that it won't be a good night for you, your children, or your animals. That's all gone. All you have to worry about now is Mary's cooking."

Helen smiled. Her first real smile in days.

"Then, ladies, this ends our group session for the day. I can use some help in the office. Whose turn is it?"

"Mine," the young girl named Delphine said as she struggled up from her chair. Helen watched her limp painfully behind Mona. Her eyes were full of questions, but she said nothing.

"The dumb-ass guy she was living with threw her down a pair of steps and broke both her hips. But not before he knocked all her teeth out," Connie said flatly.

"How . . . how . . . does anyone know how many women have come through here, or is that something I'm not supposed to ask?" Helen said.

"There's a chart in the office. When we leave, we sign it. Thousands."

A second golf ball settled in Helen's throat. "My husband is a computer genius. He knows how to crack . . . you know, tap into *anything*. I saw a whole bunch of computers in the office when I got here."

"We went on manual ten days ago. New software is being designed by one of the top firms in Silicon Valley. It should be operational in a few weeks. I don't think you have anything to worry about. This house is armed with the latest high-tech gadgetry, and did you get a good look at the doors? Two layers of solid mahogany with steel bars in between. The windows are shatter-proof, and there are bars on the inside. They open with a key. Mona keeps them. The keys, I mean. Do you feel better now?"

"I guess so. Does our benefactor ever come here?"

"I've been here two months, and I've never seen her," Ardeth said. "But to answer your question, I don't think so. She's supposed to be very rich and owns some big toy company. No one really knows anything about her, and Mona is tight-lipped. She's right, though, the less we know the better off we are. I'm just grateful there is a person like Miss Tyger."

"I know I was told at some point the way this all works, but that was such a bad time for me. It's all a big blur. I have so many questions. What happens if you don't like where they're sending you?"

"Then you'll just have to suck it up. Anything is better than what I came from. My children are my top priority. What's best for them is best for me. Life is whatever you make it. We're all getting a second chance here. I plan to keep up my end of the bargain, so you see, it doesn't matter where I go as long as my children and I are safe. I want you all to remember something. Those men that abused us are in their third stage of behavior right now. Revenge. They're out there looking for us. You know it, and so do I. That's the way it works. Sorry to skip out on you, but I promised the kids I'd play Monopoly with them this afternoon," Ardeth said.

"I hope we're doing the right thing, Lucie. I don't see any other option right now. Even if it is pretty and comfortable here, we just might have traded one prison for another. It's *for now.* Later will take care of itself."

The little dog licked her hand.

"I keep getting this eerie feeling that someone is watching me," Isabel Tyger said as she looked over her shoulder. "Maybe what I need is a good stiff drink."

"Sounds good to me," Arthur King said, holding up his hand to signal the waiter. "What will you have, Gerry?"

"A double vodka collins."

"A double scotch straight up," Isabel said.

"Double bourbon on the rocks," Arthur said. He waited until the waiter was out of earshot before he spoke. "I fired him."

Isabel clapped her hands. "There is a God after all. You did it just like that!"

"What other way was there? I had him cold. I wish you could

have seen him sweat. In a million years I never would have believed Daniel Ward was capable of such a thing. How could I have been so wrong? I thought I had good judgment."

"Don't be too hard on yourself, Artie. People like Daniel and Helen Ward go to great lengths to hide a shameful secret like that. In time, Helen is going to be just fine. It's her husband who is going to be a problem. He's about to go into his revenge mode about now. He'll see his job loss as his downfall and blame Helen. Soon he will realize blame isn't good enough. He's going to want to find her so he can punish her for your firing him. The word *punish* to Daniel Ward at this stage may even mean finding Helen and killing her."

"What kind of man was he?" Gerry asked.

"The perfect Silicon Valley computer whiz. CEO material. There wasn't anything he couldn't do. He worked long hours, was always in early and left late. Never took time off, never called in sick. He dressed well; he was always immaculately groomed. Shoes polished, fresh haircut, car always clean. I thought of him as a perfectionist. I had no clue, none at all, that he was capable of such behavior. I don't know anyone who is his equal when it comes to software design. He was being groomed to step into my shoes. He was always pleasant, affable, got along well with his coworkers. He's a Jekyll and Hyde. In many ways he wasn't what we call a team player. Other times, he was. Why didn't I know?"

"You weren't supposed to know. We still wouldn't know if he hadn't gone after Helen's dog. A dog he gave her, mind you. Everyone has a breaking point, Artie. The dog was hers. I'm sorry the poor animal had to go through what she went through, but it was a blessing in disguise. Helen is free of him now, and she's safe. I've made the decision not to tell her he was fired. Right or wrong, I'll live with it. She knows this man. She knows he's going to leave no stone unturned in his quest to find her."

"I barred him from the building and the grounds. I don't think he'll show up again. He was too angry, but it was a controlled anger, something I'd never seen in him. He denied it to the end, said his wife was shopping in Los Angeles. I told him to clean out his office. The only thing he took was his liquor and Helen's picture.

It was a fuck-you gesture. That I did recognize. You can keep her safe, can't you, Izz?"

"As safe as she'll let us. I wish you could see the way she holds that little dog. It breaks my heart. I remember . . ."

Gerry interrupted her. "I think we should have another drink since Izzie had us chauffeured to this fine establishment."

Arthur signaled the waiter again and waved around the table. "Tell me what you want me to do, Izz. Do you want me to put the word out in the field? Is our game plan that he doesn't work in this business again? What? I need to know. Hell, every one of my competitors in the valley will do cartwheels to sign him up. He did threaten me with a lawsuit if I did that. You could come in for some trouble, Izz, if we go that route. I don't think those high-priced lawyers or all your money will make a difference. We need to think about this."

"I'd go to my grave before I give up anything that concerns the shelters. Let it be. If he runs true to form, he isn't going to be looking for a job right now. He's plotting and scheming. Men like him don't give up. Helen and Lucie are safe. She's a wonderful little dog, isn't she, Gerry?"

"Izzie."

"All right, Gerry, all right. I'm so lucky to have friends like you two. Sometimes I wish I had children. Helen is young enough to be my granddaughter. What do I have? I have a network of people who resemble superspies, thousands of women in fear of their life, a dead-ass toy company, two friends, a big old house that is like a barn, and too damn much money."

"Cut her off, Gerry. No more liquor for you, my friend. Let's eat."

Later, over coffee, Isabel said quietly, "I'm going to be Helen's counselor when the time is right. I can help that young woman. I know I can."

"You're breaking your own rule," Gerry said briskly. "Everything works now because you go by the rules. Break those rules, and you're headed for trouble. Tell her, Artie."

"He's right, Izz, but you aren't going to listen, are you?"

Isabel squared her plump shoulders until the glasses perched on the bridge of her nose started to jiggle. "You two fine men know squat when it comes to women. I'm not even sure you know anything about men. I've been doing this for forty years. Give me some credit, please. If I run into problems, you'll be the first ones I call. By the way, what are my shares of ComStar worth today?"

"One-seventy a share. With all the splits, how many shares do you have, Izz?"

"Five hundred thousand. You're making me richer by the day."

"Without you there would be no ComStar," Artie said. "I'm forever grateful to you for believing in me and helping me get started."

"Me, too, Izzie. I'm not in either of your leagues, but you helped me set up my practice; you take care of all those animals no one wants. Most important, you're a good and loyal friend."

Isabel flushed. She was never comfortable on the receiving end of a compliment. "Well, boys, this old girl wants to go home. It's been a long day. How about brunch at my house on Sunday."

"I'm your man," Artie said.

"I'll be there," Gerry said.

Isabel clapped her hands. "Good. I just love it when you two agree with me."

Helen poked her head into the office. "Is there anything I can do, Mona? I'm not used to sitting around. I would like to make myself useful."

"You could pick some flowers for the dinner table. It's early, but you could set the table if you like. Other than that, we're running on schedule. Tomorrow will be different. Ardeth will be gone, and you can step into her chores. Some new magazines arrived today. They're on the coffee table in the living room."

Helen nodded as she headed for the kitchen, Lucie trotting alongside. "I almost forgot the magazine Billie gave me this morning. We'll do what Mona said, and then I'll check it out. Daniel used to read that magazine from cover to cover. There must be something in there she wants me to see."

"Do we eat in the kitchen or dining room?" she asked the girls in the kitchen.

"Dining room. Dishes are on the sideboard and silver is in the top drawer. Napkins in the drawer underneath. There's a vase for flowers on the bottom."

Helen smiled. "How did you know?"

"Routine. All the new guests start out this way."

Thirty minutes later, Helen headed for her room, Lucie in her arms. She found the magazine and flipped it open to scan the contents. What was it Billie wanted her to see? The Silicon Top 100? Daniel's dream of being named to the 100? Quickly she scanned the list. She wasn't sure if she was happy or fearful when she didn't see his name on the list. Ted Wexler's name was the third from the top, though, and Daniel hated Ted Wexler with a passion. Ted was a team player, and Daniel wasn't, something she thought Arthur King worried about. Daniel was a glory hound who knew his business, but Arthur was a family man.

"I would imagine Daniel is about ready to go up in smoke if he has read this article, Lucie. However, it isn't our problem any longer." She flipped to the back page and a column headed "This just in . . ."

Theodore Wexler of ComStar Industries was named COO by Arthur King, CEO. The industry expressed surprise, because rumor had the title and the job going to Daniel Ward. Neither man could be reached for comment as we went to press.

Helen dropped the glossy magazine in the wastebasket next to the bed. "I just bet, Lucie, there are a lot of holes in the walls of the house we used to live in. That isn't our problem anymore either. Someday, Lucie, you and I are going to be fat, happy, and sassy. We'll take our new world by the tail and give it a wild swing. We're on the way, thanks to some very wonderful people. You know what, I just realized? We missed Christmas! We aren't going to worry about that now either. Our next Christmas is going to be wonderful. I'm going to make cookies. We're going to have a real tree with pine needles all over the place and a centerpiece that smells heavenly. I'll make you a stocking and fill it with treats and we'll sing 'Jingle Bells' until we're hoarse. You can bark all you want. That's a promise, Lucie. I never break a promise. A little nap now might be nice. Just you and me in this big old bed.

"Just you and me, Lucie."

5

Helen looked around the room that had been hers for two long months. She'd cleaned it from top to bottom, changing the sheets, even washing the windows. It was now ready to give solace and comfort to the next guest. Earlier she'd carried her bags downstairs in preparation for leaving. She took a careful look around to make sure she'd left nothing behind. Her sketch pad was under her arm, her shoulder bag under the other arm. The room was as clean, as bright and pretty as it was two months ago when she first arrived.

She knew she was postponing the inevitable moment when she had to descend the stairs for the last time. She was safe there. Lucie was safe. Now she was going into uncharted waters, to a place she didn't know, a place that wouldn't be revealed to her until the moment she stepped into the dark blue van. Hot tears pricked her eyelids. Lucie whimpered at her feet.

In many respects the previous two months had been the happiest of her life. She'd learned how to speak her mind, to talk openly of her abuse, to show her scars and the few deep bruises that remained. She'd learned to trust, to put that trust in other women's hands. As Mona said last night, she was fit as a fiddle health-wise. She now knew a smattering of martial arts and felt like she could hold her own should she ever need to take defensive action. She could shoot like a pro at the rifle range in the basement. As Mona put it, we're evening the odds should you ever find yourself in a tricky situation. Just knowing these things, she'd said, builds confidence. Her head was clear, her dog was as fit as she was. Helen even had a new name now, Nancy Baker, a driver's license, a credit card, and a bank account. She knew they were forgeries and would never get by in a court of law. They were for now, to get her to a safe location at which point a second set of papers would be issued—still forgeries, but a better quality. Everything was *for now*.

She wished there was something she could leave behind to show her gratitude, but she had nothing. Maybe she did have something after all. She dropped to her knees and spread out her sketch pad. She flipped through the pages until she came to the one where she'd sketched Gerald Davis and Billie. Just last night she'd added Lucie to the picture. She debated a moment before she signed her real name. The name she was born with. Helen Marie Stanley. It was all she had to give.

"Come on, Lucie, it's time to go. Just let me fasten the strap on this backpack and you get a free ride. Easy, girl, easy. Okay. Get comfortable."

Downstairs, Mona was waiting at the side door. "The van is ready, Nancy."

"Thanks for everything, Mona. Perhaps someday we'll meet again."

Mona smiled. "I hope not."

"Would you give this to Billie the next time you see her? I know I shouldn't have signed my name, but I did. It's who I am. I couldn't give a gift with someone else's name on it. She can tear it up or burn it. I just wanted . . . you know, to leave something behind. Something that says you helped Helen Marie Stanley. Stanley was the name I was born with. Good-bye, Mona."

"Good-bye and good luck, Nancy. You too, big girl," she said, patting Lucie's head. "You take care of this lady now, you hear? And I'll be sure to give this to, uh, Billie."

Helen, her eyes burning, didn't look back as she walked down the hall and through the kitchen until she came to the garage door. The blue van with the dark, tinted windows waited silently for her to enter. She slid back the doors and climbed in. The garage door slid upward, the van backed out smoothly. The driver was someone Helen had never seen before. She would probably never see her again after that day either.

"What happens now?" she asked boldly.

"I'm going to drive you to the campus of the University of Santa

Clara. There will be a car waiting for you. The registration and insurance card are in the glove compartment. The car is registered to Nancy Baker. There's a map on the front seat with your travel route all laid out for you, complete with stops and which motels you will be staying in. You will pay cash for your food and lodging. Keep your receipts."

"Where is it I'm going?"

"New Jersey."

"That's clear across the country! I've never been outside of California."

"You were never in a woman's shelter before either. You'll be fine. Just follow the route that's mapped out. Drive no more than eight hours a day. Do not, I repeat, do not exceed the speed limit. Be ever mindful of your gas tank and have the oil checked several times en route. Get the car washed at least once along the way."

"Where am I going in New Jersey?"

"To a town called Woodbridge. We secured a one-bedroom garden apartment for you. The rent is paid for three months. Across the road from the apartment complex is a large shopping mall called Woodbridge Center. You have a job in a lingerie shop called Fine Things. It's a high-end shop. You are to start work ten days from today. The utilities and the phone are in your new name. Pay these bills promptly when they come in. You will be banking at First Union, which is right down the road. Everything is very convenient. We want you to enroll at Middlesex College to take business courses at night. It's less than nine miles from your apartment. There's a packet in the car that will explain everything to you. When you reach your apartment, you'll find a computer all set up for you. You'll be notified through regular mail when the system will be operational.

"Once a month, between the first and the third, forty-three dollars will be automatically deducted from your account. While you don't have a bill per se, it is mandatory that you pay something back to the foundation for all the help that has been given you. You have health insurance for six months as well as dental with the foundation. That will cease when your new employer's insurance takes over.

"There is a veterinarian on Oak Tree Road in Edison where you can take your dog if need be. A file has been started for your animal. The vet's name is Dr. Lo. An appointment has been set up for your pet for the second day after your arrival. A map showing the location of the clinic will be in your packet. I think that just about covers everything. There's fifteen hundred dollars in your bank account, and there will be five hundred dollars in cash in the glove compartment of the car. If there's anything you want to ask me, ask now."

There were a million things she wanted to ask. She stroked Lucie's head, and said, "No, I understand everything you said."

"If for any reason you have car trouble, call Triple A. There's an emergency card attached to the insurance card. You can use the credit card to pay for repairs."

"Where . . . how far is the grocery store?"

"Not far. You can go in any direction and you'll find one. Your kitchen cupboards and refrigerator and freezer have been stocked. There's also a supply of dog food, dog vitamins, and dog toys for your pet. Miss Tyger is very thorough."

Helen closed her eyes. A new life. Everything taken care of. All she had to do was step into that life and she would become Nancy Baker. Would she ever be Helen Marie Stanley again? If she were to die tomorrow would the name Nancy Baker be on her tombstone? She almost blurted out the question. Instead she bit down on her tongue and squeezed Lucie closer to her chest.

"Have you ever been to New Jersey?" Helen asked.

"You can take the train from Metro Park to New York City. The station is close to where you will be living. I understand the trip is less than fifty minutes. No, I have never been to New York City either."

Helen leaned forward, trying to see what the driver of the van looked like. The tinted shield between the back passenger seats and the front seats was as darkly tinted as the windows.

"Sit back please, you're obstructing my view," the driver said.

"Are you a case or a volunteer?"

"Does it matter?" the driver asked.

"It matters to me when other people control my life and my every movement."

"It didn't bother you before you came into the program. You were in harm's way then. Today, you are in the arms of angels who only want what is best for you. You can leave anytime you want." The voice was suddenly cold and frosty.

"I didn't say I wanted to leave. Forget I said anything."

"It's forgotten. Relax and enjoy the ride." The voice gentled, and to Helen's ears she thought she detected a hint of tears. Nothing in the world was the way it seemed. Nothing. *For now.* She had to hold on to those two little words: *for now.*

Five days later, Helen slowed the Volvo to a crawl as she approached Exit 11 on the New Jersey Turnpike. She paid the toll, asked for directions, turned north toward the Garden State Parkway, where she got off at Exit 131. From there she followed the signs to Route 27 and then to Route 1, where she almost missed the turnoff to the apartment complex. She heaved a sigh of relief when she drove around the parking lot and located the building she wanted.

She was home.

Five trips later, Helen slipped off the pet harness and lowered Lucie to the floor. A second later, leash in hand, they made their way down to the first floor and outdoors. Lucie sniffed, squatted, and was ready to go back inside.

Helen was happy to see the dead bolt and two other locks on both doors of the apartment, all of which she put into place immediately.

It was time to check out her new home. The first home she and she alone would be responsible for. The grungy efficiency she'd once lived in simply didn't count. Here, in these small quarters, she could do as she pleased, when she pleased. If she wanted to walk around in her underwear, she could. If she wanted to leave dishes in the sink, she could. She could leave the television on all night. She could play the radio all day. She could eat cereal for dinner if she wanted. She could leave the sheets on the bed for two weeks instead of changing them every day the way Daniel insisted.

There was no Daniel in her life telling her what she could or couldn't do. From this day forward she was responsible for her own life and Lucie's as well.

Life was going to be worth living after all.

"I have some wonderful ideas, Lucie," Helen said, sitting down cross-legged on the floor. Lucie jumped into her lap. "As soon as the computer is hooked up, I'm going to see about selling lingerie on-line. Pretty, sexy stuff. Mona encouraged me. I know the computer pretty well now. I just might make enough money so I can pay back all that's been given to us. I want to be independent. I don't want to be a taker anymore. We're going to give back, too, just as soon as we can turn a profit. Maybe I won't have to work at the store if shopping on-line becomes profitable. Daniel said it was the wave of the future. Maybe he was right. I did say we were going to check out our new digs, didn't I? Come on, girl, let's see what our new home looks like.

"We aren't going to get lost, that's for sure," Helen said as she walked from the comfortable living room into the bedroom. "I like this. Plain and neat. No clutter. A few plants, and it will brighten right up. God, how I hated that four-thousand-square-foot house in California. It never felt like a home. There wasn't one thing in that entire house that said Helen Marie Stanley lived there. Those four thousand square feet shrieked that Daniel Ward lived there. I have to stop talking about him, and I have to stop thinking about him. We aren't to dwell on the past. Just the future."

Helen bounced on the bed. "We are going to sleep well tonight, Lucie. Look, there's even a bed for you. And a basket of toys. I know you miss your mouse. I'll look for one as soon as we get settled. It won't be the same, but you'll adjust the way I'm adjusting."

Helen looked around, certain a woman had decorated the apartment. The flowered spread and draperies matched the pale green carpet perfectly. White wicker was feminine and not just for sunporches any longer. Even the bathroom matched the bedroom, with thirsty green towels and ankle-deep throw rugs. The shower, tub, and vanity were spotless, the chrome gleaming. Underneath the vanity were paper products, enough to last months.

One picture hung in the bedroom. Puzzled that someone would hang a picture of a lone pine tree in a bedroom, Helen studied it to see if there was some hidden meaning. At the base of the dark trunk she could make out a name. Edna Mae Trolley. Helen bit down on her lower lip. Edna Mae Trolley, whoever she was, had probably done the same thing she'd done when she gave her sketch to Mona. "As long as one person knows you're alive and well, that's all that matters, Edna Mae Trolley. I will treasure this picture because it's obvious the pine tree has some deep meaning to you.

"This sofa is so comfortable, we can both sleep on it. Hop up, Lucie. We can eat in here off trays. I always wanted to do that. Now we can. Tonight we can sit here, watch television, and eat popcorn. God, this is so wonderful." Lucie yipped her pleasure as Helen curled into the side of the wide sofa. Lucie wiggled and squirmed until she was next to her mistress. Moments later, both were asleep.

"Artie, when are the computers going to be up and running?" Isabel grumbled.

"I've had my people on it round the clock, Izz. It's not as simple as you think it is. Three more days, tops. My people are going to help your people do all the inputting. You need to relax."

"I'm not going to relax until I know Helen Ward is on-line. I want to show you something. She left a gift for me. At first I was angry. I was one step away from tossing her out on her ear until I thought about it. Tell me what you think, gentlemen."

"She's a hell of an artist," Artie said.

"She got my good side. Made you look *good*, Izzie," Gerry drawled.

"What else?" Isabel demanded.

"What else what? The dog is a perfect likeness. It's kind of sad now that I look at it," Gerry said.

"Men! The name. Look at the name!"

"So. It's her name, Izz," Artie said.

"Not anymore it isn't. She's Nancy Baker now. She's supposed to think, act, and become Nancy Baker. This is what she does."

"Jesus, Izzie, don't you understand what she was doing? She had to leave something behind, something that said who she was. She may never become Helen Marie Stanley again. Leaving that picture behind means maybe there's hope that someday she can be Helen again. That hope and her dog are all she has. Hell, even a dog marks his territory. Cats too. Listen, I *know* I couldn't give up my life, my identity. I just couldn't. I came into this life Gerald Davis and I plan on going out with the same name. I imagine Helen more or less feels the same way. What's going on is *for now*. In her mind it isn't forever."

"I feel the same way," Artie said.

"Now why did I know you were going to say that," Isabel grumbled. "I'm having it framed."

"I guess you were just talking to hear yourself." Artie grinned.

"There's something about Helen Ward that got to me. Maybe it was the middle-of-the-night call, although I've had hundreds of those."

"It was the dog, Izzie. The dog and Helen. You can't stand it when someone harms an animal any more than I can. They're both going to be fine. You could have told her who you were. Not that it would have made a difference," Gerry said.

"She has talent. I don't think we should waste that talent. She told Mona she wants to design lingerie and possibly sell it on-line. She doesn't have any start-up capital other than the money we've put in her bank account. I . . . I wanted to . . . ask if you two would approve of the foundation making a small loan to her to start up this fledgling enterprise. That way she could stay home with Lucie."

"It always comes back to the dog. Sure," Gerry said.

"It's okay with me," Artie said.

"She's a hard worker. I could tell that right off. She knows how to clean a house, and she knows how to garden. She's smart, too.

That husband just beat her into the ground until she was afraid to do anything but breathe. Good, five thousand should do it. I'll have the lawyers draw up the papers."

"Five thousand isn't going to get her past the post office, Izz. She's also going to need a better computer than the one you gave her. I'll build her one and ship it out next week. You okay with that?"

"Ten thousand and the computer," Isabel said.

"Fifteen is more realistic," Artie said.

"Then it's fifteen," Isabel said smartly.

"So that's what this command breakfast was all about," Gerry said.

"For God's sake, Izz, you could have done this without us."

"Yes, I could have, but when you're dealing with a human life, no one wants to take sole responsibility. I make mistakes, too, as you well know. I guess . . . I want her to survive. She doesn't know that black world out there, but she's going to be learning really quickly. I just want to make it a little easier for her."

"Any scuttlebutt on the husband, Artie?" Gerry asked.

"To my knowledge, no one has seen or heard from him. No one has called ComStar for a reference. You know those damn headhunters; they're forever calling. Not a peep out of any of them. Legal said we had to give him severance, and the check cleared yesterday. Other than that, I know nothing."

"Nothing is better than something," Isabel said, as her index finger traced the outline of the little dog on the sketch Helen had left for her.

"If you need me, call," Artie said. "I'll need the address so I can ship the computer. I'll put my people on it as soon as I get back to the office."

"Thanks, Artie."

"For you, Izz, anything. You know that."

"I could use some help later this afternoon if you can spare the time, Izz," Gerry said.

"I'll be there. Any new pups?"

"Six."

"Do you have homes for them?"

"Nope."

"Then they're mine," Isabel said.

Gerry laughed. "I was hoping you'd say that."

Isabel smiled. It was wonderful to have friends.

6

Helen turned off the eleven o'clock news, satisfied that all was right in the world. At least for the moment. "Come on, Lucie, time to go on-line."

The little dog scampered over to the small dining area that was now Helen's in-home office. A brand-new ComStar computer and printer took up almost the entire table. The shelves on both walls, bare when she moved in, were filled with computer books, Xerox paper, printer cartridges, a separate fax machine, her textbooks for the night classes she attended along with all the small business papers and manuals she'd applied for with the Small Business Administration, and last but certainly not least, dog treats and chew bones to keep Lucie busy while she was on the computer. There wasn't an inch of available space left.

It was her home, and she loved it, cluttered or not. It now looked like someone with an identity lived there; a real person, as she thought of herself these days. She'd spent the past weekend going to the flea market on Route 1 to buy knickknacks and green plants that had been bedraggled but were now showing signs of life with plant food and daily watering. Before long they would be lush and full. At least she hoped they would.

She'd spent $29 dollars at the flea market, $29 dollars she probably shouldn't have spent. She'd weighed the decision up one side and down the other, finally opting to spend the money simply because it was her choice and it would brighten her life. Her on-line counselor told her everything in her life was about choices. She was right, too. Once you make a choice, you take responsibility for that choice and you live with it. Step One. That night she was working on Step Two of her one hour of on-line counseling.

Helen turned on the computer and handed Lucie her first treat of the evening. She logged onto Internetx Express, typed in her password under the name of TTLS@internetx.com with her on-line name of Twinkle Twinkle Little Star or TTLS. She then e-mailed Boots@aol.com. She waited for the Instant Message to appear in the upper-left-hand corner.

Helen typed slowly. She passed a few minutes with the daily pleasantries before Boots asked her first question.

"Are you still feeling overwhelmed?"

"A little, but I think I have a handle on it. I went shopping over the weekend. I spent $29 on plants and stuff to brighten up the apartment. I feel a little guilty, but I can economize somewhere else. I needed to do that."

"Understood. How is the job going? Do you like it any better?"

"No, not really. I don't understand how people can charge so much for sleazy apparel. The name of the store, in my opinion, is a joke. There is nothing fine about the merchandise they sell. The clientele leaves a little to be desired. I think the owner is satisfied with my work."

"This is good, TTLS. You voiced an opinion, and you made a decision. I imagine it felt rather good. Once you get your own business going, you can leave the shop. Any progress on your fledgling business?"

"It really did feel wonderful, Boots. As to the business, I'm told a lot of it is word of mouth. I ordered cards, had some of my sketches put into a brochure. Once I'm more comfortable with the computer, I can make my own. I don't know what it is about computers. I hated them even in school. I just wasn't good at it. Then when I . . . Never mind, it isn't important. I study the computer books every morning before I go to work. It's a slow process, but I'm getting more knowledgeable by the day."

"It all takes time. You have your business classes, your job, and your on-line counseling. It's a full plate for anyone. Rome wasn't built in a day. You have to learn to do one thing at a time and do that one thing well. It will fall into place. Cottage industries flourish in this country. How is TTLS2 doing?" Boots asked.

"She's sitting right here next to me. She pretty much sleeps during the day while I'm gone. It's working out. She misses me, but then I miss her, too. I come home for lunch and walk her."

"That's good. Now, tell me, how are you sleeping? Are you still having your fearful dreams? Do you still look over your shoulder when you're walking on the street?"

"I still dream once in a while. Yes, I still look over my shoulder. Sometimes I'm afraid to open the mailbox. I don't know why that is. I feel better than I've ever felt. Mentally, I'm a lot stronger now. I don't exactly ooze confidence, but I am getting more confident with each passing day."

"Do you think about *him?*"

"I try not to, but yes, at times I think of him and what I allowed him to do to me. I was so afraid. I feel anxious at times but not fearful. You don't know this man, Boots. He *will* find me at some point."

"No, TTLS, he will not find you. As long as you stick to the program, there is no way he can locate you. You must trust me on this."

"You don't know him."

"Yes, TTLS, I do. I also know thousands of men just like him. Did you ever love that man?"

"I'm not sure. I just wanted to belong to someone. I wanted someone to care about me. I thought he did in the beginning. That feeling lasted for about three days, until I found out what he was all about. I should have left the first time he hit me. I didn't because I had nowhere to go. The four hundred dollars I had saved wouldn't have taken me very far. Daniel insisted I give up my job. I couldn't go back to my mother. When someone tells you over and over he is going to kill you and then describes the ways he plans on doing it so he won't get caught, you start to believe him. Fear is a terrible thing."

"Yes, it is. You're past that now. Do you miss the shelter?"

"Yes. I think about it every day. I tend to think a nunnery is like the shelter. No worries, your needs are taken care of. All you have to do is take care of your spiritual well-being. Nuns always look so serene and unflappable. I envy that. My ultimate goal is to be able to be serene and unflappable. I want to be strong and gutsy, too. Do you ever feel like that, Boots?"

"At times. Tell me, what do you think one of those unflappable, serene nuns would have done if she were in your position? Would she have done something about it, would she have prayed for guidance, what? Don't misunderstand me. I have nothing against nuns."

"I don't know. They live among women. I imagine there are some women who became nuns for that reason."

"Nuns live in very cloistered surroundings and lead very cloistered lives. If you were to take them outside of their realm, I think they would have a difficult time adjusting to the outside world. I don't think they would remain serene and unflappable for very long. This is just my opinion. You see, that's the reason we move our guests after sixty days. It is much too easy to fall into that safe, serene, unflappable trap. You have a whole new world you have to learn to deal with. It's going to be whatever you make it. I'm just here to guide you along. Tell me, did you ever have your own bank account, you know, spending money of your own while you were married?"

"No. He . . . he handled all the finances. It was always cash in stores. I had to turn over the receipts. We had a lot of credit cards, but only Daniel could use them. They were all maxed out, and he would pay one off with the other. It was just a vicious circle. One time a dollar fell out of the zipper compartment of my purse, and I didn't notice it. He went into such a rage, I ended up in the emergency room for six hours. I think it took me six hours at the flea market to spend that $29. I got such pleasure out of walking along, picking and choosing and finally deciding what to get. Do the . . . other women . . . are they getting a grasp on things better than me? Am I too slow, too . . . fearful? Is there some kind of time frame where I wake up one morning and suddenly realize I'm like Superwoman or something?"

"Each person is different. The flip side of that particular coin is some women are better at covering up. Everyone isn't up front and in your face. Once again, TTLS, you can put this all behind you, but it is never going to leave you. Eventually it will be a very pale memory, but it will never go away. You need to know that and to accept it."

"I do."

"Good. Now, let's get down to business . . ."

At the end of the second hour, Helen smiled when she signed off and shut down the computer. She loved "talking" to Boots, her on-line counselor. The smile stayed with her when she picked up Lucie, who was sound asleep on the chair next to hers. "Go get your leash. Five minutes and then it's time for bed. It was a good night. We covered a lot of territory. I feel very good. Attagirl, Lucie. I didn't think I would be on-line so long tonight. We spent almost two hours. I think Boots likes me. Quiet now. Everyone is sleeping."

They were back indoors and bolted in less than ten minutes. Lucie scampered to the bedroom. She waited, her new mouse in her mouth. Helen giggled when she looked at her bed and all the toys Lucie had spread out. "There better be room for me." Lucie immediately scattered the stuffed toys and took her place on the opposite pillow.

The small night-light in the socket near the floor cast a comforting glow so that Helen could see the dim outlines of everything in the room. She stared at it as though mesmerized as her mind wandered back in time. . . .

Helen looked around the long narrow room of the trailer. It looked so trashy, and it smelled terrible. She'd done all she could with air fresheners and sprays, but nothing worked. The furniture was old and had deep-down smells that even soap and water could never get out. It was a mean-looking place, and she hated it. After today, she wouldn't have to worry. She moved by rote then, emptying overflowing ashtrays, picking up beer and wine bottles and empty food cartons. She'd done the same thing yesterday and all the days before that. She often wondered what would happen if she didn't clean it up. Would her mother or the man she lived with do it? Maybe when the trash was up to their knees they would kick it out of the way.

Since she was leaving with no plans of returning, it was important to Helen to leave the trailer tidy if not clean. "Where's Harry?" her mother asked as she breezed in the door.

So that was what his name was. "I don't know where . . . Harry is. Mom, I need to talk to you."

"About what?" Phyllis Stanley asked as she popped the cap off a bottle of Budweiser and drank greedily.

"I'm moving out. Today. Actually, right now. You and . . . ah . . . Harry can have the place to yourselves."

Phyllis Stanley's eyes turned mean as her lip curled. "Yeah, sure, move out. At least I won't have to worry about you coming on to my man anymore. I could use some rent money. I thought the deal was you were going to get a job in the diner and help out a little. You owe me, kid."

"What do I owe you, Mom? Nothing, as far as I can see. You never took care of me. I took care of you. I hate this place. I hate it that you bring strange men here who look at me like I'm a piece of meat. Can't you see what they do, what they think? You work hard, I'll never deny that. Where does all your money go? It certainly never went to me. All I ever had was hand-me-downs from the neighbors, food in cartons. You never bought me a hair ribbon or a new pair of shoes. I never had a date the whole time I was in high school. Do you know how bad I wanted to go to the senior prom? Even if someone had asked me, I wouldn't have had the money to buy a dress. I don't have one pleasant memory, Mom, and that's sad."

"Whine, whine, whine," Phyllis snarled, her heavily made-up face almost a caricature of something Helen had seen in the funny papers. "Where are you going?"

"I got a small efficiency. I'm going to work full-time in a boutique and go to college at night. I want better than this, Mom. If I have to work my butt off, I will. I just wanted to say good-bye."

"Don't let the door hit you on the ass on your way out," Phyllis screeched. "Do you care that I was counting on that hundred bucks a month you were supposed to pay in rent? Hell, no, you don't."

"Mom . . ."

"Go on, get out of here. Don't come back either. I don't ever want to see your face again."

Tears rolled down Helen's cheeks. "I tried to love you, Mom. I really did. I wanted to hug you and have you kiss me and tell me one day things would get better. I knew they wouldn't, but I hoped. A lie would have *been better than nothing. All I ever wanted was to belong to you. You acted like I was some stray you picked up off the street. You never called me sweetie, or honey, or dear. It was always, hey kid. I'm going. I'll send you my address in case you ever need me."*

"Yeah, right. Go on, get out of here."

Helen jerked upright. She swung her legs over the side of the bed and headed for the kitchen, where she opened a bottle of soda.

She hated thinking about the past, hated thinking about her mother. If there was at least one good memory, maybe she would feel better. A moment later she was lost in thought again as she relived the moment in time when she finally received her BA degree.

"Helen Stanley." The dean's voice rang clear and true. Helen accepted the rolled-up diploma, smiled for the photographer, and made her way back to take her position next to her classmates.

A whole new world awaited her.

A smaller, nicer furnished apartment, a new job in a graphics-design firm, and then Daniel Ward were her rewards for six long years of hard work and studying.

It was all so long ago. A different time, a different life. She could barely remember the worn, cozy, comfortable apartment with the bamboo blinds on the windows and the rows and rows of green plants she'd tucked into corners. The firm she'd worked for was wonderful, the people outgoing and friendly. She was just getting to know them when Daniel came into her life and turned it upside down.

Helen gulped at the cold soda. She didn't want to think about Daniel Ward. Daniel Ward was dangerous to her mental stability. She shook her head to clear away her negative thoughts. "I have a new life now. A second chance. You're just someone I used to know, Daniel."

Helen slipped between the covers and said the short prayer she said every night. The little dog listened to the words, her head between her paws.

The moment Helen's breathing evened out, the little dog inched closer and placed one paw on her mistress's shoulder, but not before her eyes pierced the semidarkness. Satisfied, she, too, closed her eyes and was asleep within seconds.

* * *

Helen dusted her hands dramatically. "We are going to eat like queens tonight, Lucie. Roast chicken with all the trimmings. I can't believe we're finally on a work schedule that gives me some free time, and it only took us nine weeks. It's spring and the world is looking really good right now. The April showers really did bring out all the May flowers. Our little balcony looks like a rainbow."

Lucie trotted off to the corner of the room where she kept her stash of toys to return with a long braided rope. It was time to play. Helen dropped to the floor and played tug-of-war with the little dog, who growled ferociously. Helen rolled and romped, laughing and tickling the terrier. It was a special time of day for them both. "Okay, okay, I give up. You won!" Lucie growled playfully.

A moment later Helen froze in her tracks when the doorbell sounded. An alien sound, a sound she'd only heard once in the ten weeks since she'd moved in. She wasn't even sure if it had rung that first time because she had been sitting on the stoop waiting for the computer technician to hook up the new computer. Lucie raced to the door, her tail between her legs as she growled fiercely.

Helen walked to the door, her shoulders stiff, her eyes wide with alarm. She was relieved to see all three locks in place. Did she dare risk looking in the peephole? What if another eye on the outside was glued to it? She took a deep breath. "Who is it?"

"Sam Tolliver. I'm your neighbor in 6-B. I was wondering if I could borrow some dog food."

Open the door? Don't open the door? Boots would say open it. "Just a minute, Mr. Tolliver." Her hands were shaking so badly, she immediately jammed them into her jeans pockets as soon as she undid the bolts and opened the door. Lucie hugged her ankles, the hair on the back of Lucie's neck on end. "Come in, Mr. Tolliver."

"Sam. Call me Sam. Only my students call me Mr. Tolliver. And you're Nancy Baker."

"How . . . how do you know that?"

Tolliver looked perplexed for a moment. "Your name is on your mailbox and your mailbox is next to mine. I've been meaning to come over and introduce myself and maybe bring you a welcoming cake or something, but I don't know how to bake, and the bakery is out of the way. Finals at school, you know. You need to help me out a little here. I feel like I'm intruding and talking to the wall. You look . . . petrified. Would you like me to leave the door open?"

Her first one-on-one encounter in the privacy of her home. With a *man*. Boots would say lighten up, you knew it would happen. She tried to relax. "No, it's not necessary to leave the door open. Would you like wet or dry dog food?"

"Max will eat anything. I'll replace it on Saturday if that's okay with you. I like what you did with the place. When Jim lived here he had a roll-out bed, two stools, and a futon. He was the guy that had the apartment before you. It's homey. Maybe sometime you'd like to take a crack at my place. Green plants make all the difference and all those . . . what *do* you call that stuff?" he asked, pointing to her array of knickknacks.

In spite of herself, Helen smiled. "Flea-market junk. How about a little of both?"

"Huh?"

"Dog food. A little of both."

"Yeah, sure. Something smells really good in here."

Helen smiled again. "Roast chicken. You're smelling the stuffing."

"Stuffing is for Thanksgiving. You're making stuffing in May in the middle of the week?"

"Yes." Boots was going to approve of this encounter. Big-time. "Don't you cook?"

"Eggs. I usually pick up something on the way home. Or I wait for some kind soul to take pity on me and invite me for dinner. Max has great table manners. Hint, hint, hint."

"Are you asking me to invite you for dinner?"

"I thought you'd never ask. We accept. Should I bring something? Wine, beer, orange soda. Max likes orange soda. I think it's the fizz."

She almost said Lucie likes grape soda but stopped in time. "My dog likes grape," she said, closing the bag of dry dog food. "Do you still want this if you're coming for dinner? My dog eats what I eat, vegetables and all."

"No kidding. What's her name?"

"Nine-A."

"Weird name."

"She was one of a litter of nine. I put the A on for individuality," Helen lied smoothly. *I'm doing it, Boots, I'm doing it.*

"So what time is dinner?"

"Seven-thirty."

"You don't talk much, do you? Sometimes I'm overwhelming. That's what my students tell me. I rarely pay attention to what they say except in instances like this."

"I don't know you," Helen said flatly.

Sam snorted. "That's hardly surprising. You've been here ten weeks and the reason I know that is Jim moved out one weekend and you moved in the next. No one on this floor knows you. We're kind of close up here in the clouds. You know, we borrow, we hang out, we gossip, we talk about our animals. Friendly bunch. We all kind of figured you didn't want to be bothered with anyone. Hell, I wouldn't have bothered you either, but I needed the dog food. Everyone else on this floor has cats. That's a kick-ass computer if I do say so. ComStar, huh? What do you do, Nancy Baker? Or is that none of my business?"

"I work part-time in a shop in the mall, and I design and sell lingerie on my own. I eventually want to have my own shop somewhere. It's not that I'm antisocial. I just haven't had any free time. I work, go to class four nights a week, and on weekends I work on my designs."

"Where are you from, Nancy?"

"Where are you from, Sam Tolliver?"

"That's Dr. Sam Tolliver, ma'am. Born and bred right here in the Garden State. How about you?"

"Walterboro, South Carolina. It's a small, old historical town."

"A Southern belle, huh? What happened to your accent?"

"I don't have one. You're nosy, aren't you?"

"I call it being friendly." Sam grinned. "Does your family still live there?" he queried.

"I don't have a family. Where is your family?"

"Got a sister somewhere in Peru digging out ruins. She and I haven't spoken in years. I'm thirty-three. Never married. This is all my own hair, and my teeth are in great shape. When I get to know you a little better, I'll show you my birthmark. You got any? Birthmarks. We might want to show-and-tell later on."

"Nope. Blemish-free."

"I guess I should be going so you can get back to whatever it is you were doing. Sounded like you were having a good time when I rang the bell."

"I was playing with my dog."

"Oh. Listen, Max is lonely being cooped up all day. Maybe we could arrange a play day the way parents do with kids. He's really gentle. He won't hurt that little fluff ball of yours. Jesus, what the hell kind of name is Nine-A? Does she really answer to that? How about Tiffany or Samantha or even Myrtle? Your eyes are sparking. Okay, I'm taking the dog food and leaving. I do have one question, though. Does Max eat here with us and Nine-A, or should I feed him this deplorable stuff?"

"I guess it depends on how much you eat. I eat one slice of white meat and almost all of the stuffing."

"Then I guess I'll see you at seven-thirty. It isn't dress-up, is it?"

Helen stared at the tall man hopping from one foot to the other. Rangy, a Clint Eastwood type, sandy hair, weathered skin, a few freckles, raggedy Villanova sweatshirt, ratty sweatpants, beat-up sneakers, and the clearest, brightest blue eyes she'd ever seen in her life.

"Nah. Come as you are. Just wash your hands."

The moment the three locks were in place, Helen picked up Lucie and ran into the bedroom, where she flopped on the bed. Only then did she let her nerves take over. *Is Sam Tolliver who he said he is? Did he really live here before I moved in? Is he truly a Ph.D.? Does he teach at Middlesex College? Do I dare trust him?*

"What did you think, Lucie? I kind of liked him, but then I kind of liked Daniel, too, in the beginning. He has a dog. That's got to be a plus. He's the right age. Boots says we have to learn to trust, and she's right. All men aren't like Daniel. He seemed nice. If we decide we don't like him or his dog, we won't have to see them again."

Lucie burrowed against Helen's chest. "I hate calling you Nine-A but we have to do what we have to do. Now, though, we are going on the Internet to see if Dr. Sam Tolliver is who he says he is."

7

Helen risked a glance at her watch: 10:50, and they were still sitting at the dining-area table, their dinner plates in front of them. She felt her stomach muscles bunch into a knot. How was she going to get Sam to leave without coming across as weird? Boots would be logging on soon, and here she was with her dinner dishes still in front of her, entertaining a stranger and his dog. She risked a side glance in the other direction to where the chocolate Lab was playing with Lucie. All her toys, even her treasured new mouse, were in a pile in the middle of the living-room floor. Obviously she trusted the big dog and his owner as well.

"Your dog is beating up on my dog," Sam said. "Notice that he is being a gentleman and only offering gentle swipes at her, whereas she is determined to bite his tail in two."

"Are you trying to tell me my dog isn't a lady? She's sharing all her toys, even her favorite mouse. Your dog brought nothing to the party. And, speaking of parties, tomorrow is a workday, and I still have to clean up."

"I'll help. We can have this cleaned up in no time," Sam said, jumping up. "I'm a whiz-bang in the kitchen. Max wanted to bring his blanket, but I wouldn't let him. I didn't want you to think he was a sissy."

"No, you don't have to help. I do better in that department myself. I know where everything goes and you don't. I try to be in bed by eleven-fifteen. That's a blunt hint that you should leave now."

"There's nothing bashful about you, Nancy Baker," Sam said good-naturedly. "I guess I overstayed my welcome. I enjoyed the dinner immensely and the company as well. I'd like to do it again sometime soon. I think Max is in love. Look at the way they're mooning over each other."

"My dog is . . . she's *fixed*," Helen said desperately, her eye on the kitchen clock.

"Yeah, so is Max. I'm going, I'm going. Do you live by the clock or something?"

"Or something."

"So, can we do this again?"

"Well . . ."

"I'll cook. How about day after tomorrow?"

When the minute hand of her watch hit the twelve, Helen would have promised anything. "Yes, day after tomorrow. Fine, fine. I like your dog. Good night, Sam."

Sam's eyes narrowed slightly as he called his dog to his side. In the end he had to pick up the 110-pound dog and carry him through the open door. "I know you must have someone in the closet that comes out at eleven on the dot," he grumbled, as Helen slammed the door shut.

Her nerves jangling, Helen raced to the computer and turned it on. In minutes she was logged on and waiting for Boots to Instant Message her. She was only three minutes late. *Oh, God, I forgot your chewie, Lucie. You have to wait a minute until Boots comes on. I see now I need better control. I'm so nervous.* Her shoulders slumped when she read the two short words, "You're late."

"I had unexpected company. Time got away from me."

"What kind of company, TTLS?"

"A neighbor. I checked him out. Dr. Sam Tolliver, Ph.D. He came over to borrow dog food and more or less invited himself to dinner. I didn't know how to get out of it. He has a dog, Max, a big chocolate Lab. Nine-A loves him, and he loves her. Everything he told me is true. He teaches at the college. Actually, he heads up the Accounting Department."

"How did the evening go?"

"Very well. He's easy to talk to. He likes to eat. No personal questions. Mostly dog talk and accounting methods. I didn't get nervous till ten minutes of eleven. I'm sorry I was late."

"It's okay. Is it safe to say you have a friend now?"

"He invited me to dinner at his place day after tomorrow. I said yes so he would leave. I can see him being a friend. Nine-A liked him a lot. She even let him pick her up."

"What did you think of him, TTLS?"

"He made me laugh. Once I got over my nervousness, I relaxed and enjoyed his company. He wants to introduce me to some of the other neighbors. I don't know if I'm ready for that yet. Do you approve or disapprove?"

"It's a step in building your new life. Be cautious. Now, tell me, how is TTLS2 doing? We've made a lot of progress these past two months, so we can ease up a little tonight. In fact, I'm thinking we can cut down the counseling sessions to three times a week. If you aren't comfortable with that suggestion, we can continue as before for a while longer."

"I'd rather continue."

"All right, we'll continue. I want to hear all about your latest list of orders and about TTLS2's latest antics."

"I have six orders for teddies, the lacy ones with the smocked straps. And, I have orders for seven camisoles. I must have dropped a potato or else the bag had a hole in it because she snatched it right up and carries it everywhere. I think she thinks it's her old mouse or else it smells like her old mouse. She keeps it in her bed. She showed it off to Max tonight. He wasn't impressed. All he did was sniff it. Sam wants to know if we can have play dates for the dogs since both of them are left alone so much. I said yes but only here. I won't take her there."

"Good thinking. How did she react to Sam?"

"Very well. I thought . . . I was concerned that a man, any man, would make her schizy. Dogs are very shrewd judges of character. Did you ever have a dog, Boots? Oops, sorry, I know, no questions of the counselor."

"And your own fear?"

"It's there, but it isn't there if you know what I mean. It's like even though I'm busy, I'm still lonely. I miss . . . other places. My bad dreams are easing up. I rarely get them now. I think I'm really excited about Sam. I do like him. I'd like to know him better."

"That's normal."

"I know this is a question but I have to ask it. Do you . . . is there any news of . . . of . . . you know?"

"It is a question, and no, you do not have to ask it. That part of your life is behind you. You have to stop thinking about it. You're safe."

Then why don't I feel safe? Why do I check the doors and windows three times before going to bed? Why am I fearful when I take the trash out? Why do I jump out of my skin when Lucie barks for what seems like no reason? "I guess I'll get used to it eventually."

"Would you like to call it an early night?"

"Yes, I would if that's all right."

"We'll talk tomorrow evening."

The sigh escaping Helen's lips was so loud, Lucie woke up and whimpered. "It's okay, baby. I'm just going to clean up this mess and then we'll go out. Get your leash and wait by the door." The little dog jumped from her perch on the kitchen stool and trotted over to the door for her leash. Ten minutes later, Helen fastened the leash to Lucie's collar. The warm air was like a balm as she quietly walked down the steps and out to the patch of grass that was Lucie's favorite spot.

"Hurry, Lucie, it's late. No barking, it's almost midnight, and everyone is asleep. Ah, good girl, Lucie. Good girl. What's wrong?" Helen looked over her shoulder, straining to see in the darkness. Was someone out there? Obviously Lucie thought so. Someone else walking their dog? Someone *spying* on her? The thought sent shivers up her spine.

And then Lucie let loose with an earsplitting bark as she strained at the leash, dragging Helen forward to a dark shape at the far side of the parking lot. A matching bark echoed her own, but deeper and more menacing.

"Nancy, is that you?"

"Sam!"

"Yeah, yeah, it's me. Easy, Max, easy. I took him out when I left your place but he must have known you were out here with Nine-A. He kept slamming up against the door so I brought him out again. Who's Lucie?"

Her dog's name on her neighbor's lips sent another shiver up Helen's spine. She took a deep breath. "Lucie who?"

"That's what I'm asking you. I heard you talking to someone named Lucie. I thought you were calling Nine-A."

"It wasn't me. Maybe someone else is out here walking their dog," Helen lied smoothly.

"Listen. I have an idea. How about if I take Nine-A for the night or you take Max. They seem smitten with each other. Max just sat by the door when we got home."

"I'll take your dog. Listen. I have to go in. It's late and getting later by the minute. I get up early."

"Okay. But it's my turn next time."

"I don't think so. My dog gets homesick. She doesn't like to be away from me, and I don't like being away from her. You can pick him up at six."

"Since we both work and leave early and the dogs are alone, would you mind if your dog stays at my house during the day with Max? You know, for company."

"Yes, I mind. No."

"Prickly, aren't we?"

"It's late. I just met you, for heaven's sake. Already you invited yourself to dinner, and now you want me to baby-sit your dog."

"I'm reciprocating. Okay, okay. I thought . . ."

"I know what you thought. Another time, okay?"

"Sure, another time. Listen, would you like to go fishing on Saturday? Up to Round Valley. It's just an hour or so away. The fishing is pretty good. We could make a campfire and cook what we catch. I always take food in case they aren't biting. The dogs can run and romp. Good exercise. This little walk in the parking lot doesn't quite fill the definition of exercise. You can let me know tomorrow."

"I'll think about it. I have some orders I have to deliver. I think Lu . . . my dog might like a good romp. Good night, Sam."

"Okay, Max, go with this pretty lady, and I'll see you in the morning. I have to get his blanket, though. Wait right here."

This is crazy. I'm crazy for agreeing to this. Then she looked down at the two dogs tussling with each other. Lucie was so happy, so playful. How could she deny this little animal anything? She reached down to scratch the Lab behind the ears. He licked her hand. Helen felt hot tears prick her eyelids.

"I found him alongside the road. He could hardly stand up he was so malnourished, and whoever had him, beat him. I guess he knows you're a good person. I haven't seen him lick anyone's hand but mine. He's gotten me through some bad times. In case you're interested," Sam said softly.

"I'll take good care of him," Helen said in a choked voice.

"It's okay. It really is an imposition. I'll make his breakfast."

"No, it's okay."

"Does this mean we're friends again?"

Helen shivered as she unlocked the door and reached for Max's blanket. "Yes," she said simply.

"Whew, that's a load off my mind." Sam grinned.

"Good night, Sam."

"Night, Nancy. C'mere, big guy, and give me five!" Helen smiled when the Lab smacked his paw against Sam's open palm. She watched as they tussled a moment before Sam turned to head back to his apartment.

Helen slid all three bolts home. The Lab watched her expectantly until she said, "Okay, Lucie, show Max where we sleep. Take his blanket. I'll be there in a minute."

Helen sat down on the kitchen stool and fired up a cigarette, something she only did when she was under incredible stress. There had been questions in Sam Tolliver's eyes under the parking-lot lights when she called her dog Lucie. Did her lie convince Sam? She doubted it. God, how easy it was to make a slip of the tongue. She made a mental note to be more careful.

The lights off. One last check of the door, and she was ready for bed. She brushed her teeth, washed her face and hands, then pulled on her pajamas.

Helen burst out laughing when she entered her bedroom. There they were, stretched out on the bed, side by side, Lucie's tiny head in the curl of the Lab's neck, both of them on Max's blanket. "I'm glad you saved me some room," she said, crawling into bed. "Night, Lucie, night, Max."

* * *

Helen woke slowly the following morning, aware that something was different in her life. The something different was the 110-pound Lab lying next to her, one heavy paw across her chest. She smiled when Lucie reared up to lick her face. Max waited, his gaze curious, until Lucie was finished, at which point he gave Helen's cheek a tentative lick before he bounded off the bed. Both dogs waited expectantly to see what her next move would be.

Helen smiled. "Here's the drill, guys. You wait while I use the bathroom. In five minutes, if your master is on time, you go for your walk. If he's late, I do it, and then you get your breakfast."

The moment Helen finished brushing her teeth, the doorbell rang. Max bounded toward the door, Lucie in pursuit, Helen bringing up the rear.

Helen blinked. Dressed in a lightweight camel-colored suit, pristine white shirt, and casual loafers, Sam looked every bit the college professor. She amended the thought to handsome college professor. She liked his steady brown gaze and the dimple in his chin. On top of all that, he smelled delicious. She said so and then flushed a bright pink.

"I clean up nicely," he quipped.

"I see that. And it's still early. You can leave Max here today."

"Are you sure? I don't want to take advantage."

"Sure you do. It's okay, though. Better walk him."

Lucie whimpered at her feet, her bright red leash between her teeth. "In a minute, baby. I have to get dressed."

"I'll be glad to walk your dog with Max. It looks like that's what they both want."

Helen panicked. "Well . . . no, that's okay . . . I'll . . . I'll do it. C'mon, baby, let's go." Before Sam could blink, she had Lucie's leash on and was running down the steps, her slippers making slapping motions on the rubber tread. Lucie howled her displeasure at these strange goings-on. Max jerked free of Sam's hold and sailed down the steps, his paws barely touching the concrete.

"C'mon, Lucie, pee before someone sees me in my robe." The Yorkie obliged and a moment later, Helen was racing breathlessly up the steps.

"Hell, I guess you didn't need me after all," Sam grumbled.

"I have a handle on it. C'mon, guys, let's go." Helen shrugged at Sam's blank gaze as Max tore down the hall to Helen's door.

"I'll pick him up tonight."

"Okay." Helen closed and bolted the door.

Normally a neat, tidy person, Helen slammed her way through breakfast. "You're getting dry food, Max," she said, pouring kibble into a big bowl. She carried her coffee into the bathroom with her. She exited twenty minutes later, dressed for work. A quick glance at her watch told her she was going to be ten minutes late if she took the time to send Boots an e-mail. In the scheme of things, ten minutes didn't seem all that important.

The e-mail was short and terse. "Boots, a new development. Can we go on-line at nine tonight? Thank you. TTLS."

Helen filled the dogs' water bowls, set out more dry food in another bowl, and issued the same warning she did every day. "Don't get into any trouble, and be good until I get home."

In the parking lot Helen realized she would be fifteen minutes late instead of ten minutes the way she'd originally thought. She started to shake and tremble when the car's engine refused to turn over. Maybe the battery was dead. Did she dare go back to the apartment and call a garage or should she simply cross the busy highway and walk to work? Run would be more like it. She opted for the latter and got out of the car. At the least, she would be thirty minutes late. In the past she'd been slammed against the wall and kicked for being two minutes late. Perspiration beaded on her forehead as she set out on foot for the mall.

Thirty-seven minutes later, Helen walked into the lingerie shop. As always, she stared at the shop owner to gauge her demeanor, much the way she'd stared at Daniel for years and years. Her insides quivered. "I'm sorry I'm late. My car wouldn't start, so I had to walk."

"I'm not interested in your problems, Nancy. I have enough of my own. On time means on time. I was going to keep you till the end of the week, but I changed my mind. I don't find you an asset to Fine Things. You aren't upbeat enough. You don't smile, and you're always looking at your watch like you have somewhere to go. Customers pick up on things like that. Don't think I haven't heard about your little side business either. Here's your pay. Don't try to collect unemployment either. I'll fight it if you do try."

"You're firing me?"

"Do you have a problem with your hearing, too?"

"No, ma'am, my hearing is fine. What isn't so fine is what you said about me. It is rather hard to be upbeat when people come in here to buy your tawdry merchandise. All they want to do is get it in a bag and to leave. They don't want chitchat and happy, sappy smiles. I learned that the first day I was here. Yes, I do look at my watch. I count the minutes and seconds until it's time to leave. I don't like your shop, and I despise this sleazy merchandise you call fine things. I also don't like your return policy, which is no returns at all. Is this check going to bounce?"

"Of all the nerve!" the woman sputtered.

Helen sighed. "Where's your happy smile, Mrs. Peters?" she called over her shoulder as she exited the store for the last time. *Way to go, Helen. I stood up for myself. I told it like it is. So I got fired. So what?*

In the mall, she walked aimlessly, finally taking the escalator to the second floor, where she sat down at an outdoor table and ordered coffee. She longed for a cigarette.

The waitress, a young girl she'd talked with often, set the coffee in front of her. "You look like you lost your last friend."

"I just got fired. Do you know of anyone looking for help here in the mall?"

"Yeah, me. We pay the same as all the other shops. Tips are all yours. I don't think you're the waitress type, but a job like this will tide you over till you can find what you're looking for. We all get along swell. Six-hour shifts. It's all fast food, no heavy trays or anything like that. You gotta wash your hair every night, though. If you're interested, I'll talk to my boss. He doesn't come in till noon. I open."

"Do you think I could work ten till four?"

"Sure. That's what I work."

"I don't even know your name," Helen said, suddenly shy.

"Susan Little."

"Nancy Baker," Helen said, extending her hand.

"Pleased to meetcha." Susan giggled.

"Likewise." Helen laughed. "When do you think I can start?"

"How about tomorrow. I know Mr. Donner will welcome you with open arms. The kids he hires aren't dependable. He keeps looking for mature adults. You're a mature adult, like me. Right?"

Helen wasn't sure about the mature part, but Susan definitely was an adult. "Right."

Another decision, another hurdle and she'd weathered both of them. Thank you, God.

8

Isabel Tyger threw back the covers and swung her legs over the side of the bed, but not before she looked at the bedside clock. It was five minutes later than the last time she'd looked. Long years of poor sleeping habits told her there would be no more sleep for her that night. She might as well get up and make some coffee. Or tea. On the other hand, a double slug of bourbon might be just what she needed.

The toy poodle sleeping on the pillow next to her yawned and stretched as though to say, aren't we sleeping *again?*

Isabel slipped into a worn, comfortable, ageless flannel robe. Her feet slid into equally worn and comfortable slippers. She picked up the little dog and nestled her inside her robe against her ample breast. It was amazing, she thought, how comforting the little dog was. Her very own security blanket. Artie and Gerry laughed at her, but she knew they understood.

"I hate this house. I really do. I don't know why I ever stayed here. I should move into a condominium where other people do everything for you. Why do I need this mausoleum? It holds nothing but bad memories for me." It was a litany she went through each time she woke and couldn't go back to sleep.

At the beginning of the long, dark corridor, Isabel pressed a keypad and the entire house sprang to light, shining down on the austere-looking portraits of her father's side of the family that hung on both sides of the long hallway. Mean-looking men, her father included, and blank-faced women with pursed lips and high-necked plain dresses. "Someday I am going to burn every last one of these damn pictures and hang circus pictures all the way down to the end of this hallway," she muttered. It would never happen, and she knew it. Her shoulders slumped.

Tyger house had always been a house of men. First there was her great-grandfather, and then her grandfather, and then her father and brother. The women who'd had the audacity to marry the Tyger men had all died within the first few years of their marriages for some strange reason. Secretly, she always thought they'd died to get away from the Tyger men. She was the only female Tyger to survive. Gerry and Artie said it was because she had grit. Whatever it was, here she was, approaching her seventieth birthday, alone in a house she hated with no family and no one to leave the Tyger toy fortune to.

She wished now, the way she always wished on her sleepless nights, that she had someone to talk to, someone to tell her she mattered, that she counted for something. Artie and Gerry told her all the time that she was special, but it wasn't the same. Now, even her brother was gone, buried in some godforsaken part of the world. A brother she'd barely known even though he was only four years older, a brother who'd given up his share of Tyger Toys to her because he wanted to be a free spirit and travel the world. She'd inherited nothing from her father, just the promise that she could live out her life here in this ugly old house. She hoped her father was spinning in hell for the way he'd treated her.

Isabel walked into the fluorescent-lighted kitchen and blinked. State-of-the-art. Every appliance known to man was there, and all she ever did was make coffee and tea. She really had no clue as to how the kitchen operated. The cook, a cranky curmudgeon like herself, was the only one who knew how the appliances worked. She firmly believed if the cook went on strike, she would starve to death. She firmly believed a lot of things that Artie and Gerry said were nonsense.

Isabel shook her head to clear her thoughts as she poured generously from the bourbon bottle she kept in the cabinet under the kitchen sink. She moved on to her second vice and lit a cigarette from the mangled pack in her robe pocket. Bourbon, cigarettes, and her father's money had gotten her to this point in time. She wasn't about to spoil a good thing. The toy poodle slept peacefully inside her robe.

"I really hate this time of day," she mumbled. The night was still alive, and the new day hadn't been born yet. This was the time of day, according to articles she'd read, when God made His choices. Her father had died shortly before dawn. And if the reports the embassy had passed on to her were accurate, so had her brother.

The day her brother had turned over his inheritance to her, she'd gone to the cemetery and danced a wild jig on her father's grave. Even then the plan to provide sanctuary for battered and abused women must have been in her mind. She poured more bourbon and fired up a second cigarette from the stub of the old one. She wasn't supposed to smoke and she sure as hell wasn't supposed to drink. She gave an unladylike snort to show what she thought of her doctor's orders.

Maybe she needed to go on-line. She could surprise Helen Ward with a long e-mail she would get in the morning when she turned on her computer. She jammed the bourbon bottle into the pocket of her robe and trotted down the hall to her father's old office, a room she'd hated all her life. A room she hadn't dared to change just like the rest of the house. Why, she didn't know.

Well, by God, tomorrow, today really, that is going to change. As soon as it gets light, I'm going to call in a contractor and redo the whole damn house from top to bottom. "Whatever time I have left is going to be filled with sunshine and wildflowers," she said aloud as she took her place at the desk and turned on the computer. While she waited for the computer to boot up, she looked around at the shelves with all the toys that had been manufactured over the years. There wasn't even one that remotely appealed to her. There wasn't a single toy suitable for a little girl.

Tyger Toys was a stodgy, old-fashioned toy company known for its durable products, toys that were guaranteed never to wear out and guaranteed to survive every torture test a child could come up with. Toys passed down from one child to the next. Toys that were strong and sturdy like her father, hateful old man that he was. Maybe that's why she wasn't interested in the toy business, preferring to leave it in the capable hands of all the buttoned up MBAs she paid outrageous salaries to.

The computer screen said it was okay to type her letter. What did she want to say to the young woman who had touched her heart? Be brave, be careful. Be extra careful with this new man who has entered your life. Talk about her little business, explain that it wasn't the end of the world that she'd gotten fired. Build up her self-esteem. Ask about the dog and the dog next door. Get minute details. Tell her she can always count on you and the shelter.

In the end she typed nothing. Instead, she turned off the computer and poured herself a third drink, this one stiffer than the one before. She gulped at the smoky-tasting bourbon. "Sixty-two god-damn years later and it still haunts me," she said, slurring her words.

Somehow the phone found its way to her hand. She dialed Gerry's number and wasn't surprised to hear him pick up after the first ring.

"Can't sleep, Izzie?"

"Guess you can't either. Maybe we should call Artie and have a three-way conference call."

"I wouldn't do that if I were you. He treasures his sleep. His arthritis is bothering him a lot lately. How much have you had to drink?"

Isabel chose to ignore the question. "As soon as it gets light, I'm calling in a contractor to renovate this damn house. I need sunshine. I hate this place. Tell me again, Gerry, why I stay here. Never mind. I'm going for a walk. Go back to bed." She hung up the phone before her old friend could respond.

How many times had she gone for this same walk? Hundreds? Thousands? Maybe hundreds of thousands of times. She could find her way in the dark even if she wore a blindfold.

As she walked along, she slurped from the bottle in her robe pocket. Courage in a bottle. It was such a crock. She didn't know the first thing about courage and guts. If she did, she wouldn't be walking down this well-worn path.

Isabel was almost to her destination when she saw headlights arc to the left of where she was walking. Gerry. Or Artie. She kept walking.

He was there before she was. But then maybe that's why she'd called him. Sometimes she just didn't know the why of things.

"It's four-thirty in the morning, Izzie."

"It will be light in another hour. Why are you here?"

"Because you need me, that's why. You have to stop this. It isn't good. It sure as hell isn't healthy. It was a long time ago."

"To me it was yesterday. Guess you called Artie, huh? I thought you said he treasured his sleep."

"You're more important than Artie's sleeping habits."

"That's nice of you to say that, Gerry. Want a drink?"

"Why the hell not," Gerry grumbled.

"We have to stop doing this, Izz," Artie said as he, too, walked through the undergrowth in his pajamas and slippers, his hair standing on end. "Pass that bottle to me. You already have a snootful, don't you, Izz?"

"What if I do?" Isabel said smartly. "I didn't ask you to come here. Go home."

"And leave my best friend in the whole world here crying? I don't think so," Artie said.

"That goes for me, too, Izzie. We were part of it. We were only eight years old. There was nothing we could do. As it was, your father ran us off. We came back as soon as we could. Don't you understand, there was nothing we could do?" He wondered how many times he'd said these same words and how many more times he would say them during the course of his life.

"I should have kicked him, screamed at him to make him stop. I could have done that."

"You did do that. We all did. You just blocked it out. You were like a wild tiger that morning. Artie and I screamed every cussword we knew. Why in the goddamn hell do you think I became a vet? Why do you think Artie designed all those computer programs for vets and that database as well? We were just kids. And if you think for one minute, I don't think about that day every day of my life, you're wrong. I know I speak for Artie, too. Sixty-one years later and we still think about it. You're losing it, Izzie. You need to get a grip on things. It's the Ward woman that's doing this to you. Damn it, I wish I had never called you that night."

"How many times are we going to go over this?" Artie said, sitting down on the ground.

"There are just some things you never forget. If you two hadn't attacked him he would have . . . I saw his eyes. You saw his eyes. Maybe we were just kids, but all three of us couldn't be wrong. You're right, Gerry, Helen Ward brought it front and center. She's just like me. I can't ignore that."

"You are helping her. You gave her a new life. The rest is up to her," Artie said. "By the way, her husband moved out of his house. I heard he has a small apartment in town. He cashed in his pension. Took a big hit on taxes and penalties. Rumor has it that our competitors are trying to sign him up. I thought you might want to know."

"I have a real bad feeling about him. I'm worried about Helen. He *will* find her. I don't know how, but he will. That man isn't like the others we've had to deal with. This one is *smart*. I feel like I've lied to her. I keep telling her she's safe, and we all know it isn't true."

"Can we talk about this tomorrow, Izz? I'd like to go home now. I have a breakfast meeting at seven."

"I'm going to stay here for a while," Isabel said.

Artie dropped back to the ground. "Damn, I'm going to be thinking about this all day now."

"Let's get to it, Izzie."

Isabel got up and walked over to a small clearing full of wild-flowers and manicured shrubbery. She dropped to her knees and started to cry. Artie and Gerry watched helplessly as Isabel moved among the old stones where they'd scratched numbers one through nine. Eyes wet, they also dropped to their knees. All three were children again as they relived the most horrific moment of their young lives. The day Anson Tyger had drowned Isabel's pet dog and her nine new pups in front of their very eyes. And when he'd stretched out his long arm for Isabel, they'd turned into instant warriors.

"It's an omen, don't you see," Isabel cried. "Helen Ward came to you with Lucie that night. What are the chances of that happening ever again? She was the ninth person to enter the shelter in December. Lucie was Nine-A. That has to mean something. I think it means I am to guard her with my life. I don't care what you two big strapping men think. Do you hear me? I don't care. And furthermore, if I want to come here and bawl my eyes out at four-thirty in the morning, I will do so. I will continue to come here until the day I die. And when I die, if you two are still alive, I hope you will come in my place. That dog was my best friend. She made my life bearable. I promised to take care of her and her pups. I promised just the way Helen Ward promised. I would have, too. She trusted me, she depended on me, and I couldn't help her. She had the most beautiful, soulful eyes. The pups were precious. I loved each and every one of them. I loved them more than I loved the man who was my father. I hated him. I still hate him. I danced on his grave. I was next. We all know it. That's what we've never been able to forget. He would have drowned me, too. If I was a man, I would have pissed on his grave."

"We did it for you, Izz," Artie said gently.

"Yeah, we did, Izzie," Gerry said just as gently.

"Good for you. Good for all of us. This calls for a drink," Isabel said, handing over the bottle to her friends. "Do you agree? It's an omen?"

Both men shook their heads.

"Then gentlemen, you may each take one of my arms and walk me back to my house that is shortly going to be redone. I have a plan."

"Ah, she has a plan," Artie said.

"I love a good plan. Especially when it comes together. Why don't you skip your breakfast meeting and Izzie can have her housekeeper make us some of her famous Belgian waffles?" Gerry said.

"Okay. I'm certainly dressed for it," Artie said, pointing to his pajamas and slippers.

Isabel stopped in her tracks. She turned around to face her two old friends. "A person is rich if he or she can claim one good friend.

I'm rich beyond measure since I have two such good friends. I don't know what I would have done without you two."

"It's the other way around, Izz. Gerry and I are the lucky ones. Whoever would have thought, all these years later, we'd still be coming here and still be friends," Artie said gruffly.

"Let's eat on the patio," Isabel said.

"Sounds good. I can't wait to hear this plan of yours," Gerry said, his eyebrows knitting into a straight line across his wrinkled forehead. "It's about Helen Ward, isn't it?"

"Yes. It's about Helen Ward."

"So are you ready?" Sam barked through the closed door. "C'mon, the fish are biting, and I want to eat fish tonight. I'm going to load the car. You bring the dogs and whatever you think you might need, okay?"

Helen opened the door. "Are you always this cheerful in the morning?" Overhead, birds chirped as the sun began to peek through the new growth on the trees. It was going to be a wonderful day.

"I'm trying to make up for canceling our dinner the other night."

"I told you I didn't mind. It's still dark out, Sam."

"It's getting light. Sometime I'll take you night fishing. Just you and the moon and the stars. No stress, no strain. Just you and the fish."

"I'm throwing mine back if I catch any."

"You're what?" Sam said, pretending horror.

"I could never kill something and then eat it."

"You eat meat, don't you?"

"Hardly ever. I'm basically a vegetarian. The chicken I made the other night was the first meat I'd had in months. I *never* eat red meat."

"I'm carnivorous." Sam grinned. "I packed us a lunch just in case."

"I'm ready. Does Max bring his blanket with him?"

"No, leave it behind. He'll be so busy chasing squirrels and rabbits, he'll forget about it, and he has your dog to play with."

"Are there ticks there? If a dog gets a tick on his spine, it will paralyze him until it's taken out."

"I didn't know that. We'll keep a sharp eye. How do you know about that?"

"I saw it on the Internet."

Helen picked up Lucie and settled her on the backseat of Sam's Chevy Blazer. "Be a good girl now and don't jump off." She smiled when Max leaped onto the seat and nudged her hand away from Lucie.

"I think he's trying to tell you something." Sam laughed.

Helen frowned. "Your dog is very possessive. I'm not sure I like that," Helen said defensively.

Sam slammed the door of the cargo hold and stared at her. "You're serious, aren't you?"

"Yes, I am."

"I don't understand. The dogs like each other. You should be glad, like I am, that they have someone to keep them company all day when they're alone."

Helen felt flustered as she walked around to the passenger side of the 4 x 4 and climbed in.

"Is this something you don't want to talk about, or is it none of my business?"

"Both," Helen said.

"I guess I can respect that. Would you rather talk about the world situation or how about that business you're starting? By the way, how's the job going?"

"Waitressing isn't easy. The tips aren't what I thought they would be. The people are nice, though, so that helps. I can eat and drink all I want. The hours are good, too, so I can't really complain. It isn't my life's work. What are you going to be doing this summer?"

"I teach a few courses at Rutgers a couple of days a week for extra money. I'm helping a couple of my more promising students study for the GMATS. Like you, the hours allow me to do other things. Max likes to hike, and I fish or just get in the truck and go. I do some tent camping a few times during the summer. All things considered, I lead an uneventful life. Then there are the barbecues and the blind dates my friends insist on."

"Oh."

"Oh? That's it, oh? Does that mean you don't like blind dates or you don't like me going on blind dates?"

"Do blind dates ever develop into anything?"

"Not for me. You know what my true test is when I meet a young woman?"

"No. What?"

"Max. Some women just aren't animal people, dog people in particular. I cross them off my list right away. I can't imagine life without an animal in it. Sometimes they pretend they like old Max, but I can see through that right away. If he doesn't warm up to someone I bring home, I don't bring her home a second time. Take you. He liked you right away. Hell, he even licked your hand. There was only one other female he liked, but she didn't like me. She told me right to my face accounting people were boring and unimaginative and she didn't want to waste her time on someone like me."

Helen laughed. "Did she really say that or are you making it up?"

"So help me God. She designed galoshes. You know, rubber boots. Fishing boots and rain boots. All the colors of the rainbow, red, purple, bright yellow. Those babies sell like crazy, too."

Helen continued to laugh.

"You should do that more often. You're pretty when you laugh."

Lucie barked sharply, Max joining in. Helen laughed again. "I'll have to remember that."

"You were supposed to say I'm handsome when I laugh. No, no, don't say it now, it's too late."

"Actually, what I was going to say was I admire a sunny disposition so early in the morning. Truly, I admire anyone who can get up early and be cheerful. I'm pretty much of a grouch until I've had three cups of coffee."

"You're forgiven. Do you know how to cook fish?"

"You mean a whole fish or a filet?"

"Either-or?"

"Assuming we catch some fish and assuming you clean them

up and fillet them, I think I can do my part. What did you pack in the picnic basket?"

"Tell me what you packed first," Sam said craftily.

"I asked you first." *God, I'm flirting.* A warm feeling spread up and down Helen's arms. A nice feeling, she decided, and long overdue.

"Peanut butter and jelly sandwiches and apples. Good stick-to-your-ribs food. What'd you bring?"

"Tuna and egg salad. I wasn't sure which one to make so I made both and then mixed them together. Overall, it's an interesting taste. Nut rolls that I made myself last night and some apple wedges and orange slices. I bought some treats for the dogs. Lu . . . my dog loves them. I guess none of us will starve," Helen babbled, aware that she'd almost slipped again. She risked a glance at Sam to see if he'd picked up on the slip. He seemed oblivious.

The balance of the ride to Round Valley was made with small bursts of chatter mostly centering on the weather, Sam's students, and tales of both dogs.

"Wow, I thought we'd be the first ones here. Just goes to show the fish must be biting. You are going to get an education today, Miss Baker."

"I can hardly wait. What about the dogs?"

"Just let Max take over. He knows the boundaries, and he knows the rules. I assume you brought your whistle."

Helen yanked at the string around her neck. "Two toots and they come back. One toot means they have to bark to give us their location, right?"

"You got it," Sam said, taking the fishing poles from the back of the Blazer. "You're like an overanxious mother. Is there a reason for that?"

"Yes."

"Oh. Hey, hold on a minute. You need to carry your share," Sam said, reaching for Helen's arm to pull her toward him.

Helen's face drained of all color as she flinched and cowered close to the Blazer.

"Whoa," Sam said, backing up, the palms of his hands straight out in front of him. "Easy, Nancy."

"I . . . I . . . I'm . . . sorry. I don't . . . what it is . . . I don't like to be . . . *touched.*"

"Okay. I can respect that. Are you okay?"

"I'm . . . okay."

"Then I say, let's go fishing."

"Sam . . ."

"It's okay, Nancy. You don't owe me any explanation. You ready to fish?"

"I'm ready to fish. And, I'm ready to make a bet. A dollar. I bet I catch more fish than you."

"You are on, lady. Show me the color of your money."

Helen forced her facial muscles into a smile as she withdrew a crumpled dollar bill from her jeans pocket. "Let's see yours."

"You're gonna have to trust me. I locked my wallet in the glove compartment."

"I hope you didn't pull that tired old excuse on the lady with the rubber boots."

"Ya know what, she was the boring one. I'm a fun guy, don't you think?"

"Absolutely." Helen giggled and flushed a rosy red.

"Why do I get the feeling you don't laugh much?"

"Oh, I can giggle with the best of them," Helen said flippantly.

"You can, huh? I'm going to remember that."

He was flirting with her. It was going to be a wonderful day.

As she trudged alongside Sam, she was aware of how bright the new sun was, how pungent the pine-scented air had become, and how beautiful the water was with the sun shining down on it. Simple things. Things she'd never paid attention to. Now, all of a sudden they were in her face just the way Sam was in her face. Oh, yes, it was going to be a glorious day.

9

Helen turned on her computer and waited, hoping Boots would be on-line that evening. She had so much to tell her, so much to share since they'd last communicated. Her gaze went to the small desk calendar sitting alongside her computer. Was it really three days since she'd logged on to talk to Boots? She'd sent almost a dozen e-mails, with no response to any of them. She was worried because it was unlike Boots, who was so conscientious about the on-line counseling. True, it was a little over fifteen months since she'd moved there and begun the late-night counseling sessions, and it wasn't imperative that she cleanse her mind every single night. At least that's what Boots had said in her last e-mail, but surely Boots didn't think it was time to cut her loose. Her heart took on an extra beat at the mere thought of being totally on her own, with no support to fall back on. Certainly Boots would have discussed a major decision like that with her. Besides, it had to go through channels, and Isabel Tyger had the final say in such matters.

She wished she knew more about her faceless counselor. What she did know, she liked, and plans were in the works, providing the shelter's board agreed, for a meeting in Asbury Park between her and Boots. It was something she looked forward to, something she anguished over when she sent her letter to Isabel Tyger asking for permission to meet with her counselor. All she wanted was one day and the opportunity to thank Boots in person, to walk on the boardwalk and the beach and maybe get a hot dog. It was supposed to be a great day for Lucie and Max, too. Boots loved animals, and said she would love to meet Lucie and Max. Come to think of it, the last sessions were more about Lucie and Max than about her. That was okay, too. She loved talking about the dogs. Anything she had to say on the on-line sessions was now redundant. Except maybe her fears, fears she knew would never go away until the day Daniel Ward died. Sam was helping with all those emotions, though. There were now days, sometimes weeks, when she didn't think about Daniel at all. *Where are you, Boots?*

Helen's fingers flew over the keyboard. She checked her old mail, checked to see if mail she'd sent to Boots had been opened and read, checked to see if she'd missed any mail during the past days. Everything came up negative. She frowned. Something was wrong, she could feel it, sense it. Once again, her fingers flew over the keyboard. She entered the private chat room where she and Boots talked for hours on end. The room was empty. She felt her shoulders slump, and she wanted to cry. Instead she clicked on her e-mail to compose a new letter to Boots. She typed quickly, expressing her concerns and ending with, "I have this eerie feeling I'm being watched. I'm not afraid, though. My dog is nervous. That, more than anything, worries me. I want to talk to you about Sam Tolliver. Our friendship this last year has progressed to where I think he's expecting more than I think I'm ready for. I was very up front with him. I told him all I wanted at this time was friendship, and it has been a wonderful friendship. He's introduced me to things I'd only read about. He never makes demands. I trust him. I really do. He doesn't ask questions aloud. His eyes say it all. I like him. A lot. He's good for me. I know that. He makes me get out and about. We do things as a couple. I like that, too. We went to New Hope, Pennsylvania, and bought all kinds of stuff. Mostly junk, but it was fun. We colored eggs for Easter and he made me an Easter basket.

"Sam said he might be going away for six weeks. He has a teaching opportunity somewhere in Vermont. He wants me to go with him. I told him no.

"The business is building slowly and steadily. I'm about to the point where I need to think about renting some store space. The apartment is so full of boxes and materials, it's hard to maneuver. The three ladies I have sewing for me are having a hard time keeping up with the demand for Sassie Lassie undergarments. I'm going to have to hire more help. I'm still waitressing, but I cut my hours to four a day and just do the lunch trade. It's paying the rent. I haven't really touched the funds Ms. Tyger's foundation lent me.

"I guess that's it for now. Good night, Boots." She signed the e-mail the way she signed all her correspondence—TTLS.

Helen turned off the computer and sat for a moment staring at the blank screen. It was amazing, she thought, how a piece of electronic equipment and a person she'd never met face-to-face, could literally help her become a sound, normal, mentally healthy person again. *Where are you, Boots?*

"Time for bed, Lucie. We'll clean up this mess tomorrow when we pack up our deliveries. We'll have some walking-around room once all this stuff is out of here. Get your leash and we'll go outside."

Lucie ran to the door and tugged at the leash hanging from the doorknob. Helen fastened it to her collar. "Let's make this a quick one, girl. I'm really tired tonight. You miss Max, don't you? I miss him too. I even miss Sam. I never thought I'd say something like that. He's a good friend. Good girl. Okay, run!"

Lucie ran for the steps leading to the second-floor complex and then ran to Sam Tolliver's apartment door, where she sat down and whimpered. Helen bent down to pick her up. She crooned to her as she made her way to her own door. "Just a couple more days, baby. I bet Max misses you as much as you miss him. Sam had to go away. His best friend is getting married, and Sam is the best man. He didn't want to make the trip without Max. You get a cookie, and then we're going to bed."

The little dog waited patiently until Helen fastened all three locks on the door before she entered the kitchen. "Okay, two cookies!" Lucie took them daintily and walked off to the bedroom, where she would chomp on them while Helen brushed her teeth and put on her pajamas.

In bed with Lucie snuggled tight against her, Helen turned off the light. As tired as she was, sleep eluded her. She felt wide-awake. Wide-awake and worried. She'd had many nights when she wasn't able to fall asleep but this time she felt something different tugging at her. Did she miss Sam *that* much? Was it possible that she was beginning to feel something besides friend-ship for the college professor? Or was it something else entirely? Boots? Or Daniel?

Helen shifted Lucie and rolled over on her side. She shouldn't even be thinking of Daniel. Not hearing from Boots these last three days had pushed Daniel forward in her mind. Had he surfaced somewhere? Did Boots's absence mean Isabel Tyger's people were taking care of things to ensure her safety? *Damn, it always comes back to Daniel. Always.*

Maybe what she needed to do was really think about Daniel. Instead of pretending he never existed, maybe she needed to break the rules and let her mind remember all the terrible things he'd done to her. Maybe she needed to do that. Maybemaybemaybe. Boots and the others said Daniel Ward was in the past, someone she used to know, someone not worthy of her thoughts and feelings. "The thing is, Lucie, I don't want to be Nancy Baker. I want to be Helen Stanley again. Not Helen Ward but Helen Stanley. I wish I was divorced. I'll never be free of him as long as I'm still married to him. I worry that all these phony credentials are going to catch up with me. I'm just not a good liar. If the authorities confront me, I'll fall apart. If Sam confronts me, I don't know what I'll say or do. It's not like I have good or fond memories of Daniel. I just don't want anyone to *know*. It's my dirty, little secret. I feel so ashamed, so inferior, so . . . stupid. Sam would never understand someone like Daniel. He would never understand a woman allowing something like that to happen to her. Perhaps once, but not repeatedly. If I don't understand it, how can I expect someone like Sam to understand it?"

How could she ever explain to Sam the fear she lived with? His first question would be, why didn't you leave? Why?

Helen stroked Lucie's head as she forced her mind to recall each and every slap, every punch, every kick. She roll-called every bruise, every laceration, every broken bone, every fracture, and every trip to the ER, every trip to all the different doctors she'd used, every lie she'd ever told to protect her husband.

Lucie moved and bellied up to the top of Helen's pillow. "Stay, Lucie. I'm going to make some tea and go back on the computer."

The time flashed on the bottom line of the computer: 1:36 A.M. She logged on and waited. She checked her buddy list to see that RB, better known as Robin Bobbin, was on-line. She immediately sent her an Instant Message. Do you know where Boots is?

No.

Helen sent another message. I'm having a hard time today. I need to talk. Want to go to the chat room?

Sure, came the reply.

Robin Bobbin was a four-month *newbie* to the on-line counseling sessions. *Newbie* was a word computer people used for first-time computer users. Boots was also her counselor. Helen thought she could smell the woman's fear.

A rapid-fire series of questions flew from Helen's fingers. RB's responses were curt and always in the negative. "I'm scared," she wrote.

"Me too. Just follow the rules. Someone will be in touch. Something must have happened. Maybe the computer system is down. It's happened before. Boots might have some problems or she might be away. Keep sending your e-mails, and if you have fears or questions, put them in the e-mails, too. Someone from the foundation will be in touch. I'm waiting just like you are. You can always reach me after ten. My sessions are scheduled for eleven o'clock. If I hear anything, I'll e-mail you. Relax. Everything will be okay. Listen, this might sound silly, even off-the-wall, but do you have a pet? No? Get a cat or a dog. They make all the difference. Go to the pound and rescue an animal. Boots will approve. I'll e-mail her to explain it was my suggestion. Tomorrow is another day. That's kind of funny now that I think of it. It is today. Is there anything else I can help you with in Boots's absence?"

"I'm afraid of my own shadow. I hear sounds, voices, and I think . . . I think he found me somehow."

"Sometimes I still feel like that. I have three locks on my door. It's over fifteen months. It's rather like waiting for the other shoe to drop. If you follow the rules, he will not find you. Do you have family?"

"Yes. That's what makes it so hard. I miss them. I read a book once on the Witness Protection Program. This is just like being in that program."

"I know. You're alive. That's how you have to think of it. You need to get a pet. You need to be able to love something again. It's a start."

"Thanks. I'll do it tomorrow. Maybe I'll get two pets, a dog and a cat."

"Make sure the cat is a kitten and the dog is a pup so they learn to get along. LOL," Helen added—the symbols that meant "laughing out loud."

Helen signed off, finished her tea, and fixed another cup. She smoked two cigarettes as she stared at the dark screen of her computer.

Somewhere, something was wrong. It was the same kind of feeling she always had when she knew Daniel was going to use her as a punching bag. She was so wide-awake, it was scary. Rather than waste her time just sitting, Helen reached for her computer book.

For weeks she'd been again toying with the idea of setting up a web page and selling her Sassie Lassie lingerie on-line. Sam said it was a terrific idea and volunteered the services of one of his students to design the web page. If she did that, she would have to quit her job in the mall and really concentrate on getting store space. She'd been reading up on Internet selling, and if her little business took off, she would be working twenty hours a day filling orders. As Boots said, nothing ventured, nothing gained.

The biggest hurdle would be finding enough people to do the sewing. Again, Sam had come to the rescue, saying some of his students would be likely candidates. She agreed. She was on a roll now, excited with the prospect of branching out. Perhaps the three seamstresses on her payroll could cut the patterns and the college girls could sew them at her new location. She could sew and sell under one roof. Packaging could be done in the back of the store. Sam said it would only take a few days to get a working version of the web page on-line. You can fine-tune it as you go along, he'd said, and then volunteered to keep her books. All in the name of friendship.

She really needed to talk to Boots. She knew she was capable of making the decisions, of working hard to make the small business work. Still, she wanted . . . no, she *needed* Boots's approval.

Could she do this? Was she capable of starting a business and making it work? Oh, yes. Maybe if she worked really hard, one day she would be in a position to buy a small house with a backyard for Lucie to run in. A house with a real kitchen, where she had room to move around. A house with a family room and a fireplace that burned real wood. If there was extra money left over after her bills were paid, she'd donate to the animal shelters in the area. She vowed then, at that precise moment, to give back as much as she could to make some other woman's life a little easier.

Helen pulled out her sketch pad. Her pencil raced across the pages as she drew pictures of sexy, lacy underwear. She giggled when she thought of the college student looking at the garments, taking pictures of them, and then scanning them onto the web page. It was going to be fun. She was going to need some power words to attach to her web page. Decadent. Delicious. Sensual. Sassy. Definitely sassy. Feathers. She was going to need feathers on the web page. Maybe eventually she would need live models. Uh-huh. She giggled again. Life was starting to look really good.

It was four o'clock when Helen stacked all her sketches and her lists into a neat pile. She took a last look around the apartment, checked the doors again, and turned off all the lights.

Lucie squirmed off the pillow, making room for Helen's head. She fell into a deep, dreamless sleep, with her arm around her beloved pet.

Up to her neck in boxes, materials, books, and ledgers, Helen stopped what she was doing when Lucie suddenly let out an ear-splitting howl. The fine hairs on the back of her neck stood at attention. At the same moment she dropped to a low crouch to hide behind one of the larger packing boxes. "Lucie, get over here. Shhhh. Come here, girl!"

Someone was coming to her door. Friend or foe? "Come here, Lucie," Helen said a second time. The little dog scampered over to where she was hiding and leaped into her arms. "Shhh, Lucie.

No barking." She placed the open palm of her hand loosely over the dog's mouth. It was something Lucie knew and understood from their days back in California. The Yorkie trembled in her arms.

They waited for the inevitable knock on the door. When it came, Helen started to shake as hard as the little dog. She struggled for a deep breath, her heart knocking inside her rib cage. Was it always going to be like this? Of course it was. A stranger would always be a stranger.

The knock was loud on the metal door. Overly loud. Way too loud. She hated the sound.

Helen almost fainted when she heard a voice shout, "Miss Baker, I'm Les Webster from the college. You called about your web page a couple of days ago. Professor Tolliver sent me."

"It's okay, Lucie, Sam sent him. This time, it's okay."

Helen wove her way through the boxes to the door. "I'm sorry, Les, I was in the other room," she lied. "Come in." Her hold on Lucie was secure.

"Cute dog," the young man said. "Great computer. Top-of-the-line. I like this," he said, sitting down and flexing his fingers. "With what you told me on the phone and what Professor Tolliver said, I think I'll just get to it if that's okay with you. Just go on with what you were doing. I won't bother you."

"That's it? You don't want any input? You don't want me to sit next to you and tell you how I see it all?"

"Nope. Sex sells. We know that. I have all the pictures right here. Sexy underwear. I'm your man. I have five sisters. You want flash, pizzazz, bright colors, and lots and lots of *sass*. Like I said, I'm your man."

"Oh," was all Helen could think of to say.

"My sisters seem to think you need something ethereal if you want to go with the feathers for your, ah, innocent line. Clouds, lots of lace, and a demure whatever-that-thing-is."

Helen watched the gangly young man as he clicked and clicked at the keyboard. Lucie barked once and then again.

"Cute dog. We have three dogs at home," Les said absently.

"Big dogs. They eat a lot. Do your best to keep yours quiet. I have to concentrate."

Helen nodded until she realized the boy couldn't see her. He couldn't be more than nineteen, and it was doubtful he'd shaved yet. His hair was a richly burnished copper color. There was no part, no effort to control the corkscrew curls that stood straight in the air. They were a perfect match for the millions of freckles that peppered his face and arms. His jeans had so many rips and tears in them Helen had to fight herself not to offer to sew them for him. The rugby shirt was worn and faded and looked extremely comfortable. Sam had one just like it. The sneakers he wore looked like Sam's, too, half–beaten to death, worn, and dirty, the laces frayed and just as dirty. He turned and smiled. "Did I pass muster?"

"Uh-huh." Helen decided she liked him. "Would you like something to drink, a Coke, coffee, or tea?"

"Maybe some herbal tea, but later."

Helen knew the moment the words were out of his mouth, she was forgotten. He was so engrossed with what he was doing, the building could cave in and he wouldn't notice.

"Okay, Lucie, let's me and you go for a walk. Get your leash, baby."

"Professor Tolliver was just parking his car when I got here," the kid threw over his shoulder as Helen opened the door.

"Really," was all she could think of to say. Sam was back. Lucie would be so happy. She felt giddy at the thought. She'd missed the big Lab. She'd missed Sam, too. *God, I really missed Sam. A lot. More than a lot.*

Lucie jerked forward, dragging Helen down the walkway to Sam's door, where she let out a ferocious bark. An answer came through the door. The Yorkie danced and pranced until Sam opened the door. She was inside in a flash, running to Max and tumbling all over him.

"Too bad her owner doesn't greet her neighbor the way her dog does," Sam grumbled.

"Hello, Sam. It's nice to see you. We missed you. I missed you. I really did. All she did was mope around."

"That's what Max did. I thought he was sick at first. Then I showed him a picture I had of all of us. You remember the one I took when we went fishing at Round Valley. I stapled it to his blanket. He was kind of okay after that. Did you really miss me, or are you just saying that?"

"No, I really missed you. I knew the dogs would miss each other. What will we do if one of us moves away?"

"I'm not going anywhere," Sam said. "Are you planning on moving?"

"Not right now. Someday I hope to buy a little house with a yard so Lu . . . so Nine-A can run around." Damn, it was still hard to keep thinking of Lucie as Nine-A.

"Someday could be a long way off," Sam said glumly. "Want to come in for coffee? I brought back some flavored, the kind you like."

"Sure. I guess I'm kind of in the way in my apartment. I can't wait to get a place where I can store all this stuff. I feel like I'm living in a warehouse. By the way, I quit my job yesterday. I was going to ask to borrow your newspaper to look for a store location. Want to come with me?"

"Okay, but I don't know what you're going to find on a Sunday afternoon."

"I'm just looking. Once the web page goes up, I'm going to need the space. I'll feel like I'm going to work if I have a place of my own. I hope this works. I'm so nervous about it all. I've never done anything like this before. It's kind of scary."

"You have to start somewhere. How about if we rent a video tonight. We can order in, pizza or Chinese. My place of course. Les will work straight through the evening. We'll have to feed him."

Helen felt flustered. There was a look in Sam's eyes she'd never seen before. "That . . . that sounds good," she managed to say.

"We could have a sleepover." Sam grinned. "We could share secrets. We *could* pretend we're married and do all the things married people do. Hell, I'm up for *anything*."

Helen knew the color drained from her face, and it felt like an army of ants were marching around inside her stomach. "You mean . . . well . . . listen, Sam, I thought we had a clear understanding about our friendship."

Sam took her face in both his hands. "I do have an understanding. I like you a lot, Nancy. You know that. Jesus, I consider you to be one of my best friends. I enjoy your company more than that of any of my other friends. Sometimes friendships change into something more meaningful. Maybe this one won't. I'm hoping it will. However, I don't see that happening if you don't open up to me. I'm not stupid. I'm not deaf, dumb, *and* blind either. I know you aren't exactly what you pretend to be. I even suspect your dog's *real* name is not Nine-A. We are never going to get beyond this point if you don't open up to me. You can trust me, Nancy."

"I know that, Sam. Sometimes I wish I'd never met you and your dog. Then the other times, I am so glad I did. I just can't . . . it isn't that I don't . . . I can't," Helen said flatly. "When the time is right, you are the first person I'll run to. I want you to trust me. Can you do that, Sam, for just a little while longer?" *Until I get hold of Boots and she tells me it is okay.*

"Okay, let me get this straight. We're going to do the video and the ordering in. We are not going to have a sleepover. We are just going to watch the video, hold hands and snuggle and maybe eat some popcorn while our dogs cavort around us."

"That's pretty much it," Helen said. "It has to be this way, Sam."

"I'm okay with it, Nancy."

Well, I'm not okay with it. I wish I could tell you how much I want you. I want to feel your arms around me. I want to make love to you. I want us to wake up next to each other in the morning and then make love again. I can't go to bed with someone who thinks my name is Nancy and calls me Nancy. When I make love to you, it will be as Helen Stanley. Not as Nancy Baker, and never as Helen Ward.

10

Sam Tolliver looked in the mirror. "So you aren't Brad Pitt or George Clooney," he grimaced. "By the same token, Brad Pitt and George Clooney aren't college professors with a 110-pound chocolate Lab." He stuck his tongue out at his reflection. Max growled and swatted his tail against his master's leg. It was his way of saying, get a move on.

The call had come in just minutes ago from Les, saying Nancy's web page was finished and up and running. His first inclination was to run down the hall to Nancy's apartment and tell her. Then he decided to get a sneak preview. He'd whistled at the clever graphics and had felt his neck grow warm at the foxy-looking underwear Sassie Lassie featured. This definitely called for a celebration.

Wine bottle in hand, freshly shaved, wearing a clean shirt, clean socks, and underwear, he was ready to celebrate. He hoped Nancy felt the same way. Maybe he should have gotten her some flowers. Where the hell did you find flowers at ten o'clock at night? Nowhere he knew of. The wine would have to do.

"Yeah, yeah, we're going, Max. First, though, I need to . . . plan my . . . you know, my presentation. This is a biggie for Nancy. I want her to know I'm as excited as she is about her new business. Plus, I think I'm falling in love with her. If I tell her, though, she'll back off. She's spooked enough as it is. Two weeks ago when she told me she might move I thought I was going to pass out. That means she'll take her dog with her. Where does that leave us, Max? Out in the cold, that's where. If she even *thinks* I'm putting a move on her, she freezes. Enough of this. Let's go!"

Max was at the door, his tail swishing furiously, before Sam could get off the kitchen chair. He barked at the door to Helen's apartment before Sam had time to close and lock his own door.

"I have news! Good news! Wonderful news!" Sam shouted as he entered Helen's apartment.

The moment the door closed behind him, Sam playfully dropped to a low, menacing crouch, the wine bottle swinging wildly in his hand. And then all hell broke loose as Lucie leaped through the air to grab at Sam's shirtfront as she strained to reach his throat. Helen backed to the door, her face whiter than the ceiling she was standing under. She cowered, her arms crossed over her chest, her eyes fearful. Max skidded across the floor to reach up and grab Lucie by the scruff of the neck. He barked wildly, circling Sam first and then Helen. It was clear he didn't know what to do, whom to protect.

"What the hell!" Sam exploded. "Your dog almost ripped out my throat! What are you doing, Nancy? What's wrong? You look like you think . . . oh Jesus, I think I know what you and your dog are thinking. Down, Max. Easy . . . Nine-A. That's a good girl. Nancy, come over here and sit down. *Now*, Nancy! You thought I was going to strike you, didn't you? I would never do that. I think it's time for us to talk. Really talk."

Helen drew a deep breath as Lucie leaped to her lap. She was trembling so badly, Helen opened her sweater and covered her, holding her close. "It was just an instinctive reaction. I'm sorry. You looked so . . . threatening there for a minute. I wish I could talk to you, but I can't. I have to follow the rules. If I break them . . ."

"What happens if you break them?" Sam asked gently.

"I . . . won't . . . I can't expect you to understand. Maybe it's better if we don't see each other anymore."

"Oh, no! That's bullshit. I'm not leaving here till you tell me what's going on. I think I can pretty much figure it out myself, but I'd like to hear you tell me. I'd like you to trust me enough to tell me on your own. I give you my word, I won't let anything happen to you or your dog."

Helen held the little dog tighter. "I do trust you, Sam. I really do. I just can't say anything to you until I get approval to do so.

When you break the rules, the program doesn't work. It's that simple. Can we leave it at that?"

"No. If I didn't care for you, maybe. As it is, I think I'm falling in love with you. I even think you care for me, odd as that may sound, but there has to be trust on both our parts; otherwise, it isn't going to work. I think I would trust you with my life. Hell, I trust you with my dog. I never let anyone keep my dog. Nine-A likes me. She lets me pick her up, cuddle her, and she comes willingly to my apartment even if you aren't there. What in the hell happened here a few minutes ago? Are you in the Witness Protection Program? I need to know. Please tell me, Nancy."

Helen made an instant decision when she saw the concern in Sam's eyes. She knew she would regret it, but she didn't care. She licked at her dry lips. "My name isn't Nancy Baker. I truly, truly hate that name. My name is Helen. It was the way you came into the apartment, crouching low and swinging the wine bottle. My husband beat my dog so badly she almost died. He beat me, too. I had broken bones, fractures, wounds of all shapes and sizes. I went to the doctors and the emergency room so many times I lost count. The night he attacked . . . Nine-A was my breaking point. I ran with her and a very kind motorist picked us up and took us to a vet. He saved her life, fixed me up, and managed to contact a women's shelter. They took me in, and I didn't look back. They did all this," Helen said, waving her arms about. "They set me up here, got me a job, got me phony credentials, you know, a driver's license, a Visa card, a new social security card. All I had to do was follow the rules, and I just broke them. That means I can no longer stay in the program."

"Jesus, why didn't you tell me?" Sam said.

"I wanted to. I couldn't. I owe my life and my dog's life to those people who cared enough to help us. I'll have to leave now and find my own way. I can't put any of them in harm's way. Once you break the rules, you're out of the program. That's the first thing that's drummed into your head."

"I'll never tell anyone. I told you. You can trust me. I'll never breathe a word of this to another soul. No one ever needs to know you told me," Sam pleaded.

Helen started to cry. "I'll know. We do mandatory on-line counseling. I've been doing it since the day I moved here. Something is wrong, though. I can't get through to my counselor on the net. I've sent dozens of e-mails, and she isn't responding. If they were cutting me loose, I think I would have been notified. I have a bad feeling and don't know what to do. It's with me every minute of the day. I'm thinking my husband somehow found me, or he's getting close. He will find me, it's just a matter of time. Why haven't you asked me why I didn't leave?"

"Because I know why. You were afraid, you had nowhere to go, and that bastard said he would kill you if you left."

"How . . . how did you know?"

"When I was studying for my doctorate, I volunteered in a crisis center. I saw and heard it all."

"I used to pray he would have a car accident. I prayed for him to die. I hate myself for that, but it helped me to think like that. In my own way I was just as sick as he was. I got help. He didn't. I can't stay here now."

"Oh, yes you can. You aren't going anywhere, Helen. You know what, you were never a Nancy. I never did think that name fit you. Nine-A," he snorted. "That doesn't even bear discussing."

"We were the ninth guests the month of December at the shelter. We went by a number until our credentials came through. I was Number Nine and she was Nine-A. I slipped so many times and called her by name. You heard me, but you pretended you didn't. If you had brought this to a head a while back, I would have cut and run in the middle of the night."

"And now?" Sam held his breath waiting for her response.

"I don't know, Sam, I just don't know. I guess I have to stay put until I can reach Boots. She's my on-line counselor."

"And then?"

"Then I guess I'm on my own. They'll take away the credentials, tell me to leave. I'll have to give back the money they lent me."

"You could marry me. You'd have a new name. I have enough money in the bank for a down payment on a little house somewhere. You can get a new identity as my wife."

"Sam, that is so nice of you, but I can't marry you. I'm not divorced. You see, my . . . husband is one of those computer wizards, among other things. Divorces are a matter of public record. He'd find out some way, somehow. It was better to simply disappear and let sleeping dogs lie."

"Who's next in command after Boots? Can't you go to that person?"

"I don't know who that person is. Besides, questions were taboo. The rules say I have to wait for someone from the Isabel Tyger Foundation to contact me. That's the procedure. I betrayed the very people who helped me. It's unacceptable."

"Will you relax? I am not going to tell anyone. I am not going to put any moves on you. I am not going to call you Helen in public, and I am not going to refer to your dog as Lucie. Read my lips, Helen; no one knows you said a word but the two of us. You are still safe. Nothing has really changed. Why don't you check your e-mail and see if Boots has contacted you today?"

"I did check it, right before you came over. I'll go on-line at eleven since that's my scheduled time. I log on and then log off. When you came in you were excited. What happened?"

"Your web page is finished. Les called me and wanted me to tell you. I brought wine to celebrate."

"Oh."

"That's it, oh!"

"I didn't mean it like that. I can't get excited since I don't know what's going to happen to me. How am I going to operate an online business if I'm on the run? It was a good idea, but now I don't think it's going to work. With the situation the way it is, I can't make a commitment to a new business."

"Why don't you check it out just for the hell of it? You might even have some orders since the site has been up and running for a few hours. Personally, I can't wait to see it."

Helen turned on the computer. "Did Les give you the address?"

"Yep. It is *www.sassielassie.com.* All lowercase. Les said he added some music for effect."

"Oh my God!" Helen squealed. "Look at that!"

"I'm lookin', I'm lookin'." Sam grinned. "What does . . . ah . . . that little number with the feathers go for?"

"Seventy-five bucks," Helen said. "A lot of stitches go into it. Feathers are hard to attach."

"Uh-huh. Do you have any . . . ah . . . samples?"

"A whole box. It comes in white, black, and red," Helen said, scrolling down the screen with her mouse. "This is really fantastic. Les did a wonderful job. The music is . . . sensational. Don't they play that kind of music in strip joints?"

"You're asking me? You know what they say about accountants and professors who teach the subject. Remember the lady with the galoshes? We are supposedly the most boring people on earth. My answer is, I don't know."

"All those feathers! All those fluffy clouds. I guess this is the ethereal page. The stuff really looks demure, chaste, kind of virginal," Helen said thoughtfully.

"Helen, there is nothing demure about a garter belt trimmed in lace. Fishnet stockings are not virginal even if they're white. Ask any man. What's with those *strappy*, spike-heeled shoes? I didn't know you sold shoes, too!"

"I don't. I don't sell stockings either. We just put them in for effect. Then again, it might pay me to buy some accessories. Tell me something, Sam. If you clicked onto this web page, and if you were married or had a serious girlfriend, would you be tempted to order something?"

Sam sat back in his chair and leered at Helen. "I would order one of everything! Didn't you tell me you were going to show me a sample? Let's see the real thing."

Helen got up to rummage through the boxes in the living room. For the moment she forgot about her personal troubles in her excitement. "What color?"

"Black," Sam shot back.

Helen stood up, her right hand twirling the filmy garment in the air. A feather worked loose and sailed upward. Both dogs watched it curiously but no more curiously than their owners.

"Oh yes, I could see that being a best-seller," Sam drawled. "How about modeling it for me?"

"I don't think so. I'm not . . . what I mean is . . . I don't wear this kind of stuff. I just plan on selling it. Maybe some other time."

"I'd like to make love to you," Sam blurted.

Helen licked at her dry lips. "It's been . . . I don't know if . . ."

"It's like riding a bike. It all comes back to you. Trust me," Sam said breathlessly.

"The dogs?"

"They stay out here, we go in there. We close the door. Simple, eh?"

Before she could say yes or no, Sam swept her into his arms and was carrying her into the bedroom. He kicked the door shut with his foot.

"You feel something for me, I know you do," Sam murmured against her hair. He turned her gently to face him and then began to nibble at the base of her throat, his hands working beneath the opening of her skirt. "Do you like it when I touch you here?" His fingers skimmed lightly over the smooth skin of her inner thigh. "And here?" His lips blazed a trail to the satin-smooth valley between her breasts.

He nuzzled the pulse spot at the base of her throat, feeling it race beneath his lips. He wanted her, wanted to feel her skin warm beneath his hands. He could already anticipate her passion. Each curve and hollow of her body beckoned to his lips and hands. Her long dark hair twined through his fingers as he turned her to face him. When his mouth claimed hers, she welcomed him feverishly. He deepened his kiss, searching for an answering response. It came when he whispered her name, when his fingers gentled on her flesh, when he breathed his need for her. Then, with a little moan, like the sound of a stricken child, she turned into his embrace, offering her mouth to his, yielding beneath his touch.

Suddenly she was naked, the last obstacle between his hands and her body had been discarded. He took her hands in his and placed them on his belt, invoking her without words. His jeans fell away beneath her fingers; she left his newly exposed flesh warm from her kisses, continuing until he was as naked as she was. Their passions rose like the wildness of a summer storm, hungry mouths searching, feverish hands touching.

They tore at each other, each seeking what only the other could give. There was no yesterday, no tomorrow, only the here and now. And when their passion had abated, lips swollen from loving and bodies glistening with the sheen of desire, they lay in one another's arms glorying in the journey they had shared. Kiss-softened mouths, tender exploring caresses, bodies still warm from passion's fever, they basked in the afterglow of a moment only two could share.

"Sam," Helen whispered.

"What?" Sam whispered in return.

"I didn't know . . . I never . . . it was never like that before. Sam, I love you. There, I said it. I've been wanting to say those words for months, but I was afraid. I love you. Sometimes love hurts when you can't do anything about it. I'm glad you pushed me into telling you everything. I'm so tired. Are you tired, Sam?"

"Worn to a frazzle. Let's take a little nap."

"Oh, that sounds so good. The best part will be waking up next to each other. Stay the night, Sam."

"You'd have to drag me kicking and screaming to get me out of here. I'm staying."

Helen snuggled into the crook of Sam's arms.

The lovers slept peacefully and dreamlessly.

It was two o'clock in the morning when Helen took her place at the dining-area table, her eyes sparkling. "Well? Do you think this model will sell?" she asked, grinning from ear to ear.

"I'll take a dozen," Sam said.

"Be serious."

"I am being serious. I'll give them to all the female department heads for Christmas. Anonymously of course. I still can't believe you're going to sell crotchless underwear!"

"Supply and demand. Frederick's of Hollywood sells it. It's not really crotchless. There's . . . an extra piece if . . . if a person wants it."

"Oh. That makes all the difference in the world." Sam grinned. "Want some wine? The wine we were supposed to drink earlier?"

"Sure."

"Where do we go from here, Helen?"

"How about the bedroom?"

"Are you serious?"

"I'm serious."

"When? I mean, now? We just came out of the bedroom."

"Unless you have something else to do," Helen quipped.

"Me. No. I never have anything to do at this time of night. This is supposed to be the time when you . . . you know, do stuff like this . . . like that. Isn't it? I don't think it matters if we just did stuff like that, you know before. Hell, we took a nap and everything."

"I think we should go for it. You are the sweetest, the most gentle man I've ever met in my life. Caring and loving, too. Did I leave anything out?"

"Handsome. I'm ready," Sam said. "What about the dogs?"

"Why don't you take them over to your apartment. I want to take a shower and get ready."

"Ready. Yes, you need to get ready. Yesirree, you do need to get ready. Everyone needs to get ready. Yes indeedy. I'll do that. In fact, I'll do that right now."

Helen handed over a box of dog treats.

The moment the door closed behind Sam, Helen beelined for the packing boxes for the leftover bag of feathers. She upended the bag all over the bed and then galloped down the hall to the bathroom where she took a five-minute shower. Wrapped in a towel, she stared at her reflection in the mirror. "I am Helen Stanley tonight. I am not Helen Ward, and I am not Nancy Baker."

Clutching the towel in front of her, she waited for Sam to round the corner into the hallway.

"Oh, Sam! What's your feeling on feathers?" The towel slid seductively to the floor.

"I love feathers," the glassy-eyed professor mumbled, as Helen shoved him onto the bed.

"Me too. Somehow I knew you were a feather man. They tickle, don't they."

"Oh yeah."

"You are going to be so surprised at what I can do with these feathers."

"You know, I never really thought much about feathers. I see your point, though. Oh, God, do that again. Don't stop."

11

Helen thrust her arm under her pillow, careful not to wake Sam. She squeezed her eyes shut against the darkness. According to the little travel clock on the nightstand, the sun would be up shortly. A new day! What would it bring? Terror or finally a measure of peace? Both? Was that even remotely possible? She'd broken the rules. Yes, she trusted Sam. How could she not trust him? She'd made love to this wonderful man, not once, not twice but three times during the long night. She'd given herself to him completely. Something she'd never done with Daniel. What was going to happen to her now?

Sam stirred and whispered, "I know you're awake. What are you thinking, Helen?"

"I'm thinking about how wonderful it all was and wondering what's going to happen now. The sun is about to come up. It's a new day. Nothing has been touched yet so that makes it brand-new, kind of sparkly, if you know what I mean. Things have changed. I have to make decisions now. The truth is, I don't know what to do."

"Do you love me?"

Of course she loved him. "Yes," she said, her voice ringing with happiness. "Yes, Sam, I do."

"And I love you. That's what counts. We'll work from there. We need to do some serious talking, Helen. We can do it now or later. Personally, I opt for later."

Helen rolled over. She smiled. "Let's talk first and get that out of the way. We have all day to do other things. It's the weekend, remember?"

"So it is. Tell me all about you, from the day you were born."

Helen's stomach rumbled. "That far back?"

"Uh-huh. Were you a cute little kid?"

"Probably not. I was all legs and stringy hair as I recall. My mother wasn't . . . she wasn't much of a mother. Most times I took care of her. She used to call me a little old lady. She was . . . different. She didn't want to get old. She wore sexy clothes and lots of makeup. There was always a man around. Half the time I didn't know their names, and when I did learn them they were gone and there was someone new. I never knew my father. We were trailer-park trash according to the kids I went to school with. It was hard living with that as a kid. I was always shabby but neat and clean. I never had cookies and milk waiting for me when I came home from school. I was lucky there was milk in the icebox. Mom was a cocktail waitress, and she'd bring food home in Styrofoam containers. We never had a grocery shopping day like most families. I don't ever remember my mother making a bed or dusting. She never did the dishes either. Mostly there were just glasses to wash because the Styrofoam trays got thrown out. The forks and spoons were plastic. My clothes came from thrift shops, Goodwill, and the neighbors."

"How about your teen years? What about high school?" Sam asked.

"It was worse," Helen said flatly. "I clerked in a drugstore for spending money and clothes. Cheap stuff because I didn't make much. I used to leaf through the magazines in the store and for some reason lingerie fascinated me. It was always so pretty and feminine. I promised myself I would have stuff like that someday. It was a dream, but it kept me going. My mother kept getting older and the thick makeup she used started to make her look even older. She lost her job to a younger, prettier cocktail waitress so she worked in a diner, where her hands got rough and red. She always smelled like fried food. I used to wish she would wash her hair more often. The men she brought home changed to rough types who slapped her around and stole her money. I always kept what little money I had in my locker at school. I had vouchers for a free lunch at school so I made sure I ate everything possible for nourishment. Trailer-park free-lunch kids didn't exactly have friends. I guess you could say I was a loner. All I wanted to do was get out and make it on my own. I counted the days, the hours, the minutes until I graduated.

"Things started to change in my senior year. The last man my mother brought home started to look at me in a different way. It made me nervous, and I told my mother. She accused me of flirting with him and leading him on. I used some of my savings to buy a dead bolt and one of the stockboys from the drugstore put it on for me. I didn't get much sleep that year.

"I moved out the day after I graduated. I got this tiny little efficiency apartment and worked in a boutique and went to school nights to get my degree. It took me six years, but I did it.

"I got a job with a graphics-design firm. Then I met Daniel Ward. He was older, polished, and seemed very nice and dependable. After we'd dated for a while, I showed him the trailer park I grew up in. I wanted to be up-front with him. He didn't say a word about it. He said something like that was then, this is now, and it isn't important where you used to live. He was like a white knight to me. I was so impressed. He seemed to like me. He took me to dinner, to concerts, bought me little gifts. He courted me. Three months after graduation, I married him. I wasn't in love with him. I just wanted to belong to someone. I don't expect you to understand that kind of feeling. I needed someone in my life who cared about me as a person. I thought he did. I had this new, tiny little apartment and I loved my job. If things had been normal, I would have made him a good wife. I knew how to keep house and how to cook. I thought I would learn to love him. I was so stupidly naive it makes me sick when I think of it now. I want you to know, though, I would have stuck to my bargain. I am so glad we never had children. Don't misunderstand, I love children. I just didn't want Daniel Ward's children."

"You should have left, Helen."

Helen propped herself up on one elbow. "That's so easy to say and not easy to do. Go where, Sam? Back to the trailer? Back to that tiny little apartment? I tried talking to a counselor at the neighborhood church. He told me I needed to honor my husband. I spoke to the parish priest, and all he wanted to do was talk about forgiveness and turning the other cheek. At that point in time, Daniel seemed to be the lesser of two evils. I tried talking to my mother, but she told me I made my bed and now I had to lie in it. In other words, I wasn't to even think about returning to the trailer. I grew up watching men abuse my mother. Maybe down deep, I thought that's the way it was supposed to be. I know that's sick thinking, but I did think that. There, now you have it all. I don't ever want to talk about this again, Sam."

"Didn't you have any relatives?"

"No. There was no one. In the beginning, Daniel would just jab at me, maybe slap me once in a while. He was always contrite the next day. I started to think I deserved it because I married him without loving him. I guess I wasn't in a good mental place at the time. When the abuse really started, I became afraid. He was so violent, so threatening, I feared for my life. Unless you've been there, you can't possibly understand."

"You're free now," Sam said, reaching for her.

"You don't understand, Sam. I will never be free of him. He's looking for me right now. He is not the kind of person to ever give up. Never, ever."

"I think you're giving this guy too much credit. How can he possibly find you? Your people spirited you away. I'm sure they left no signs anywhere. He'd have to be Houdini to find you."

"He's a computer wizard. There's nothing he can't do with a computer. He is literally a wizard. You need to believe me."

"All right, I believe you. What are you going to do?"

"I don't know. I must be a very weak person to have spilled my guts to you," she said flatly. "I have to get in touch with Boots."

"Then let's get up and log on. Isn't there anyone you can call? Don't you have a go-between?"

"No. Just the e-mail. There is someone I can call if I get desperate. The vet who helped me and Lucie. I promised I would never call him. If I do call him, that means I've compromised the foundation. I don't want to do that. Talking to you is bad enough. Who gets the shower first?" Helen asked, hoping to change the subject.

"You go first. I'll walk the dogs. Looks like it's going to be a beautiful day. Let's go on a picnic."

Helen stared at Sam as though he'd sprouted a second head. "Picnic? With all this staring me in the face, you want to go on a picnic?"

"Yeah, I do. It will be good for both of us. Maybe we can come up with some ideas on what you can do. A picnic is not a bad idea, Helen. Sometimes you have to stop and smell the roses. The dogs will love being able to run for a while."

Helen's shoulders slumped. "Okay, but first I have to see if I can reach Boots. I have the store to get ready, a million things to do. Okay, okay, we'll go on a picnic."

"Attagirl. We'll be back in a flash. We never got to do those other things."

"I know." Helen twinkled. "There's always later. Isn't that all part of going on a picnic?"

"Yeah, yeah. Okay. I'll throw an extra blanket in the truck."

Helen stepped into the shower. She lathered up and then let the water sluice over her body while her mind raced. She was pulling on khaki shorts and shirt when Sam was ready to enter the apartment with the dogs. She blew him a kiss as she sat down to log on to the computer. No e-mail from Boots or anyone else for that matter. The chat room was empty.

Helen clicked on her e-mail and typed furiously. The message was short and sweet. "I'm leaving the program unless someone gets in touch with me. Tell me how you want to handle this and where I should return the money lent to me by the Tyger Foundation." She signed it, Nancy Baker < TTLS >. If she didn't hear back on her e-mail, she would call Dr. Davis that evening.

"Okay, let's get this show on the road," Sam said.

"Sam, when are you leaving for Vermont?"

"Oh, didn't I tell you? I turned it down last week. I'm staying here. I'm not letting you out of my sight."

"I can't let you do that, Sam. You said you needed the money."

"I don't need it that badly. I might sign on with a construction crew. I like working with my hands. I used to do it on college breaks. Hell, I don't think there's anything I haven't done in the name of money. It's not a problem. I want to help you, Helen. I'll do whatever it takes. All I want is your promise that you aren't going to do anything stupid like running out on me. By the way, you never said where you were from."

Alarm showed on Helen's face. "Why do you want to know that?"

"I just do. Isn't it part of the whole story? It's called trust."

"I'm not telling you, Sam. That's one thing you don't need to know. Besides, it's better if you don't know. If I promise not to run, will you promise to stop asking questions?"

"Yeah, I guess so."

Helen crossed her fingers behind her back. She wondered if she was telling a lie. "Oh my God, Sam, I forgot to check the Internet to see if any orders came in. I keep forgetting I'm selling on-line now. Damn, this is all so new to me. I need to get it together, and obstacles keep getting in the way."

"Tell you what, you stay behind and check, I'll get the groceries I never got yesterday. By the time I get back we can load up and be off. Is that okay with you?"

Helen stood on her toes to kiss him lightly. "Whatever did I do without you?"

"Beats me. Run around in circles? You keep the dogs, okay? Don't forget, we need food for the picnic."

"Yes, sir." Helen smiled as she snapped off a smart salute.

Helen felt the blood pumping in her veins as she sat down to turn on the computer. Would there be lingerie orders? How could she not have looked earlier? Perhaps it was all so new to her she just didn't believe she could earn a living on the Internet. Either that or she was totally stupid and out of her mind. Both, she decided, while she waited for the web site to boot up. Why else would she have blurted out her life story to Sam?

Some of the tension between her shoulders lessened when she remembered their lovemaking during the long night. He'd been so kind, so gentle and so very passionate. Sex had never been good with Daniel. All he'd ever wanted was instant gratification. *Please, God, don't let anything go wrong. Please don't let Daniel find me and ruin things. Please, please, please.* She smiled as her web page came into focus with the shower of white feathers cascading down the screen. She continued to smile as she clicked her mouse to scroll down her limited inventory. Satisfied that the page looked as tanta-lizing as it did the first time she viewed it, she clicked on her e-mail to see if there were any orders. She blinked in amazement as her index finger on the mouse started to tremble. She counted in a shaky voice. Eleven orders for the black bustier, nine for the white lacy teddy, eighteen orders for the black camisole and match-ing garter belt, and four orders for the black, underwire push-up bra with the lace straps. She clapped her hands in glee as she continued to scroll down the credit-card page. She sat back in her chair and whistled when she started to read the inquiries for the spike-heeled shoes and fishnet stockings.

Helen fixed her gaze on the two dogs staring at her intently. "Ladies and gentlemen, I do believe we are in business!" She clapped her hands again. Lucie howled, and Max tried to jump on her lap, at which point Lucie bit his tail. A moment later they were chasing each other around the apartment, barking.

Pencil and paper in hand, Helen computed the material, the sewing, the shipping to see what she would have left in the way of profits. She gasped. Two thousand dollars, and that didn't include the spike-heeled shoes and fishnets. She wouldn't think about federal taxes or state taxes or any of that accounting junk right now. Sam could take care of that for her.

"And the best part of all this is if I do decide to leave the program and move, I can do Internet business anywhere. I can rent a small house somewhere with a garage to store supplies and packing materials," she muttered to the dogs, who had skidded to a stop at her feet when she started to mumble. "Please, God, don't take this away from me. Please let me make it on my own. Please let me be Helen Stanley again."

Helen clicked off the web page to check her personal e-mail. Nothing. She fired off another e-mail saying the same thing she'd said in her earlier letter. If they didn't care about her, why was she anguishing over her situation with Sam? Wasn't it supposed to be a two-way street? Did she dare call Gerald Davis? Of course she dared, but would she do it? Certainly not from her apartment phone. Where? There was a pay phone outside the Shop Rite super-market. She could call from the market later that night. It might even be better to call later because of the time difference in California and the fact that the vet was an admitted "night owl." She felt strangely exhilarated at the prospect of talking to him. Surely he would know what was going on at the foundation since he admitted to being a personal friend of Isabel Tyger.

"Forty-two orders, guys. I am now a bona fide, legitimate business owner. It's so wonderful! How about a treat for you two?"

The word *treat* sent the Lab flying into the kitchen, where he sat up on his haunches. Lucie barked once and took her position next to the big dog. "Ladies first, Max," Helen said, opening the vanilla cookies. Lucie immediately bit into hers while Max lay down, the cookie between his paws, and proceeded to do what Sam had taught him, pry the wafers apart and lick the filling. Helen was laughing in delight when Sam was at the door.

"He knows how to dunk. We used to sit together, before you came into my life, watching the *X-Files*, dunking our cookies. It only took him fifteen minutes to learn how to do it."

"Lucie can't seem to get the hang of it." Helen giggled.

"Max will teach her, won't you, big guy?"

"Sam, there are forty-two orders on the net. And inquiries about the shoes and the fishnets. I'm so excited. Getting that web page set up was the best thing in the world. Do you think it will continue?"

"Absolutely. Word of mouth is going to be your best advertising, and all those search engines Les signed you up for aren't going to hurt either. Congratulations!"

"Sam, the picnic is off. We have to look for a store location. I have to fill these orders. I can make us a late dinner if that's okay with you."

"Whatever works for you, Helen. I was thinking on the ride back that I haven't been this happy in a long time."

"I know. Me too. Okay, I'm ready to go out looking. Are you taking the dogs or should I?"

"Lucie gets too nervous when I take her. She needs to be able to see you. She lets me walk her as long as your apartment door stays open. It will be better if you take them."

"Okay, then let's do it! This is such a good day, Sam!"

"Does that mean you're okay with the confession then?"

"I'm okay with it. For now."

"Why is everything with you for now?"

"Because that's the way it has to be."

"Okay, Helen, I can live with it. For now!"

12

Isabel Tyger shifted her weight on the hospital bed, causing the stacks of paper spread all over the bed to slide to the floor. She cursed ripely, bringing her private-duty nurse on the run. "I want my laptop, and I want it now! I don't want any excuses either. Fetch it!" she growled.

"Now, Miss Tyger, you know I can't do that. Doctor said . . ."

"I don't care what the doctor said. I'm sick of these inane soap operas and the game shows. I'm sick of being doped up. No more pills. I'm sick of you, too. I want out of here and I want out of here *now*. That's as in right away, this very minute," Isabel said, her nostrils flaring while her eyes flashed sparks.

The young nurse took the tirade in stride. She'd been hearing it for days. "I'm sick of you, too! You are the crankiest, the most obnoxious patient I've ever had. You are a curmudgeon," she said cheerfully.

Isabel grimaced. "It's true. I can't deny it. Will you please put a call in to my doctor? I want to see him. I want an appointment where he will sit and listen to me, not run in here on the fly and then run out. He does it on purpose. And when you do call him, tell him if he doesn't show up within the hour, my bequest to the geriatric ward is off. That should bring him on the run. He's probably out on some damn golf course hitting little balls all over the place. Damn it, I want out of here! I'm sick to death of all these people staring and poking at me."

"Actually, Miss Tyger, I think Doctor's on the tennis court." The young nurse twinkled.

"Same thing," Isabel snapped. "All this bad humor of mine is being wasted on you, is that what you're saying?"

"Yes, ma'am. Ah, here's the mail. That should keep you busy for a while. I'll see about your lunch while you read it."

"I'll have a roast beef sandwich, some pickles, some chips, and some chocolate ice cream on top of chocolate cake."

The nurse grinned devilishly. "That's what I'm having. You are having the mixed vegetable plate with crackers and Jell-O for dessert. Your cholesterol is still way too high."

"Go already!" Isabel shouted as she ripped at the manila envelope Mona had sent from the shelter that morning. Another week's worth of e-mails from TTLS and Robin Bobbin. She frowned at the increasingly desperate tone of each of the e-mails. They were much worse than the last batch. She needed to do something and she needed to do it *now.* She pressed the buzzer on the side of the bed. Her private-duty nurse appeared in seconds, her eyes full of questions.

"Get my clothes! Call someone, an ambulance if necessary, to take me home. I mean it, Maggie. I'm not waiting for that yuppie to shower after his tennis game. Now, goddamn it! I signed myself in here, and I'm signing myself out! Why are you still standing there? Move, girl!"

Maggie left on the run for the nurses' station, where she had Isabel Tyger's doctor paged. When the page was returned within minutes, she started to babble. She knew she was unprofessional, but she didn't care. "She's leaving, Doctor, and she isn't waiting for you to take a shower. I'm just repeating what she said. She wants me to call for an ambulance. I'm going to go with her if she wants me to. I don't have another case so it will work out well. She also said you can forget her bequest to the geriatric ward. I'm sorry you don't like what I'm telling you, Doctor, but I am just the messenger and have no control over what your patient says and doesn't say. Personally, I think she's stayed here about one week too long. I know all about deep pockets and paying patients. Good-bye, Dr. Evans," Maggie said, slamming the phone back into the cradle.

Maggie looked around at the other nurses, who were staring at her in awe. "He's a wise-ass," she said smartly.

"A good-looking wise-ass," one of the nurses said.

Maggie turned around and smirked. "He wears a hairpiece! Whataya think of that?"

"No!"

"It must be a good one. You can't tell."

"How do you know?" another nurse asked.

"I know," Maggie fibbed.

"Wow!" the three nurses said in unison.

"Miss Tyger, I think Dr. Evans will be here shortly. Are you really determined to leave because if you are, I'll get your things ready. It isn't going to be easy for you at home. You need to know that. Then again, I've seen patients do remarkably well once they are in their own surroundings. I'm more than willing to go with you. However, if you have someone else in mind, that's okay, too."

"I know all about that. I didn't get to be this age without learning a thing or two. I'll sleep downstairs. I can get around with my walker. It's just a broken hip, for God's sake. There's nothing wrong with the rest of me. All right, all right, so my blood pressure is a little high, my cholesterol is out of whack, and my tonsils are enlarged. All those things are fixable. I guess you're as good as anyone. I need a telephone," Isabel said tartly.

"You should have fought for that one," Maggie grumbled.

"At first I didn't care. I didn't want people calling me all hours of the day and night. I care now, so get me a phone."

"It's against doctor's orders, Miss Tyger."

Isabel stopped stuffing the e-mails back into the envelope long enough to say, "I think you already know my position on that matter. A phone please. Now!"

"Yes, ma'am."

The instant the phone was plugged in, Isabel started dialing. The first call was to her housekeeper, instructing her to call for a hospital bed to be set up in the den. The second call was to Gerry and the third one to Artie. She dusted her hands dramatically when she hung up the phone for the last time.

He was tall and he was handsome, hairpiece or not. "So you took a shower after all!" Isabel said, pointing to the doctor's wet slicked-back hair. "While I waited. I'm leaving, Dr. Evans. I'm sick of being doped up so that I don't know what day it is much less what time it is. No more dope medicine, do you hear me?"

"So I heard. Do you think that's a wise decision on your part? I haven't discharged you."

"According to you, no. According to me, yes. There's nothing wrong with my head or my brain. I broke my hip. I can walk with the walker. I am capable of going to the bathroom myself. I can take the medication you prescribed at home just the way I take it here. I will have a nurse at home just the way I have here. The same nurse in fact. I'm discharging myself. Now what the hell is our problem here?"

"The problem is I want you watched carefully. You are not in the best of health, Miss Tyger. I know you haven't been happy, but isn't it better to be well and on the road to good health? You require supervision."

"Cut the crap, Dr. Evans. All this hospital wants is my twelve hundred dollars a day for this fancy suite of rooms I am not allowed to walk around in. How do you expect me to get better if you don't let me get up and walk around?"

"The bones needed to knit. You know the first two tries were unsuccessful. You do know you have osteoporosis. People like you have to be very careful."

"That does it! That really tears it. Just because I'm small in stature doesn't give you the right to refer to me as people like you. I'm relieving you of your responsibility. One more day of this place will put me in the loony bin. Don't you understand? I can't take it anymore." She was so angry she was on the verge of tears.

"When I said people like you, Miss Tyger, I was referring to people who have similar conditions. Your height and weight had nothing to do with my comment," the young doctor said testily. "Furthermore, Miss Tyger, there are procedures . . ."

"You know what you can do with your procedures, Dr. Evans. You should have discharged me a week ago. I know it, and you know it. I'm discharging myself. Now, if you want to continue seeing me as your patient, you will have to come to the house. That will be all, Dr. Evans."

Maggie turned her head to hide her smile. She heard the handsome doctor scuff his feet on the tile floor, felt his indecision, sensed his humiliation. "Do you have any new orders, Dr. Evans?"

"Ah, no. I'll review Miss Tyger's case and call you tomorrow. Follow the same routine when you get your patient home. Where did that phone come from?"

"It was a gift," Isabel said blandly, when it looked like the young nurse was about to confess to going against the doctor's orders. "Am I going in an ambulance or private car?"

"I'll call for an ambulance right now and pick up your discharge papers on the way. I think it will be better if you go in your robe if that's okay with you. I'll help you dress when you get home," Maggie said.

"That's fine with me. I can't believe I'm finally going home. I used to hate my house. Then I remodeled it and it became a real home. The word *home* is truly a wonderful word. It really is true when people say there is no place like home. Don't you agree?"

"Yes, ma'am, I do."

"You were a good nurse to put up with me, Maggie," Isabel said slyly, watching the nurse carefully.

"Thank you. Are you going to follow the doctor's orders, Miss Tyger, or are we going to do it the difficult way? It is for your own good, you know."

"Yes, I will follow the doctor's orders as long as they aren't unreasonable. I'm not ready to pack it in yet. I still have some living to do."

"Now, that's what I like to hear," Maggie said. "I should have everything ready to go in say, twenty minutes. Then you are homeward bound and you can peck away at your laptop all you want."

"I just hope it isn't too late," Isabel mumbled.

"I have friends coming for dinner, Maggie, so you can have the evening off. Go into town and go to a movie with that new boyfriend of yours. My dinner is a broccoli-and-salmon casserole with diet sherbet for dessert. I will have one glass of wine as per the doctor's orders, and I will take my medicine. My housekeeper will help me into bed. Go and enjoy yourself. You've been cooped up here for days. You need to get out and about."

"Are you sure, Miss Tyger? He isn't exactly a new boyfriend. I've been dating him for six months or so."

"I am very sure. I want to spend some time with my two best friends, and I don't want you hovering over me. You can trust me. The question of the moment is, can I trust you with that boyfriend of yours?" Isabel's eyes were flat and hard as she waited for the nurse's response.

"I don't think you have to worry about me. I am going to worry about you though, because you can be pretty crafty sometimes, Miss Tyger."

"I'm going to take that as a compliment."

Maggie laughed. "I think my fella is going to be delighted that I finally have an evening off. It's kind of hard to keep a romance alive when you work around the clock."

"Make tonight count then. This is absolutely perfect the way you arranged this chair and my computer. Go on now and have a good time. Tomorrow I want to hear all about it."

"It's a deal. I think I hear your guests. I'll let them in, and then I'll leave. When I get back, I'll check in on you even if you're asleep."

Isabel nodded as she turned on her computer. The nurse was forgotten a moment later when her e-mail screen came into view.

"Three days, Izz, and you're on the computer. Are you supposed to be doing that?" Artie demanded as he strolled into the room.

"Of course. Hello to both of you. Fix yourself a drink and pour me some tea. That's another word for bourbon. I have to be careful what I say and whom I say it around," Isabel said tartly.

"Are you permitted to drink, Izzie?" Gerry asked, a frown spreading between his eyebrows.

"Of course not. This is a little celebration. One drinks when one is having a celebration. I'm home. I'm having a cigarette, too. Then I'm going to have a shitty dinner while you two men eat prime ribs. It's a trade-off. Will you two stop looking at me like that? When it's my time to go, I'm going to go, bourbon or not. Are we clear on this once and for all?"

Gerry sighed. "We're clear, Izzie. Now, what's up?"

"Artie?"

"I'm clear on it, Izz."

"Good. What's up is Helen Ward. She's getting ready to fly the coop. She's done very well during the time I was in the hospital. She's frantic now because I haven't been in touch with her. Three weeks is not an eternity. I don't think she would be alarmed if it wasn't for this man she met. She met this man and . . . do I have to tell you the rest?"

"You said he was okay. You said he checked out."

"I did say that, and yes, he is who he claims to be. He's in love with Helen and I think Helen is in love with him. She's selling lingerie on the Internet. Come here, I want to show you her web page. No drooling, gentlemen."

"Uh-huh," Artie said.

"Very . . . ah . . . nice," Gerry said. "I always did like feathers. That lace is kind of nice. There's something about red underwear . . ."

"This girl has a brain," Isabel said, ignoring Gerry's flushed face. "When that impossible person she worked for fired her, she got a job waiting tables. We all know that's hard work and definitely underpaid. She managed to get this web page up and running and according to this last e-mail from her, the orders are coming in fast and heavy. She's rented store space and is hiring more seamstresses. Lucie is doing well and Mr. Tolliver's dog is with Lucie all the time. They play together. Isn't that nice? Helen says they moon over each other, and if they're separated, they cry by the door. I wasn't wrong about her. She did break the rules, though. I guess I can understand that. If you go to bed with a man, you want it to be for all the right reasons and you don't want to start off a relationship that might eventually lead to marriage with a lie."

"Where is this going, Izzie?" Gerry demanded.

"She's honest and a hard worker. She's caring and loving. Part of it is my fault because I didn't keep up with the sessions on the net. I left her to flounder, but it was only for twenty-one days. Considering the circumstances, I think she did very well. Now, do we let her stay in the program knowing she told Sam Tolliver who she is or do we cut her loose? Since we're only a three-person board, you each have a vote. I vote to keep her."

"Keep her," Artie said.

"I agree," Gerry said.

"Then it's unanimous."

"What would you have done if we voted no?" Gerry asked.

"It would have broken my heart, but I would have gone along with you."

"Do you know anything new about Daniel Ward, Artie?" Isabel asked.

"He's been doing some consulting work for Lomax Industries. Strictly freelance stuff. One of my managers told me he saw him at a steak house a few weeks back. With a woman. He said he didn't look like he used to look when he worked for us. He said he looked like someone down on his luck."

"What is he doing?" Isabel fretted. She hated it when things didn't go according to plan. Tripping over the housekeeper's scrub bucket wasn't something she had planned. Breaking her hip was not in her game plan, but she had to deal with it the best way she knew how. Now she was going to have to deal with Daniel Ward on a more personal level, and Helen as well.

"I'll tell you exactly what he's doing. He's trying to find his wife. He's scouring every database in this country and probably outside the country, too. He's hoping that sooner or later she'll slip up, and then he'll pounce. Maybe you should relocate Helen now, Izz. She's been in Jersey for sixteen months," Artie said.

"I don't want to do that unless I have to. Upheaval is a trauma in itself. Helen has had enough of that. So has Lucie. There are new factors in the equation now, Mr. Tolliver and his dog. If he's the kind of person I think he is, he isn't going to let anything happen to Helen. When you're in love, you take care of those you love. I'm putting a private investigator on Daniel Ward. Around the clock. I wish I had thought to do it earlier. I can't imagine why I didn't."

"You didn't do it because Daniel Ward was here and Helen was safely out of state. Ward is still here, so that means he has no clue as to Helen's whereabouts," Gerry said.

"She's special. Don't look at me like that. You saw her that night, Gerry. Tell me she isn't special."

"I can't. I thought the same thing myself. You're getting personally involved, and we all agreed we wouldn't allow that to happen, Izzie. The truth is you were involved from the get-go."

"Some rules are meant to be broken," Artie said. "I think hiring a private dick is a very good idea. Ward could flip out, he could take off in the middle of the night and we'd be left sucking our thumbs. If he didn't think he was on to something, he would have taken one of the lucrative jobs that was offered to him. He can't live on consulting fees, and since he cashed in his 401K, he's going to be hurting for money pretty soon. They were in hock up to their eyeballs. It's amazing the things you don't know about people," Artie complained. "By the way, I've made up my mind to retire the first of the year."

"It's about time!" Isabel said. "Now you can spend more time with us."

"You're making a mistake, Artie," Gerry said. "When you retire you get fat and lazy. You *say* you're going to do all these wonderful things but you don't. First thing you know, you're watching TV fourteen hours a day, eating junk food, and complaining about your neighbors' kids and all the noise they make because you can't snooze any old time of the day. Don't do it!"

"I'm doing it! For your information, I don't plan on lazing my days away. I'm going to help Izz, and I also plan on helping you at the clinic. I'll probably be working harder than I do now. That's providing you two want or even need my services."

"Commendable, Artie," Isabel said.

"I could certainly use the help," Gerry said.

"See, everything always works out for the best. I'm going to call Helen tonight. We're agreeing then that Helen stays in New Jersey for the time being. I'm hiring the same agency to keep track of Daniel Ward that your firm uses for surveillance, Artie."

"When are you going to tell Helen Ward who you really are?" Gerry asked.

"Never. She knows me as Boots, and that's all she needs to know. With Boots, she's free to be herself. Isabel Tyger would scare her to death. Don't ask me how I know that. I just do. I think it's time for dinner, gentlemen. No, no, I can make it on my own. It just takes me a little longer. Besides, I am in no hurry to face that miserable food the doctor insists I eat. I don't want to hear either one of you say it's for my own good either."

"Then we won't say it, will we, Artie?" Gerry grinned.

Artie stopped in his tracks and turned around. "Izz, I want you to live forever. I cannot imagine my life without you and Gerry in it. How hard can it be to follow the doctor's orders? If you won't do it for yourself, do it for Gerry and me. Do it for Helen and Lucie. They need you as much as we do. That's the end of my speech. Another thing, when you invite us to dinner, we eat what you eat. We aren't special."

Isabel's faded blue eyes filled with tears. "If only you knew how very special you are. I love you both so much I ache with the feeling sometimes. After all these years we're still best friends. It's amazing."

"I think it's a damn miracle." Gerry guffawed. "Especially since you are the crankiest, the orneriest, the stubbornest woman I've ever met in my life."

"I second that," Artie said, thumping Gerry on the back.

"See. That's why I love the two of you. You tell it like it is. Unfortunately, I am all those things."

"You are also the most generous, the most caring, the most humble person I've ever had the pleasure of knowing," Artie said.

"That too," Isabel quipped.

"I need some downtime, Sam. That means you need to go home. I have a lot of thinking to do. You can leave Max if you like," Helen said.

"You aren't going to do something wild and crazy, are you?" Sam said, taking her in his arms.

"I wouldn't know wild and crazy if it slapped me in the face. The answer is no. I can't think around you, Sam. When you're around, I want to rip off your clothes and make love to you. I want to snuggle with you and the dogs. I have things I have to do, things to take care of."

"We did everything days ago. Your shop is open. You signed up for security, your merchandise is packed neatly in the cases, all your deliveries are up-to-date. Your new computer is hooked up in the back room. With your new ISP, you can send the orders directly to your seamstresses. If you tell me what it is that is so pressing you don't want me around, I'll understand. Nothing kills a romance faster than one or the other wanting to be joined at the hip twenty-four hours a day. I'll settle for twenty."

"Not today you won't. I want to try and reach Boots, and I might get up the courage to make that one phone call that might shed some light on matters. I need to wrestle with my conscience over that call. Suddenly I feel like my direction has been ripped out from under me. I need some reassurance. Now, go, Sam."

"Okay. Call me if you change your mind. I'm two doors away. Max can stay. Now, kiss me until our teeth start to rattle."

"Oh, no. I know where that's leading. Come over for breakfast, okay? I promise to dream of you. All night long."

"Okay."

"You gave up pretty easily," Helen said testily.

"My best friend always said to leave them wanting more." Sam grinned as he opened the door.

"Is that the same friend who has been married four times?"

"Yep, that's the one," Sam called over his shoulder before he closed the door behind him, leaving Helen to stare blankly at the metal door.

"Whatever," Helen muttered as she slid the three locks into place.

While the dogs tussled and pretended to fight over a rawhide chew, Helen made a fresh pot of coffee. While she waited for it to drip through the machine, she turned on the computer and clicked on her e-mail. She grew faint when she saw that she had e-mail. Not just any e-mail, but e-mail from Boots. "Thank you, God. Thank you."

Helen stared at the screen in front of her until the coffee finished dripping into the pot. She toyed with the idea of not opening the mail and waiting for morning. What did Boots write? Did her threat of leaving the program prompt her on-line counselor to finally respond? Or was she responding because she had confessed to breaking the rules? Was this e-mail her termination letter?

Worms of fear crawled around inside Helen's stomach as she poured coffee, added sugar and milk. Here it was, the letter she'd been waiting for the past three weeks. Still, she was reluctant to open the e-mail. Was her safety net going to be ripped out from under her? Do it! Just do it and get on with it! her mind shrieked.

Suddenly Helen felt sick to her stomach. A feeling of light-headedness overcame her. She reached for the edge of the dining-area table for support. Get on with it, Helen. Open the damn mail and read it. She obeyed her own instructions and clicked, READ.

It looked like one of Boots's regular e-mails. Not too long, not too short. She closed her eyes for a minute and then opened them. She read the mail slowly, savoring each and every word.

Good evening, TTLS,

First things first. I apologize for your anxiety but circumstances beyond my control did not allow me to continue our counseling sessions. No, it was not a test as you suggested in one of your e-mails. It was simply life getting in the way of life.

Several of your e-mails disturbed me greatly. You broke the rules, TTLS. That in itself is automatic dismissal from the program. My first reaction was to gather up the forms, fill them out, and send you on your way. The foundation board voted to give you another chance if I recommend it, even though you failed our trust. While I understand how you feel, it doesn't make what you did right. You jeopardized your very safety. Possibly the safety of others. How can I trust you again?

The foundation ran a check on your neighbor, and he is exactly what and who he claims to be. That means you are safe. For now. What if HE slips, TTLS? This is new to him. In his zeal to protect you, he might inadvertently make a mistake. Then what? I'm not saying he will. I'm saying, what if? I hope you realize you are putting his life in danger as well as your own. Love is a powerful emotion. I understand what you are feeling, what you are going through. You need more time, TTLS. You are still adjusting to a new way of life. The board understands your falling in love. What they don't understand is why you felt the need to bare your soul. We need to know, in a return e-mail, exactly what you told this

*person, when you told him, and his precise reaction. Do not even
think about lying to us. I thought you had more guts, TTLS. You
have disappointed me greatly. In the end it is my opinion that counts.
I will wait to hear from you. You will be notified of the decision,
one way or the other.*

The e-mail was signed, Boots.

Helen clicked off the e-mail and then turned off the computer.
She sat back, numb from head to toe. A sob caught in her throat
and erupted in a loud, choking sound, bringing the dogs on the
run. She slipped off her chair to the floor, the hard sobs tearing at
her body as both dogs tried to comfort her.

A long time later, when she couldn't cry anymore, Helen cuddled
and stroked the dogs. Her hands were wet, the animals' fur wet
with her tears. She was so tired. She curled into the fetal position,
Lucie against her chest, and closed her eyes. She was asleep in an
instant.

The dogs looked at one another before Max trotted into the
living room for his blanket. He tugged and dragged it until he had
it where he wanted it, over Helen's shoulders. He listened to Lucie
whimper and then stretched out alongside Helen, his front paw
on Lucie's back, his eyes glued to the locked door—Helen's self-
appointed protector.

13

~

Helen woke, aware of an enormous weight on her body. She struggled to take a deep breath. What was wrong with her? Was she
having a heart attack? Where was she? She tried to move, the heavy
weight shifting slightly. Max! "Move, baby. It's okay, Lucie," she
whispered. She rolled over, the two dogs watching her expectantly.
Moonlight shone through the part in the draperies. That had to
mean it was still night. The luminous hands on her watch glowed
in the semidarkness: 3:10. She needed to get up, take a hot shower
to ease the ache in her bones. "To what end?" she mumbled. Her
eyes felt like hot coals as she staggered into the bathroom to turn
on the shower. Her reflection in the mirror made her gasp.

Wrapped in a thick robe, Helen padded out to the kitchen, where
she made fresh coffee. Behind her, the computer waited. Boots was
waiting. The board members were waiting for her response. What
should she say? Even if she found the right words, how could she
simply type them in such an impersonal way? Wasn't it Boots who
said you can do whatever you set your mind to doing? All she
had to do was get a mind-set and run with it. So easy to say, so
very hard to do.

Sensing Helen's strange behavior, Lucie tugged at the hem of
Helen's robe. She bent down to pick Lucie up. Max pawed Helen's
shoulder. "C'mon, we'll sit on the couch until the coffee is ready.
I can't pick you up, Max. You're too heavy." Lucie continued to
whimper as Helen curled into the corner of the couch, Max at her
side, Lucie in her lap. The Lab nuzzled her open palm, an indication
she was to scratch behind his ears. "I don't know what to do."
Lucie bellied off Helen's lap to snuggle against Max. "I guess that's
my answer. Okay, guys, coffee for me, treats for you. It's okay. It

really is. We'll make this work for all of us. I don't know how, but we will.''

This time there was no hesitation when Helen sat down in front of the computer. She turned it on, clicked on her e-mail and started typing her response to Boots's last e-mail.

Dear Boots,

I'm glad you are okay. I was worried about you. At first I didn't know what to think. At some point I thought perhaps you were testing me. I realized rather quickly what a stupid thought that was. I felt incredibly alone and vulnerable when I didn't hear from you for so long. Three weeks is a very long time to me. I became so fearful it was hard to sleep. I think it is unforgivable what you put me through these past weeks, unintentional or not. In your vast organization there must have been one person who could have sent me an e-mail telling me things were all right. After weeks of careful thought, I came to the realization that I cannot accept your explanation.

There are no words for me to tell you how appreciative I am for everything that was done for me by all of your people. I stuck to my bargain, obeyed all the rules. When I did fail, it was because there was no support left for me to draw upon. I suppose that makes me a weak person. The very reason you had to help me in the first place. I'm not that same weak person any longer, thanks to you and all the people who give so generously of their time and themselves. I may be a little frightened but I am young and I am healthy. I am not afraid to work hard. There are only two things I am afraid of. One, that something will happen to my pet. Two, that I forget who I am and why I was in this program in the first place. I can't blame anyone for my weakness, only myself.

Yes, I've fallen in love. That alone is a miracle in my eyes. Sam is a kind, gentle man and he cares deeply for me and my dog. I feel the same way about him and his dog. If this is about trust and truth, then yes, I do deserve a second chance. However, I'm going to turn it down. I realize you didn't ask me to give up the man I've fallen in love with. It's what you meant, though. He understands the situation. I think he would protect me with his life if he had to. My pet as well. I would do the same for him if the situation were reversed.

Last of all, Boots, I cannot separate the animals. They have become attached to one another, and it is beautiful to see. I could never be the one to rip them apart. I don't expect you or your board members to understand such feelings. It's the way it is. I cannot and will not change how I feel in this regard.

I will return the business monies advanced to me as soon as you tell me where to forward the check. If you care to give me a tally of all the monies expended on my behalf, I will pay them off also. It will take some time, but I will honor my obligations.

I'm sorry, Boots, that we aren't going to be able to meet in person. I guess some things are just not meant to be.

I don't know if I have the right to ask this or not, but I won't know if I don't ask. Will you please express my thanks to Isabel Tyger? Tell her I will be forever grateful that she saved my life and my dog's life as well. I talk to Lucie all the time and tell her what a wonderful lady Miss Tyger must be. I think she actually understands. I regret that I failed you, Boots. However, I didn't fail myself or my pet. That's the bottom line for me.

I'm going to have this on-line service canceled. It's an added expense I will no longer be able to afford. If you should ever want to reach me, do it through my web site. Thank you again for everything.

TTLS and TTLS2.

Helen bit down on her lower lip as she turned off her computer. Another chapter of her life closed. She wished she knew what the future held for her. And for Sam. Sam was now built into the equation called her life. Then again, maybe it was better that she didn't know what the future held. One day at a time, Helen, she told herself. Just take it one day at a time.

Helen looked down at the dogs lying at her feet. "It was the right thing to do. I didn't really have any other options. We'll be okay. I'll take care of us. I promise. I think we should all go to bed now. Come on, it's late, and Sam's coming for breakfast. Things might look brighter in the morning. I seriously doubt it, but it's worth thinking about," Helen said wearily as she made her way down the short hall that led to her bedroom.

Three thousand miles away in California, Isabel Tyger prowled the long hallway, her walker making thumping sounds as she stomped it down on the thick carpeting. Another sleepless night. She felt totally useless when she gingerly lowered her bulk into the comfortable chair behind her desk. She strained to see out the library window to see if Maggie Eldridge's car was parked anywhere near the garage. She took a moment to wonder what kind of personal life her nurse had. She was no prude, and she pretty much had a live-and-let-live attitude, but it *was* four o'clock in the morning, and her nurse wasn't home. To her, giving someone the night off meant that person should be back by midnight. Were things done differently these days? Maybe she should have been a little more specific where the nurse's duties were concerned. "At least she's out from under my feet," she muttered when the computer came to life. She wished she knew what Helen Ward thought of her e-mail. Would she respond immediately or was she going to take time to think about it? She blinked when she saw her e-mail envelope flashing. Helen?

Isabel read the e-mail three times before her fist shot in the air. "Yessss," she chortled. A moment later the phone was in her hand. "Wake up, Gerry. My bird told me to kiss off. Isn't that what young people say today? I heard that expression on one of those soap operas when I was in that damn hospital. Told you she had some spunk. I knew I was right about her. She plans to leave the program, so we'll let her think she is, but we'll stay on top of things. She said she won't separate the dogs. Now, isn't that something? God, Gerry, I just love it when I'm right. Why aren't you saying anything? You weren't sleeping, so don't pretend you were. Say something."

"I love it when you're right, too, Izzie. Listen, will you marry me?"

"We don't have time for marriage, Gerry. Not right now. Maybe later. Besides, we have too much to do. I'm not saying we'll spoil our lives if we get married, but things will change. I've always loved you. I believe you when you say you've always loved me. Why should a piece of paper come between us? The answer is no."

"One of these days I'm going to stop asking. You'd have someone to play checkers with at four in the morning if we got married."

"The nurse isn't back yet, Gerry. I gave her the night off. When you give someone the night off, doesn't it mean they have to be home by midnight?"

"That would be my thinking. These young kids today don't think anything of staying out all night, coming home for breakfast, and then going to work. If I did that, it would kill me."

"That's because we're old, Gerry. Today I feel very old. I don't feel good either."

"What does that mean, Izzie?" Gerry asked, alarm sounding in his voice.

"It means I don't feel like myself. I think it's all that medicine they have me on. I'm not taking it anymore."

"Then don't take it." From long years of friendship, Gerry knew the minute he agreed to something, Isabel would do just the opposite.

"Why don't you come over for breakfast, Gerry?"

"Okay. Do you mind if I go back to bed now?"

"Don't you want to talk to me?"

"About what, Izzie?"

"About you know who. Isn't it remarkable what she's doing?"

"No. It's damn stupid."

"She doesn't think she's being stupid. She thinks she's taking control of her life. She's going to be a success no matter what we do or say. She's got grit and spunk. I know she's got to be scared out of her wits. She's right, though, she isn't that same weak person she was when she came to you that night. She's the one who used the term *weak*, not me."

"How do you like the word reckless, Isabel?" Gerry demanded.

Isabel blinked. Gerry only used her birth name when he was upset with her.

"I don't like it at all, *Gerald*."

"What are you going to do about it?"

"I don't know. I need to think about it."

"Fine. Now, can I go back to bed?"

"Go ahead, sleep your life away," Isabel snapped as she broke the connection.

Isabel did her best to curl into the corner of the old comfortable chair she was sitting in. Each time Gerry asked her to marry him she went through the same turmoil. "Sometimes I wish I had married him. We might have had children, a big family, a loving family," she muttered. It was possible. Gerry saw past what she considered her ugliness and her gimpy leg. Oh, no, she couldn't let go of the past. Her father and his wicked tongue had seen to that. All the cruel things he'd ever said to her came flooding back. Horse-faced, buck-toothed, scraggly, homely as a mud fence. And those were the kindest things he'd said. The ugly things he'd said were only allowed to be thought of in total darkness so no one could see her shame, not even herself. Feeling it, living it was bad enough. Seeing it would push her over the edge. Was his hatred of her due to that awful day when she'd been born or when she screamed, *"When I'm old enough I'm going to kill you for what you did!"* She'd meant it, too. She almost wished she'd followed through.

For a long time she'd thought Gerry felt sorry for her, and that's why he kept proposing. Then she'd moved on to thinking he was grateful for her helping hand in putting him through college and setting him up at his clinic. Then, when her father lay dying and refused to have her in his room, she knew the very sight of her offended him; therefore, she must offend other people as well. Even Gerry and Artie, although they said it wasn't true. When her inheritance was cut off, she was suicidal. They were there for her every minute of the day and night. Friendship. Friendship wasn't love in her opinion. "You are one screwed-up old broad, Isabel Tyger," she mumbled.

Headlights flashed on the study wall. Isabel quickly switched off the light and struggled to her feet. She thumped her way down the hall to her room and got into bed.

She waited.

The house was quiet. Almost too quiet. Since the renovations, nothing creaked or groaned. Thick padding and deep carpeting muffled everything.

Fifteen minutes passed and her door, which she'd left ajar, didn't move. By craning her neck Isabel was able to look out her bedroom window in the direction of the L-shaped wing where her study was located when she noticed the light go on. She frowned. What was the nurse doing in her study? At 4:45 in the morning, did she have reason to believe her patient would be on the computer? Was it possible she was searching for a book? After an all-night date, what kind of person would want to read a book? Was she going through her desk, and, if so, what was she looking for? Was she spying on her?

Isabel kept her eye on her bedroom window, the large digital clock with the two-inch red numerals directly in her line of vision. It was 5:25 when the study light was turned off. Isabel rolled on her side to better see the door. There was just enough light from the small night-light in the socket to the left of the door. The fine hairs on the back of her neck twitched. When the door finally moved, she closed her eyes, pretending to be asleep. She smelled Maggie's perfume and something else. Cigarette smoke? Pipe tobacco. Artie smoked a pipe, so she was familiar with the scent of good tobacco. What *was* she doing in her office? Satisfied, the nurse adjusted the door to its original position.

If the nurse had tried to use Isabel's computer for some reason, she would have been thwarted almost immediately, since she didn't know her password. The moment the computer booted up it asked for a password. Suspicious by nature, Isabel discounted the nurse's searching the shelf for a book for forty minutes that would lull her to sleep. No, she was interested in the computer for some reason.

Isabel swung her legs over the side of the bed and grappled for the walker. This time she slid it, shuffling her way to the study, where she knew the room by heart. The first thing she did was to draw the heavy draperies so no light would shine through. Then she closed and locked the study door. She turned on the computer, waited for the password line to appear. She logged on and sat back to wait. She typed furiously and waited again until the last entry sprang to life. Isabel looked down at the last entry, 5:02. Her suspicions were right: the nurse had tried to use the computer. The question was why.

Isabel sat quietly, her mind racing. Every possibility under the sun surfaced. Most she rejected; others she gave serious thought. Was the pretty, cheerful nurse a spy of some sort? Who would she be spying for? Gerry and Artie would laugh their heads off if she even mentioned such a thing and say she watched too much television, when in reality she rarely watched television, much preferring a good book.

Isabel closed her eyes to bring her night table into view. Bottles of prescription drugs and a pitcher of water. At least six different vials. Her eyes narrowed. As long as she was running with all these crazy thoughts, she might as well run a little further. Telephones. There were extensions in every room in the house, even the bathroom and the garages. Since she was becoming so paranoid, she would call the phone company that day and change the situation. If necessary, she would get a switchboard. Only private lines in her office and bedroom so no one could listen in. Maybe she should disconnect the intercom system, too, in case she forgot to turn it off in one of the rooms. Fear gnawed at her insides.

What did she really know about the young, cheerful nurse? Nothing. When she'd been admitted to the hospital after her fall, she'd been out of it for a few days. When she'd been more alert, the nurse was just there, sitting on a chair, knitting. Gerry said he'd hired her. Probably from some nurses' registry. She'd never been an alarmist, but she was alarmed now, right down to the tips of her toes.

"I'm a veritable sitting duck. Or else I'm losing my mind," she grumbled as she turned off the computer. She parted the drapes looking to the horizon. Pale pink and lavender signaled the start of a new day. The light of battle glittered in Isabel's eyes as she yanked at the drapes. The new day spread before her.

Ninety minutes later, Isabel was seated at the kitchen table finishing her breakfast. Promptly at seven o'clock, Maggie Eldridge entered the kitchen, a huge smile on her face. "I was going to bring breakfast to your room, Miss Tyger."

"I'm not an invalid, Miss Eldridge. I need to be up and about. I need to return to my life and do what I can."

"What *do* you do, Miss Tyger? You never said," the nurse said, pouring coffee.

"I sit on various boards, take care of the toy business, my charities, e-mail my friends, that sort of thing," Isabel said blandly. "Tell me about your evening. Did you have a good time?"

"A wonderful time, but I felt guilty leaving you alone."

"You shouldn't feel guilty since I wasn't alone. My housekeeper was here."

"How did you sleep last night?"

"Like a log." Isabel smiled. "How about you? Are you used to the bed yet?"

"You were sound asleep when I came in. I did check on you as I promised. I, too, slept like a log. I never have trouble sleeping. The bed is fine."

"Where did your beau take you?"

"To a lovely Chinese restaurant and then we rented two movies to watch. We had some wine, cheese, and fruit, at which point I had to leave just as it was getting interesting." Isabel clucked her tongue to show what she thought of that statement. "I was in by twelve-thirty."

"Those sleeping pills must have really knocked me out. I didn't hear a thing."

"That's why the doctor prescribed them. You need your sleep. How are you feeling this morning?"

"Quite wonderful."

"Are you ready for your bath and a massage?"

"Absolutely," Isabel said.

"Tell me what you ate for breakfast. Some of your medication has to be taken after a meal. We don't want to do anything wrong here."

"I had fat-free yogurt, half a grapefruit, and two slices of toast with low-sugar jam and herbal tea."

"See, now you're getting it." The nurse beamed.

Isabel wondered what this smiling, lying woman would think if she'd told her she ate two eggs, four slices of bacon, and then swilled down three cups of coffee. "No, no, I can do it myself. I think I'm ready for the pronged cane."

"We can try it, but I don't think so."

"I'm not getting a sponge bath either. I'm taking a shower."

"All right," the nurse said agreeably. "I'll stand outside the shower and wait."

"Suit yourself," Isabel said, swinging her walker around in a wide sweep, narrowly missing the blue-eyed nurse. *Lying little shit,* she thought.

Isabel made her way to her bathroom. "You can wait here in the dressing room. I prefer to do this myself if you don't mind. If I need you, I'll call for you." *Vanity, thy name is woman,* she thought as she struggled out of her nightgown and robe. She burned with humiliation each time she had to view her naked body. Yet Gerry didn't seem to mind her gimpy leg, her rolls of fat, a protruding stomach, and pendulous breasts. An ugly body, she'd once heard her father say when she was little. As soon as she learned the meaning of the word *ugly,* she'd learned to dress to cover what she considered her flaws.

Inside the shower, Isabel sat on a round plastic bench that had rubber suction cups on the legs to keep it in place. The warm steamy water felt wonderful, soothing and comforting. *Lying little shit. What is she up to?* How far off the mark would she be if she told Artie and Gerry she thought the young nurse was seeing Daniel Ward? Not far off, she decided.

"Are you all right, Miss Tyger?"

"I'm fine. I love the feel of warm water. Tell me more about your evening. I love to hear about young people's romances. Are you sleeping with him?"

"Miss Tyger!"

"Well, are you?"

"When I have the time. That's rather personal, don't you think?"

So is trying to use my computer and lying to me. "No. What does he do? What's his name? Maybe I know him."

"I doubt that. He does consulting work. He's also a computer troubleshooter."

"I know everyone in San Jose. Who is he? Why don't we invite him to dinner?"

"He's much too busy. He more or less has to fit me into his schedule as it is. I don't find that romantic at all. His name is Donald McDermott. Do you know him?"

"No!" Isabel shouted to be heard over the running water. *I bet I know his real name,* she thought nastily. *Lying little shit.*

Isabel stood up and stepped out of the shower, letting the water continue to run. She managed to dress herself, but she was exhausted when she was finished. She turned off the water just before she called out, "I'm finished."

"Goodness, I'd hate to have your water bill."

"I'm rich. I can afford it," Isabel said, staring intently at the nurse to see her reaction to her blatant words.

"That's what Donald said. I had no idea you were the person who owns the toy company. What's it like to be rich?" the nurse asked.

"It's a better feeling than being poor. I give away more than I keep. There are a lot of needy people out there who require my help."

"Donald said you donate a lot of time and money to battered women's causes. He said he read about you in some newspaper. I didn't know any of that. I moved here to San Jose when the cold weather back East got to me. I can't ever imagine letting some man use me as a punching bag."

"That's what they all say in the beginning," Isabel snapped.

"Maybe I'll donate my weekends at one of your shelters. I like to give back a little."

"There's no need. Believe it or not, we have all the volunteers we can handle. Can you withstand an investigative check of your background from the day you were born? And everyone in your immediate circle?"

"Of course," the nurse snapped. She smiled to take the sting out of her sharp retort.

"I need you to do a few things for me. I want you to go to the bookstore and pick up some new novels I ordered. I also need some toothpaste and shampoo. While you're in town, you can pick up my dry cleaning. I'll be fine. I'm going to sit here and finish my last book."

"Miss Tyger, I mean no offense, but I am not an errand girl. I'm a nurse. I don't think your doctor would approve of me leaving you alone."

"It goes with the job. Take it or leave it. I don't much care what that doctor thinks. I thought we were clear on that. Don't ever make the mistake of thinking I'm a fool."

"Goodness gracious," the nurse said, flustered. "Wherever did you get an idea like that? Are you sure you slept well last night?"

"From you, that's where. I said I slept like a log. Now, are you going to run my errands or not?"

"If that's what you want me to do, then I'll do it," the nurse said, her smile gone.

"Good. My list is on the kitchen table. The bookstore will charge the books, so will the dry cleaner and the drugstore. Take your time. Eat lunch out."

"Why do I have the feeling you're trying to get rid of me?"

"Because I am. I don't like people who hover over me. I'll be right here when you get back. If I get tired, I'll take a nap. Why don't you surprise your boyfriend with a pizza for lunch."

"First you have to take your medication."

"I already took it," Isabel lied. "If you don't believe me, check the bottles. I told you. I'm not a fool. I know the medication helps me. I just saved you the trouble of handing it to me. Jot it down on your chart. By the time you get back my next dose will be due."

"This is so irregular. I'm not sure you need a nurse at all." Maggie pretended to pout.

"I agree. We'll work on that. Perhaps all I need is one of those in home aides who come to check on you every other day. You know, they check your vital signs, help you with your bath and dressing. They stand around much like you're doing," Isabel snapped, hoping to rattle the nurse.

"You certainly are cranky this morning. I'll be back in an hour or so. Is there anything I can get for you or do for you before I leave?"

"Not a thing. I'll be fine."

Isabel waited until she was certain Maggie had left the grounds before she made her way to the study, where she immediately dialed a private detective service she had used before. "This is Isabel Tyger, and here is what I want you to do . . ."

14

Helen gathered the last of her belongings and carried them to the door, wondering if she would miss the small apartment that had been home these many months.

"Is that the last of it, honey?"

Helen smiled. The only time Sam called her by name was in bed. She kept on smiling when she closed the door behind her.

"Share." Sam grinned. "I want to know what makes you smile. This is like an adventure. It's not too late, you can change your mind, you know."

"I was thinking you only use my name when we're in bed. I know you're afraid you might slip. As long as you really know who I am, everything is okay. This is right for me. I didn't leave a forwarding address, Sam. I did notify Boots, though. They'll do whatever they have to do, and I will do what I have to do. Life will go on. It's that simple. I think the big question is, are you sure you want to move in with me?"

"Try and keep me out of your life. I'm certain. Max is certain. He's got his blanket. We're ready to rock and roll."

"It's a good thing you own furniture. We'd be sleeping on the floor otherwise. The stuff in my apartment came with it. I'm not sure how I'll adjust to beanbag chairs and a ten-inch television set, though." Helen smiled.

"You're gonna love it."

Helen stopped and turned around. "It's true, Sam, I will love it. As long as you and Max are there it will be the next step on my long road to a new life. I need you to understand something, Sam. I agreed to you moving in with me because I love you. I didn't agree to it because I'm afraid or I want you to protect me. If Daniel manages to find me somehow, I'll deal with it. Me, not you. I want us to have a clear understanding on the matter."

"I'm good with everything, honey. If things look like they might be getting sticky, we can always relocate to Vermont. I have a teaching job there anytime I want one. Tuck that in the back of your mind somewhere. Another thing, if you sense anything, if you feel threatened in any way, I want your promise you will tell me. Two heads are better than one. Mine is a little cooler in this matter than yours. Whatever you do, don't panic. That's what I want *you* to understand and agree to."

"I do, Sam."

"Then let's get this show on the road. Les and a few of the guys from school should have the furniture in the house by the time we get there. We can unpack the boxes anytime. Let's go to the Garden State Art Center tonight. We can hear the concert on the lawn, and we can take the dogs with us."

"If I go, will you help me with the orders? We're two weeks behind, Sam."

Sam grinned. He liked that *we* business. It meant they were a unit, a couple. She was finally letting him into her real life. "Les and the guys are going to help when they finish unloading the furniture. I can't believe it's been three weeks since that . . . you know."

"That we made love and a week later I signed off on the program? It seems like yesterday." Helen laughed. "I still can't believe I modeled that bustier for you."

"I can believe it." Sam leered. "Okay, let's go! Next stop, our new rental two-bedroom, two-bath house, complete with eat-in kitchen and wood-burning fireplace and fenced-in yard for our two adorable pets."

"You sound like a real-estate agent. I'm ready." Helen grinned as she climbed into the front seat next to Sam. She couldn't remember ever being this happy. Never, ever. She offered up a prayer that nothing would go wrong.

"Metuchen, here we come!"

"Do you know the town, Sam?"

"A little. It's nice. Lots of trees on the streets. Nice shopping.

They have their own library and police station. You can walk to everything if you need to. It's close to Roosevelt Park. We can take the dogs for runs there. They ice-skate on the pond in the winter. They sleigh ride, too. There's a mall at the top of the hill. We're just a spit from Route 1 and Highway 27. I can drive to school in ten minutes. It's close to your shop. Ten minutes tops in driving time for you. There's a good vet you can take Lucie to, now that Dr. Lo has shut down his practice. I think we're both going to like it."

"I think I've been blessed, Sam. The orders are coming in so fast they boggle my mind. Yesterday I had to ask my supplier for an extra delivery. And then there's you. In my life, I've never been this happy. I just wanted you to know that, Sam."

"Me too," Sam said, reaching for her hand. "Me too."

Isabel Tyger walked slowly, the pronged cane slightly ahead of her as she matched her steps to the thud of the heavy cane. There was a murderous look in her eyes that matched the menacing clouds outdoors. Heavy rain slashed against the windows of the sunroom to a frenzied beat that set her teeth on edge. In her hand was a manila folder that had just been hand-delivered.

"You are doing remarkably well, Miss Tyger. I never would have believed it was possible. Another week or so, and you won't need the walker at all. And you certainly won't need me. I feel guilty taking your money as it is," Maggie Eldridge said, setting aside the paper she'd been reading.

"Do you now?" Isabel snapped, her mind on the contents of the folder in her lap. "What is it about me that makes you feel guilty, Maggie?"

"You're doing so well. You can shower by yourself. You take your own medicine. You eat what your cook prepares. You're an excellent chess player, and you've beaten me each time we play. I'm just here to make sure nothing goes awry. I'm used to working for my money. This is a vacation for me compared to other cases I've been on. And all that free time you give me is so generous of you. As I say, this is almost as good as a vacation. Do you feel all right, Miss Tyger? You look ... *angry*."

Isabel looked across the sunroom at the young nurse. Her eyes were so very blue and so incredibly guileless. Isabel shifted in her chair. "The truth is," she said, whacking the envelope against her leg, "I'm *very* angry. Do you know what I have here in my hand?"

Maggie giggled. "Now, Miss Tyger, how could I possibly know what's in that envelope? It was just delivered. I saw the messenger coming up the walk a little while ago."

"What about all the other envelopes that were delivered the past two and a half weeks? And what about the envelopes that were delivered to me while I was in the hospital?"

"I don't understand. Are you asking me a question, or are you trying to tell me something?" Isabel noted that some of the sparkle seemed to leave the nurse's eyes and voice at the question.

"Both," Isabel retorted.

"I'm afraid I don't understand." The guileless eyes were now wary and suspicious.

"Let me spin a little story for you. When I'm finished, you tell me if I'm right or not."

"All right," Maggie said, the color leaving her face. Round spots of rouge stood out starkly.

"When I fell and broke my hip, the event made the local newspapers as well as the local television news. When you were hired by a friend of mine to do private duty for me, your picture was also in the local papers. Some photographer snapped you walking into the hospital. I would imagine shortly after that your new boyfriend came into the picture. It was probably a chance meeting in the lobby or one of the local restaurants."

"Actually, Miss Tyger, I met Donald at the laundromat. We were both trying to get the last dryer. I won."

"He was handsome," Isabel went on. "Very cavalier. He invited you to a movie or dinner and you accepted. You told him what you did for a living, and he told you what he wanted you to know. The truth is, you don't know anything about the man you've been seeing. Since you've been here, the information you took out of my home was meant for your eyes only. For want of a better word, I set a trap for you. You see, I know what you've been doing since the first day we got home. I saw you going through my study the first night I gave you off."

"Miss Tyger, what are you saying? More to the point, what are you accusing me of? Why are you so interested in my boyfriend? Why are you prying into my personal life? That wasn't part of my job description."

Isabel knew she was on to something by the nurse's jittery tone of voice.

"Nor is spying part of your job description. What were you doing in my study?"

"Looking for a book," Maggie said feebly.

"Bullshit!" Isabel said succinctly. "I'm going to ask you one question, and, for your sake, I hope you have the good sense to tell me the truth. If you don't, I'll find a way to prosecute you," she lied. "You'll lose your nursing license. You're a good nurse, Maggie. I'd hate to see that happen to you."

"What . . . what's the question?"

"Ladies, ladies, ladies, why so serious? The two of you look like you lost your last friend," Arthur King boomed as he strode into the sunroom, his golf umbrella dripping all over the carpet.

"In a manner of speaking, we have. Maggie was just about to answer a question for me. Pour yourself some coffee, Artie. Now, Maggie, while I was under your care in the hospital, did you read the e-mails and photocopy them to give to your boyfriend, Donald McDermott?"

Arthur King choked on the coffee he was drinking. He grappled for a pile of napkins on the serving cart, his eyes on the young nurse and what she was about to say.

"Yes."

"I can't hear you, Maggie. Speak louder."

"Yes," the nurse said miserably.

"For God's sake, why?" Artie demanded.

"He asked me to. I . . . I wanted to please him. They were just chatty letters, there was nothing serious in them. I even read them. I couldn't imagine what he wanted to do with them."

"What did he tell you he was going to do with them?" Artie asked coldly.

"He said . . . what he said . . . was, he wanted the e-mail addresses so he could send out advertisements on the net. I know it wasn't right, but he said it was cheaper for him than it was to buy a list of names. I'm sorry I did it. I knew it was wrong when I did it. I don't have any excuse, and if you want to fire me, I deserve it. I would like to ask some questions," she said, bravely meeting Isabel's eyes. "Why would you hire a detective to spy on me or on Donald? Does this have something to do with industrial espionage? Is someone trying to steal your toy designs?"

"No, Maggie. Your boyfriend is trying to steal someone's life."

"Donald? Trying to steal someone's life? That doesn't make sense. How can you steal someone's life?" Maggie sputtered.

Isabel sighed. "I'll leave it to you, Artie, to explain the situation. I need to go on the computer. Where's your boyfriend right now, Maggie?"

"I think he's home, getting ready to go on a business trip. Are you going to have him arrested? What's going on?"

"Tell her, Artie," Isabel said as she made her way across the room. "Tell her Donald McDermott's real name and keep her here until I get back."

In her study, Isabel sat down with a thump. She felt dizzy and faint at the nurse's betrayal. The whole program was compromised now. Wizard that he was, Daniel Ward could find out anything he wanted to know by using the e-mails and his computer skills. And there was nothing she could do to him. Nothing she could prove. Bastard that he was, he probably had something set up whereby he would pretend to do what he'd told Maggie, sell on-line names and addresses. It was done all the time. Daniel knew it, and so did she.

"This is all my fault," Isabel mumbled. "Why did I insist Mona bring me the e-mails, the records from the shelters? Because," she answered herself, "you have to have your damn fingers in everything. You think you're the only one who can do things right. Now you can see what that attitude and that kind of thinking has gotten you."

The computer came to life. Isabel shifted her weight in the chair as she waited for the e-mail screen to come to life. She typed in the address for the Sassie Lassie web page and waited for the revolving envelope so she could send off an e-mail to Helen.

Would Daniel Ward's prying eyes see this e-mail? Possibly. Still, somehow, she had to warn Helen. She wrote: "I'd like to order both versions of your TTLS and TTLS2. It is imperative that you call me as soon as you receive this message as these are special-order gifts. My number is . . ."

The walk down the hall to the sunroom seemed to take Isabel forever. Her eyes narrowed when she saw the young nurse in tears.

"Are you crying for what you've done, or are you crying because that jackass you thought was so wonderful is who we said he is?" Isabel snapped.

"I showed her the company picture we had taken the last year Daniel was with us," Artie said.

"Do you have any idea what you've done?" Isabel snapped again.

"I'm sorry. I'm truly, truly sorry."

"That's not going to get any of us anywhere. How did you leave it with him? What are you supposed to do next?"

"I usually call him at lunchtime. If he's free for the evening, and I can get off, we meet somewhere for dinner or a movie. Sometimes we go back to his apartment. If . . . if there's anything, you know, special, he wants me to do, he usually tells me at night. For the most part he just says for me to keep my eyes open and to go through your mail. He . . . he got very angry when I couldn't get your password to open the computer. He wanted me to give you some medication and ask you for your password while you were medicated. I refused. I can't believe this is the same person. He was kind, caring, gentle. Yes, he gets angry sometimes, but then so do I. You get angry, Miss Tyger. Everyone gets angry at some point."

"There are different kinds of anger, Maggie. Daniel Ward's anger almost killed someone. The same thing could have happened to you, but it didn't. Thank God you had the good sense not to medicate me," Isabel said. Artie winced at her tone.

"Are you going to call the police?" Maggie asked fearfully.

"I don't know. What I do know is you aren't going anywhere

for the time being. You're going to stay right here under my nose. Artie, call the detective and tell him to come over here and baby-sit this young woman."

"You're keeping me here against my will! That's illegal," the nurse sputtered, her eyes full of anger.

"Would you rather I call the police and the hospital, a hospital I endow rather handsomely? The police commissioner is a friend of mine. The choice is up to you."

"I'll stay."

"I thought you'd see it my way. I want you to change out of that nurse's uniform. It offends me. Personally, I don't think you deserve to wear it. Go upstairs with her, Artie. Disconnect the phone in her room and make sure she doesn't have a cell phone."

Artie nodded. "By the way, some of my best people are on their way over here to check out your computer. We'll have the latest system in by the end of the day. He won't be able to tap it."

"What about . . . ?"

"It's in the works. Move, young lady!" Artie said in his best G-man voice.

Helen tidied up her work area, stacking everything neatly. She looked around. It felt so good, so wonderful finally to be on her own. She missed the dogs, though. She missed Sam even more. He'd called her three times. Maybe it was four times. She smiled at the thought. Tonight they were going to make spaghetti. Together. Sam had promised to make his famous garlic bread. What that meant was he was going to stop at Shop Rite and buy a frozen loaf of bread and doctor it up. He tried. That was the important thing.

Helen took one last look at the showcases to make sure the lingerie looked fresh and pretty for morning. The glass gleamed from Windex, usually the last thing she did before leaving. Today she'd only had six customers in the shop, but they had bought a total of $720 worth of merchandise. The Internet orders were quadruple those of the store. One last check for orders, and she could leave. She tapped her foot impatiently while she waited for her web page to soar to the full screen. It took another minute for her to scroll down the order-form page. She read the e-mail attached to the order form three times before she started to shake. She was reading it for the fourth time as she dialed the number on the e-mail. Something was wrong. Her breathing turned ragged-sounding as she waited for the voice on the other end of the wire.

"Hello."

"This is Sassie Lassie calling about your order," Helen managed to gasp.

"I've been expecting your call," Isabel said.

"Is this Boots?"

"Yes, I'm Boots. I'm afraid I have some bad news."

Helen listened, her face turning as white as the snowy undergarments in the showcase. She sat down on the stool behind the counter when her legs refused to hold her weight.

"I'm sorry this happened, TTLS."

"Damn it, Boots, call me by my name. My name makes it real. What do you want me to do?"

"I want you to move. We can have things operational for you by tomorrow. I want to know you're safe. This is my fault, and I take full responsibility."

"It's not your fault. I told you, one way or another, Daniel would find me. I'll handle it, Boots. I'm not moving again. I like where I am. The dogs have a yard to run in. The house is nice. I love Sam. I have a small business. I'm not giving it up. I have a life now for the first time ever. I refuse to give it up."

"He could snuff out your life. Or Sam's life. Is that what you want? You need to give some thought to that yard where TTLS2 runs."

"I don't want to hear this," Helen screamed. "I'm getting a gun. I'll protect myself. Your people turned me into a crack shot."

"Your husband is getting ready to leave on a business trip. Since he doesn't have meaningful employment, one has to wonder where he's going. We're watching him from this end, and we have a private detective on the case. I want you to stay alert. I don't want anything to happen to you or . . . those close to you."

"I refuse to listen to any more of this. I appreciate your concern. I have to get on with my life the best way I can. You take care of yourself, Boots. Stop worrying about me and get well. Perhaps we'll talk another time. By the way, did the foundation ever okay that personal meeting?''

"No. They thought it was too risky. I was looking forward to it myself.''

"I was, too, Boots. Maybe when this is all over . . . It won't be over, will it?''

"No. Promise me you'll be careful and that you'll stay alert.''

"I promise.''

Tears flooded Helen's eyes as she hung up the phone and turned off the computer. How was she going to tell all this to Sam? Maybe she shouldn't tell him at all. But if she didn't tell him, his life might be placed in danger. He needed to be careful and alert, too. How long would he be able to handle living like this before it got to him?

Helen squared her shoulders and stiffened her spine. She knew in that one split second of time that she was capable of killing. If she had to, she would kill to protect what she was building for herself. The first thing she was going to do in the morning was apply for a permit to purchase a gun.

Using what name? An inner voice queried. *Helen Ward?* If she did that, she might as well send Daniel a road map to her house. The Nancy Baker name wouldn't hold up. Nor could she withstand a background check. Helen felt a tremendous surge of relief when she realized she wouldn't be getting a gun after all. Guns killed people. No, that was wrong. The National Rifle Association said people killed people.

"I'll just have to kill you with my bare hands, Daniel, if it comes down to that. I have enough hate in me to do it, too.''

The declaration left her feeling wobbly and light-headed. Time to go home to Sam. Sam would make her feel better. She could hold Lucie all night if she wanted to. Tomorrow she would bring both dogs to the store. They could play in the small storage room, and she would walk them every hour or so. There was no way she was letting Lucie out of her sight.

"I hate you, Daniel Ward! I hate you with every bone in my body.''

* * *

"How long are you going to keep me here, Miss Tyger?" Maggie Eldridge asked.

"You are free to leave anytime you want."

"If I do leave, are you going to have someone watch me?"

"Yes."

"Even though I gave you my word that I wouldn't see Donald . . . Daniel, whatever his name is?"

"Yes." Isabel looked out into the darkness, her mind clear across the country in New Jersey.

"You listened to my call at noontime. I told him you were leaving California on a trip. He knows I won't be able to feed him any more information. I'm useless to him now. What if he comes after me?"

"People like Daniel Ward never give up. You need to know that," Isabel said wearily.

"I guess there's no point in me staying here. I'm so very sorry, Miss Tyger. I wish I could undo what . . ."

"Spare me your sorrow. I'm not in the mood. It's late. If you're going, go."

"If there's any way I can make up . . ."

"There isn't. My housekeeper packed your belongings. Your bags are by the front door."

"Good-bye, Miss Tyger," Maggie said tearfully.

Isabel ignored the nurse as she stared out the wide bow window at the darkness beyond. She finally turned away when she heard the nurse's engine roll over. She'd never felt so alone in her entire life. She knew if she called Gerry or Artie, they would come running. Such devotion. There were times when she wondered if she deserved their love and dedication to a friendship that was forged years ago when they were children.

Isabel turned off the lights and made her way down the hall to her bedroom, where she did something she hadn't done in years. She struggled to lower herself to one knee. She prayed fervently.

She asked for nothing. She promised nothing. She simply prayed.

At three o'clock, when she couldn't stand tossing and turning another minute, she got up and dressed. She reached for a wool shawl she kept hanging on the hook of her bedroom door.

She walked slowly even though she knew where each pebble, each blade of grass stood. *This is what my life has come to,* she thought sadly. *Walking about in the middle of the night. Talking to a dog that died sixty-one years ago.* She wondered if she was crazy, if she was losing her mind and no one had the nerve to tell her. Maybe she needed to be locked up somewhere. "You're nothing but a stupid, silly old woman, Isabel Tyger," Isabel muttered as she lowered herself to the ground. She took a moment to wonder if she would get hemorrhoids sitting on the cold ground. Like hemorrhoids would really affect her life one way or the other. "Bullshit!" she said, uttering her favorite word.

Isabel sat quietly, her back against a tree, her legs stretched out in front of her. She knew she would have a devil of a time getting up later, but she didn't care. This was the only place on earth that gave her any kind of real comfort. She talked then, to the dog named Boots and her nine pups, who were buried next to where Isabel sat. When the pain came, as she knew it would, sharp and fast, she heard the sharp bark of welcome overhead. "I'm coming, Boots, I'm coming."

15

Helen angrily tossed the newspaper she was reading on the floor. Tears rolled down her cheeks. She wanted to call someone, to demand she be allowed to attend the memorial service being held in California for Isabel Tyger. Why had the woman's family waited over ten weeks before holding a service? She'd sent three dozen, possibly more, e-mails to Boots's e-mail carrier requesting permission to attend a service when it was held. She had expected a reply, but none had been forthcoming.

She hadn't even known of the toy heiress's death until Sam told her he read about it in the paper a week later. She'd been depressed for days, unable to shake off the feeling that she'd betrayed her benefactor, who had spent her life helping battered and abused women.

Helen stared now at the e-mail glaring at her from her Sassie Lassie web page.

> *Miss Tyger's memorial service is to be a private affair attended by close friends. The foundation rules are still in effect and will continue as before. Your condolences are appreciated by Miss Tyger's friends, who were near and dear to her heart. Your well-being and your safety are paramount to the program. Life must go on. It was and still is Miss Tyger's legacy to all of you who were helped by her insight and her generosity.*

The e-mail was signed by Arthur King and Gerald Davis. Didn't they know she was no longer in the program?

Helen ran to the back room, where sobs ripped through her body. Another part of her life was gone, ripped out from under her.

Helen stared at the wall phone. She could pick it up and call Arthur King, Daniel's old boss. She was almost certain he would take her call. Or, she could call Dr. Davis. She wasn't in the program any longer, so there was nothing to prevent her from calling. She needed to do *something*.

She could make the call person-to-person from a pay phone. All she needed was a pocketful of change. She could get that at the First Union Bank two doors from her shop. There was also a pay phone a block away.

Instead of listening to her own thoughts, Helen picked up the phone and dialed the information operator. She scribbled down the two numbers before she sucked in her breath to ask the operator to make the calls person-to-person.

Five minutes later, Helen's shoulders slumped. Arthur King was out of town. A recording came on at the Davis Veterinary Clinic that said the clinic was closed indefinitely and that Dr. Charles Goodwin was overseeing Dr. Davis's practice.

Helen slid to the floor to be next to the dogs. "You see. This is what I mean. I have no rights. I'm still not my own person. If I was my own person, Dr. Davis would have called me. Or, someone from Miss Tyger's foundation would have called. Boots doesn't even care about me anymore." She continued to stroke both dogs' heads as they slept. "It is what it is. I can't change anything," Helen mumbled as she got to her feet. "Up and at it, guys, I think we have time for a short walk. We'll just go out the back. I have a lot of work to do this afternoon."

Both dogs yipped their pleasure at being outdoors. They strained at their leashes when a yellow tabby pranced out from behind a Dumpster. The feline stared at them contemptuously as she continued her leisurely stroll to the end of the back lot. Max stopped his frenzied barking when Lucie started to whine and whimper. He tried to lick at her tiny face before Helen bent down to pick her up. She knew something was wrong, and it wasn't the tabby cat that had upset Lucie. In the blink of an eye she had both dogs inside her storeroom and the door locked. She then ran to the windowed front door, checked to make sure it was still locked, and pulled down the shade.

Fear was a terrible thing. Lucie trembled in her arms. Helen crooned softly to the little dog before she set her down next to Max. Unlike her mistress, Lucie did not spook easily, especially when Max was around. The little dog's fright merely intensified the strange feelings Helen had been having for the past several weeks. So many times she'd felt that someone was watching her. Just yesterday, when she'd gone next door to the bank to make a deposit, she'd felt someone staring at her. The day before, when she'd walked across the street to the deli for a sandwich, she'd felt the same way. The sensation of unseen eyes boring into the small of her back was so strong she'd galloped back to her store and locked herself in the storage room with the two dogs.

Daniel?

Had her husband finally found her? Was that why Lucie was so spooked a little while ago? Dogs had a natural instinct in matters like this. She suddenly felt icy cold. She was rubbing her arms for warmth when the phone rang. Answer it? Don't answer it? It might be Sam. She picked up the receiver. "Sassie Lassie," she said briskly. When there was no response, she said, "Hello, is anyone there?" When there was no response, she hung up the phone. She started to shake so badly she had to hang on to the counter for support.

Daniel?

Helen looked down to see Lucie snuggled between Max's two front paws, his big head resting lightly on her back. She offered up a prayer of thanks for the beautiful Lab. She knew that Max would protect her and Lucie with his life. Suddenly she wanted to lash out, to hit something, to smash something out of sheer frustration.

Helen felt vulnerable in the store. All she wanted to do was go home and lock all the doors and wait for Sam. A moment later she realized she could do just that. "I own this store," she mumbled. "All I have to do is lock the door, and we can go home." *If Daniel is out there somewhere watching me, he's going to follow me,* she thought. *If I do leave, I'll be leading him right to my house.*

Helen almost jumped out of her skin when someone rattled the front door. Raising the shade, Helen saw two giggling teenagers wearing sweatshirts that said J.P. Stevens on the front. She unlocked the door and let them in.

"Do you have any thong underwear?" one of them asked.

"I don't have any in the store, but we do have some on our web site. They're pretty much a special order. Would you like me to bring up the web page for you to see what we have?" This was normal. This was business. Shift into neutral, Helen. Help the girls and then you can go home.

"Yeah," both girls said in unison.

"Here we go," Helen said, twirling the monitor around for the girls to view. She half listened to them as her gaze raked the street outside the store. Everything looked so normal. "Do you see anything you like?"

"Do we ever! I'd like one of everything," one of the girls said.

"Me too," the second girl said.

"I'll take seven pairs," the first girl said. "Two black, two pink, two red, and one white."

"I'll take the same thing," the second girl said.

"Are you sure? They're very expensive. Eighteen dollars a pair to be exact. I'll need a deposit," Helen said. She wondered where high-school girls came by this kind of money.

Both girls whipped out their wallets and laid down fifty-dollars each. Helen typed in the order and printed out a receipt. "They should arrive in about three days. Do you want me to mail them out or do you want to pick them up?"

"We'll pick them up," both girls said in unison.

When the door closed behind the girls, Helen wondered if they did their own laundry and what their mothers thought of thong underwear. As if it was really her problem. She thought back to her own schooldays and the long walk home that took her past a fashionable lingerie shop. Each and every day she'd stop and stare, marveling at the sheerness, the minuscule hand stitching, the beauty of the items that were changed daily in the window display. At one point she convinced herself the owner changed the window display just for her because she stopped each day to pretend she owned the beautiful things. In those days she was lucky she had JCPenney cotton underwear.

"We're going home," she announced to the dogs. Neither animal moved. They knew they never went home until they heard the lock click on the front door and the computer screen saver chirped good-bye. Only then did they yawn, stretch, and stand up to wait for their leashes.

Helen carefully locked the back door to the shop, her grip on the leashes secure. Lucie whimpered again. "Show me, Lucie. Show me what's bothering you."

Lucie trotted ahead, Max at her side as she sniffed the ground and the corners of the building. When they reached her van, the little dog kept moving forward. Max let out a sharp bark to let Helen know they passed the van and what kind of strange goings-on was this? "Shhh," she said to the big Lab.

The moment Lucie stopped in her tracks, the Lab started to paw the ground. Lucie barked, her little body shaking from head to toe. The Lab lifted his leg and squirted the exact spot Lucie had been pawing.

"So there!" Helen said dramatically. "Good boy, Max. Good boy." If it was Daniel spying on her, the Lab now had his scent. "Okay, into the van, Max," Helen said, sliding the door of the Ford Explorer. She unhooked the dogs' leashes and settled them on the backseat. "Buckle up, Max." She always smiled when Max buckled Lucie in first and then himself, something Sam had taught him to do.

The smile left Helen's face almost instantly when she steered the van out of the back parking lot. She crossed Route 27, taking a back street to Central, where she drove around in circles trying to see if anyone was following her. She passed St. Joseph's High School, Charlie Brown's restaurant, and then turned right on Stephenville Parkway. A brown Ford Escort and a dark blue Honda stayed with her until she turned right on Calvert and followed it all the way to Grove, where she turned right again, then made a left onto James Street. The blue Honda was still with her, but there was no sign of the brown Escort. She crossed Lincoln Highway at the light and drove up Parsonage Road to the Menlo Park Mall. The Honda was still behind her when she pulled into the underground parking lot. She drove out almost immediately and headed for the traffic light, where she crossed Parsonage Road again and drove into the Target parking lot. She steered the Explorer to a parking space and craned her neck. There was no sign of the blue Honda.

Helen waited ten minutes before she pulled out of the lot and headed home, her eyes constantly searching the rearview mirror.

If it was Daniel's scent Lucie picked up, he probably knew already where she lived. He was probably lurking somewhere near her house at that moment. Lucie knew, though. All this past week the little dog had acted strange at certain times of the day and evening. Just last night she'd refused to go outside for the last walk of the night. Instead, she'd peed on the paper Helen left by the back door for "accidents" during the night.

Helen slowed down and swerved into the driveway to park next to Sam's Chevy Blazer. He was home early. "Thank you, God," she murmured.

"We're home, guys." She smiled again as she watched the Lab use one paw to tap the seat belt. Lucie leaped over the backseat to land in Helen's lap. The Lab did the same thing the moment he was free. "Okay, a quick run in the backyard and then inside. Go!" she said, unlocking the gate with the key on her key ring. She relocked the gate and entered the house through the garage.

"Smells good. What is it?" Helen said.

"Ann Landers meat loaf. I cut the recipe out of the paper years ago and every so often I get a fit for meat loaf. It ain't bad." He leered at her. "What's wrong? I can tell by the look on your face that something happened. Sit down. I'll make us some coffee. First I have to let the dogs in. Yo, big guy," Sam said, as the Lab threw himself against his body, pushing him backward until he was against the refrigerator. Lucie yapped and then sprang into his arms.

"Lock the door, Sam," Helen said.

"Maybe we should have a beer instead," Sam said, stretching his arm to lock the door.

"A beer is good. Beer's fine. I like beer. I really do."

"Uh-huh. Okay, tell me what happened," Sam said as he twisted the caps off two bottles of Budweiser. Helen told him.

"You didn't see anything? It's just a feeling?" he queried.

"That, plus Lucie's strange behavior. He's here, Sam. I know it. I feel it. So does Lucie."

"Do you want to go to the police?"

"That's the last thing I want to do. If he is here, he hasn't done anything. What am I going to say? I have this feeling my husband is out there spying on me because I'm living with another man. How's that going to look?"

"Did you try Boots again?"

"I've been e-mailing for days. I tried again today. I even tried to call Arthur King and Dr. Davis. The clinic is closed indefinitely, and Mr. King is out of town. I didn't call because of Daniel. I called to see if they would give a message to Miss Tyger's family or friends. I keep forgetting that she had no family. I needed . . . I wanted . . ."

"I know what you wanted. I guess you are going to have to leave it alone. Boots will get back to you the way she did the last time. You were worried then, too, but she was in the hospital. Perhaps she had a relapse."

"She called to warn me, Sam. It's been over two months. I'm telling you. Daniel is here. For all I know he could be standing in the bushes outside the house."

"What will he do, Helen?"

"That's just it, Sam. I don't know. Batterers go through stages. Boots said he could be in the kill mode. I know that sounds dramatic, but that's the way it is. He wants to get even with me for leaving him, and for losing his job, and whatever came afterward. Daniel is very clever. He fooled everyone all those years. They almost named him man of the year at the company one time, but Ted Wexler got it instead. Daniel was so magnanimous at the ceremony that night. When we got home, his rage took over. Ted Wexler's honor cost me a broken collarbone."

"Jesus H. Christ, Helen! You should have left right then," Sam exploded.

"I couldn't walk, Sam. Look, that was then, this is now. I warned you this would happen. You said you could handle it."

"I can handle it. I'm upset for you. I hate it when you tell me how that son of a bitch hurt you."

"He can't hurt me anymore. You know what I would really like to do, Sam. I'd like to go back to California and get all my records. I want my driver's license. I want my own credit card. I want mine and Lucie's medical records. I want to go to a lawyer in California and file for a divorce. Dr. Davis has pictures he and his friend Billie took of me that night. I'm sure Mr. King can help me find Dr. Davis so he can turn the pictures over to me."

"I can get your records for you by mail, fax, or over the phone. I can't leave, and I don't want you to go without me. You can file for a divorce here. Someone from the foundation will help you, won't they?"

"No, Sam. They won't. I can't bring them into this. I gave my word."

"Sometimes I'm confused, Helen. Are you in or are you out of that program?"

"I'm technically out, but I'm still in. I don't have any papers saying I'm Helen Stanley Ward. All I have are bogus papers saying I'm Nancy Baker. Until my own identity is given back to me, I am still, in the eyes of the program, Nancy Baker. I can't live like this. It's not fair to you."

"Let me worry about what's fair to me. We need to put our heads together and work out some kind of plan. We're safe here since the house has an alarm system. The ADT sign out front should deter anyone from even thinking about breaking in when we're home. From now on we set it when we leave for work."

"Daniel could dismantle it in a heartbeat. I don't want you to underestimate him, Sam. I had a hangup at the store today, too. It's possible it was a legitimate wrong number. Whoever it was on the other end didn't hang up when they heard my voice; I was the one who hung up."

"Helen, I know all about wackos. I know how to deal with a lunatic. It's you I'm worried about. You're starting to unravel. If you fall apart, you're lost before you start. You need your wits about you."

"I know that, Sam. You know how people always say when something goes wrong they wait for the other shoe to drop? Well, since I entered the program, I've been waiting for that shoe. My mind, my heart, my gut tells me the shoe has dropped. Lucie knows it, too."

"Do you want to talk about relocating to Vermont?"

"No, Sam, I don't. I'm not running anymore. I can't do that to you. Your life is here. So is mine. When and if I move . . . we move, it will be for the right reasons." Helen wondered if what she'd just said was the truth or just wishful thinking.

"Do you have any idea how much I love you, Helen?"

"Probably about as much as I love you. We can make this work, can't we, Sam?"

"Damn right we can."

Helen reached across the table for Sam's hand. "You and Max are the best thing that ever happened to Lucie and me. Now, what else are we having besides Ann Landers meat loaf?"

"Baby carrots, little green peas that look like emeralds, and mashed potatoes. Gravy of course. You have to make the salad."

"What about dessert?"

"You, my dear, are the dessert." Sam grinned.

"The end to a perfect dinner." Helen laughed.

He absolutely glows, she thought. *I will not allow you to spoil this, Daniel. I will not.*

16

Helen gathered up the mail from the foyer floor beneath the mail slot and slapped it down on the kitchen table, not bothering to look at it. She let the dogs out and then put on a fresh pot of coffee before she changed into her sweats. Maybe she would surprise Sam and make a pot roast. He loved it when she cooked an apple with the roast, saying it gave the gravy a tangy taste. The meal would take care of itself once she added the carrots and potatoes. Since she wasn't a red-meat eater, she would eat the vegetables and salad and Sam would have cold sandwiches the rest of the week. While the meal cooked, she could pack up the Internet orders in the garage so she could spend more time with Sam later on.

Helen took a minute to look around the kitchen. Sam's and her kitchen. They spent wonderful hours in here cooking or baking together, cleaning up or having a cup of coffee. Sam and Max were her whole world now. Her gaze swept to the colorful calendar hanging next to the refrigerator. The red X's told her it had been almost a month since she first felt like someone was watching her. Maybe it had been her imagination after all. Lucie hadn't acted weird in almost a week now. There had been no hangups at the store, none at all at the house. She was starting to relax again. She didn't know if it was good or bad on her part. Sam was fond of saying, you snooze, you lose. That meant she had to stay alert.

The coffee finished dripping. Helen poured and carried her cup to the table, where she shuffled the mail, arranging the catalogs, the flyers, and the junk mail on the bottom and the first-class mail on top. Sam would weed out what he wanted to keep and what he wanted to throw away. When she saw her name on a cream-colored envelope, she frowned. The letter was addressed to Nancy

Baker, and the return address was that of a law firm in San Jose, California: Johnson, Carlisle & Stevens. Her heart took on an extra beat. It was a law firm she'd never heard of. The law firm the Tyger Foundation used was Spindler & Spindler.

Helen stared at the letter, moving it away from Sam's mail, which she'd piled on top of yesterday's, which he hadn't seemed to read yet, so it wouldn't contaminate it. She used her napkin to edge it closer to her coffee cup. She wondered what would happen to it if she ripped it up and put it through the garbage disposal. It would probably clog it up. Maybe she should burn it. Flush it? She longed for a paper shredder. In the end she opened it and read the two short, curt sentences.

> Dear Ms. Baker,
>   Please call this office as soon as possible to discuss a matter of the utmost importance.
>   Please feel free to reverse the telephone charges.

The letter was signed, Seymour Johnson.

"In your dreams," Helen muttered as she tore the letter to shreds and burned them in the oversize ashtray on the counter. She watched the crinkly paper curl into black, dead ash. She carried the mess to the sink and turned on the disposal. She added a lemon to take out the evil smell of burnt paper.

Helen moved by rote then. She browned the pot roast, peeled vegetables, handed out chewies to the dogs, then made her way to the garage. Shift into neutral, don't think about the letter. Do what you have to do. Don't think about the letter. Don't even think of mentioning it to Sam.

She worked feverishly, unpacking boxes, sorting what had to go to the seamstresses, what had to be packaged for UPS, and what she had to take to the shop. She was on her third cup of coffee when Sam strode into the garage.

"Whatever you're cooking smells wonderful. I thought tonight was leftovers. I missed you today," Sam said, holding out his arms.

Helen melted into his embrace. How good he felt. How wonder-

ful and right. "You deserve better than leftovers. Oh, do that again."
She sighed happily.

"You feel tense. How about a nice shoulder rub?"

"I'd love a nice shoulder rub. I'd love other things, too."

"You must think I'm easy." Sam grinned as his fingers dug into
her shoulders. "How was your day?" It was a casual question but
one that demanded a response.

"Fairly routine. Not much store traffic, but there are enough
orders on the web page to keep me busy all evening. Each day I
seem to pick up three or four new orders, and the repeat business
is great. It's above expectation."

"So why are you so tense?"

Helen shrugged. "Lucie goes to the vet tomorrow. Does Max
need anything?"

"Nope. He's up to snuff on everything. Did you burn something
today?"

"Yes, Sam, I did. A letter came addressed to Nancy Baker from
some lawyers in San Jose. I burned it and rinsed it down the
disposal." So much for not telling Sam.

"What did they want?"

"They asked me to call their offices on a matter of the utmost
importance. I don't think so. That part of my life is over."

Sam turned around and dropped to his knees. He took Helen's
hands in his. "Is that wise, Helen? What if it doesn't have anything
to do with your husband? What if it was about your mother or
Boots?"

"I don't want to know, Sam. My mother doesn't know my alias,
so it isn't about her. The foundation uses a different law firm. My
appointment is next Monday with a lawyer here in town to file for
divorce. Why do you suppose it's taking so long to get a duplicate
of my driver's license from California?"

"The answer is on the kitchen table, Helen," Sam said wearily.

"You got a response? Good. Then I can go to the Bureau of
Motor Vehicles on my lunch hour tomorrow. God, I am so relieved."

"You don't understand, Helen. It was a letter saying you're
deceased. That has to mean the people at the foundation filed a
death certificate somehow, some way. There's a big rigamarole you

have to go through. When you go to the lawyer, tell him everything. Let him do the paperwork. They'll pay more attention to a letter from a lawyer than one from you or me. If we try to do it, we'll just be spinning our wheels."

"Dead?"

"Dead," Sam said. "You'll have to get a copy of your birth certificate, your social security card, and any church records that might be available. I don't think the foundation would fool with the social security office or the department of records. A driver's license is something different. You said they told you the credentials they gave you would never stand up in a court of law."

"Dead? That's terrible, Sam."

"I guess on the surface it does sound terrible. I'm assuming your situation called for strong measures. It's possible it's the foundation policy."

Helen glared at him. "To declare someone dead!"

"In a manner of speaking, Helen Ward is ... was dead. They gave you a new identity. Your benefactors had every reason to believe that you would remain in the program and continue to use the new identity they provided you. You were never supposed to go back to being Helen Ward. It was safer to have her declared dead."

"They never told me that."

"Perhaps they thought you understood what a new identity meant. If you get another letter, Helen, respond."

"I don't think so, Sam. Are we going to argue over this?"

"No, we aren't going to argue. However, I think I can be a little more objective than you."

"No, Sam, you can't. You love me. Don't tell me you can be objective."

"We could probably work this up to a real fight if we tried. I hate fighting. All fighting does is cause hard feelings. You know what they say, make love not war."

Helen giggled. "Who said that?"

"Sam Tolliver, one of the smartest men in New Jersey, that's who. What do you say, are you up for a little predinner hanky-panky?"

"Best offer I've had all day. Should I turn the stove off or leave it on?"

"Turn it off," Sam said as he slung her over his shoulders. Helen giggled all the way to the bedroom.

Dinner that night was served at ten-fifteen.

The next day, Helen closed the store a half hour early to allow enough time to get Lucie to the vet. "It's okay, Max. You have to stay in the van. We won't be long. Lucie just needs her rabies shot and her heartworm pills. You watch the van." Helen cranked the windows a half inch and locked the Lab in the van before she scooped up Lucie. "Shhh, it's going to be okay. Nothing is going to happen."

Helen opened the door of the Shady Elm Animal Clinic and was relieved to see the empty waiting room. That meant they would be in and out in minutes if she didn't chitchat.

When the vet was finished with Lucie, Helen withdrew thirty-five dollars for the office visit and handed it to the receptionist.

"You don't owe us for the heartworm. Your husband paid for it when he was in here last week. He's very protective of Lucie, isn't he?"

Helen wondered what color her face was. Was it as white as the knuckles on her hands? "Yes," she managed to say. She turned and headed for the door. "Tell the doctor I'll call for my next appointment."

The moment Lucie was safely in the van, Helen walked around to the side and dropped to her haunches to put her head between her knees to ward off the light-headed feeling that was threatening to overcome her. Daniel had found her. There was no doubt in her mind that it was Daniel in the office last week. Sam took Max to the vet on Park Avenue in South Plainfield. If Sam had stopped to pay for the heartworm medication, he would have told her.

Helen had no idea how she drove home. The moment she was safely inside the house, she looked around, wondering how she'd gotten home in one piece. She blinked at the mail lying on the foyer floor. A small yellow notice for a certified-mail pickup appeared to be stuck to a flyer for Pizza Hut. There was also another cream-colored envelope from San Jose, California. This time she ripped the cream-colored letter and the certified notice into pieces and flushed them down the toilet without reading the letter. Thank God Sam had insisted on an unlisted telephone number. If he hadn't, it would probably be ringing off the hook by now.

The dogs watched her, backing out of the bathroom to give her space. She seemed unaware of their presence as she paced up and down the hall. From time to time, she lashed out at the wall with either her fist or her foot. She ignored the pain that ricocheted up her arm and her leg.

Fear and anger raced through her veins. Damn, maybe Sam was right. Maybe she should have read the second letter from the lawyer. She snorted. What could they possibly tell her that she didn't know? That Daniel Ward had found her? She already knew that. Should she tell Sam? Should she pack up and run? Should she call the shelter? More to the point, should she call the police? "No, no, no," she muttered. *Calm down*, she chided herself. *You aren't that old Helen anymore. You're strong now. You have guts and stamina. Don't give in to your fear. That's what Daniel wants. You don't do what Daniel wants these days. You are your own person. You can outthink him.*

Helen raced to the bedroom and yanked open a dresser drawer. Inside the toe of one of her wool socks was a stash of money she'd been squirreling away for just such an emergency. She counted the money carefully—thirteen hundred dollars. It was enough to get her and Lucie back to California. *Sam will never understand if I cut and run.* She started to cry. Sam was too easygoing, too trusting. He had no idea what Daniel was capable of. If she left, would Sam be safe? If Daniel was watching her, Sam, and the house, he would know if she bolted. Would he follow her or stay behind and harm Sam?

Red-hot anger, unlike anything she'd ever experienced before, rivered through her. She had to do the right thing. For everyone concerned. Before, it was just herself and Lucie. Now she had to worry about Sam and Max. How could she possibly keep this from Sam? He was so attuned to her. He would know something was wrong the minute he walked in the door.

Dear God, what would life be like on the run without Sam? "I hate you, Daniel!" she screamed. Tears streamed down her cheeks. Frightened, Lucie leaped into her arms. Max pawed at her legs. Realizing she was scaring the dogs, Helen dropped to the floor and gathered them close. They cuddled, trying to comfort her.

A headache started to hammer away at the base of her head. Before long she would have a full-blown migraine, the kind of headache she used to get back in California. The kind she hadn't had since moving to New Jersey. The only thing that helped was a dark room and sleep. Three days in a dark room and hopefully she wouldn't throw up the way she had in the past. Three days to do nothing but think. Three days to plan. Maybe this headache was the reprieve she'd been looking for.

On her way to the bedroom, Helen wondered what had happened to all her good intentions. "I can't jeopardize Sam and Max. I just can't. I love them too much," Helen murmured as she crawled between the cool sheets, Max on one side of her, Lucie curled into the crook of her arm. "I just love them too much."

"What in the hell are we doing sitting here in a cemetery in the rain, Gerry?"

"I don't know what your excuse is, since you're supposed to be on vacation, but mine is I'm sitting here reading Izzie's will. I'm also getting drunk. Do you have a problem with that, Artie?"

"Pass the bottle, Gerry."

"What about your ulcer?"

"Screw my ulcer. We're probably both going to get pneumonia and die, so my ulcer means diddly. I worry about you, Gerry. We can't bring her back."

"I know that. I know every single thing you're going to say so save your breath. Why didn't you go on that vacation you planned?"

"I didn't feel like it. My arthritis is bothering me. My ulcer is bothering me. I'm grieving. What kind of vacation do you think I'd have? You think you know someone and then bam, you don't know them at all. It's still sticking in my craw that I was so wrong about Daniel Ward. I didn't want to leave you to handle all of Izz's affairs by yourself."

"I'm too drunk to understand something like that. You have to be more speee-cif-ic."

"In all the years we were married, my wife had never once said a negative word about Isabel. Then one day, out of the blue, she finally let loose. I always knew she resented Isabel and our friendship. I never realized she hated her with such passion. She hated you, too. I never knew it, just like I didn't know Daniel Ward was such a bad person. Marie's been dead some time now. Why am I thinking like this? Am I finally losing it?"

"No. Gimme that bottle."

"She said, and this is a direct quote, 'I hate her guts.' She never understood, Gerry. She never even pretended to understand. Does that make me dumb as shit or just plain stupid? Both, I guess. I went to six different shrinks, Gerry, over the years. None of them could figure me out. On top of all that, Marie used to volunteer at the shelter. Izz said she was a godsend."

Gerry nodded sagely. "I got your number. Here, drown your ulcer and maybe it will stop hurting." He handed over the bottle with a flourish.

"Liquor isn't the answer," Artie said, reaching for the bottle. "I hope you brought an extra one. This one is almost empty. Why are you reading the will?"

"Because you and I are the executors. We have to do what Izzie wanted. It's in the works. This is going to be a full-time job. I closed the clinic indefinitely. That twerp Sanders wants to buy me out. He wears penny loafers, Artie. Those damn yuppies think they know everything."

"I'm retiring. I'm not even waiting till January. Seventy is time to hang it up. Do you agree?"

"Yep. So what are we going to do?"

"See that Isabel's instructions are carried out. Oversee everything. She's going to want an accounting when we meet up next. You know how she is . . . was."

"He was going to drown her that day after he finished with the dogs. Right there in that water trough. He would have, too, if we hadn't popped out of the bushes and attacked him. Why didn't we ever talk about that? We should have talked about that, Artie. If we had talked about it, dealt with it, Izzie might have died a happier woman. Did you ever tell *that* to those six shrinks?"

"Christ, no! We didn't talk about it because we were just little kids, and maybe we thought we were wrong. I don't think Izz realized . . ."

"The hell she didn't. She knew. She's the one who brought it up first. She mentioned it the last time we were out here together. It's over now. Life is going to go on. How do you think this will is going to go over when it's made public?"

"Like a lead balloon. Do you care, Gerry?"

"All I care about is carrying out Izzie's wishes. After that, I don't care what happens. Do you?"

"Not really. We're just two old codgers coming down the home stretch. Seems like we should do something, you know, memorable. For some damn reason I thought Izz would be here forever and outlive both of us. I wasn't prepared. There's this . . . this . . . tremendous void in my life now. I wake up automatically at four in the morning and wait for the phone to ring. We're soaking wet, Gerry. I know you have a key to Izz's house. Let's go up and dry out. We can make some coffee and sit in the kitchen like we used to. I need to show you the detective's report on Daniel Ward. The truth is, there isn't any report. He lost the son of a bitch weeks ago.

"I was thinking, Gerry, why don't you and I go East and see Helen Ward. We can tell her the news firsthand. If you don't like that idea, let's call her."

"Izzie wouldn't like that, Artie. Izzie liked to go by the book. With the exception of those times when she added a new page," Gerry said, struggling to get up from his cramped position on the wet ground.

"It's hell getting old, isn't it?" Artie said.

"It beats the alternative," Gerry said, swinging the bottle around in a circle. "We've both had enough of this." He upended the bottle, watching the amber liquid puddle at his feet. "She's here, you know. All around us. And there's that little bit of her we buried with Boots. This is *our* place, Artie." Gerry shook his head to clear it. "What did we decide? Are we going to let the lawyers handle it, or are we going to go against Izzie's wishes?"

"I say we let the lawyers handle it. We might screw it up."

"Okay," Gerry said agreeably as he lurched his way back to the Tyger house.

"I feel like bawling," Artie said.

"Then bawl."

"Okay, I will."

"Me too, Artie, me too. It's never going to be the same again. I thought the golden years were supposed to be wonderful. I wonder who started that lie. I'd like to pop him right in the nose."

"Izz said it first, as near as I can remember," Artie said, blowing his nose lustily.

"Oh."

17

"Honey, it's time to sit down and talk. It's been three weeks since you received those legal letters, and you haven't said a word about what you're going to do. Everything in our life feels like it's been put on hold. Even me. I've respected your feelings, but I think it's time we move on here. You're jumpier than a cat in a rainstorm. I'm starting to get jumpy myself, so I have an idea of how you must feel. Even the dogs are picking up on your feelings. Now, let's talk."

Helen reached for her coffee cup. She had to give serious thought to curtailing her caffeine these days. "If you mean what am I going to do about those two legal letters, the answer is I'm going to do nothing. I don't know anything about that law firm. The only way they can know anything about me is from Daniel. Therefore, I am not going to call them. Are you saying if you were in my place you would call?"

"Hell, yes, I would."

"That's easy for you to say, Sam. There is no Daniel Ward in your life."

"Then let's get him the hell out of your life once and for all. You've been waffling these past weeks, and you canceled your appointment with the attorney in town. We need some kind of game plan, Helen."

Helen stared out the kitchen window. "I understand how you might think that, Sam. The truth is, my airline ticket arrived today."

"When were you going to tell me?"

"That I was leaving or that the ticket arrived?" Helen asked, stalling for time.

"Both," Sam snapped.

"I was going to tell you this evening. I knew you would ask a lot of questions, Sam, and I don't have any answers. I'm leaving next Tuesday. If you travel in the middle of the week, the fare is cheaper."

"When are you coming back?"

"I don't know. I can't give you a specific time or date, but I will be back. When I return, I really will be Helen Stanley."

"You're Helen Stanley now," Sam said adamantly. He finger combed his curly hair, causing it to stand on end.

"No, Sam. The law says I am Helen Stanley Ward, deceased. I'm going to change all that. I have my wits about me now. Those letters . . . Lucie . . . I got thrown off stride for a bit. I know what I have to do, and I'm going to do it. You have to let me do this my way."

"Okay, honey. I bought something today for us."

"A present?"

"Not really. I got us beepers. I'll feel better if you have one. I got one for Les, too, in case I can't get to a phone right away. You just hang it on your belt. They're real easy to use. We can practice later till we both get the hang of it. Let's build a fire tonight and pop some corn."

"Sounds good. A night off from packing merchandise is okay with me. It was sweet of you to get the beepers."

"That's because I'm a sweet guy. Now, let's go rake some leaves. The dogs can run in the yard. Don't look at me like that, Helen. We are not going to hide out. We're going on with our lives."

"Do we get to jump in them when they're piled up? I saw some of the neighborhood kids doing that when I drove home."

"Absolutely. It's kind of nippy out so layer your clothing. The truth is, it feels like snow."

The rest of the day and evening passed in a blur for Helen. She slept fitfully and was up an hour before Sam staggered into the kitchen. "What did I miss?" he mumbled.

"Nothing, Sam. Lucie had to go out so I figured I might as well stay up. I can get in an hour or so of packaging so UPS can pick up early. I can make some pancakes if you like."

"Not for me. Just coffee. I have a seven-thirty meeting. You okay, honey?" Helen nodded. "Don't forget to take your beeper with you."

"I won't forget, Sam."

In her pajamas and fuzzy slippers, Helen worked steadily packaging and labeling her orders. The moment Sam left the house, she headed for the shower.

At nine-thirty she was ready to start her new day. Her heart took on an extra beat as she carefully loaded her packages in the back of the Explorer and helped the dogs into the backseat. She sat quietly for several minutes, craning her neck to look out the rearview and side-view mirrors for any vehicle on the street that looked like it didn't belong. Satisfied, she backed out of the driveway and headed toward her shop.

Fifteen minutes later, Helen settled the dogs in the back storage room, put on a fresh pot of coffee, and turned on her computer.

This was the part of her business day that she liked the best. Knowing she was in her own shop, doing business, selling her own creativity and actually earning a living. Something Daniel Ward said would never happen. She liked sitting in the small cubbyhole she designated as her office, drinking coffee, smoking her first cigarette of the day, and watching the hands on the clock. She had forty-five minutes until it was time to open the blinds and unlock the front door. Forty-five minutes of Helen time as Sam called it. She looked at the clock now. Sam would be calling soon, something he always did before she opened the doors. She continued to watch the hands on the clock and started her countdown. Rarely was she more than a minute off either way. The phone rang almost immediately.

"Sassie Lassie," Helen said briskly.

"Hi, honey."

Helen's voice dropped to a throaty murmur. "Hi, yourself. I was just thinking of you, Sam. I love you so much. I just wanted you to know that."

"I do know, honey. I love you just as much. You wearing your beeper?"

"Yes, Sam, I am. Are you wearing yours?"

"You bet. Makes me feel important. Gotta run, honey. I have

another meeting in ten minutes. I hope you sell everything in your store today."

"Me too. Love you, Sam."

The hands on the clock read 10:50 when Helen rinsed her coffee cup and crushed out her cigarette. She was about to open the door leading to the interior of the little shop when she heard a knock on the front door of the shop. A customer? Daniel? Who? Lucie struggled to sit up as did Max waiting expectantly to see what she would do. By cracking the door a half inch she could peer into the dimness of the shop. She took a deep breath when she saw the handle of the door turn. The specialty locks Sam had installed were in place. She let her breath out slowly as she continued to stare at the door. The parchment shade on the door showed her the outline of two men. She thanked God for the bright October sunshine. Two? Why would two men be coming to her shop? In all the time she'd been open for business she'd only had three male customers, and one of them had been accompanied by his wife.

Helen knew she was being ridiculous when she kicked off her shoes and dropped to a low crouch, but she didn't care. She slithered out the door and crab-walked behind the counter to the small front window. By squinting she could peek through the tiny openings of adjustable strings on the parchment shade. Two strangers. One old, one young. Both carrying briefcases. They looked like bankers or Wall Street types. She bit down on her lower lip.

The door handle moved again followed by more solid knocking. Helen crab-walked her way back to the storage room, leaving the door slightly ajar. "Shhhh," she said to the dogs. "Here, chew on these," she said, handing out two rawhide bones.

Helen poured fresh coffee, aware that her hand was steady. She marveled at how calm she felt. When the phone rang she almost dropped the cup of coffee. So much for being calm. When it stopped ringing she deflated like a pricked balloon. With shaking hands she dialed the number that would give her access to her voice mail and then pressed the numbers for her code. She followed the directions to listen to her messages, saving the business messages by pressing the number 2. She held her breath while the operator gave her the date and the time of her last call. She listened to the message, saved it, and then played it back three times.

Miss Baker, This is Seymour Johnson. I'm an attorney in San Jose, California. There is a matter of the utmost importance that I must discuss with you. I'm making this phone call from the front door of your shop, which appears to be closed. I'm staying at the Clarendon on Highway 27 in Edison. Please call me as soon as possible. In addition, I've been leaving messages for you everywhere I could think of, your Internet e-mail, certified mail, and regular first-class mail. We need to talk, Miss Baker, before the newshounds get hold of this story.

Helen took a long, deep breath before she doubled over. Newshounds? What story? The story of Isabel Tyger's program or the story of her miserable marriage to Daniel? She looked down at the beeper attached to her brown-leather belt. She found herself shaking her head ever so slightly. She couldn't involve Sam in this. No matter what he said, she couldn't jeopardize his job.

She needed to go home, and she needed to go home *immediately*. First things first, though.

She logged on to her computer and clicked on her web page, where she quickly typed a notice to be posted within the hour. It was simple and to the point.

To All Sassie Lassie customers,

Due to the heavy demand for our merchandise we are curtailing all Internet orders for the time being. The moment our suppliers can match the demand for Sassie Lassie apparel, a notice will be posted. Thank you all for your patronage. We all look forward to a quick solution to what we hope is a temporary delay.

Helen spent another fifteen minutes downloading all her files and copying them onto disks. She slipped the small packet into her purse. Helter-skelter, she yanked and pulled at the gossamer apparel in the showcases, leaving empty boxes and tissue paper strewn everywhere. A tight knot on the heavy-duty trash bag meant she was ready to go.

It was time to move on.

Without Sam.

Both dogs whimpered in the backseat. "Everything is going to be all right," Helen repeated over and over until she started to believe the words herself. How could anything ever be all right again with Daniel stalking her? And he was stalking her. She could almost *smell* his presence.

Helen hit the automatic garage-door opener attached to her visor three doors from her rental house. She sailed up the driveway and into the garage. She hit the button a second time. The door closed within seconds. Safe.

"Into the house, guys. Quick. Cookies for everyone," she cajoled when it looked like Max was going to balk at these weird goings-on. The mention of his favorite treat made him pick up his feet to follow Helen into the house.

Helen wasted no time once she was inside the house. She immediately ran to the bedroom and packed her bag. The sock with the money went into her purse. Lucie's carry-bag, her mouse, and a ragged washcloth she was attached to went on top of her own things.

Should she leave a note for Sam? Of course not. The less he knew, the safer he would be. *I'm so sorry, Sam. So very, very sorry. I can't risk Daniel hurting you. I wish it didn't have to be like this. You don't know Daniel. If you did, you would run for cover.* A lone tear dropped onto the back of Helen's hand.

Helen was carrying the nylon travel bag through the kitchen to the garage when the doorbell rang. She almost fainted, the sound shattering any and all feelings of calm she might have previously felt. "Shhhh! Not a sound. Shhhh," she hissed. "Stay, Max. Watch Lucie."

The doorbell pealed a second time just as Helen ran down the hallway to the bedroom, where she peeked through the skinny miniblinds. The same two men with their identical battered brief-cases stood on the stoop ringing her bell. Then she looked across the street at the silvery car parked at the curb. Daniel!

She almost lost it then. She would have if the two dogs hadn't run to her, toppling her onto the floor. She clung to both of them as she fought the dizziness that threatened to engulf her. "Shhh, we have to stay here so they won't see us. We need to be quiet. Very, very quiet." Lucie crawled into her lap, whimpering and whining. Max prowled around the room, his growls deep and hoarse, but he obeyed Helen's orders not to bark.

Were the two men with Daniel? Or was it the other way around, and Daniel was with them? Did the three of them follow her from the shop? Maybe it was a parade and everyone was following everyone else. Did they know she was here, hiding from them? Or were they just staking out the place? She clenched her teeth as the red-hot anger she'd felt so often of late took over.

What are my options? Helen wondered. *Few to none,* she answered herself.

Helen hugged her knees, Lucie cuddled in her lap. She could call Sam or Les and they would come on the run. She knew instinctively if she did that, something terrible would happen to Sam and the young computer whiz. She couldn't risk calling either one of them. Three against one woman and two dogs. Not good odds. Try and make a run for it. Go somewhere public. And then what? You have a plane ticket. Maybe you can go on standby to California. All you'll have to do is pay a fee for changing the ticket. What was Newark Airport like? She'd never been there. She would have to park the car and walk. Alone. If she left the car at the door, it would get towed. She was right the first time. As far as options went, they were few to none.

Unless . . .

Helen's arm snaked out to reach for the phone on the nightstand. She dialed a number she knew she would never forget as long as she lived. She waited, hardly daring to breathe, for someone to pick up the phone. The voice was bright and cheerful. "This is Mona, how can I help you today?"

"Mona, this is . . . this is Nancy Baker. My husband found me. Right now he is sitting outside my house in a silver car. I think it's a Nissan. There are two strange men ringing my doorbell. They came to my shop earlier today. I didn't open the door. I just left and came home. I know there is a shelter here somewhere. Can someone come and get me? Please, I need your help."

"Give me your number, Nancy. I'll call you back in fifteen minutes."

"Okay." She spoke slowly, enunciating each number carefully.

She sat back to wait. After two minutes, the men at the front door left. Five minutes later, she heard a car drive away. But when she looked outside, Daniel was still there. Precisely fifteen minutes after Mona had hung up, the phone rang.

"Listen to me carefully, Nancy. This is what I want you to do . . ."

An hour passed and then another hour. It was two-thirty when Helen heard the sound of a police siren on the street. She peeked through the blind to see a police officer walk up to the silvery car. Ten minutes later the police cruiser escorted Daniel down the road, his lights still flashing, the siren silent.

"Come on, Max. I have to put you in Sam's room. God, I don't want to leave you, but I can't take you with me. If I could, I would. I'll find my way back here someday. I promise. I'll bring Lucie back. I don't know when that will be. Damn it, I can't leave you. You're part of my life, too. Sam will just have to understand. Come on, you can come with us. Hurry. Get your blanket, Max. Good boy," she said, stuffing it in the nylon bag. "Into the garage. Quick now. Someone is picking us up. You need to be quiet and you need to be good." *Forgive me, Sam. I don't know what else to do. You know I'll take good care of Max.*

Lucie whimpered and clung to her mistress.

Helen paced, the two dogs curled next to each other at the side of the bed. They watched her. From time to time she stooped down to pat them on the head. She muttered to herself, or was it to the dogs? She didn't know and didn't care. She was safe. The dogs were safe. Where was Daniel? Did the police arrest him? What a stupid thought. All he was doing was sitting in his car. Daniel could charm the wings off a butterfly if he wanted to. And the two men, where were they? More to the point, were they the attorneys they pretended to be? Did the people from the shelter take care of them, too?

Helen sat down when her legs threatened to give out on her. The dogs crawled on their bellies to lie next to her. "It's almost the same as the other shelter, Lucie. Remember how safe we felt when we were there? I don't know if we're in or out of this program.

I don't know if we can stay or not. For now this is the best for all of us. Later will take care of itself."

She wanted to cry, to yell and scream. In short, she wanted to take a page out of Daniel's book and act out her rage. Thinking about it was one thing, doing it like Daniel did was something else entirely.

Helen sipped at the lukewarm herbal tea as she looked around the cozy room. The gas fireplace had been turned on earlier by the woman who escorted her up the steps. Unlike the bright, airy room she'd had in California, this one was cozy and welcoming, a winter room with draperies and deep carpeting. Two Sherpa dog beds, one large, one small were in front of the fireplace. A safe haven.

The house, what she'd seen of it on her arrival, was laid out much the way the one in California was. She'd asked if there was a walled garden and was told yes but it wasn't used in the winter months. She would, however, be allowed to walk the dogs outdoors. She'd seen the large sunroom that ran the length of the walled garden where the guests gathered for their counseling sessions. There was a large fieldstone fireplace that looked like it burned real wood at the far end of the room. She wished she could go there now, but she had to wait to be processed.

Helen dozed in the comfortable rocker. When the timid-sounding knock on the door came, she jumped up from the chair, her heart racing. Max, his teeth bared, waited for her command. "Easy, big guy. Easy. It's okay. Come in," she called.

She was a mousy little woman whose face bore the scars of her ordeal. She reminded Helen of a frightened little bird as she eyed the dogs warily. If she weighed eighty pounds, it was a lot. She stumbled once and apologized as she righted herself. "I'm not totally healed yet," she murmured.

Helen felt the urge to cry all over again. "I remember what that was like. For a long time I didn't think I would ever heal. I did."

"Then what are you doing back here?" the woman asked.

"My husband found me."

"Oh."

"What am I supposed to do now?" Helen asked.

"Julia sent me to fetch you. Julia runs this shelter. We're having tea in the sunroom. We talk, we unload, we vent. If you were here before, then you know how it works. Do you want to walk the dogs? I used to have a cat."

"Used to? Didn't you bring it with you?"

The woman's eyes filled with tears. "I couldn't bring a dead cat. I wanted to. Actually, I tried to but . . . he . . . what he did was . . . he threw her through the living-room window. While he was doing that I ran out the kitchen door."

"Good for you! What's your name?"

"I don't have one yet. I've only been here four days. To you, I'm number Eight. You'll be number Nine." She pointed to the two dogs, and said, "Nine-A and -B."

A chill ran up Helen's arms. An omen?

"We're having Irish stew for dinner. We're baking bread and apple pie. The food here is so good. That . . . that person I used to live with drank up all our money. Most times there wasn't much left for food."

And there but for the grace of God go I, Helen thought.

"I'm ready," Helen said.

"No, you aren't," the woman snapped. "Those are just words. None of us are ever ready. It doesn't work that way."

"What I meant was, I'm ready to go downstairs."

"Oh."

Both dogs hugged Helen's legs as they made their way down the hallway to the staircase leading to the first floor.

In the foyer, Helen eyed the stout front door that she knew held steel bars between the layers of mahogany. She risked a glance at the windows and noted the mesh grills. Safety came in many different ways.

The air was fragrant with baking bread and Irish stew cooking in the kitchen. She realized how hungry she was. What was even more amazing to her was that she could even think about food at this particular time.

Helen held back for a minute, listening to what sounded like normal conversation within a small group of women. She heard the words *Thanksgiving* and *pumpkins.* She heard someone say the temperature dropped twenty degrees in the past few hours. She did her best to smile at the introductions, but received none in return. She hadn't smiled that first time either. "I'm going to take my dogs outside for a bit if that's all right with you."

"Put your jacket on. It got very cold," the woman named Julia said.

Helen nodded. Julia was so like Mona it was incredible. She knew when she returned to the sunroom Julia would have told the women what she wanted them to know about her. Second visits were rare. The women would probably view her return visit as scary and would question the shelter's safety rules.

The dogs were jittery, walking around the yard sniffing and growling. They didn't run; nor did they tussle with one another. They kept turning to look at her to make sure she hadn't deserted them. She spoke quietly and soothingly. "This is just for now. We aren't going to stay here forever. It's only for a little while. We can handle it. We're together. You have your blanket, Max, and Lucie has her mouse, and I have both of you. I'll take care of you. I promise. It's time to go in. They're waiting for us." The dogs obediently followed her into the house and sat down next to Helen's chair, their eyes alert, their tails tucked between their back legs.

Helen listened as the women talked. She'd heard it all before. She'd *lived* it. Her mind wandered to thoughts of Sam. How was he? What was he doing? Was he home? Did he even know that she'd left? She wished now that she hadn't left the beeper behind on the dresser. Or had she? Had she thrown it in the nylon bag at the last second? She simply couldn't remember. What difference did it make anyway since she had no telephone access here at the shelter?

As the discussion droned on, Helen stroked Max's head as she half listened to the women seated around her. For some reason she felt outside the group this time around. She felt like she didn't belong, that somehow she'd cheated. She blurted out the words before she realized she'd said them aloud. The women stared at her, their faces blank.

"We never turn anyone away. We're here to help each of you."

The words tumbled out faster than bullets. "I fell in love. That's what I did wrong. He's a fine man, a wonderful, caring person.

At first I thought I wasn't good enough for him. But I grew as a person during those months. I realized my life was going to be whatever I made of it. You gave me my start on this new life. Still, it was and is a lie. I tried to explain that to my counselor, but somehow things went wrong. She had some personal problems and left me to flounder. At least that's what I thought at the time. I don't want to be a fictitious person. I have every right to be the person I was born to be. Everyone said ... the person ... that person ... would never find me. In my heart and in my mind I wanted to believe that. I needed to believe it, but there was always one small part of me that knew somehow, some way, he would find me. And he did. That's why I'm here. If it was just me and my dog, I wouldn't have asked to come back. I'm here because I'm afraid for the life of the man I fell in love with. I was doing just fine. I started my own little business that was earning me a living. I had love and compassion for the first time in my life. I didn't want to lose that. I was so happy. I'd finally become the person I always wanted to be. All my dreams that I'd put on hold were working out. Now that's all gone. You said he wouldn't find me. You promised me safety. And now I'm sitting here asking where it all went wrong. Was it me? Was it him? Was it you? I need to know what went wrong. I need to know, so I can get my life back. I don't want to be here. I don't want to stay here. All I want is my life. I don't want to be Nancy Baker. I hate Nancy Baker. I want to be Helen Stanley. Listen to me, everyone. That's my name. Helen Stanley."

"That's enough, Miss Baker," Julia said, her hands fluttering in the air. "Don't say any more."

"No, it isn't enough. I played by the rules until you people let me flounder. I had nowhere else to turn, so I told that wonderful man I fell in love with the truth. You know what else. I'm not sorry. I'd do it all over again. And the next time you promise your ... whatever we are, that they will always be in touch, that they're only a click away on the computer, you damn well better mean it. All that stuff you fed me the first time was just a bunch of words. I kept my end of the bargain. You didn't. Now, if you want me to leave, I'll leave, but I will need some kind of vehicle."

"Drink some tea, Miss Baker," Julia said.

"I don't want any damn tea. I want some answers. I want them now. I deserve to know what is going on with my life. I have these two animals to take care of. I have strange men with briefcases knocking on my door. That sadistic bastard I was married to was sitting outside my door. I'm not even divorced. I want to be divorced. I want this man locked up. I want to press charges. I want my day in court. I want my goddamn name back. I can't get my name back because you people had Helen Ward declared dead. *Dead!* I'm not dead. I'm sitting here in front of you. I'm talking to you."

At some unseen signal, the women got up and left the room. Helen leaned back in her chair, her eyes burning with unshed, angry tears.

"Drink your tea, Miss Baker."

"You had no right to declare me dead. You never got around to mentioning that to me. If you had, I wouldn't have agreed to any of this. Helen Stanley can't get married to that wonderful, caring man because she's dead. I want to get married, and I want to have children, but in order to do that I have to get divorced. I can't do that either because I'm dead, and don't tell me to live in sin. Don't tell me the end justifies the means."

"Yours was an extreme case, Miss Baker. Miss Tyger herself was the one who made the decisions where you were concerned. At the time we all thought it rather strange, but one never questions one's benefactor. I'm not trying to pass blame here. You asked what happened, and I'm telling you. I don't know how your husband found you. We're working on that right now. I also don't know who the two men were with the briefcases. For all I know they could have been salesmen. What we promised you was safety. You are safe. Are you not?"

"What about Sam? What's going to happen to him?"

"I don't know. Our people have been alerted. You should have left his dog behind. Dogs are a great deterrent."

"I should have done a lot of things, but I didn't. We need to start fresh here. I want answers, and I want them now. You must have people who can give me some kind of explanation. Let me go on your computer. Let me make a phone call. Either that or give me a car so I can leave."

"You can't leave. You know the rules."

"Are you telling me I'm a prisoner here in this house?"

"In a manner of speaking. Think about those two animals you have. Where are you going to go? You're safe here. We'll get you the answers. You just need to be patient. I know how hard it is . . . Helen. Give us a chance to fix this."

Tears rolled down Helen's cheeks. "I don't think you can fix this. Come on, guys, let's go upstairs," Helen said, turning away from Julia.

"Yo, troops, I'm home," Sam bellowed as he opened the garage door leading into the kitchen. "I'm expecting tantalizing smells and sweet kisses!"

He knew immediately that she was gone. He didn't need the absence of tantalizing smells or the sound of happy barks and wet kisses to tell him the house was empty. The dark house had been his first clue when he pulled into the driveway. Helen would have turned the heat up when the temperature dropped. The house was cold, almost frosty as he walked from room to room. He whistled for Max, knowing the big Lab was gone. Helen wouldn't have left him behind to pine for Lucie. A note. Maybe there was a note someplace. He knew there wouldn't be, but he looked anyway. The first place he looked was under his pillow. Helen often left him little Post-it notes saying how much she loved him. Sometimes she stuck a note on his can of shaving cream or on a bottle of Budweiser. Hoping against hope, he checked the vanity and the refrigerator.

The house was too neat. Too tidy. Yet she'd been there because her car was in the garage right next to his. He ran from room to room looking for Max's blanket. He heaved a sigh. She'd taken the Lab and had the presence of mind to take his blanket. That had to mean she wasn't abducted. She'd left of her own free will. *Now, Sam Tolliver, what in the damn hell does that say about you?*

God, Helen, why didn't you trust me enough to call me? I promised to take care of you. We could have found a way to make it work. His eyes started to burn when he bent down to pick up one of Max's rawhide bones. He stuck it in his pocket as he made his way to the garage. He hit the automatic button alongside the kitchen door. The moment the heavy door slid upward he climbed into his truck. He backed out and then waited for the garage door to close. He almost jumped out of his skin when his neighbor tapped on the passenger-side window. Sam pressed a button until the window was halfway down. "Something wrong, Harry?" God, was that strangled-sounding voice his?

"I was going to ask you the same thing, Sam. My wife told me the cops were here this afternoon and made some guy in a silver car move. She said she thought he was watching your house. In addition, two other guys knocked on our door and wanted to know if she knew when you guys would be home. Jill said she didn't keep track of your whereabouts and closed the door. She wanted me to tell you. We're a friendly group around here. I don't want to know your business, but if you need my help, just give a shout, okay?"

"I'll do that, Harry. Thanks for telling me," Sam said in the same strangled-sounding voice. He waited until his neighbor walked across the yard, an overweight poodle trundling alongside him, before he backed completely out onto the road. Maybe there would be a clue or a note at the shop. He knew there wouldn't be, but he hoped against hope.

Thirty minutes later, Sam turned the switch that lit up the store. He blinked at the empty glass cases. He turned on the computer, typed in Helen's password, and waited for the Sassie Lassie web page to surface. He blinked again when he read the terse message. Helen had planned this. She'd taken the time to shut down her business and yet she hadn't taken the time to leave him a note. She'd cleared out all her merchandise, and yet she'd left the most expensive items of all, the computer and printer. Without thinking, he disconnected the cable wires and the phone jack. It took him three trips before he had everything loaded into his truck. He wondered if he should put a sign on the door saying the store was closed due to a family emergency or something equally dire-sounding. In the end he opted to lock everything up and to keep the parchment shades drawn.

With nothing better to do with his time, Sam cut through the bank's parking lot and walked across the street to the deli. Unless Helen brought a sandwich from home, she usually ordered one from the deli. He shivered as he ran across the street and into the steaming deli. He spotted an empty booth in the back and headed for it. Did she ever sit in this booth? Maybe the one in the front. Or did she take carryout. He wished he knew.

Sam looked up from his reverie when the waiter standing next to his booth cleared his throat. "Sir, would you mind sharing this booth with another customer?"

Yes, he did mind, but it seemed selfish to take up seating for four when there were people waiting. He nodded as the waiter beckoned a man standing next to the register.

"Appreciate this," the man said sitting down. "Donald McDermott," the man said, offering his hand. Sam had no other choice but to hold out his own hand.

"Sam Tolliver."

"Pretty cold out there all of a sudden."

"It's that time of year," Sam said curtly. He wished he had a newspaper to read so he could discourage conversation.

"Another week and it will be Thanksgiving. That means Christmas is just around the corner. I'm partial to that particular holiday myself."

"Most people are," Sam said. *How the hell long does it take to make a sandwich and fill a bowl with soup? If I were eating, I wouldn't have to talk.*

"Live here long?" the stranger asked.

"All my life. You?"

"Not long. I got transferred. My family won't get here till next week. How about you?"

"Family is scattered."

"No wife and kiddies?" the man joked.

"Nope. Not even a dog."

"Too bad. Well one of these days when you're least expecting it, the right one will show up."

Without meaning to, Sam Tolliver then blurted out the words that saved his life. "Oh, she showed up all right, and then she took off. And took my dog with her. You can't trust women. They say one thing and then do the exact opposite of what they say."

"My wife isn't like that. She's perfect. She knows I won't stand for anything less than perfection. I don't mean for this to sound like I'm bragging, but my wife lives for me. All she wants to do is please me. It's as though it's her mission in life."

"Really," Sam said sourly. "What do you do for her?" he asked.

"What do you mean?"

"Well, if she does all that, what do you do for her? Isn't it a two-way street?"

"Oh, I see what you mean. I give her an allowance she doesn't have to account for. She gets manicures, pedicures, and has her hair done. She doesn't have to work. She has a charge card and can pretty much buy whatever she wants. It's a good swap. It works for us," the stranger said.

"Doesn't this jewel of yours want her own career? All women seem to want to do their own thing," Sam said.

"No, not my wife. Taking care of me is a full-time job. I like my shirts ironed at home. She presses my tee shirts, and even runs the iron over my socks. She likes doing all that. I like the sheets changed on the bed every day. She does that. I like a complete breakfast as well as a complete dinner. That all takes time and preparation. My wife worships the ground I walk on."

"Sounds like a slave to me," Sam muttered as he reached up to accept his sandwich from the waiter. Good. Now he wouldn't have to keep up his end of this stupid conversation.

"A willing slave." The stranger chuckled as he, too, accepted his sandwich. "Tell me, the one that got away, what went wrong?"

"I don't have a clue. She just split. With my dog." Sam's eyes started to water from the hot mustard.

"Maybe you were too lenient. Sometimes women need to be put in their place."

Sam swallowed half a glass of water in one gulp before he scraped the mustard off his sandwich. He snorted to show what he thought of the man's comment. "This isn't the Dark Ages.

Women do what they damn well please, and that's okay with me. I think I'm going to take this soup to go. Nice talking to you."

"Yes. You too. Have a nice Thanksgiving."

Sam didn't bother replying as he handed over the bowl of soup. "I'd like this to go, please. Make me another sandwich without mustard this time. Put it in with the soup."

Sam was pocketing his change when his dinner companion walked up to the counter to pay his bill. "See ya," Sam said.

"I doubt it," the man muttered under his breath.

Sam ran across the street and through the bank parking lot. He didn't look back. Inside the truck with the heater going, his shoulders started to shake.

Would he ever see Helen and Max again?

18

The dogs at her side, Helen walked into the small, cozy office where the woman known as Julia sat at the computer. She cleared her throat to announce her arrival. Julia held up her hand to signal she would be with her in a minute. Helen shuffled her feet as she waited, her eyes boring into Julia's back. This small windowless office was so much like the one in California it was uncanny. The plants looked the same, the file cabinets and chairs all neutral in color. Now that she was a little more computer-literate, she could tell that all the electronic equipment was state-of-the-art.

Julia swung her chair around to face Helen the moment the screen in front of her turned blank. "What can I do for you this afternoon?"

"What you can do for me is tell me how you are going to undo a death certificate and when can I expect some sort of vehicle. You owe me that. I refuse to accept anything less. I'm not here for sanctuary the way I was the first time."

"It doesn't work that way, and you know it," Julia said patiently.

She's a pretty woman, Helen thought. *She's comfortable in her own skin. Was she once a battered woman or is she a regular employee? She looks like she doesn't have a care in the world.*

"I know how it's *supposed* to work," Helen snapped. "Tell me something, were you declared dead? Are any of the other women here declared dead, or am I it?"

"I don't know. No, I wasn't declared dead. I don't know this for a fact, but yours must have been an extreme case for the foundation to resort to such a drastic measure. You know I'm not supposed to discuss these things with you. I sent out an e-mail and I called the foundation. I'm waiting for a reply. The next in the series of viruses we've had to deal with just hit. I don't know when I'll get a response. That's all I can tell you."

"And still my husband found me. Someone needs to explain that to me. Look, I will never deny the help the foundation gave to me. I am the person I am today because of that help. I went by the rules until your side broke down. I guess it was meant to happen this way. At least I know now you can't keep me safe since my husband found me. I bet he's the one responsible for your virus problems. I need to leave here to find my own way. There are people here who are in harm's way if I stay. Please call again. If you don't have a response in the next hour or so, I'm leaving. I'll find my way back to my house to get my car. Are we clear on this? By the way, where is everyone?"

"They're in a special group-therapy session in the dining room. It will last all day. I just made some fresh coffee. Some new magazines came this morning. Go into the sunroom and relax. The fire probably needs replenishing by now. You look like you could use a nap."

Helen didn't bother responding. She'd had so much coffee her nerves were twanging. A nap sounded wonderful since she'd spent a sleepless night, but she knew she wouldn't sleep.

In the sunroom Helen poked at the fire and threw on several logs. A shower of sparks shot upward. Max growled ominously. Lucie pawed at Helen's legs, a sign she wanted to be picked up.

What was one more cup of coffee? She poured and then laced the heavy mug with real cream and sugar. The glossy cover of the latest *People* magazine beckoned. Like she really cared what happened to the beautiful people of the world when her own world was in such upheaval. Where was Sam? What was he doing? Did he hate her for running out or did he understand? Was his heart breaking the way hers was? Did he understand she ran because of him? She sighed so loudly that both dogs tried to jump into her lap. "Whatever will be will be," she said, stroking the dogs' heads.

Five minutes later she was sound asleep.

Helen woke instantly, aware that something was wrong. A nest of bongo drums beat inside her head as she struggled to focus on what was going on around her. The moment the room came into a sharp focus she saw Max ready to spring, his huge body quivering as he snarled and lunged, only to fall back waiting for Helen's orders.

"Easy, Max, easy. Good boy. Lucie, come here." The Yorkie needed no second urging. She leaped onto Helen's lap and started to growl. "It's okay. We're okay," she whispered. She wondered if it was a lie. Everything seemed to be a giant lie these days.

The objects of the dog's fury stood in the doorway, Julia and two men. The same two men who had come to her shop and her home. Helen sucked in her breath as she fought a wave of dizziness. It wasn't safe to trust anyone.

"Is it all right to come into the room?" Julia asked uneasily.

"No, it isn't all right. What do you want? Who are those men and what do they want? They're the ones I told you about. Tell them to leave, or I'll turn Max loose."

"Young lady, we mean you no harm," the older of the two men said quietly.

"I've heard that song before. I don't know you. I don't want to know you. Please leave." In her life her voice had never sounded so desperate.

Helen addressed her next comment to Julia, who was staring bug-eyed at her, the dogs and the two men. She wondered how the woman's eyes could be everywhere at once. "As far as protecting your guests from outsiders, this place leaves a lot to be desired. It wasn't this way in California. Get them out of here."

"We're attorneys. We sent you several letters but you didn't respond. We had no other choice but to come here in person. We'd like to come into this room and close the door. Just the two of us. Miss Julia will remain outside. Will you hold your dog?"

"Not likely. How did you find me?" Helen snapped. "You can tell that husband of mine he's wasting his time."

"We have nothing to do with your husband. We are the attorneys for Isabel Tyger's estate. But to answer your question, Arthur King and Gerald Davis, the two remaining board members of the foundation, gave us your address. Now, can we come in?"

"Why? I have nothing to do with Isabel Tyger other than she

gave me a new life and in the process had me declared dead. Can you undo that?"

"In time, with a lot of paperwork."

"I don't have a lot of time, gentlemen. My husband is trying to find me. No, that's not quite true. He did find me. That's why I'm here. While you were ringing my doorbell yesterday, he was sitting across the street watching you. I'd like to know where all the safeguards are that you people say you have. He found me. He even found me after you had me declared dead. That tells me more than I need to know. I don't have anything else to say to you."

Helen stared at the younger of the two men. He was dressed just the way Daniel used to dress. Daniel always referred to it as the power look. Cashmere jacket, pristine white shirt, designer tie, Brooks Brothers loafers. The only difference was, this man had a wary look in his eye whereas Daniel's eyes always sparked confidence as well as arrogance. "All right. Close the door and let's get this over with. For starters, I returned all the money the foundation lent to me. I do have an outstanding bill that I am making timely payments on. From the looks of things, that might take me a while until I can get myself resituated and get back to my business. Well, let's hear it. Don't get too relaxed since you won't be staying long," Helen said angrily.

"The dog—?"

"The dog stays at attention. He will do exactly what I tell him to do when I tell him to do it. Please believe me. He is capable of ripping your throat out. If you don't make any sudden moves, you should be all right."

The wary look in the younger attorney's eyes turned speculative. Helen felt a tinge of fear and wasn't sure why.

The older attorney opened his briefcase and withdrew a folded document inside a blue sleeve of paper. "This is Isabel Tyger's Last Will and Testament. We can read it to you, but I can give you the short version aside from the usual charitable bequests or you can read the will itself."

Helen made no move to reach for the will. She forced her body as deep into the chocolate-colored chair as she could while she waited. "Obviously, you think this is something I should know, but for the life of me I can't figure out what it can be. What does it say, gentlemen, and why should Isabel Tyger's will be of any interest to me?"

"The will says you are the heir to Isabel Tyger's estate. I'm surprised you don't already know this. It's been on the news for several days."

Helen blinked. The word scam came to mind almost immediately. She almost blacked out when Daniel's face swam in front of her. She wondered how much he'd paid these men and exactly how he'd arranged all this. She forced a laugh she didn't feel. "All right, the game's over. You can leave now. You must think I'm some kind of an idiot. I didn't even know Isabel Tyger, and as far as I know, I was nothing more than a statistic to her. Her people declared me dead. How does a dead person inherit someone's estate?"

"You are the sole beneficiary of Miss Tyger's estate, Miss Helen Ward, a/k/a, Nancy Baker," the young attorney said coldly.

"I don't care what it says. I don't believe you. A total stranger would never leave an estate to another total stranger."

"No, most people wouldn't do something like that, but this total stranger did exactly that. This will is genuine and has been filed for probate. You can check with the courthouse in San Jose. You can also call any of the all-day news channels and ask them yourself if they carried the story. It's been in the papers, too. Perhaps not as much here in the East, but it was certainly big news in California," the white-haired attorney said quietly.

"Whatever. I don't want it. Give it to someone else."

"It doesn't work that way. You are suddenly a very rich woman. It will take a year or so to wind things down, but in the meantime you are welcome to move into Miss Tyger's house. Money has been set aside for you to use until things are settled. As I said, you are a very rich young woman."

Helen's brain whirled and raced. Daniel was always big on watching the news to see what went on in the world. If these men were telling her the truth, that had to mean that Daniel knew. Since he had been the one to design the foundation's original database, it was entirely possible he tracked her through Isabel Tyger even though Arthur King would have updated the entire system. Wizard that he was, Daniel probably knew all about the will from the get-go.

"How rich is rich?" Helen asked. She didn't think the young attorney's voice could get any colder but it did. The speculative look was now openly suspicious.

"Very rich. You could never spend all the money in your lifetime. There's all manner of real estate, Tyger Toys, automobiles, a yacht, a private plane, a private island, stocks, bonds, and the ranch."

Maybe this was all true. Or, maybe she was having one of her nightmares. "Why me?"

"I think you might be the one to tell us that," the young attorney said.

"Tell you what? I never met the woman. I never spoke to her in my life. I'm not even sure I know what she looks . . . looked like. I'm telling you, this is a mistake. I don't know Isabel Tyger."

"You know her very well. Why are you lying to us?" the young attorney said. The tassels on the Brooks Brothers' loafers swished. "Not that it makes a difference. The will is set in stone. There is no one to contest it. Miss Tyger was of sound mind when the will was drawn up. Miss Tyger's two best friends, Arthur King and Gerald Davis, were the witnesses to the will as well as the executors."

"What do you mean I knew her very well? Who told you that?"

"She told us herself. You used to e-mail her regularly under the name Boots."

"Boots? Are you saying Boots was Isabel Tyger?" Helen asked, her face full of shock.

"As if you didn't know," the younger attorney said snidely. "We're beating around the bush here. We came here to notify you of your inheritance. We've done that, so we'll be on our way. What you do now is up to you."

"Our card," the older attorney said, handing over a small white business card.

"Wait just a minute, gentlemen." Helen fixed her gaze on the young attorney. "I don't care for your attitude. Not one little bit. I think I know what you're implying, and I resent it. I resent you, and I resent Isabel Tyger's leaving me her fortune. *If* it's even true. You are implying that somehow, some way, I coerced Boots into leaving . . . well, I didn't. I didn't know Boots was Isabel Tyger until you told me so. To me she was my on-line counselor. Nothing more. Here," she said, tossing the blue-jacketed will in the direction of the older attorney. "Take that with you. I don't want it, and I have no intention of accepting it. Not now, not ever. All I want, all I've ever wanted, is my own life. *Now* you can leave. Don't come back because I won't be here. Are we clear on that, gentlemen? Hurry them along, Max, they're dawdling."

There was no need for Max to escort the attorneys to the door. He growled, his teeth bared, his ears going flat against his head. The attorneys' feet sprouted wings. The slam of the door was so loud, Helen shuddered.

Helen leaned back into the depths of the chair. Boots was Isabel Tyger. In a million years she never would have guessed it. They'd gotten on so well. She'd shared her dreams for the future, her dark past, and all those growing-up years so long ago. Boots had understood. She'd been more than a counselor. She'd been a friend. A good friend. And she loved animals. The first question every night was how was Lucie. Or TTLS2, as she called her.

Why? Why had Isabel Tyger included her in her will? Would she ever know? She closed her eyes and thought about her benefactor's wealth and what it could mean to her if she accepted it. She could hire round-the-clock security guards to protect her from Daniel. She could move out of the country. She could sit in the sun drinking ice tea for the rest of her life. She could get manicures, pedicures, massages every day of the week. She could have someone cook for her, wait on her hand and foot. She could live the good life. If she wanted to.

All I want is my own life. I want Sam. I want to be on hand when he makes his last payment on his student loans. I want to be there when he throws away the beanbag chairs and buys a new chair. I want to go to bed with him at night, and I want to wake up next to him. I want to go to Round Valley fishing with him and the dogs. I want to keep up with Sassie Lassie. I want to do it on my own. I want to get married to Sam and have kids of my own.

"God, Boots, why? Didn't you trust me to keep secret that you were Isabel Tyger? I would never have betrayed that trust if you had told me. You didn't do me any favors, Boots. I don't know the first thing about being rich. The truth is, I don't want to be rich. I just want to be me, and to make my own way the best way I can. This is just too much for me to handle right now. It was you who told me once when you don't know what to do about something, do nothing."

The dogs listened attentively to Helen's monologue. The moment she stopped muttering, they were nipping at her to take them outdoors.

Helen was too numb even to think about looking for her jacket. She moved jerkily, her arms and legs stiff and uncoordinated as she stood outside shivering in the cold as the dogs chased each other all over the garden. Her thoughts were so chaotic she finally gave up and stared off into space.

Indoors again, she sat down by the fire and tried to think, to rationalize her situation. She could be rich if she wanted to be rich. Who in her right mind would turn down an inheritance? Was it possible to disappear and elude Daniel? With an inheritance looming on the horizon, would he double his efforts to find her? Of course he would. He worshiped wealth and power, and that's exactly how he would view Isabel Tyger's bequest to her. Didn't Isabel know Daniel would have a claim on the inheritance since she'd never filed for divorce? How does a dead person file for divorce or collect on an inheritance? Maybe in legal circles it was considered a minor technicality.

Once more, her life was changing, and there was nothing she could do about it.

Sam would know what to do. Sam could look at something and a moment later come up with the pluses and minuses of any problem or statement. *I love you, Sam Tolliver.*

"I brought you some tea," Julia said, setting a tray on the coffee table. "You look flushed, Helen. Are you feeling all right?"

"My throat's a little scratchy and I'm achy. I think it was the way I slept last night. Did you hear anything about a vehicle? Do you have any aspirin?"

"We have lots of aspirin. No, I didn't hear anything yet. I expect we'll hear soon. Did you get over your fright of those two attorneys? I'm not going to pretend I don't know what's going on. I heard about your good fortune on the news. Congratulations!"

"That depends on your point of view. I told them I didn't want it. All I want is to get out of here and get my life back. I know I must sound like a broken record to you, but that inheritance means nothing to me. I don't think they can make me take it."

"Mercy. I would certainly know what to do with something like that. Think of all the good you could do with that kind of money. You could feed all the homeless people, take care of all the wounded and sick animals no one wants, you could set up scholarships so young people can go to college. You could help more battered women. The list of good things you could do is endless. You don't have to *keep* the money for yourself if you don't want it. Think of all the children you could help. There are so many babies and children who need surgeries and are denied them for lack of funds. As I said, the list of things is endless. I'll get your aspirin."

Helen sighed. The woman was right. Now she had something else to think about.

Julia returned with the three aspirin in a paper cup. Helen swallowed all three of them in one gulp. "Earlier, you called me Helen. Why?"

Julia smiled, her plump cheeks creating deep dimples. "You said it was your name. I think you've gone past what we can do for you. I understand where you're coming from. I really do. In a way, I envy you your courage and your guts. Sometimes I forget what my real name is. There are times when I want to go home so bad I cry. The feeling passes." Her voice dropped to a careful whisper. "I think it's appalling they had you declared dead. It's so . . . so *extreme*. I'm not sure I could handle that either. It poses another question to me. The person . . . your husband . . . will he . . . ?"

"I know what you're trying to say and the answer is, I don't know. I'm not divorced. I'm dead. But I'm still married to him. My head feels so fuzzy I can't think."

"I can let you use my car, Helen, if they won't give you one. I think that's unlikely now that you are the heir to all of this. Don't those pumpkin pies smell wonderful?"

Helen sniffed. "I can't smell anything. Would you really give me your car?"

"Of course. I live here. I can use the van if I need it."

"I have a Ford Explorer sitting in the garage at home. If you can think of a way to get it without being seen, it's yours. We can trade."

"Helen, the best thing you can do is go to California. You'll be safe there. Wealth has its privileges. If you want to get your life back, then you need to go back to the beginning. Think about what we talked about and all the good you can do. This has been a terrible shock for you but I believe you can handle it. I think I see in you what Boots saw in you. Her motto hangs in the foyer. Persevere and you will prevail."

Helen smiled. "It doesn't matter where you've been. What matters is where you're going and how you get there."

Julia clapped her hands. "You got it. I'm going to bring you some fresh tea and I'm going to lace it with cognac. If you're coming down with something, you need to sweat it out."

"Thanks."

"Curl up and watch television. They're showing a rerun of *Dirty Dancing*. Everyone seems to like that movie. Don't think about anything until tomorrow. Wake up and start fresh is my motto. You rest and I'll get you some fresh tea."

Where are you, Sam? What are you doing now? Do you miss us?

Totally unaware of the frenzied activity going on in her behalf, Helen snuggled with the dogs, chills racking her body as she dozed.

"I warned her, Artie. You heard me. You warned her, too, but she didn't listen. I knew it was all going to backfire. What should we do? We can't let the young woman swing in the wind because of Izzie's shortsightedness," Gerry Davis said crossly.

"I say we call the airlines and bring her here. Or, I can send the company jet to pick her up. Tyger Toys has a jet, too. The way I see it, it's an either-or situation."

"Artie, I don't think the young lady wants to return to California.

When Julia called, she said all she wants is a vehicle. I knew this was going to happen. I told Izzie it was going to happen. The worst part is Helen doesn't want any part of the inheritance. Why didn't Izzie take that possibility into consideration? Tell me what we're going to do about that."

"If Daniel Ward is in New Jersey, it can only mean he was successful in tracking Julia's e-mail from the shelter to Izzie and now he knows where it is. He probably knows where the other three shelters are, too. I curse the day you ever hired that lovesick nurse to take care of Izzie. What she did was unconscionable."

"You don't have to rub it in, Artie. Izzie was not entirely blameless. She insisted Mona bring her all the e-mail while she was in the hospital. I don't think it would have occurred to Izzie that the nurse would betray her. The nurse's credentials were perfect. The nurses' registry is very reputable. Her résumé didn't say anything about not being able to fall in love. She was in love with that bastard or she never would have spied on Izzie the way she did."

"We can't unring the bell," Artie fumed. He continued to seethe as he exploded at Gerry. "Do you have any idea how many people's asses are going to go in a sling over this crap? You can't just go around declaring people dead. Doctors, regardless of what Izzie paid them, never should have signed a death certificate. We, Gerry, as in you and I, went along with this. We even helped Izzie make up phony letterheads with a bogus insurance agency so the mother could be paid off. I have nightmares about all of this, Gerry. We could end up in jail! Neither one of us would do well in prison garb."

The old vet's voice turned quarrelsome. "Maybe we should go on a long, extended trip. Helen Ward is not going to want to return to California. She's in love, and the man she loves is where she is. We need to remember she isn't that battered, frightened woman she was when she first came to me. Right now I suspect she's one angry woman who thinks she can take on Daniel Ward and win. Hell, maybe she can. Izzie said she was mentally healthy and sound. I think that more than anything is what bothered Izzie. She wasn't expecting Helen to make such rapid progress. You remember Izzie and how she wasn't happy unless someone needed her. I say we okay the car and let the chips fall where they may. If she needs us, we're here. Don't even think about either one of us going to New Jersey. Another thing, Artie, both of us need to get off the sauce. Alcohol isn't our answer."

"What about the mother?" Artie said, ignoring Gerry's statement and pouring two fingers of scotch into one of Isabel's favorite cut-glass tumblers.

"What about her?" Gerry said sourly.

"Shouldn't someone tell her Helen *isn't* dead?"

"She didn't seem very interested when we told her she *was* dead. All she cared about was the insurance money. She didn't even bother to make a pretense of crying. She was a heartless, uncaring woman. Now you know why I prefer animals to people."

"We're just going to sit here and do nothing!" Artie said, his voice full of outrage.

"What do you want to do, Arthur?"

"Well, Gerald, I think we should at least warn Helen that her husband knows the location of the shelter and if she's leaving she had best have a plan. I know Daniel Ward. He knows Helen is due to inherit Izz's estate. He's still her husband. He's entitled to half. The whole pie if something happens to Helen. I think Helen already figured that out and that's why she doesn't want the inheritance. If you'd get your snoot out of that bottle, you'd realize we need to do something."

"We are doing something. We're talking about it."

"We don't have a plan, Gerry. We need our own plan. We're reasonably intelligent men. We both went to college. I run a major corporation and you're the best damn vet in the state of California. Surely we can come up with something. Ideally, the best-case scenario would be to get Helen here. I say we call her and hear what she has to say. She might have a plan of her own. You know something else, we need to stop hanging out here at Isabel's house. We don't live here. We don't even belong here. Technically, we are breaking and entering. Helen Ward owns this house now. Okay, I'm going to call," Artie said.

"Then stop talking about it and just do it," Gerry said.

Five minutes later, Julia's sleepy voice could be heard on Isabel's speaker phone.

"This is Arthur King, Julia. I need to speak to Helen Ward. I know it's late, but this is important. We've given the okay for a vehicle for Helen if she still wants it after this conversation. I'll give you the details once I speak to Helen. I'll hold on, Julia."

To Gerry he said, "She's going to wake Helen. Do you want to talk to her, or shall I do the talking? You probably know her better than I do. She rarely attended ComStar's functions. You helped her dog, so she'll probably be more receptive to you."

Gerry blinked at the raspy-sounding voice. He mouthed the words, *she sounds sick.* "Helen, this is Gerry Davis. I'm sorry for waking you but Arthur King and I need to talk to you. We think your husband knows the location of the shelter. You're safe as long as you stay inside. If you leave, he's going to follow you. We would like you to come back here to California. Ideally, that would be the best situation. You are more than welcome to bring your young man with you. We understand you already have his dog. We can't force you to do anything you don't want to do. We did authorize a vehicle for you if you still want it."

"Can you undo that death certificate, Dr. Davis?"

"In time. Not right away."

"My mother thinks I'm dead. How could you people do that to me and to her?"

Gerry took a deep breath. "It wasn't an easy choice, Helen. Isabel thought it was the only way to keep you safe. She cared deeply about you. The truth is, she was obsessed with your safety. We agreed to go along with it. It will take time, but we can make it right for you. For now, your biggest worry is your husband."

"You think he wants to kill me so he can get his hands on the money Miss Tyger willed me. I don't want it. I told those two lawyers I don't want it. I refuse to accept it. Besides, how can a dead woman inherit an estate? The money is secondary with Daniel. He wants to get even with me. The only thing that will satisfy him now would be to kill me. I'm not stupid, Dr. Davis."

"I never thought you were. What are you going to do, Helen?"

"I don't know. You had no right to play with my life like this.

It was all for nothing. Daniel found me. He's stalking me. There's no reason for me to believe you can keep me safe. I'm better off on my own."

Artie leaned across the table. "Helen, this is Arthur King. Please listen to us. We only want to help. I can have our corporate jet at Newark Airport in five hours. You can be on your way here an hour later. Give us another chance to help you. There are so many things you don't know, things you need to understand. Please."

"Which one of you is going to tell my mother I'm alive?" Helen asked hoarsely.

"Both of us can tell her. If that's what you want."

"It's what I want. I know she won't care, but I want her told. Just out of curiosity, how much insurance did I have?"

Gerry winced. "Twenty-five thousand dollars."

"That must have made my mother very happy."

"It did," Gerry said. "Will you come here?"

"No. I have a life and a business. I had a man who loved me as much as I loved him. I *did* have a life, a business, and a man who loved me. I intend to get that life back. On my own with no more help from any of you. All I want from you is to get the paperwork started to get me back my identity. If you can't do that, tell me so right now."

"We'll start on it in the morning," Artie said, his voice resigned.

"Good. Now this is what I want. Are you listening, gentlemen?"

"We're listening, Helen."

19

She was almost certain it was a dream because in real life she would never, ever, have anything to do with Daniel. She wouldn't give him the time of day if he was in a dark room. She wouldn't look at him or answer a question unless he was somehow able to use physical force to make her respond. No questions. Not a single one . . .

"So, Helen, what are *we* going to do with all that money? A trip around the world would be nice. On the other hand we could try out that yacht you inherited. Ah, I can see it now, both of us standing on the deck, the sea breeze whipping all about us as we drink champagne in crystal glasses toasting our new rich life."

"Will that be before or after you beat me within an inch of my life? I hate you, Daniel. *We* aren't going to be doing anything together. You need to get that out of your head right now. I am not going anywhere with you. Not now. Not ever. If you don't leave, I'll call the police."

She'd watched him approach, and for some strange reason she wasn't afraid. She eyed the noticeable limp with pride. She'd done that, but she'd had a weapon at the time. Now all she had were two bare hands and her feet.

The moment Daniel lunged, Helen brought up her knees and then kicked out with both her feet. A second later she was on the floor, the two dogs licking at her cheeks. "It's okay, it's okay. It was just one of my Daniel dreams. I haven't had one of those in a while. Everything's okay. Ohhh, it's cold. Let's get back into bed."

Under the down comforter that did nothing to warm her, Helen realized she had a fever and chills at the same time. *I can't get sick now. I have to get out of here. I have to make sure Sam stays safe.* She tried to think back to the last time she'd had a good winter cold. Three years ago. She'd been run-down and listless, and the cold had lingered and lingered for weeks. It had taken her forever to bounce back because Daniel showed her no mercy. Just this past spring she'd had a cold, but it had only lasted a few days because Sam had babied her with hot toddies and chicken soup. He'd even taken a day off to make sure she took her aspirin and drank gallons of fluids. Sam cared about her. Sam loved her.

"Helen, are you all right? I heard a noise in here," Julia said from the doorway.

Teeth chattering, Helen tried to explain. "I had this horrible nightmare that Daniel was here in the room. I was fighting with him and fell out of bed. I think I'm sick, Julia. I can't get warm."

Julia switched on the night light and then put her hand on Helen's forehead. "You're burning up. I'll make you some hot buttered rum and get the aspirin. Would you like an electric blanket? I know we have one somewhere. I just have to find it. I'll turn up the heat, too. Stay under the covers and I'll be right back."

Julia was back within minutes. She tossed off the down comforter and plugged in the electric blanket. "I'm putting it on high for now. Once it warms up, we'll turn it down. For some reason these things make me nervous. I'll make the toddy and get the aspirin. By the way, who won the fight?"

"I don't know because I fell out of bed. I think I had the edge, though. The strange thing about the dream or nightmare was I wasn't afraid."

"Good for you. I'll be right back. You'll be warm in no time."

Twenty minutes later, Julia heaved a heavy sigh. "The rum will make you sleep, and you're probably going to sweat. I'll sit here a while. We can talk if you like."

Helen didn't think she would ever sleep again. "You talk, Julia. I'll listen. Tell me what it's like to be in charge of a shelter like this."

"It has its good days and its bad days. I do my best not to get involved with the women who come through here. It doesn't work. For instance, it bothers me, Helen, that you are so down on Miss Tyger and her legacy. All she wanted to do was protect you the only way she knew how. Yes, it was extreme. I have to believe extreme measures were called for where you were concerned. I met her once, you know."

"You did! Did she come here?"

"No, I went to California. She wanted all four managers to meet each other. We stayed at her ranch. She was warm and gracious, and she treated us like queens. I can't prove this, but I think she had an unhappy life. Some kind of tragedy went on at some point. I think she is . . . was the most compassionate woman I've ever met. We even met the other two board members: Arthur King and Gerald Davis. Mr. King owns some big computer company, and Dr. Davis is a veterinarian. Dr. Davis called Miss Tyger Izzie and Mr. King called her Izz. They were such good, close friends. You could see they loved each other. I even think Dr. Davis was in love with her. He obviously didn't care if she was short and fat and had a gimpy leg."

Helen struggled to sit upright. "Did she have warm eyes? Lots of curls? Never said five words if two would do?"

"Yes, that sounds like a good description of her. Here, I have a picture of the three of them. I thought you said you never met her."

"That's her! I didn't know I had. The night I was taken to Dr. Davis's clinic, he called a woman who came over to help. Billie. I guess they decided not to give me any way to know who she really was. She was really nice to me. And, she loved my dog. I thought she was a volunteer. The only time I saw her again was when she took me to the shelter. I know now that she was my on-line counselor, but I didn't know it when we were on-line each night. She knew how to cut right to the chase. We never wasted time. Boots was the closest I ever came to having a friend. It still doesn't explain why she chose me over all the women who came through these shelters."

"Maybe Dr. Davis or Mr. King can tell you. Do you know yet what you're going to do?"

"For starters, I'm leaving. I don't want Daniel to go after Sam. He knows I left, and he probably knows about this house and that I'm in it. He thinks I'll go on the run and try to lose him. I have to figure out a way to outsmart him. Don't even think about the police. He hasn't done anything except spook me. I can't prove he beat me. I know he's covered all his tracks. I keep telling everyone he was and is a computer wizard and that he would find me. I don't know how he did it, but he did. He's here. I saw him with my own eyes. So, you see, those extreme measures didn't work. He waded right through them. In my dream he told me he erased all the medical records of my visits to emergency rooms and to the different doctors. He could do that, Julia. I have no doubt in my mind at all that he really did do that."

"What about Sam?"

"I left so Sam wouldn't get involved or hurt. I didn't even tell him I was leaving. I stole his dog in the bargain. I wanted him to know Max was with me and that I was safe. I'm hoping he understands. I'm not the brightest person in the world, but it was all I could think of to do."

"He must be worried sick, Helen."

"He knows Max will look out for me. I care about Sam too much to put him in danger."

"Shouldn't that have been his decision?"

"Probably, but Sam is no match for Daniel. Right or wrong, I can't change things. It's done. I'm not a martyr if that's what you're thinking. I'm a woman who loves someone too much to want to see him hurt because of her past. I have to handle this myself. If I don't, all the foundation's help meant nothing."

"I'm going to get you another rum toddy. Have the chills let up?"

"As a matter of fact they have. This blanket is so toasty. You don't approve of any of this, do you?"

"I think in the end each of us has to find our own way. If you can make it work for you, then you do it. Speaking strictly for myself, I don't have the guts. I know what I have here. The unknown is a gamble I'm not prepared to take. Most of the women who come through here don't have the guts either. If I were you, I'd get back to California as fast as I could. I would hire armed guards twenty-four hours a day. I'd work night and day to get my identity back, and then I'd head off to some foreign country and live anonymously."

"That's the easy way out. That wouldn't say much for me, now would it? Those two lawyers that were here are of the opinion that I somehow coerced Boots into leaving me her estate. Not that I care what they think. Money isn't my answer. I never had much, so right now it doesn't matter. I guess you find that hard to believe. If I had to choose between Sam and the inheritance, I would choose Sam and not look back. Money cannot buy happiness."

"It could for me," Julia said, getting up. "That's why I buy a lottery ticket every week. Who knows, maybe someday the jackpot will be mine. It could happen. The odds are that it won't, but it's fun to dream about it. Do you want me to let the dogs out for you?"

"They're fine. I think I'm going to pass on the second cup of rum, though. I think I'll sleep now. I appreciate you sitting here with me, Julia."

"Sleep tight," the older woman said as she bent down to turn off the night-light. "I'll leave the door ajar. If you need anything, call out."

"I will." Within minutes Helen was sound asleep.

"We're like criminals, Gerry. We keep returning to the scene of the crime. We could have done this just as easily from my office, your clinic, or my house. Hell, we could have gone to Kinko's and done it. Oh, no, we had to come here to Izz's house to do it. What *is* that young woman going to do, Gerry?"

"I wish I knew. My best guess would be she's going to try and outfox that son of a bitch. Did you call that five-hundred-dollar-an-hour lawyer of yours?"

"I did, and he's on it. It's going to take time. I told him to put everything else aside and work on it. He said he would. Don't look at me like that, Gerry. I hate lawyers as much as you do. He also said we were stupid to allow ourselves to be a party to such shenanigans. That's the word he used, *shenanigans*. Shit, he's as old as we are so he uses words like that."

"Want to go for a walk, Artie?"

"If you mean down to the pet cemetery, no, I do not."

"We have to stop coming here. It's playing hell with my mind and my heart. Let's just get to it, Artie."

Arthur King followed the vet down the hall to Isabel's office. He turned on the computer and waited for it to boot up. "I think this is a good idea, Gerry, I really do. I kept thinking all night about Izz's nurse and Daniel. For all we know, Daniel could have wormed his way into Sam Tolliver's life and the guy wouldn't even know it now that Helen has left. I can just see that bastard trying to ingratiate himself with Tolliver the way he did with Maggie Eldridge. Even if he disguises himself, Tolliver should be able to pick up on the likeness. These pictures were taken professionally with the right kind of lighting for our catalog. It's going to scan perfectly. I have Tolliver's e-mail address at the college and his e-mail address at home. One way or another, he'll get it today. What that means is we have to stay here until he responds. You okay with that, Gerry?"

"I'm okay with it. I'm going to take a walk while you're doing that."

"If you wait a minute, I'll go with you. I just have to type out a message and attach the picture."

"I thought you said you didn't want to go down there."

"Yeah, well, a man can change his mind in five minutes. Us old codgers are known for shit like this."

"Yeah, I guess we are. Damn, this is the only place that ever felt like a real home to me," Gerry said.

"I know. Okay, it's going through. Good, it's done."

"When do you think he'll respond?" Gerry asked.

"Probably as soon as he gets it."

"We're good at waiting. I don't have anything else to do. How about you, Artie, do you have anything else to do?"

"Before Izz died, I had so much on my plate there weren't enough hours in the day to handle it all. Then it all fell apart. I don't care about any of it anymore. I think we're depressed. What exactly is clinical depression? Do dogs get that?"

"Do you want the long version or the short version?"

"Whatever. Just tell me we're going to come out of this void at some point."

"Okay."

"That's it, okay?" Artie grunted.

"I'm a vet, not an M.D."

"And a damn fine one you are. I wouldn't take my dog to anyone but you."

"You don't have a dog, Artie."

"If I did, I would bring him only to you. This is all going to come out okay, isn't it, Gerry?"

"I sure as hell hope so."

Sam Tolliver looked at his watch. As if time really had meaning for him these days. He hated going home to the cold, dark house he'd shared with Helen and the dogs. He supposed he could go to the mall and start his Christmas shopping early this year. Or, he could stay here and pretend to be busy. He could also head to the nearest bar and drown his sorrows. Better yet, he could go home, turn up the heat and turn on all the lights, and handle the Sassie Lassie orders that came in before Helen's message went up on the web page. He knew enough about the business to fill the orders, call the suppliers, and notify UPS for pickups. Yeah, yeah, that's what he would do. He'd post another notice saying something clever. Something Helen would smile over when she saw it. *If* she saw it. He could eat leftover Chinese and work through the night. There were probably a *kazillion* orders already. His eyes started to burn as he packed up his briefcase.

Damn, he hated this time of day. It was dark outside, and it was only four-thirty. The long night stretched ahead of him. All he had to do was turn off the computer, turn off the lights, and lock his office. One stop at Grand Fortune for whatever and then home to an early dinner. His gaze went to his desk calendar. Thanksgiving was less than a week away. A long four-day weekend. What was he going to do with himself for four whole days?

Sam was about to turn off his computer when his mailbox started its crazy beeping and swirling. He found himself frowning. Who would be sending him an e-mail at this hour of the day? *Get with the program, Tolliver. Open it up and see what it says.*

Sam sat down and crossed his fingers for good luck. *Please,* he pleaded silently, *let this be from Helen.* He clicked on the READ button, the frown deepening. He read the e-mail a second time before he downloaded the attachment. He stared, his eyeballs literally at attention. "Son of a bitch!" he shouted so angrily his voice could be heard all the way to the administrative offices.

Sam's fingers flew across the keyboard as he tapped out his message. He clicked the SEND button at the same moment he saw the telephone number at the end of the e-mail. A second later his phone was in his hand. He punched in the number and then let his breath out in a loud *woosh,* crossing his fingers a second time. Maybe, just maybe, he was finally going to find out what the hell was going on. His fist shot in the air the moment a gruff voice said, "Hello."

"This is Sam Tolliver in New Jersey. I just got your e-mail."

20

"It's *him!*" Artie said in a hoarse whisper. "Guess he got the picture!"

Gerry Davis grimaced. "We're breaking every one of Izzie's rules by doing this. You know that, don't you, Artie?"

"Yeah, yeah, yeah. This is the right thing to do, Gerry. Be quiet now so I can hear what he's saying."

They hunkered down over the desk to speak and listen to Sam Tolliver. "This is Arthur King, Mr. Tolliver. Thank you for responding to my e-mail so quickly. Did the picture go through satisfactorily? It did. Good. Have you ever seen Daniel Ward? You had dinner with him! That's not good, Mr. Tolliver. That's not good at all."

Gerry reached over and pressed the button of the speaker phone just in time to hear Sam Tolliver say, "I want to know everything, and I don't want the sanitized version either."

Arthur King chose his words carefully as he told Sam what he wanted him to know. Gerry nodded agreeably as he listened to what Sam Tolliver called the sanitized version. Gerry knew Artie wouldn't give up anything he felt would hurt Helen or Sam himself.

"I want to know how that son of a bitch found her. Helen used to recite chapter and verse about your organization and how secure it was."

"Mr. Tolliver, Dr. Davis and I will find out. There's something you need to know if you don't know it already. Helen ran because of you. She ran to protect you. Just like she ran that night to protect her dog. You have to deal with that."

"I don't *have* to do anything but pay taxes and die. Helen knows I would protect her and Lucie with my life."

"That's the whole point, Mr. Tolliver. Helen didn't want you to protect her with your life. She loves you too much to do that. Did she ever tell you she excelled in the self-protection program the shelters offer? Each guest takes two hours of self-defense a day, seven days a week. She's also a crack shot. Helen had eighty-five days of it. She can take care of herself. What you can do for all concerned is to sit and wait. As hard as that may be for you to accept, you have no other options at this particular moment."

"I know all about that program, and it doesn't make me feel one bit better. Lessons are one thing. Reality is something else entirely. While I'm waiting around sucking my thumb, what are you two old codgers going to be doing?" Sam snapped. "I say that with all due respect. Helen told me you're both in your seventies. I'm almost thirty-five, thirty-four if you want to be exact. I'd say that gives me an edge over both of you. Not to mention I'm fit and I am goddamn well dedicated to finding Helen. I'm also prepared to take my chances with that jerk she was married to. With that said, do you want to run that line of bullshit past me again?"

"Not was, is, Mr. Tolliver. Helen is still married to Daniel Ward. Secrecy and safety are the keystones that make the foundation work. If it makes you happy to call it bullshit, then call it bullshit. We have rules. As it is, I'm breaking one of them by being in touch with you. We weighed the consequences and decided your safety was more important than this particular rule."

"There you go. You break one rule, you might as well break a few more. I want to find Helen."

"Would the inheritance have anything to do with you finding Helen?" Artie asked sourly. He didn't like the way this conversation was going at all. Gerry looked like he didn't like it either.

"What inheritance?" Sam demanded.

The two old men looked at one another. Gerry shrugged. Artie's lips stretched into a nasty, thin line. "Isabel Tyger left her entire fortune to Helen. It's been in the papers and all over television. Are you saying you don't know? If so, I find it very hard to believe."

Both men heard Sam suck in his breath. "No, I didn't know. I swear to you on Helen's life, I didn't know. I have enough doom and gloom in my life. Lately there has been so much garbage on television and in the papers I gave up in disgust. I don't think I've read a paper in three weeks. In addition, I'm on so many committees I don't have time for anything else, much less watching television. Helen didn't say a word about that to me."

"Helen didn't know until after she left. She said she doesn't want it. All she wants is you and the dogs."

"Listen, did she really say that? Damn, I knew I loved that woman for a reason. If she said that, then she means it. Helen never says anything she doesn't mean."

"Yes. Us two old codgers more or less came to the same conclusion. However, Daniel Ward isn't of the same mind. Now, Mr. Tolliver, do you see the problems facing us?"

"Look, that crack I made about you two old codgers ... no offense. It was uncalled for and I apologize."

"No offense taken, and we accept your apology. Just sit tight. With age comes a certain amount of wisdom. Let us handle this."

"What are you going to do?"

"I don't know, Mr. Tolliver. We need to think on the matter. Helen is safe. The dogs are safe. That's the most important thing right now."

"Wisdom, huh?"

"It comes in stages, Mr. Tolliver. We'll be in touch via e-mail if we come up with anything."

"If nothing else, I want to know how that bastard found her. I should think you would want to know the same thing. Doesn't this compromise your foundation?"

"We'll be in touch, Mr. Tolliver." Arthur King broke the connection a moment later.

"I don't think that young man has a very high opinion of us, Gerry."

"Why should he? He's right. When you're right, you're right. You yourself called us old codgers the other day. Face it, Artie, we *are* old. We can't run with the sharks anymore. Half the time we can't remember things. We fuss and fret over every little thing. Our piss and vinegar ran out a long time ago. If I was Tolliver, I wouldn't have much confidence in us either. He's the kind of guy who believes in game plans, and we ain't got one. I believed him when he said he didn't know about Helen's inheritance."

"Izz must be spinning, knowing Helen doesn't want her inheritance. I wonder why she never considered that," Artie said.

"We don't know that she didn't. Izzie worked in mysterious ways. You know what I think we should do, Artie? I think you should go through Izzie's files, find out where that private dick said Daniel Ward lived. Then what I think we should do is a little B&E. I have a tool kit. That's a plan. If we get caught, we get caught. Maybe we can find out something, especially if he left in a hurry. We'll say we're his uncles. Or his grandfather. All our white hair should cover our asses on that score. What do you think?"

"It sounds like a plan. Okay, let's do it."

"Are we going to stop coming here then, Artie?"

"We'll stop when Helen kicks us out."

"Between the two of us we could buy this house from her."

"I don't want to *own* it. I just want to come here. If we own it, it won't be the same."

"Yeah, I guess you're right. Find the dick's address and let's check it out. Do we need a gun?"

"Hell, why not? Izz owned a gun, so it's got to be here someplace," Artie said. "You do realize neither one of us knows anything about firearms."

"Knowing that, people will take us seriously for fear we'll discharge it and actually *hit* something," Gerry said as he riffled through Isabel's desk drawers.

Fifteen minutes later, Arthur King held up a manila folder in one hand and Isabel Tyger's gun in the other.

"Is that thing on or off?" Gerry asked nervously.

"How the hell should I know? Does it have a switch or something?"

"I don't know anything about guns. Don't stick it in your pants the way they do on television. Izzie would know. She knew everything."

"Of course Izz would know. It was her gun. I'll just . . . what I'll do is . . . dump it in this envelope and carry it that way."

"Sounds like another plan to me." Gerry guffawed. "We're too old for this shit, Artie. We should be playing shuffleboard, or checkers, or something. Instead we're packing a gun that neither one of us knows how to shoot in preparation to breaking and entering the home of one of your former employees."

"Izz would love it." Artie grinned.

Gerry snorted. "Yes, she would. After we broke down the door, she'd probably push us out of the way and enter, gun blazing. Somehow, some way, we are going to screw this up. You know that, don't you?"

"If we don't shoot the gun, we'll be okay. Besides, he's gone. We're only taking it for protection."

"Then let's go," Gerry said. He hitched his pants higher on his lanky form. "Who's driving?"

"You drive. I'm packing the gun. Since we don't know where the on/off switch is, I need to watch it. Don't go over any bumps."

A devil perched itself on Gerry's shoulders. "Who loves ya, baby?" he said in his best Telly Savalas cop voice.

"You do," Artie said, playing along.

Sam felt like a tired old dog when he locked his office door. He'd been so hopeful when the e-mail from Arthur King arrived. Now even that slim thread of hope was gone. And to make things worse, the woman he loved was now a multimillionaire. What would she ever want with someone like him? Oh, he'd talked a good game to the old boys, but that's what it was, a game.

His guts churned as he walked across the parking lot. He was halfway to his car when he realized he'd left his jacket hanging in the office. Like he really cared if he got pneumonia or not. He longed for Max.

Thirty minutes later, Sam pressed the remote on his visor. The garage door flew upward. He drove the Blazer in and cut the ignition. *Now what, Tolliver? You had a plan to get you through the night, didn't you? One step at a time. Change into sweats and go for a run. Maybe the cold air will clear the cobwebs from your brain. Come home, shower, eat that five-day leftover Chinese food in the fridge, and then pack up Helen's orders. Fall into bed and dream about Helen and Max all night long.*

"Get on with it, Tolliver," he muttered to himself. "So what if the house is cold and dark. You turn on some lights, and you turn up the heat. If you want noise, you turn on the stereo. Get on with it."

Sam waited to be certain the garage door closed tightly before he pressed the button by the door that led into the kitchen. The moment he heard the little snick of the lock going into place, he opened the kitchen door with his key.

Nothing in the world could have prepared him for the destruction that faced him when the kitchen exploded with light. Cabinet doors hung drunkenly on hinges. The oven door was halfway across the room, the refrigerator door hanging wide open. Water puddled on the floor from the automatic defrost system. Flour, coffee, and sugar were everywhere. The long, trailing fern that Helen had nursed back to health was just a memory; the fronds everywhere, the dirt in clumps on the chairs and top of the table. A mound of it was sitting on one of the oven shelves.

Sam took a deep breath before he turned on the hall light switch. His beloved beanbag chairs from his early college days were ripped wide open, the beans everywhere. The small television and the stereo system were a mass of black plastic parts on one side of the room, some in the hall, and others crunched into oblivion. He took another deep breath as he marched his way to the bedroom he'd shared with Helen.

Everything in the room was ripped, slashed, or gouged. Drawers were splintered, the contents destroyed. The drapes hung in tatters, the blinds ripped and bent out of shape. He blinked at the sight of the toilet seat in the middle of what was once his bed. He poked his head into the bathroom to see the shower door off its track, the glass shattered and broken, half on the floor, half on the bottom of the tub. He looked down when he realized he was standing in water almost to his ankles. He stretched his neck farther and saw the tank to the toilet lying next to the vanity, whose sink was overflowing. He sloshed his way to the vanity to turn off the faucet.

Sam's shoulders slumped as he backed out of the bathroom.

There was one more place to look; Helen's workroom, where her inventory was stacked to the ceiling. Did the intruder go into that room? "Intruder my ass," Sam snarled. He knew who had ransacked his house, and it wasn't a nameless, faceless intruder. It was Daniel Ward. He knew it as surely as he knew he needed to take another breath to stay alive.

Do it, his mind ordered. *Open the damn door and see what the bastard did. Do it, Tolliver. Get it the hell over with.*

Sam's hand snaked out to grasp the doorknob. He didn't know if he should pounce, shout a warning, or turn on the light. He did all three at the same moment. *"Eiyah!"* he bellowed, dropping to a low crouch, his long arm reaching up to turn on the overhead light. He straightened, his gaze unbelieving. Tacked to every inch of wall space was Helen's Sassie Lassie lingerie with lewd printing on each and every garment. Whore, slut, and bitch were some of the kinder words. He ripped the garments from the wall, hating to touch something Daniel Ward had had his hands on. Sam took a moment to wonder if Daniel Ward always traveled with a staple gun and red spray paint. Then he got sick and bolted for the bathroom.

When he was finished, Sam sat on the edge of the bathtub contemplating the three inches of water swirling about his feet. What the hell kind of sick bastard had Helen been married to? He felt his stomach start to churn again. He fought with himself to stay calm. *Think, Tolliver. Don't react. Think.*

You have renter's insurance. It was the first thing you bought when you and Helen moved in here. You can call the Disaster Master people to come and clean everything up. The insurance company will pay for it. File a police report? Don't file a police report? He couldn't prove Daniel Ward destroyed his house. He couldn't even prove Daniel Ward was in the vicinity. Obviously the man had come in through the garage and disarmed the alarm system. Helen said he was a wizard. A real bad-assed sicko from the looks of things. He groaned then when he thought of Helen taking on the man who had been her husband. She'd said right along no one was a match for Daniel Ward, and she was right.

That night in the deli he'd fallen right into Ward's hands. He'd been bitter and angry. Maybe that's why the man hadn't pursued him. If that kind of thinking was right, then what the hell was this destruction all about? Maybe Daniel Ward thought Helen had left him for good and he was no longer any kind of a threat to his getting Helen back. Maybe the destruction of his house was a kind of warning.

He couldn't think there. He needed to get out of that crazy place. Pack a bag, go to a motel. He snorted. There wasn't anything to pack thanks to Daniel Ward and his knife and scissors. Check into the Best Western and head for the mall to buy some new clothes. When he checked in, he would go to his office and after he called the Disaster people, he would e-mail Arthur King.

His briefcase in hand, Sam turned off the lights and left the house. He wondered if he would ever be comfortable living in that house again. With or without Helen. He didn't bother setting the alarm. What was the point?

"We're here, Gerry. Kind of seedy-looking, don't you think?" Artie asked as he looked around at the rusty bicycles, wagons, and trash littering the yards of the apartment complex. He looked upward to the second level to see blinds askew, screens from the windows hanging by one clip. The window frames and the doors leading to the different apartments were dirty and scuffed, the paint peeling in long strips. Everywhere there was the stench of garbage. Rusty cars, some without tires, some without seats, were parked every which way. He found himself shivering at the squalor.

"Do you think the car will be safe?" Gerry asked anxiously.

Artie shrugged. "It's a crapshoot. The only thing we have going for us is the darkness. It doesn't look like anyone is paying attention to us. I hope that holds once we get inside and turn the lights on."

"This is the kind of neighborhood complex where people see nothing and hear nothing. I can't see anyone living here wanting to get involved. I can almost guarantee that Daniel Ward didn't know his neighbors. That means they don't know him either. That's good for us."

"Let's go and get it over with," Artie said, climbing out of the car. He cursed his arthritic knees. He did his best to breathe through his mouth as he followed Gerry up the cracked and broken walkway that led to Daniel Ward's apartment.

"It's locked," Gerry said, trying the door handle. "Do you have my tool kit? How are we supposed to get in?"

"It's your standard credit-card door. Places like this don't worry about their tenants' safety. Ten bucks tops at Wal-Mart," Artie said, jiggling his Visa card up and down. "Told you," he said triumphantly as he pushed the door open.

"I'll keep my hand on the light switch while you close the blinds," Gerry said nervously.

"Christ Almighty," Artie said the moment the room sprang to light.

"Jesus!" was all Gerry could think of to say.

The two men stared at each other, their mouths hanging open.

"He papered the whole damn room with pictures of Helen. It's mind-boggling. That poor woman. Look, Artie, no matter where he sat, no matter where he walked or even if he was standing still, Helen was all about him. Where in the hell did he get so many pictures?"

"Take a good look. These are almost all the same few pictures. He probably scanned them, making different sizes. It can all be done on the computer. Speaking of computers, this is one kick-ass machine. I bet he built it himself."

"Why'd he leave it behind?" Gerry asked.

"Because he is so goddamn cocky he didn't think we'd ever latch on to him. The guy took his laptop with him," Artie muttered as he pressed the switch to turn on the computer.

"Maybe it's booby-trapped," Gerry said, backing away from the folding table the computer was sitting on.

"No, it's not booby-trapped but he might have crashed his files. Who the hell knows the way that guy's mind works. He's probably got some intricate password we'll never guess," Artie said. "I was right. It wants a password."

"I knew it! Now what are we going to do? It smells in here. Guess that guy wasn't big on cooking," Gerry said, pointing to takeout food containers, paper bags with half-eaten fast food, and numerous pizza boxes. Beer and liquor bottles littered the grimy floor. "What are we going to do, Artie? What the hell are we doing here anyway?" Gerry asked as he stepped on a fat cockroach.

"We're trying to find out how Ward found Helen. The answer is in this computer. Daniel Ward is not a leg man, which means he wouldn't demean himself by going out there physically trying to find her. He knows, more or less, how the program works. I'm telling you the answer is right here. This is going to take a while, Gerry. Sit down and make yourself comfortable."

Gerry snorted. "You're sitting on the only chair."

"Then lean against the wall."

While Artie clicked away on the computer, Gerry wandered out to the filthy kitchen and the equally filthy bathroom and bedroom. Helen's face was plastered on all the walls. He wondered if he was going to get sick. Would the police consider something like this stalking? Obsessive? Or would they say a man had every right to paper the walls of his home with his wife's picture. What would the police say when they found out he had broken into the man's home? They'd lock his ass up is what they would do. Artie would be his cellmate. He started to shake then and felt every one of his seventy-odd years.

"Any luck, Artie?"

"No. I'm having trouble trying to think like Daniel Ward. I tried every word I could think of that might have some meaning to him. I came up with zip. It's probably a very simple word, something we would never think of. Do you have any ideas, Gerry?"

"Me? Maybe he changed his old password to something more timely to coincide with what's going on in his life now that Helen left him. He never expected that, and when it happened he didn't know how to deal with it. You said he was cocky and arrogant. He lost his job and his wife finally got out from under his control."

"Keep leaning on that wall and while you're there, think," Artie ordered.

Artie threw up his hands. "I give up!"

"You can't give up. That guy is going to find Helen and hurt her. What was his passion in life? Do you know that?"

"Money."

"Let's work with that. You said he was the one who sent all

those different computer viruses to your company's computers. You said he wiped Izzie's out, too. We know he was diddling with Izzie's computer once Maggie Eldridge gave him her e-mails. He probably picked up on the Boots password real quick. That means he had to know about her will. You're the computer whiz, Artie. How could he have found out about her will?"

"By tapping into her e-mails. She sent me quite a few, you too, about her will and what she was doing. I think you might be on to something here, Gerry. He'd view it as getting the jackpot. All he had to do was find Helen, convince her he'd mended his ways, and like all arrogant male abusers, thought she would fall right into his arms along with that big jackpot of money." He shrieked, "That's it, Gerry!"

Gerry leaned over the table and watched Artie's gnarled fingers type in the word, *jackpot*. He blinked when the screen exploded to life.

"Gerry, you are a genius!" Artie preened.

"Can you copy whatever it is you're looking for? We have to get out of here."

"Let me open up the files and see what we have. I'll copy what I think is pertinent."

"How long is that going to take? I'm getting jittery. I hate this place. I hate looking at all these pictures of Helen. I want to go home. How'd he do it? Do you know?"

"Not for certain. I think I have an idea, though. I think the son of a bitch hit every single database in the country to find out which vet Helen took her dog to. She must have switched vets recently and used the dog's real name. The foundation takes care of that sort of thing and always uses the number-letter combination. I'm not sure, Gerry, but right now it's what I'm thinking. The bastard would have had to work around the clock, seven days a week, scouring every state, every city, every vet he could find. If my hunch is right, it finally paid off for him. It's just a guess, but I feel confident enough to say that's what he did. Helen stayed out of fear. Look at you, you didn't know him, and yet being here in his quarters he is still capable of scaring the *bejesus* out of you. Fear is a terrible thing, Gerry. So is mind control. Put the two together, and I think you'll understand why Helen didn't leave."

"Is this where he lived when he was seeing Maggie Eldridge?"

"Not according to the private detective's report. He was renting a rather nice furnished condo at the time. I don't think the nurse would have given him the time of day if she'd seen this place. I'm assuming his money was running low and that's why he moved here."

"I'd like to take a picture of this place, but it would only prove we broke into it. It is something the police should have if Helen ever wants to file charges. I keep a Polaroid in the glove compartment. What do you think, Artie?"

"Go get it! I have two more files to download and copy and we can leave. As long as you're going to take pictures, get them from every angle. Nobody will ever believe this otherwise."

While Gerry finished the last of the film, Artie packed up the disks and slipped them into the envelope with the gun. "I think we can leave now."

"Artie."

"What?"

"He has Helen's picture pasted on the toilet seat. Top and bottom."

"Tell me you got a picture of that, Gerald."

"Yep."

"Then we're outta here as the young people say. Don't look back, Gerry. I don't want you to remember this place. Let's go to Izz's place so I can play with all these disks."

"The plan worked, Artie. I hope you plan on e-mailing Sam Tolliver to tell him so."

"I have to think about that."

"Okay. We'll both think about it."

21

She felt warm and cozy in her cocoon of blankets even though every bone in her body ached. While her eyes were open, it seemed as though a film of some sort dusted everything in the room, reducing the contents to gray indistinguishable shapes.

"You're awake! Wonderful! You had me worried, Helen," a cheerful voice said, from someplace far away.

She knew the voice, had heard it many times but she couldn't put a name or a face to it. She wished the haze would go away.

Something warm, wet, and somehow comforting was on her face, her neck. Then she heard the sound she recognized—Lucie's whimpers and then an even deeper whimper, Max. "Hi, guys," she managed to croak. Her rusty-sounding voice startled her and the dogs, who were suddenly everywhere on the bed.

"It's Julia, Helen. Are you feeling any better? I must say, those dogs of yours are devoted. They wouldn't leave your side. It still amazes me that they would do their business on the newspaper I managed to slide into the room. As a matter of fact, for the first day they wouldn't even allow me to do that. I had to pitch the newspaper and hoped they knew what it was for. They did."

"First day?"

"You've been more or less out of it for three days, Helen. You had us all worried."

"Three days!" Helen gasped.

The voice was so cheerful, Helen cowered under the blankets.

"You were running a very high fever. It broke last night. That's why your lips are so dry and cracked. How do you feel? Do you think you can eat some Jell-O or soup? Some tea would probably taste good. I have a special blend you might like."

"Are you telling me the dogs haven't been outside in three days?"

"We tried, but they wouldn't leave your side. The newspapers worked. In the scheme of things, it simply isn't important," Julia said soothingly.

Helen struggled to prop herself up on one elbow. "I feel like a wet noodle. Okay," she said to the dogs, "go with Julia. Now! I'm all right. I'll be here when you get back."

Lucie eyed her mistress and then turned her gaze to the big Lab, waiting to see what he would do. Helen nodded and whispered hoarsely into the dog's ear. He was off the bed in the blink of an eye, Lucie right behind him. At the door, both dogs turned to look at Helen, who said, "Shoo, go outside and get some air. I'll be right here when you get back. Julia will give you a cookie."

"Can you make it to the bathroom on your own?" Julia called over her shoulder.

"Yes, I think so."

"Is it yes to the Jell-O and soup?"

"Yes."

It seemed like the struggle of her life to roll to the side and swing her legs over the side of the bed. Helen felt a head rush when she sat upright, her body trembling. What in the world had happened to her? The last thing she remembered was Julia offering to get her an electric blanket and a hot toddy for her scratchy throat. She vaguely remembered having the chills and a fever at the same time. Had she eaten during the three days she spent in bed? She simply couldn't remember.

In the pretty blue-and-white bathroom, Helen stared at her reflection and winced. Who was this hollow-eyed, gaunt-looking person whose hair was standing on end? She peered closer to stare at her pale face and cracked dry lips. She wondered if she dared to take a shower. Maybe she would feel better if she did.

Helen was doing her best to fit her legs into her favorite flannel pajamas when Julia entered the room behind the dogs.

"I don't think that was a wise idea, Helen. However, I understand. I always feel better after a shower and some body powder. I wish you had waited for me, though. You're weak and wobbly, but that will go away as soon as you get some food in you. Just give me a minute to straighten the sheets and covers. I want you back in bed for at least another day."

"How did this happen to me?" Helen whispered wearily.

"I think you were run-down when you got here. Stress. Germs. You name it. Several of our other guests have the same thing, but not as bad as you have it. It's not the flu, just a virus. I had the doctor look at them, too. It's one of those things that has to run its course. Another few days, and you'll be up and about. I want you to eat everything on that tray and drink all the tea. The doctor wants you to take these high-potency vitamins and to drink all the fluids you can handle. The dogs are fine, so I'm going to leave you and get on with my work. If you need anything, ring the bell on your nightstand."

"Does that mean you've got a handle on the computer virus? Thanks, Julia. Have the dogs been eating?"

"I set their food inside the doorway and eventually they ate it when they got hungry. The answer is yes as far as the virus goes. We've installed all new software and so far things are working again. For a while, we had to do everything by telephone. The telephone is such a marvelous invention. Archaic in some respects but marvelous just the same. I enjoy actually talking to people."

Helen nodded. She really didn't care one way or the other. She'd tried to tell them Daniel would do something. His mission in life seemed to be to destroy everything she had any kind of contact with. It wasn't her fault they hadn't listened. "How did you get the doctor in here?"

"I put a tranquilizer in the dogs' food at lunchtime the day the doctor made his house call. I just made little cheese balls and tossed them on the bed. They were really drowsy when he got here. I had to do it, Helen. It was the doctor's suggestion. It's worn off now, and they're fine."

"I have to get out of here, Julia. Daniel knows I'm here. He's responsible for all those viruses that ate everyone's files. He'll keep at it. God only knows what the next one will be like. He's probably got your telephone line tapped, too. He probably even knows I'm sick. He's just waiting."

"Get that idea out of your head right now. You are in no condition to walk down the steps much less leave. A few more days and it will be a different story. Don't you want to be here for our big Thanksgiving dinner? Four of our guests left yesterday so there are only five of us for dinner plus the dogs. When it's time, I'll help you but not one minute before."

"He's going to come here, Julia. He's probably sitting outside right now." Helen groaned.

"Good! Let him freeze his ass off. It's twenty-nine degrees outside. About two years ago a man came here with an ax and tried to open the front door with it. He didn't succeed. He found this place because his wife went back to him, and he beat it out of her. He was going to torch the house, but the police got here in time. He had six gallons of gasoline in his truck. He's still in jail."

"What happened to his wife?"

"She's a vegetable in a state-run mental hospital. If your husband is as smart as you say he is, you're not a match for him, Helen. I don't mean for that to sound like you're stupid. Men like your husband and the one in jail are a different breed. I think that you believe you can outsmart and outmaneuver your husband. He's been planning this since the night you ran out on him. He's obsessed. You cannot bargain, cajole, or outsmart someone like that. If the FBI can link any of these viruses to your husband, they'll put him away for a very long time. If you try to do something, you're going to end up screwing up your life and Sam's life as well. Think about *that*."

Helen snuggled deeper into the comforter, the dogs next to her. "It's a lot to think about," she whispered. Within minutes she was sound asleep.

Helen woke three hours later, ravenously hungry. It seemed easier to swallow, and the dull ache behind her eyes was gone. Maybe she would survive the virus after all. She lay quietly so as not to disturb the sleeping dogs. She'd lost three whole days of her life. She'd heard people use that same phrase many times and had always wondered how it was possible to lose time. Now she knew. Three whole days. Seventy-two hours. Four thousand three hundred and twenty minutes. An awful lot of seconds. Too many for her foggy brain to handle.

She closed her eyes, trying to remember the dream she'd had just before waking. It was something about Sassie Lassie. A new product? Something to add to her line? When the dream refused to surface, Helen closed her eyes again. She wished she felt better and was able to make rational decisions. Julia was right. She was in no condition to do anything, much less think.

Isabel Tyger's fortune. Her fortune now. Could that fortune hold Daniel Ward at bay? Not likely.

A belly chain! That was what her dream had been about. A thin gold chain with a paper-thin medallion that would hang directly below the belly-button. Sassie Lassie engraved on one side, the owner's name on the other side. Fifty bucks a pop. She could buy chain by the yard, do the clasps herself, hire someone to do the engraving. Maybe $59.95. The $9.95 could eat up the engraving, the shipping, and the clasps. If she sold them for $69.95 the other $9.95 would pay for the chain and she could walk away with fifty bucks for each chain she sold. Sam would be so proud of her ingenuity. When he got done laughing that is.

Sam would absolutely flip when he saw it. She smiled when she remembered his reactions to the feathers. *Oh, Sam, I miss you so much.*

"Helen, is there anything I can get for you? More juice or tea?" Julia asked from the doorway.

"My laptop. I need to check something. I need the pouch with the disks, too."

"Later, Helen. You need to rest. Look," Julia said as she opened the blinds. "It's snowing. It will probably just be a light dusting, but it looks so pretty coming down."

"It is pretty," Helen said absently. "I would like some juice. Julia, there's nothing wrong with my fingers. I feel less woozy now. I want to go to my web page and add something to my product line."

"Is your computer safe?"

"Yes, we've had no problems so far."

"How about an hour on the computer? No more than that. I'll

take the dogs out. They might like the snow. I'm making some vegetable soup for lunch. One of the girls is baking bread."

"Sounds good." Helen found her mouth watering for homemade bread and thick soup chock-full of meat and vegetables. "Go with Julia, and she'll give you a cookie. I need my sketch pad, too, Julia."

"Your word, young lady. One hour!"

"Okay, Julia. One hour."

Helen spent fifteen minutes sketching a slim model wearing a fine gold belly chain, a lacy bra, and bikini undies. For effect she added a white ermine hat to the model. She finished off the picture with cascading white feathers.

If the shelter's scanner still worked, Julia could scan it for her and she could have it on her web page in an hour's time. If Sam checked the web page, he would know she was okay. Maybe she needed to add something to the picture. Of course, Max and Lucie trying to get the feathers as they fell. Sam would understand. She sketched furiously, so furiously that she was exhausted when Julia returned with the dogs.

"They loved it. The snow is sticking to the ground. If it keeps up, we might get a few inches. I think there's a warming trend starting tomorrow. I brought you some juice and a slice of toast. Well, well, what have we here?"

"It's a belly chain with a medallion that hangs below the belly button."

"I'll take two," Julia quipped. "Pretty sexy."

"Can you scan this onto a disk for me so I can add it to my web page?"

"I can try, but I think it might be better if I call someone to take it to Kinko's. I could have it back here in an hour or so. There's no point in looking for trouble. Do you agree?"

"Yes. Are you sure it isn't too much trouble?"

"Not at all. We have a list of volunteers who help us with things like this. Just out of curiosity, what are you going to charge for this?"

"I think $69.95."

"In that case, I'll only take one." Julia laughed.

"Yours is free. You can have as many as you want."

Julia giggled. It was a nice sound.

"Drink the juice and take a nap. When you wake up, I should have the disk for you and lunch will be ready."

Helen didn't protest when Julia closed the laptop and moved it to the little desk on the other side of the room. She was asleep before the door closed.

Sam rolled over, his arm reaching out. When there was no warm body to be felt, he rolled back over. There would be no more sleep for him that night. He got up, turned up the heat in the hotel room, and then pulled on his sweatpants.

In a few hours, when it was light, he was going to pack up his meager belongings and return to the house he'd shared so briefly with Helen. There were memories there, good and bad. If he had a mind to, he could stop at the supermarket and pick up a turkey. How hard could it be to roast a turkey? After he ate his dinner, he could make up some meals and take them to the pound for the animals. Yeah, yeah, that's what he would do. A twenty-five-pound bird would provide a lot of meals for the animals if he could add dry dog food to the mix.

His shoulders started to shake. If he didn't watch it, he'd be blubbering like a baby. He wished he had some coffee. He had to remember to buy some when he got to the grocery store. Maybe there was an all-night store open, and he could go now. He vaguely remembered Helen saying the Pathmark in Middlesex Mall was a twenty-four-hour supermarket. It was a thought that required action. He sat down and sipped luke warm Coca-Cola that was left over from his carry-in dinner the previous night. Caffeine was caffeine.

With little else to do, Sam turned on his laptop, connected it to the phone jack, waited for it to boot up, then typed in the address for Sassie Lassie. Ten seconds later, his fist shot in the air when he saw Helen's latest creation. He stared hungrily at the resemblance to Max and Lucie.

It was a message, he was sure of it. A message that said Helen and the dogs were alive and well. And then he laughed when he stared at the belly chain. Who in her right mind would order, much less wear, such a thing? Then again, what did he know about women's fashions? Just for fun, he scrolled down to the order blank page and then burst into near-hysterical laughter. Obviously a lot of people were going to wear one of Sassie Lassie's belly chains. The orders seemed to go on and on. Endless. There had to be close to a thousand orders. A new one popped onto the screen just as he scrolled to the end. Someone named Hillary Nolan was ordering two chains at 4:20 A.M. Amazing. At seventy bucks a chain, give or take a few pennies, Helen was going to make a fortune. Clearly he was in the wrong profession. What the hell was he doing crunching numbers when he could be out there marketing feathers and belly chains?

Damn, he'd missed it the first time. He peered more closely at the screen, drinking in the sight of the two dogs. The dim lamplight must have cast a shadow on the computer screen when he first turned it on. Both dogs were wearing chains, medallions hanging loosely around their necks. He squinted and was able to make out the fine script that said Sam on Max's medallion and Helen on Lucie's.

It was definitely a message from Helen to take heart. It was also confirmation of what Arthur King had told him: Helen didn't want Isabel Tyger's fortune. She was more than capable of making her own way. Be it belly chains, feathers, or sassy underwear, she would do it on her own.

Sam unplugged the computer and dumped his belongings into a duffel. He was on his way home in less than ten minutes. He was halfway home before he remembered his intention to stop at the supermarket for a turkey. He made a wide U-turn and headed back the way he'd come. *Yessirreee*, he was going to have a lot to be thankful for this Thanksgiving.

22

Daniel Ward huddled inside the silver Nissan. From time to time he turned on the ignition and the heater to warm his cold body. For days he had literally been living out of his rental car because he couldn't desert his stakeout. Fast-food bags, boxes, and Styrofoam cups littered the floor on the passenger side as well as the backseat. He detested fast food, but it was cheap. On the passenger seat next to him was his state-of-the-art laptop. Underneath the seat, half-buried by grungy bags smelling of stale greasy food, was a gun he'd bought illegally.

He hated the goddamn snow that was falling because he didn't know how to drive in snow and wasn't sure if the rental car had front-wheel drive. He stared at the ordinary-looking house, the house his wife had run to. One of Isabel Tyger's famous shelters. Arthur King had bragged about the shelters, saying they were impenetrable. Nothing was impenetrable, as Arthur King had found out. Daniel had cracked Arthur's codes, crashed his computers at least four times. And good old Arthur thought Ted Wexler was the one with the brains. "Asshole," Daniel hissed between his chattering teeth. He blew on his hands to try and warm them, his gaze glued to the Tudor-style house across the street.

He was going to give it one more day before he resorted to more drastic measures. Helen would leave soon. He was sure of it. If she didn't, then he would have to do something about it. *Helen, you are going to pay big-time for all the misery you've caused me. When I finally get my hands around your neck I won't stop until you're dead. I wish you knew how much I hate you for what you've done to me. I'm going to tell you when I finally get hold of you. I'll kill that stupid dog of yours. And the other one, too. I already took care of that*

jerk you were living with. He said you dumped him, ran out on him.
You stole his dog and left him swinging in the breeze. You didn't care
about him either. Why couldn't you just do what I wanted you to do?
Oh, no, you had to pretend you had a brain. You told everyone our
business. I didn't like it then, and I like it less now. I'm living like a
bum. I haven't had a shower in a week. I'm living out of my car like some
derelict, and all because of you. Christ, I hate your guts, you slut.

Daniel turned on the engine. He sighed the moment the heat
blasted across his chest. He eyed the gas tank; half-full. At some
point he was going to have to find an all-night gas station. He'd
search one out in the middle of the night once he was sure the
occupants of the shelter were settled. It would never do to run out
of gas just when he was coming into the home stretch.

Warm and cozy, he relaxed. Maybe he should call his mother.
Then again, maybe he shouldn't call his mother. He hated her as
much as he hated his wife. He hated his sister Amy, too. Before
he could change his mind, he rummaged in his jacket pocket for
his cell phone. He'd charged it earlier. He was still surprised that
it was operational since he hadn't paid the bill in two months.

He had to psych himself for the call. He wondered why he even
bothered to call *her*. In *her* eyes he was a failure. Once she'd called
him a reject. As a child he'd longed to hear her call him Danny,
or honey, or even son. She never had. More than once she'd called
him a sissy or wimpy. God, how he hated her. She called Amy
sweetie, or dear, or sometimes sweet cakes. Her tone of voice was
always different when she spoke to Amy. Maybe that's why he
hated his successful stockbroker sister. He wondered if their attitudes would change when he flaunted Isabel Tyger's money under
their noses. Of course their attitudes would change. Still, they'd
say the wealthy philanthropist didn't leave it to him, she'd left it
to his wife. They'd snicker behind his back and say mean, cutting
things about him. Things that seared his heart, things he could
never forget.

Once, when he was a youngster, his father had tried to explain
his mother to him. She's driven to succeed. She wants to be rich
and famous, and she works tirelessly to that end. Your mother
knows how to wheel and deal, how to press buttons, whose rear

end to kiss and how to get along in the business world. I'm not like that. I don't know why she ever married me. Probably because she would stand out more against her no-account husband.

Daniel flinched. His father was a good, kind man. Perfectly content with the small nursery he ran. Adam Ward knew everything there was to know about shrubs, trees, flowers, and grass. He loved what he did. He made a decent living, and he was an honest, hardworking man. Daniel regretted now that he hadn't been more kind, more civil to his father. He'd been so busy all his life trying to please his mother, trying to succeed so she would be proud of him, that he'd ignored his father.

He'd withdrawn during those years and concentrated on his computer, his only friend. It had all come easy to him and he'd excelled, and still she wasn't proud of him. She still made cutting, scathing remarks. Once he'd raised his hand to her in retaliation for some remark. In the blink of an eye he sailed across the room, ending up sprawled on his back with his mother standing over him, taunting him with her verbal as well as physical prowess. His sister Amy had come into the room with his father and started to laugh. His father had offered his hand to help him to his feet. He'd shrugged it off. At the age of seventeen, he'd cried like a baby behind his locked door.

God, how he hated her.

The hatred drove him to dial his mother's private line. He hated the fact that he needed to hear her voice. He hated himself for weakening and dialing the number. He hoped she wouldn't answer the phone. She did.

"Mother, it's Daniel. How are you?"

"I'm fine, Daniel. And you? You haven't called in a while. Does that mean you didn't get the promotion?"

"It means I've been so busy with the promotion I haven't had time to call," Daniel lied.

"What's your salary now?"

"Certainly far short of what your firm pays you, Mother, but I stand to be the next CEO. It all takes time."

"It certainly does where you're concerned. Amy made her first million by the time she was twenty-five. Because I got into the workforce late, I was thirty-eight before I made my first million. Your father is still working on his as we all know. When do you think you'll make yours?"

"Soon," Daniel lied again.

"How's your wife, Daniel? She didn't send a Christmas card last year, or a birthday card. I was offended. Are you two having marital problems?"

"Certainly not. Actually things couldn't be better. I would have thought you would be in touch when you heard the news."

"What news? Are you having a child?"

"No, Mother. Helen and I inherited Isabel Tyger's fortune. It was on all the news stations, although for certain reasons I can't go into, Helen was referred to as Nancy Baker. How could you have missed hearing that? I'm surprised Amy didn't mention it. Every brokerage house in the country has been after us."

"I think I did hear something about that. What exactly does the word fortune mean, Daniel?"

"It means around three hundred million dollars plus real estate. That kind of fortune."

"And you inherited it all. That's the funniest thing I ever heard. Why would somebody like Isabel Tyger leave you and that little trailer-park bitch you married all that money?"

"She was grateful for my help, and she adores Helen. We now have a yacht and a private jet not to mention a whole fleet of cars. There's a house in Switzerland, one in Hawaii, one in Aspen, and a villa in Spain. Chew on that, Mother. Where's Dad?"

"I see. Perhaps you'll be so kind as to send me a copy of the will, Daniel. You always were a liar. I have no idea where your father is. He's probably outside watching some of his night-blooming flowers. I'll tell him you called."

Daniel listened to his mother's trilling laughter before the connection was broken.

"Fuck you, Mother," Daniel muttered.

Once Isabel Tyger's money was his, he would buy a helicopter and set down on his mother's lush front lawn. That should set her back on her ear. Damn, that's exactly what he would do. She'd be laughing out the other side of her face if he did that. His sister would sneer at him, her face full of jealousy. His father . . . Well, his father would look at him with his sad eyes and worry that the helicopter would ruin the grass.

Daniel turned off the heater and cracked the window to squint through it. The shelter had gone dark in the past few minutes. That had to mean everyone had retired for the night. He frowned. Nine o'clock was too early to go to bed. For the past week the lights hadn't been turned off till ten minutes past eleven. Just enough time to turn on the late news to get the day's headlines and weather. Then it was lights out.

Something was different tonight. No chink of light showed through any of the blinds on the upstairs windows. The light next to the front door was out also. Darkness, as he well knew, could be an enemy or a friend. In this case he rather thought it was going to be Helen's friend.

He thought about the three-car garage and the sensor lights overhead. Would they go on if the garage door opened? Not likely. There was probably a switch inside the garage that turned them on and off manually. He'd seen three different vehicles enter the garage, a van, a smaller car, and a 4 x 4 that had driven in four days ago. None of the vehicles had left the garage in the last twenty-four hours.

He wondered what he would do if all three vehicles left at the same time going in different directions. Which one would he follow? He snorted. The last vehicle, the 4 x 4, the Pathfinder. They were so obvious they were pathetic. Didn't they know who they were up against?

He waited.

"Helen, this is a mistake. I know it as surely as I'm standing here. Right now you have nothing going for you. It's snowing out, you're recovering from a virus, and there's someone out there waiting for you in the darkness. Is there anything I can say to make you change your mind?"

"No, Julia, there is nothing you can say."

"Will you at least give me a clue, a hint, as to where you're going so I don't worry? Remember, you have all of Miss Tyger's money at your disposal. Dip into that. I wish you'd fly to California."

"I would never fly these dogs in the cargo hold. I've heard too many horror stories. I can't tell you because I don't know."

"Are you saying you don't have a plan?" Julia asked, outraged.

"That's what I'm saying. Daniel expects me to have a plan. He's trying to outthink me."

"Why didn't you call California and ask to have Miss Tyger's plane flown here? That way the dogs could have flown first-class. At least you'd be safe, for God's sake."

"Julia, thanks for being a friend and thanks for tossing out the rules where I was concerned. I'll be forever grateful. Don't worry about me. I'll call when I can. You don't really think Max will let anything happen to me, do you?"

"I know he'll do his best."

"I will tell you one little secret, and it will make you feel better. That package you gave me. It was from Arthur King. I asked him to get me a gun. The kind I learned to shoot back in California when I was in the shelter the first time. Those defense courses Boots made us take will come in handy. I did okay on the shooting range, too. I'm not a lamb going to the slaughter, so wipe that look off your face. If I don't take charge now, Julia, it was all for nothing. I want my life, and I'm the only one who can get it back. Time to go."

"Promise you'll send that belly chain." Julia grinned.

"I promise," Helen said solemnly.

"Then go with the angels, Helen."

Helen watched with tears in her eyes when the two dogs allowed themselves to be hugged. "Come on, into the truck."

"Julia, I'm going to need a few minutes. Don't open the doors until I flash my lights, okay?"

"You got it."

Arthur King sighed when he hung up the phone. "Helen left the shelter, Gerry. And it's snowing in New Jersey. I think she's on her way to California. Don't get excited. It's just a guess on my part. I think she's going to try and lure Daniel back here. This is where it started, and this is where she wants it to end. When it's all over she can call Sam and tell him she's free. I think she's viewing it as something she has to do herself with no help from anyone. Who are we to say otherwise? We don't walk in her shoes. I think Boots was right about her. She's a hell of a person. The few times Daniel let me meet her, I liked her. My wife liked her, too."

"Have you heard anything from the lawyers about Helen's problems?"

"They're working on it. It's costing some big bucks because we made it a top priority, and everyone is walking the papers to where they have to go instead of using the mails and waiting weeks for responses. If I'm right, and Helen is heading here to California, it will take her four or five days. We should know something by then. When this is all over, Gerry, what are we going to do?"

"Something that counts. Something Izzie would approve of. You know, meaningful," Gerry said. "I'm hoping Helen will let us help her with what she's going to be going through with Izzie's estate. In the end I think she'll accept because she's good at heart, and she'll want to make things better for other people if she has the chance. It's just a guess, but I'm hoping. I do know one thing, though, Artie, she will never let this inheritance come between her and Sam Tolliver."

"I wish I knew what the hell she was up to and how she thinks she's going to outsmart that bastard. Lookeee here, Gerry, we have an e-mail from Sam Tolliver."

Artie pushed his glasses upward as he read the e-mail addressed to Gerry and himself.

"Okay, this is it. Call him and tell him what's going on. I don't care if you give him the address of the shelter or not. Call Julia and warn her that he's going to be coming by."

"It's late, Gerry."

"It's not that late. Do it, Artie. Do you have his phone number?"

"Yeah, he gave it to me in that first e-mail."

"Call him." Gerry handed Artie the portable phone.

"Arthur King, Mr. Tolliver. I'm sorry if I woke you. Oh, you weren't asleep. That's good. I have something to tell you. Listen carefully."

At the end of the conversation, Artie held the phone away from his ear so Gerry could hear Tolliver cursing a blue streak.

"It wouldn't have done you any good to go there. We all have to respect Helen's wishes. I'm sorry about your house. If that's the worst thing the son of a bitch does, we can all live with it. She knows how to shoot the gun. She is very good at self-defense. The Pathfinder is new so she won't have car trouble. She has the dogs. I think, and this is just a guess or maybe it's wishful thinking on my part, but I think she's headed here to California. Get a map and try to figure out the route she would take. I'm going to give you the address of the shelter, but you won't find out anything we don't already know. I'll call Julia now to tell her you'll be coming by. This is the first time in the history of the foundation that we're okaying a visit like this. We're doing it against our better judgment, Mr. Tolliver. It is my personal opinion that you'll be wasting your time going there. Our advice is to try and figure out the route Helen would take and head out. Her car is a hunter green Pathfinder. The license plate is LMB-465. Daniel Ward is driving a silvery-looking car and no, we don't know the make of it nor do we know the license-plate number. I understand it's snowing there, so Helen will be driving carefully. Daniel Ward, on the other hand, is a Californian and isn't familiar with snow. Tell us what you're going to do, Mr. Tolliver."

"I'm going to strangle the two of you when we finally meet up. I don't care how damn old you are. You got that? I'm going after her. You should have called me sooner. I thought she was okay and would stay put when I saw those belly chains with the gizmos hanging off them. Even the dogs were wearing them. That's what I'm going to strangle you with *after* I engrave your names on those *doohickeys* that hang below the belly button. We're wasting time here, King. I'm outta here. You damn well better hope she's okay because I am holding you personally responsible. You got that?"

"Yes, Mr. Tolliver, we have it. Godspeed."

"Godspeed?" Gerry hissed.

Artie shrugged. "They always say things like that in the movies. It seemed appropriate. He's going to strangle us with belly chains that have our names on them. What the hell do you suppose that's all about? He said he knew she was all right when he saw the belly chains. We are old. If we weren't old, we'd be able to figure that out, Gerry," Artie said fretfully.

"Maybe we should have told him sooner."

"The rules say no. We never broke them before. As it is, we're going to have to account for this."

"To whom? We're it, Artie."

"That's true. I'm tired. What is a belly chain anyway?"

"Maybe it's something Helen sells on the Internet. Check it out, Artie."

"Uh-huh," Artie said later, his gaze glued to the screen in front of him.

"Oh, my goodness," Gerry said. "The dogs are wearing them. What do those little round circles say?"

"One says Helen and one says Sam."

"That's what Tolliver meant by Helen being all right. She must have added this . . . item recently as her way of letting him know she was okay. It makes sense," Gerry said. "We might be old, but we aren't stupid. Don't forget to mention this the next time we have a communiqué from Mr. Tolliver. Maybe he'll think twice about strangling us."

"We need to stop being so damn flip. This whole thing is serious beyond anything we imagined. The worst part of it is we have no control. All we can do is sit and wait and pray Helen knows what she's doing. What do you think Izz would be doing if she were here?" Artie asked.

"The same thing we're doing. Waiting. Her money would be on Helen."

"We wait then," Artie said.

23

Toasty warm inside the Pathfinder but definitely uncomfortable with her heavy, winter jacket, Helen turned around to look at the dogs. "Look, it's just for a little while. We're going to get this thing settled once and for all, and I'm the one who is going to be doing the settling. It's the best explanation I can offer." The Lab growled his displeasure. Helen shrugged. "It is what it is," she murmured.

Helen glanced down at the road map on the front seat next to her. Arthur King had been as good as his word. Before she left the shelter, she had marked the exact same route she'd taken when she left the shelter in California to drive to New Jersey. As long as she could read the road signs, she would be all right. At some point, her memory would kick in for the highways she'd used on her trip east that first time so long ago.

Helen strained to see through the windshield the road ahead. It didn't look like the white swirling snowflakes would do anything serious. There was no accumulation on the ground, and the farther south she drove the warmer the ground would be. The only problem was, she was only going as far south as Washington, DC, at which point she would head west. From that point on, the weather would be anyone's guess.

As far as a plan went, this one out-and-out sucked, big-time. She smiled then when she realized it was Sam's favorite expression. She couldn't think about Sam. Sam was the prize at the end of the road. *If* she ever got to the end of the road. What was her game plan? To drive away from the shelter and hope Daniel would follow her. Then what? Stop so she could accost him? If necessary, pump a few rounds into him and then call the police. She'd do some jail time, get out, and get on with her life. Stupid, naive thinking at best. Incredibly stupid and incredibly naive at the worst. She wasn't capable of shooting anyone, and she knew it. She wouldn't do well in prison without Lucie, and Sam would never want a jailbird for a wife. The gun was a scare tactic, nothing more, and she knew it in her heart. Daniel, on the other hand, would shoot to kill. Daniel loved guns and was an expert marksman. Back in San Jose he'd had an impressive gun collection he liked to brag about. She'd hated it, and she hated polishing the cabinet and cleaning the glass panels. How often he'd threatened her with one of the guns. Once he'd held one of them to her temple and removed the safety. She'd fainted right on the spot the moment she heard the ominous click. He'd kicked her clear across the room that day when she came to. Impressive and terrifying. Daniel had impressive, terrifying collections of a lot of things. She wondered where all those collections were now. Probably in some pawnshop somewhere.

She was glad now that she had slept the better part of the afternoon in preparation for driving all night long. She felt alert, and the two thermoses full of coffee would ensure that she stayed alert. If Daniel was following her, and she was certain he was, he'd wait till she stopped to use the bathroom or to get gas before he pounced. Daniel liked surprises as long as he wasn't on the receiving end of the surprise. When you were in control, a surprise could throw you out of control, and that was something Daniel would never allow to happen.

She thought about the silver car her husband was driving and what kind of capabilities it had. She was almost certain it would be no match for the Pathfinder. Daniel knew *diddly* about snow. She didn't know much herself, but Sam had taught her tricks about driving in snow, tricks she hoped she wouldn't have to put into use.

I should have asked Arthur King to send Boots's plane. She could still do that if she wanted to, but it would have to be readied and that could take as much as a day or two. A flight plan and all kinds of things to throw kinks into a plan. Either she was going to accept the inheritance or she wasn't. There would be no half measures. The Pathfinder didn't come under the heading of accepting the inheritance. The Pathfinder was an instrument to right the foundation's screwup by having her declared dead. Her backbone stiffened. "Either I do it on my own, or I don't do it at all," she mumbled. "Daniel Ward is my problem. No one else's problem."

Helen slowed the Pathfinder as she approached the toll booth that would lead her onto the New Jersey Turnpike. She reached for the ticket. "Ma'am, can you see a silvery-looking car behind me?"

The attendant craned her neck. "No, miss. I can't really see in all this swirling snow. Is something wrong? Do you want me to call one of the troopers?"

Helen looked at the lapel pin the woman was wearing. Tyree Pullen. She wondered what kind of name Tyree was. So different from plain old Helen. "No, that isn't necessary. I thought I saw someone I knew a while back. It's possible he passed me earlier, and, like you said, it's hard to see in this swirling snow."

"Drive safely. The weather forecast isn't exactly rosy."

"I will. Have a nice night and stay warm."

The attendant nodded and raised the barrier. Helen barreled through, trying to see the cars in the rearview mirror as they approached the ticket booth. All she could see were headlights and swirling snow. She steered the Pathfinder to the right lane and settled down for the long drive to the last exit, where she would pick up Interstate 95. Both dogs were sound asleep. There was just enough traffic to give her a sense of security. She sighed, her shoulders relaxing.

It was going to be a very long night.

Julia Martin knew what she was doing was foolish, even dangerous. Following Helen Ward was going to get her bounced right out of the program. Calling in one of the volunteers, saying only that she had somewhere to go, was never going to work. As if she really cared at this point. Meeting Helen Ward, breaking all the rules, and helping her was something she was never going to regret. "It's time for me to make my own way. I've lived behind bars, locked doors, and walled gardens long enough. I want to breathe again. I want my life back, too," she murmured as she turned on the radio and cracked the window.

As near as she could tell, she was four car lengths behind Helen and in the same lane of traffic.

A quarter of a mile behind Helen Ward and Julia Martin, a silver Nissan crossed driving lanes, the driver's eyes on his gas gauge. He cursed ripely and violently when he tore his gaze away long enough to check the cars in the right lane.

"This is a dumb-ass move if ever there was one," Sam muttered as he tore down the New Jersey Turnpike. "I'm driving blind with no destination in mind," he continued to mutter. "Furthermore, it's the height of stupidity. On the other hand, it could be a brilliant move." He continued with his monologue as he smoked one cigarette after the other.

He'd tried calling the shelter, but there had been no answer. Maybe he should have gone there, but instead he'd opted for trying to think like Helen. The old man was probably right: Helen would be driving cross-country. If he had to guess the why of it, the only thing he could come up with was Helen wouldn't subject the dogs to the cargo hold in a plane. They'd discussed it once, and she'd been adamant about not ever shipping a dog on a short or a long flight. He could still see the expression on her face if he closed his eyes. No, Helen would drive so the animals would be safe. Helen would put their safety first just the way she'd put his safety ahead of her own.

Sam cringed at the thought. He wished he knew what was in Helen's mind. What did she hope to accomplish? Was she just going blind and hoping for the best, or did she have plans to blow away her abusive husband at the first opportunity that presented itself?

Sam shivered at the thought, perspiration dotting his brow. If anyone was going to blow away the son of a bitch, it was going to be him.

He drove steadily, his eyes on the lookout for a hunter green Pathfinder and a silvery-looking car that could possibly be a Nissan, a Honda, or even a Ford of some sort. Thank God, the snow was abating. Visibility would be better.

Sam hunkered down for what he thought was going to be the trip of his life.

A light rain was falling when Helen turned off her headlights and hit the exit ramp at full throttle so her backup lights wouldn't go on. The dogs needed to be walked, and she had to use the bathroom.

It was three-thirty in the morning when Helen's car exited the turnpike and Julia Martin's dark blue Honda continued down I-95, as did the silver-colored Nissan.

The service area was almost deserted, with the exception of two truckers just getting into the cabs of their eighteen-wheelers. Helen walked both dogs, gave them water and biscuits before she settled them back into the Pathfinder. The gun in her jacket pocket, she looked around before she headed up the walkway to the brick building and the bathroom facilities. She was back in the car in less than seven minutes. She was breathing so hard she had to take great gasping breaths until she felt calm enough to start up the 4 x 4.

Sam Tolliver was five car lengths behind her when she inched her way onto the interstate.

Helen drove steadily for the next forty minutes. She slowed when she saw flashing blue-and-red lights ahead in the distance. A knot started to form in the pit of her stomach as she crawled forward, noticing that the flashing lights were northbound as well as southbound. Both dogs reared up on the backseat. Max growled ominously as Lucie cowered against him, whimpering. Was it an accident or a roadblock? More than likely an accident since the snow had turned to rain and the roads were starting to ice over. She heard an ear-piercing siren and then deafening noise directly overhead. A medivac helicopter? That alone had to mean the accident was serious and would tie up traffic for hours.

Helen eyed the median strip between the south and northbound lanes. She swerved without thinking, following a huge Dodge van, riding alongside it. Other cars followed suit. Within minutes she was driving north, her eyes peeled for an exit sign. It would be light in a few hours, and she could read the map and get her bearings then. The worst-case scenario would be to drive fifty or so miles out of her way until she could pick up the southbound interstate farther down the road.

Helen rummaged in her carry-bag for two rawhide chews that she tossed onto the backseat. "It's just a temporary setback. Sit back and enjoy the ride. Be a good girl, Lucie," she said lightly so the little dog wouldn't pick up on her anxiety.

Helen settled herself more comfortably, her eyes alert for a silver car.

Julia Martin heard the crash behind her. She slowed and pulled over to the shoulder of the road and waited. She wasn't sure why. Other cars ahead of her did the same thing. She was about to open the car door when a silver car streaked past her. She leaned her head back, her breathing ragged with fear. Her hand on the car door was frozen in place.

Somehow she'd lost Helen. She was almost certain the Pathfinder was no longer ahead of her. Helen wouldn't risk driving fast in this weather with the dogs and the kind of credentials she was carrying. She must have stopped at the last rest stop. With visibility so bad, she hadn't seen the Pathfinder turn off. Should she forge ahead or cross the median strip and hope for the best? She answered her own question in disgust. There was no point crossing into the northbound lane since the accident had shut down both lanes. The best she could do was to keep going, get off at the next exit, and wait by the entrance to I-95, hoping she was right and Helen would get back on the highway. She wondered at what point the occupant of the silver car would come to the same conclusion she'd just come to.

Daniel Ward knew he was driving on little more than fumes when he slowed to get off at the first exit he saw. It was raining harder, and the temperature gauge inside the Nissan said it was thirty-six degrees outside. While he stared at the gauge it dropped to thirty-five.

Up ahead of him he saw the bright lights of a Texaco station at the same moment he saw a dark Pathfinder winding its way down the road. He cursed so loud he startled himself. He had no alternative but to head for the station and gas up. He wanted to put his fist through the pump when he saw that it was self-service.

Even though there was a roof of sorts over the row of six pumps, the rain drenched him in less than five minutes. He shivered violently. All he wanted to do was get in the car and *go.* He looked across the concrete apron and could see the cashier watching him. Did he dare drive away without paying? Should he get soaked to the skin by running to the cashier? The decision was made for him when a State Police cruiser rolled into the parking area.

Rain dripped down the inside of his collar and into his shoes. He hated cold feet. When your feet were cold and wet you caught a cold. At least that's what Helen used to say. Helen said a lot of things. Most, if not all, were bullshit little ditties that he never paid any attention to. He paid for the gas and ordered a large coffee to go. He smiled at the trooper and made an inane comment about the weather. The trooper grunted as he ordered his own coffee.

Rather than go back outside so the trooper could see him get into the Nissan, Daniel looked around for the rest room. It would be better if the trooper left first. When he exited the rest room he was stunned to see the trooper sipping his coffee as he talked to the cashier. The Nissan was the only car in the lot. "Fuck," he hissed as he shouldered his way through the door.

"Take it easy out there, sir. The roads are icing up." Daniel raised his finger to show he heard the trooper's words before he ran toward the car, the scalding coffee sloshing down his pant leg.

Daniel drove on until he saw the entrance to I-95. He stopped the car, debating with himself. Did Helen get back on the interstate or was she sticking to the secondary road? The old Helen would have stayed on the secondary road. The new Helen would be gutsy and go the interstate route. He'd whip this new Helen back into shape as soon as he got his hands on her. He risked a glance at the temperature gauge. It now read a degree lower than the last time he looked. "Goddamn pissy-ass car," he seethed. He should be in one of the bigger rigs, like Helen. He wasn't going to think about the accident back on 95. It could have been him. Too damn bad it wasn't his fucking wife. All his problems would have been solved. He shivered. Even though the heater was turned full blast, he felt cold and clammy. His feet were like blocks of ice. Helen would be warm and cozy inside the big rig she was driving. His shoulders started to shake with cold rage at the circumstances he found himself in. "I swear to God, Helen, you're going to pay for this. I won't tolerate this kind of behavior."

He drove on, careful to stay in the same tracks the Ford Taurus and the cars ahead of him made. Slush was better than ice. Slower but safer.

He was nine cars behind the Pathfinder and the small blue Honda Civic driven by Julia Martin.

The moment Sam saw the flashing blue-and-red lights and the medivac helicopter, he knew he had to get off the highway. Without taking his foot off the gas pedal, he swerved to the left, crossed the median strip, and headed north. If it was a mistake, he would have to live with it. There was no way he could sit in traffic for hours. For all he knew, Helen could have done the same thing he was doing. Get off, follow the road, and watch for an entrance sign to I-95. It couldn't be more than one town away. At the moment it seemed his only option.

Thirty minutes later he was back on the interstate, the accident miles behind him.

He cranked up the heater and wondered if he would die from all the smoke inside the Blazer. He opened the window. By God, when this was all over he was going to get one of those nicotine patches and quit smoking once and for all.

"Damn!" The single word exploded from his mouth like a gunshot when he saw the rain literally turn to snow in front of his eyes. His eyes started to water when he remembered past winters when he and Max romped in the snow. God, how he missed that dog. Helen wouldn't let anything happen to Max. Max wouldn't let anything happen to Helen. He smiled when he thought of the little fur ball named Lucie and how she liked to lick his face. It had taken the Yorkie a long time to warm up to him, and the day she finally let him pick her up was one of the highlights of his relationship with Helen. They were a family, goddamn it. No asshole wife beater was going to change that. Not if he had anything to say about it.

Ahead of him were pinpoints of red. Somehow, in his reverie, he'd let up on the gas pedal. He pressed downward, turned on his left-hand signal, and moved into the middle lane. It was impossible to see the cars on his right or his left. For all he knew he could be driving alongside Daniel Ward or Helen. He kept his gaze glued to the tiny red dots in front of him as he wondered where the hell he was.

24

Helen cracked the window a bit and was rewarded with a fine spray of snow. The dogs reared to attention as some of the snowflakes spiraled backward. "It's okay," Helen said soothingly. "I just need a little fresh air. I hate to tell you this, but I have no clue as to where we are at the moment." A quick glance in the rearview mirror told her the dogs were listening intently to her voice. She risked another glance at the big Lab, who reacted to her soothing voice by lying down. She continued to watch as he moved one big paw to draw Lucie closer to him.

It would be light soon, at which point the world would turn white and dangerous. She needed to get off the interstate and head to safety. She hadn't seen one of the green road signs for a long time. She worried that she might have missed it. She realized how tense she was, how very tired she'd become during the past hour. She wasn't sure, but she thought she felt feverish. She did her best to convince herself that it was the heat in the car and the heavy jacket she was wearing that were making her feel sweaty and chilly at the same time.

Helen reached across the console for the second thermos. She settled it between her legs for a secure grip and unscrewed the top. It wasn't hot, but it was still warm. She gulped at the strong brew. Afraid to take her eyes off the road in front of her, her hand snaked out again to her purse on the seat. She rummaged until she found the aspirin bottle. Somehow she managed to unscrew the cap and tilt the bottle to her lips. Capping the bottle wasn't as easy as uncapping it, but she managed. She didn't feel one bit better.

She saw it then, the huge green sign high overhead. She wondered what would happen if it fell from its cables. Probably kill everyone in its path, she decided. According to the giant sign, an exit was one mile down the road on the right. She slowed the Pathfinder until the lights ahead of her were pale pink blurs in the distance. She didn't want to lose sight of the comforting lights entirely, so she increased the pressure on the accelerator. Her grip on the steering wheel was sweaty. Her neck and back felt stiff from sitting hunched over the wheel.

The outside world grew brighter and lighter. The snow was all about her. A world of whiteness. A deadly world of whiteness.

Helen pep-talked herself as she inched the Pathfinder along the clogged highway. *This, Helen, is probably one of the stupidest things you've ever done in your life. Second only to marrying Daniel Ward.*

He was out there. Probably close by. Would he follow her when she got off the exit? If he could see her, if he knew what kind of car she was driving, he would be right on her tail. It was also possible that he had kept on going when she stopped at the last rest stop. Maybe Lady Luck was on her side and he was ahead of her instead of behind her. Maybe those lights ahead of her were his. She shivered inside the warm vehicle.

Minutes later, Helen veered to the right just in time. She broke out in a sweat when she realized she'd almost missed the turnoff.

Snow surrounded her, but at least it was light out, the world a grayish white, making it impossible to distinguish the sky from the ground. She drove carefully, trying to follow the tracks in front of her. Her biggest fear was driving off an embankment. The ache between her shoulder blades intensified. Her eyes were dry and itchy from the heat in the Pathfinder. She thought it strange that she should feel parched since her hands were clammy with sweat.

She saw the motel, the gas station, and something called Truckers' Haven through a gossamer veil of snow. "Thank you, God," she murmured as she inched the Pathfinder to the cutoff that would lead her to the array of colored lights ahead. Her body was shaking badly when she turned off the engine in front of the motel. She had to close her eyes and take deep breaths until she felt calm enough to gather her purse and open the door. "I'll be right back," she said to the dogs.

The heat of the motel lobby slammed her in the face when the door closed behind her. Helen's vision blurred when she read the small sign on the registration desk. "This is a child- and pet-friendly establishment." She registered for two nights and paid cash along with a hundred-dollar deposit for any damage the dogs might do.

Helen jammed the key into her pocket. Her next stop was Truckers' Haven, where she bought a container of piping hot vegetable soup, a large coffee for herself, and hamburgers for the dogs.

The last thing she did was walk the dogs through the hard-driving snow before heading to the sanctuary of the motel. She counted four cars in the parking area. None of them appeared to be silver. Later on, she would check the parking area again.

Inside the cozy room, she double-locked the door and towel-dried the dogs. She fed them slowly before she placed the Styrofoam takeout tray filled with water on the floor.

Helen ate every drop of the soup and crackers before she gulped down two more aspirins with the coffee. She turned on the television for noise and a small sense of normalcy as the dogs prowled and sniffed every inch of the strange room before they hopped on the bed where they watched her expectantly.

She felt like she should do something. Maybe this was the time to call Sam to let him know she was all right. She should probably call Julia, too. Sam would be getting dressed for work, perhaps showering. Julia would be in the kitchen helping with breakfast. Both of them would be doing what they did every day of their lives.

Instead she headed for the bathroom. Perhaps she would feel better after a nice hot shower and a few hours of sleep.

Helen lingered under the hot shower until the water started to cool. Even though she'd turned up the thermostat, she shivered. Both dogs were panting with the heat in the room. Shaking, she turned it down before she crawled between the sheets. The minute the dogs snuggled next to her, her trembling body relaxed. Her last conscious thought before falling asleep was to wonder how she would dig out the Pathfinder if the snow continued.

Helen opened her eyes. She knew in an instant where she was. The red numerals on the bedside clock said it was 3:10 in the afternoon which meant she'd slept almost eight hours. She felt better, less achy, and she could move her neck without pain. She dressed quickly so she could walk the dogs.

It was still snowing lightly. Helen gasped when she opened the door and snow blew into her motel room. Lucie whined and backed up, while Max strained at his leash to go forward. In her life, she'd never seen this much snow. She picked up Lucie, her grip on Max's leash secure as she tried to avoid the deepest snow. Snowblowers whined and wheezed as the maintenance crew struggled to clear the parking lot.

"And here I am with no gloves, no shovel, and no boots," Helen mumbled. She walked to the end of the building and around to the Dumpster, where Max lifted his leg and Lucie squatted.

On her way back to her room, Helen's gaze searched out the parked cars. A sigh of relief escaped her lips when she realized there was no silver car in the lot. It was entirely possible such a car could be parked on the other side of the motel, but she wasn't about to tramp through the knee-high snow to find out. She tapped one of the maintenance men on the back. "Is the interstate open?"

"Road crews have been out all day. Traffic is moving. It's letting up some. If you aren't in a hurry, I'd wait till morning."

"I am in a hurry," Helen said.

"Then drive carefully." The snowblower whined to life again.

Helen picked her way over the packed snow to her room. "I'm going to get some coffee and a sandwich. Be good and don't bark while I'm gone."

At Truckers' Haven, Helen ordered a large coffee, another container of soup, and a double order of meat loaf for the dogs. While she waited for her food order, she listened to a conversation between two truckers on the road conditions. According to one of the men, the northbound lanes were clogged with slow-moving traffic with very little sand. The southbound lane was wet and clear twenty-five miles farther on. It was this last statement that convinced Helen to move on.

When she got back to the motel, the dogs prowled the room, sniffing out the bathroom, all the corners as well as the closet before Lucie bellied under the bed while Max growled his displeasure. Helen watched through the window as the maintenance crews cleared the cars in the parking lot. They were working on hers now. The minute it was finished, she would check out, head for the interstate, and hope for the best.

Twenty minutes later, Helen loaded her baggage and the dogs into the Pathfinder and went to settle her motel bill. While she waited for the manager to inspect the room in regard to dog damage, the reservation clerk stared at her until Helen became uncomfortable. "Is something wrong?"

"Aren't you the lady with the two dogs who checked in early this morning?"

"Yes. They didn't do any damage. Both of them are well trained. Why do you ask?"

"Someone was looking for you earlier. He described you perfectly. We aren't allowed to give out any information regarding our guests, and there are other people staying here with animals." At a nod from the manager, the clerk handed Helen her hundred-dollar deposit.

Helen bit down on her lower lip. "Did the man ask for me by name or did he tell you his name?"

"He didn't seem to know your name, but he did describe you and one of the dogs, whose name he said is Lucie. He didn't stay here if that's what you want to know."

Helen felt a lump of fear form in her chest. She struggled to clear her throat. "He must be looking for someone else. My dog's name is Sugar. The other one is Duke. I hope he finds whomever he's looking for. Did you by any chance see him leave or what model car he was driving? Maybe it's someone I met back on the road at the last rest stop."

"No, I'm sorry. It's been wild here. A lot of our help haven't been able to get in, so we're working with a skeleton crew. I really didn't pay attention to anyone in particular. Work crews, the police, the troopers, and stranded motorists took all my time. We let them use some of the empty rooms to get a few hours' sleep. At one point we had twelve cots set up in the lobby."

Before hitting the road, Helen returned to Truckers' Haven to have the two thermos bottles filled with hot coffee. At the last second she picked up a pair of red mittens and a wool scarf from a rack next to the cash register. She paid for her purchases and once again started up the Pathfinder. She thanked God for the excellent heater. Even though she had half a tank of gas, she steered the 4 x 4 to the gas pump and was grateful that it was a full-serve station.

"Be careful," the attendant said as he pocketed the twenty-dollar bill and handed out change. "Nice-looking animals," he said as an afterthought. Helen nodded and inched her way forward so she could turn and head out of the area to the interstate.

It took her exactly two minutes to realize just how bad the roads were. She realized she'd made a serious mistake in leaving the warm, comfortable motel.

While the roads had been sanded earlier, they were still treacherous as new snow kept falling. There was no shoulder on either side of the road. Snow was piled high, possibly a foot or more, she judged. She crawled forward, her eyes straining to see ahead of her. She knew there were cars ahead of her—she could see pale blurs in the distance—but there didn't appear to be any cars behind her. If there were cars, they didn't have their lights on. *This was a dumb move, Helen. A really dumb move,* she thought.

Two things happened simultaneously when Helen reached the ten-mile marker. Max reared up and barked, his huge paws slamming against the window. Helen almost jumped out of her skin with the ferocity the big dog showed. She saw him then. Sam! She slammed her foot so hard on the brakes the Pathfinder fishtailed and then swung around entirely. "Sam!"

"Easy, Max, easy," Helen said excitedly as she reached over the seat to open the back door. The Lab bounded out into the snow, knocking Sam off his feet just as a gust of wind blew the door shut.

Lucie whimpered, cowering against the back of the seat. Helen pressed the button that opened the window in time to hear Sam shout, "Helen! Helen, is it really you?" Sam laughed from his position in the snowbank. Max continued to growl, bark and lick his master's face.

"Sam!"

"Jesus, Helen! I've been riding up and down this interstate for hours looking for you. I skidded into this snowbank about four hours ago. I've been waiting for a tow truck ever since. Do you have any idea how worried I've been? Shit, who cares, I finally found you. Did I tell you how good it is to see you? Jesus, I love you, Helen. I don't even care if you're rich."

Grinning from ear to ear, Helen took that particular moment to glance into her side-view mirror, conscious of the fact that she was blocking traffic in her lane. A second later, her rear wheels started to spin as she pressed her foot to the gas pedal. Free of the snow, the Pathfinder slewed ahead almost abreast of a silver car, whose driver was Daniel Ward.

Another dumb move, Helen. Beyond dumb, it was stupid. You can't do anything right. Daniel was right about you when he said everything you touch you manage to screw up. Why didn't I wait one minute longer to give Sam and Max time to get in the truck? Why? God in heaven, how could I be so stupid. Because he would kill Sam. Maybe Max, too.

Helen risked a glance at the car almost abreast of her in the opposite lane. Daniel Ward smiled at her and blew her a kiss. She jerked her neck forward just as Lucie leaped over the seat, onto the console, and then into her lap. "Shhh, it's going to be okay. It's okay, Lucie. He's not going to hurt you. I'll kill him first. I mean it. Just lie still, baby. Max is okay. He's with Sam."

Where was her gun? She couldn't think. Had she put it in the console or was it in her purse? She'd been so rattled she simply couldn't remember. She shifted to a more comfortable position, allowing the little dog to lie in the space between her legs. She was shivering uncontrollably. It was in the deep pocket of her jacket. She could feel it pressing into her hipbone. She took her right hand off the wheel, fumbled with the flap of the pocket until she felt the cold butt of the gun. She withdrew it slowly and placed it in her lap.

Helen realized suddenly that it had stopped snowing. Patches of the road were wet and clear. The trucker back at Truckers' Haven had been right. There was so little traffic, she almost had the road to herself. There was nothing ahead of her now—just Daniel across from her and a few cars farther back on the road.

Daniel was fully abreast of her now, tapping lightly on the horn to get her attention. Helen continued to concentrate on the road ahead of her, refusing to glance at her husband. He sounded his horn again. This time it was a sharp blast to get her attention. Lucie squirmed in her lap. The road was entirely clear now and wet from the runoff of the snow, enabling her to drive with one hand. She lowered the window next to her and then picked up the gun in her right hand. The moment she had Daniel's attention she brought up her hand with the gun so he could see that she was not defenseless. He laughed, a sound that in the first days of their marriage she had found endearing. Now it made her blood run cold.

"Get off at the next exit, Helen," he shouted through his open window. "If you don't, I'll get behind you and shoot out your tires. The playing field is level now," he said, bringing up his own gun to show her. "Do as I say, Helen. I just want to talk to you."

Helen pressed the button to raise the window. Moments later, when she looked into the rearview mirror, she saw the silver car behind her. He *would* shoot out her tires.

She would have to do what he wanted. Another dumb asinine move on her part. In the scheme of things, what was one more wrong move going to do? At least Sam and Max were safe. In the same scheme of things, that was more important.

Helen drove steadily, aware of the car behind her as she watched for one of the green road signs she'd come to depend on.

She thought it incredible that she was so calm. *Do people feel this way before they die? Do they feel this way before they kill someone?* She wondered if she was going to turn into a killer or if she would be killed. Where would it happen? How would it happen?

Helen took a mighty breath as she turned on her signal light and hit the off-ramp. Ahead of her were colorful signs for two different motels, two different gas stations, and a huge homemade wooden sign that said GET YOUR XMAS TREES EARLY. She had the crazy urge to drive into the tree lot and order a tree. Instead, she veered to the shoulder of the road as Daniel Ward pulled ahead of her. Obviously, she was supposed to follow him.

25

Her heart pounding in her chest, Helen stayed a car length behind her husband. It was almost dark out, and a low-lying fog was starting to move in. She shivered at the eerie sight highlighted by Daniel's parking lights. Red fog. Considering the circumstances, it seemed appropriate.

Helen cuddled the little dog next to her, stroking her silky head with her left hand as she steered the Pathfinder in Daniel's wake. She crooned and sang "Twinkle, twinkle, little star . . ." in the calmest voice she could muster. Lucie trembled as she tried to press her small body as close to Helen as possible.

The moment she turned off the ignition, Helen slipped out of her heavy jacket. "I'm going to leave my jacket on the seat for you, Lucie. You have to stay here. I won't be long. I'll bring you a treat."

Helen almost jumped out of her skin when she turned to see Daniel standing next to the car door. He rapped sharply on the window. Lucie cowered against the plush seat as she tried to burrow into Helen's jacket. She whimpered and cried, a heartbreaking sound to Helen's ears.

Daniel knuckled the window a second time. That meant his patience was running out. Daniel never gave second chances. She stared straight into his eyes as she watched him try to open the car door. His mouth tightened into a thin line when the door wouldn't yield to the pressure of his hand.

Helen pressed the lock and got out of the Pathfinder. She hit the remote button on the key chain, locking Lucie inside. She'd cracked the window in the back earlier for Lucie's comfort.

"You know I hate to be kept waiting," Daniel said.

Helen shouldered her way ahead of him. "Ask me if I care what you think or what you want." She was glad the area was well lit, light spilling from the buildings in every direction. She still felt calm, almost cocky, as she pushed the palms of both hands against the plate-glass door to open it. She didn't bother holding it for her husband; instead she let it swing back to hit him full in the face. She smiled at his muffled curse. This was the Daniel she knew and hated.

Inside the steamy restaurant, Helen walked toward the row of booths on the left side of the room and bumped straight into the arms of Julia Martin. In doing so, Daniel plowed into her, forcing her forward and Julia backward.

Helen's eyes widened in shock and surprise. What did Julia's presence mean? She managed to mutter an apology of sorts at the same time swinging around to face Daniel. "I have to use the rest room, Daniel." She made her voice purposely loud enough for Julia to hear everything she said.

"Then give me the car keys. This table hasn't been cleared," Daniel said, his face full of fury and disgust.

"No to the car keys. As you can see, it's crowded. The waitress will get to it when she can. Order me a black coffee, a cup of soup, and a grilled cheese sandwich."

"The keys, Helen," Daniel said forcefully reaching for her arm.

"The car is mine. That means the car keys are mine, too, Daniel." Helen turned to leave a second time when Daniel physically blocked her path and Julia's as well.

A burly trucker wearing a baseball cap that said, Lulu's Bait Shack on it, sized up the situation and pushed Daniel into the booth. "The lady said to wait till they cleared the table, and she has to use the rest room. Ladies are funny that way. What part of what the lady said didn't you understand? You go ahead, ma'am, I'll see that the gentleman waits for you."

"What kind of place is this?" Julia muttered for Daniel's benefit as she shouldered past him and the trucker. She beelined for the bathroom right behind Helen.

Inside the small rest room, Helen wrapped her arms around Julia. "What are you doing here? How did you find me? You followed me, didn't you? Do you want to get yourself killed?"

"You're right. I followed you. I've been up and down this inter-state so many times I'm dizzy. I was about to turn around and go back when you walked in here. What are you doing, Helen?"

"There's no time for explanations. Lucie is in the car. Take her with you. Take my jacket, too, and her little bag. Sam was stuck in a snowbank back on the interstate. I let Max out when I saw him. Almost immediately Daniel pulled alongside me and I just took off. I don't know if Sam realized it was Daniel or not. I couldn't take the chance. Here's the car key. I have an extra one. Take care of Lucie for me. You might have to sing 'Twinkle, twinkle, little star,' till you get hoarse. It's the only thing that calms her down. God, what if he saw you coming in here with me?"

"The trucker blocked his view. You go out first, and I'll wait. Maybe there's another way out of here. Where should I go, Helen?"

"Back to the shelter."

"I'm out. Once you leave of your own accord, you have to leave. You know the rules. You were the lone exception. Are you headed for California?"

"Yes."

"Then that's where I'm going. The car's in good shape. I have enough money."

"Okay. When you get there, go to ComStar and ask for Arthur King. Tell him I sent you, and tell him what's going on. I'll get there when I get there."

"What about Sam?"

"I can't worry about Sam now. He has Max. He's smart enough to figure this all out. He'll probably be waiting for us when we get there. Promise me you'll take care of Lucie for me."

"Helen, I will guard that little dog with my life. Go on now, get out there and do whatever it is you're planning on doing."

"Thanks, Julia," Helen said, hugging her tightly.

The bustle of the restaurant sounded so normal. Pies and cakes that always tasted like cardboard sat under the glass domes all along the long counter that was full of tired-looking people waiting for their food. Waitresses, all of them weary from being on their feet, did their best to be cheerful for their customers as they carried the heavy trays. Conversation swelled until it bounced off the walls. Daniel, a murderous scowl on his face, stared at her as she approached the table. The trucker lumbered to his feet and smiled. "I kept your seat warm, ma'am."

"Thank you." Helen smiled.

"You be careful out there now, you hear. It's warming up, and the fog is going to be really bad."

"I'll be careful."

"Don't you *ever* talk to me like that again in front of people," Daniel hissed venomously the moment the trucker was out of earshot.

Helen leaned across the table, a smile on her face. Her lips barely moving, she said, "Kiss my ass, Daniel." She moved back and leaned against the back of the booth. "What are you going to do to me, Daniel, knock my teeth out, bust my kneecaps? On your best day, you bastard, you couldn't take me."

"Stupid bitch."

Helen leaned across the table again, the same smile on her face as she repeated her statement a second time. "Don't *ever* confuse me with the old Helen you used to beat to a pulp. You don't scare me anymore because I see now what a pathetic person you really are. Look at you. You look like a derelict. I'm ashamed to be sitting here with you."

"You have a short memory, Helen."

"On the contrary, my memory is long and detailed. I documented each and every abuse where you are concerned. I'm going to see to it that it never happens again."

"You're dead, Helen."

"You can't scare me, Daniel. Not anymore. I will never forgive you for what you did to Lucie. I take full blame for letting you beat on me because I feared for my life. Lucie is a defenseless animal. Any man who beats an animal in my opinion is scum of the earth. You, Daniel, are scum of the earth."

"Then what are you doing here?"

It was a good question. Because she wasn't a natural-born liar, Helen opted for the truth. "I figured it was the only way to keep Sam safe. I'm divorcing you and marrying him as soon as Arthur King gets the paperwork straightened out. I wanted to tell you that in person. I also wanted to tell you that I am going to file charges against you the moment I get to California. I will not rest until you're locked up for what you did to me and Lucie. You are never going to get your hands on Isabel Tyger's fortune. You're insane. I don't know why I never saw that. Maybe I did, but I was so afraid of you back then I didn't want to act on it. As I said, I'm not that Helen any longer."

"You're my wife," Daniel said as he bit into his grilled cheese sandwich.

"Only on paper, Daniel. I'm going to leave now. I'm not going anywhere with you. I know you have a gun. I have one, too. I know how to use it. There's a state trooper sitting at the counter. Make a fuss, don't make a fuss, it's up to you." Helen fumbled in her bag for her wallet. She signaled the weary waitress and handed her a twenty-dollar bill. "Keep the change."

"Sit down, Helen."

Helen smiled. "Go to hell, Daniel." As she struggled out of the booth, she felt her shoulders tighten up. Would Daniel pump bullets into her back? Not likely. He'd wait till she got outside.

She ran like the hounds of hell were on her heels.

"Whoa, little lady. What's wrong?" the giant with the Lulu's Bait Shack cap asked as he stiff-armed her in the middle of the parking lot.

"Listen, can I ride with you? Where are you going? I have to . . . I have . . . oh, God, here he comes!"

"I knew that dandy was trouble. Sure you can ride with me. I'm going to Raleigh, North Carolina. How far do you want to go?"

"Just to the nearest airport. I'll be glad to pay you."

"You stay right here with me. I have to pay for my gas. That's my rig over there, and, yes, you can ride with me. I can take you right to Reagan National Airport. Will that help you?"

"You just saved my life. I don't even know your name. Mine is Helen Stanley."

"Most folks call me Big John. My wife calls me honey, and my kids call me daddy."

"How about if I just call you John?"

"Sounds good. Will that pipsqueak follow us?"

"Yes."

"Then we'll have to do something about that. What kind of car is he driving?"

Helen relaxed. She knew she was in good hands.

When they got into the eighteen-wheeler, John got on his CB radio, put out a call to any truckers in the vicinity, and told them, "Here's what I want you to do . . ."

With no baggage to claim, Helen walked past business travelers from the early-morning flight in search of the exit, where she could pick up a cab. She had no hope that Arthur King or Gerald Davis would be there to meet her, even though she'd called from the plane. When she heard her name called, she turned, a look of fear on her face. She relaxed a moment later when she stared at the objects of her thoughts.

"Thank God you're all right, young lady. Izzie would never forgive us if something happened to you," Gerald Davis said. At Helen's frown, he explained. "From childhood, I called her Izzie. Arthur here called her Izz. I thought you would know who I was referring to."

"Oh. I did. My thinking hasn't been too clear of late."

"Where would you like us to take you?"

"The nearest hotel or motel. I don't have much money left since I bought my ticket at the last moment. Something cheap until I can figure out what to do."

"Would you like to go to Izzie's ranch? It's yours now. I know you said you didn't want any part of it, but it would solve your immediate problem. In addition, we need to talk and not be interrupted. If you don't like it there, you can leave. There are several cars at your disposal. Think of it as a plan or an immediate solution," the vet said.

Helen nodded. "Okay, but just for now. Mr. King, have you had any luck untangling my legal status? Am I still dead?"

"We have in our possession a copy of your birth certificate. It has a raised seal, so that's one item off our list. The death certificate is proving to be a little dicey. According to the records you were cremated and then laid to rest in a mausoleum. That's also a little dicey. What Izz did was claim a homeless person from the morgue and said she was you. Yes, it was wrong of her to do that. In her zeal to protect you, she simply didn't think straight. She considered it a means to an end. She claimed a body no one wanted, cremated it, and then gave it a proper burial. She did pay attention to you when you said your husband would eventually find you no matter what was done. She didn't want that to happen. We're going to correct the mistake. Doctors and morticians are not the easiest people to deal with when their reputations are at stake, and that's as it should be, too. Your mother could be a big help to us, but she flat out refused to help. As far as she's concerned, you're dead. All she would talk about was the insurance money. It will be up to you, Helen, to enlist her aid."

"My mother?"

They were at the car now. Arthur King held the door for her.

"My mother?" Helen said stubbornly.

"She thinks you're dead, too. Isabel said you had a $25,000 life-insurance policy and she was given the money. She . . . ah . . . she didn't ask any questions."

A knot formed in Helen's throat. "Did she . . . did she . . . cry?"

"Perhaps she cried in private. Grief is a private emotion sometimes, Helen."

"Does she still live in the trailer park?"

"No. She moved to an apartment complex," Arthur said.

"I want to go there. Now. Do you know where it is?"

"More or less."

"Then take me there," Helen said. "Please," she added.

"Are you sure you want to do this right now, Helen?" Gerald Davis asked, his voice full of concern.

"I'm sure."

"How is Mr. Tolliver, Helen? He's been communicating with us, but we haven't heard from him in a few days."

"The last time I saw him he was stuck in a snowbank along I-95. Sam can take care of himself."

"Then you don't know that your husband had dinner with him one evening. Of course Sam didn't know who he was at the time.

Then your house was broken into and literally destroyed. Sam had to move to a motel until it could be put to rights."

Helen gasped. "Daniel destroyed the house?"

"And all your inventory."

"I was afraid he would kill Sam. That's why I ran. I thought if Daniel thought I walked out on Sam, he would leave him alone. Daniel is insidious. On top of that, I think he's insane."

"We quite agree with you on that score. Tell her, Gerry, what we found when we went to his apartment. The truth is, we broke into his apartment."

Helen listened as Gerry recounted his and Arthur King's visit to Daniel's apartment, ending with, "and he had your picture pasted on top of the toilet seat and the bottom of the seat."

"We have photos of it," Arthur said smartly. "They'll help you once you get to court."

"My God!" was all Helen could think of to say.

Thirty minutes later, Arthur King slowed the car and entered the parking area of the Cherry Tree Apartments. "I remember Izz saying your mother lived in the third building. Perhaps her name and apartment number will be on the mailbox. Would you like us to go with you, Helen?"

"No. Just wait for me."

Helen walked around to the third building, checked the mailbox, and saw the name Phyllis Stanley on one of the boxes and then the number four.

Uneven numbers on the first floor, even numbers on the second. She climbed the steps and rang the bell on the door with a big bronze number 4 alongside the bell. When there was no response, she rang it a second and then a third time.

Helen stepped back when a bleary-eyed man who appeared to be in his sixties opened the door, and barked, "D'ya think we're deaf?"

Helen eyed the dirty gray undershirt, the equally dirty gray boxer shorts and the slovenly-looking man wearing them, who reeked of stale liquor, cigar smoke, and body odor. She finally found her voice, and said, "I'd like to see Phyllis."

"Why?" the man barked.

"She's my mother."

"I'm not fallin' for that old line. The daughter died." He was about to slam the door shut, when Helen said, "Fetch her or the insurance company will come here demanding she return the money. As you can see, I'm very much alive."

"You wait right there," the man said. The door slammed in Helen's face and was opened a minute later by her mother.

"Mom, it's me, Helen. Can I come in?"

"No. No, you have to get out of here. They said you were dead. I spent the money. They said you were dead."

"Mom, I'm not dead. Aren't you glad I'm alive? Don't you care? My God, what kind of mother are you?"

"You lit out on me. You didn't care about me. You married that fancy-pants computer fella and didn't care a hoot about me. They said you were dead. They said I could do whatever I wanted with the money."

"Mom, I don't care about the money. They aren't going to make you give it back."

"Then what are you doing here? Are you sure I don't have to give back the money?"

Helen sighed, her eyes filling with tears. "No, Mom, you don't have to give it back. I thought you would want to know I'm alive. I thought you might care. The truth is, I wanted you to care. I'm sorry I bothered you. I won't bother you again."

"See that you don't. Those insurance people spy on people. You can't trust them."

Helen wiped at her eyes. "Good-bye, Mom."

The door slammed shut. Helen blinked. *Well, what did I expect? Maybe a loving hug, a welcoming smile? Yeah, right.*

Helen was tight-lipped when she climbed into the back of Arthur King's car. "How far is it to Miss Tyger's ranch?"

"About forty minutes from here."

"Then I suggest we go there right now."

26

Helen stepped from the car, her arms and legs trembling with weariness. She was tired and hungry to the point of exhaustion. She did her best not to think about her mother's reaction to her early-morning visit. She hadn't expected a warm greeting, but she had expected civility and possibly relief that her daughter was alive and well. She tried to shake off the thoughts and to pay attention to what the two elderly men were saying.

"This is the Tyger ranch," Arthur King said. "I believe there are about three hundred acres, but don't ask me where the boundaries are. What do you think of the house, Helen?"

"It's beautiful." It was low and sprawling with multipaned windows that glistened in the sunlight. Built entirely of fieldstone, the irregular stone formations added charm and a certain coziness. The rainbow of flowers cried out for sunglasses as Helen held her hand to her eyes, the better to observe the brilliant beds of poppies and every other flower indigenous to California soil.

As she walked up a long winding walkway whose stones matched the exterior of the house, she could see the magnificent stained-glass door ahead of her. "It's beautiful," she repeated a second time.

"Izzie hated it," Gerald Davis said flatly.

Helen blinked at the vet's tone, her eyes full of questions.

"Izz had the entire house redone a while back. It's more modern now. She wanted light and air and bright colors. I tend to think she knew back then that she was going to be leaving all of this to you. Once she got an idea into her head, neither Gerry nor I could shake it loose."

"I don't think I'll ever understand that kind of generosity. She only met me that one time. There's no way I can accept all of this."

"Perhaps when you know a little more about Isabel, you'll change your mind. Come, come, let us give you the tour unless you'd rather have something to eat and maybe a nap."

Helen looked at the two men, who, she knew, were dying to show her Isabel Tyger's house. Her house now. She could wait for food and a nap. "No, no, I can wait. I'd like to see the house."

"It looks larger than it really is. Rooms were added over the years although none were added during Izzie's father's lifetime or hers for that matter. Some of the rooms are small. Some don't even have closets.

"At one time, the walls in the hallways held pictures of Izzie's male ancestors. They're all gone now. In the upstairs hallway there is one picture. I think you're going to like it. The day it was given to her, Izzie had it framed. She stood over the man while he did it. I think she valued that picture more than anything in this whole house. She was a kind, generous, remarkable woman. If she made mistakes where you're concerned, she made them because she cared deeply about what happened to you and Lucie."

"Lucie? What does Lucie have to do with any of this?"

Both men sighed as if on cue. "Lucie is the reason Izz took such an interest in you. Lucie is the reason for everything," Arthur said gently.

"I don't understand," Helen said.

"You will, but later. I think when you know everything, you'll forgive Izz for taking your life away. I think you will also change your mind and accept her legacy.

"This is the room where Izzie spent most of her time. It's a sunroom, a den, a family room. Izzie pretty much lived in it. She dearly loved a fire in the winter months or when the sun went down and the air turned chilly. She'd curl up here with her books, papers, and ledgers and work through the night. She had great difficulty sleeping."

Helen gazed at the homey, cozy room. She could well understand why her benefactor loved the room. The cavernous opening in the fireplace reached almost to the ceiling. It was big enough to roast a whole side of beef. Wood was stacked neatly into an opening between the fieldstones. *Enough for at least a week,* Helen thought. *Maybe two weeks.* Bookshelves with hundreds of brightly jacketed covers adorned one wall. Isabel Tyger must have loved to read, the way she did. Watercolors adorned a third wall. They were colorful; an ocean scene, a field of poppies, a large golden sun surrounded by blue skies and marshmallow clouds. Happy pictures. Over the mantel was a picture of Isabel, Arthur King, and Gerald Davis. "When was that done?" she asked.

"The year Izzie turned sixty-five. Her father's picture used to hang there. It was the first thing she burned along with all the other ancestors' pictures when she had the fireplace rebuilt. The artist did it from a photograph," Gerry said.

"The three of us spent a lot of time in this room," Artie said. "It was like coming home in a way. We always knew we were welcome. We ate in here, watched movies, or just sat and talked. Sometimes all night long. We thought about asking you if you would sell this house to us, but decided it wouldn't be the same. We'd like to come by from time to time if that's all right with you. When you get to be Gerry's and my age, it's difficult to let certain things go. This is one of those things that has been a part of our lives since we were children."

Helen didn't know what to say, what to think, or where to look. They looked so sad, so woebegone, she wanted to run up and hug them. "I like the French doors," she said.

"So did Izzie. She always kept them open. It took her weeks to pick out the furniture, the carpeting, and the drapes. Every single piece of furniture she chose is fit to sleep in and guaranteed not to give you a crick in the neck. As you can see, she loved bright colors and green plants. Artie and I have been watering them a couple of times a week. I retired. Artie is on a leave of absence, and retires after Christmas."

"I didn't know that. What do you do with your time?"

"We come out here and moan and groan. Since we're the executors of the will, we've taken a few liberties. Sometimes we have lunch here, have a beer, walk around, go down to the . . . you know, just being here makes us feel closer to Izzie. I hope you don't mind. Now that you're here, we'll call ahead," Gerry said.

This time Helen did hug them. "That's not necessary. Come here anytime you want. I'm sure Miss Tyger would want you to feel at home. It's only mine on paper. It's more yours than it will ever be mine. We have to work something out where all of this is concerned."

"All in good time," Artie said as he led the way down the hall to show off the rest of the house.

"That's all for the downstairs. It's more or less your normal floor plan, huge eat-in kitchen, formal dining room, the den, Izzie's office, two bathrooms, and an extra room for junk as Izzie put it. This staircase is solid mahogany. You'd never know it because Izzie had it painted white to go with the new, bright, airy look she was striving for. She painted all the wainscoting white, too."

"I like white," Helen said, more to have something to say than anything else.

"This is the picture I was telling you about downstairs," Gerry said.

"She hung it up! It's framed and everything! This is the last thing I ever expected to see," Helen said, her voice choked, her eyes filling with tears.

"There are no words to tell you what this picture meant to Izzie. Later when you're rested and thinking clearly, we'll tell you more about her. There are five bedrooms up here, four small ones and Izzie's room. You can take your pick. On this side of the hall, there's a bathroom between the two bedrooms. It just has a shower, no tub. It's the same on the other side of the hall. Izzie's room has a private bath and her room is a little larger. You can explore and freshen up while Artie and I go downstairs to rustle up something for lunch."

It was hard for Helen to tear her eyes away from the picture hanging on the wall. She thought about the day she'd rolled it up and handed it to Mona. Her first act of defiance. "That sounds good. I am rather hungry. Would you mind calling your office, Mr. King, to see if Julia Martin called? I'm worried about Lucie."

"I'll do it right now. Take your time, young lady. We're in no rush," Artie said.

Helen poked her head in each of the rooms as she made her way down the hall. Each small room was a delight. A single bed with colorful spread and matching drapes. A white wicker rocking chair with matching cushion and one small dresser. A slipper chair and a small table with a reading lamp. Cheerful but restful.

Isabel Tyger's room was different. It was done in various shades of pink and white. It reminded Helen of pictures she'd seen as a child in the Sears Roebuck catalog. The kind of room she'd hungered for as a child. The pink, lacy canopy bed, the frilly dressing table with a pink-tufted velvet stool. The rose-colored velvet chaise that matched the rose-colored carpet was positioned to take advantage of a pristine white cabinet that housed a television set. Green ferns in white wicker stands stood in every corner of the room. Here, too, there were French doors that opened onto a small terrace that held colorful blooms and more ferns in stands.

Helen jammed her hands into the pockets of her jeans as she stared at the one picture hanging on the wall. It was a picture of a very young ballerina with worn dancing shoes dressed in a pink, frilly tutu and leotard. It was the kind of picture that could be purchased in any Target or Wal-Mart store for less than ten dollars. This picture, though, had a gold frame that probably cost several hundred dollars. She knew she was looking at something dear to Isabel Tyger's heart. Did she want to be a ballerina? Did she love pink? Was this the room she'd never had as a child?

Who were you, Boots? she cried silently. *What is it you want from me? What is it you think I can do and how can I do it? Why me? What does Lucie have to do with all this? Do those men downstairs have the answers?* Tears rolled down Helen's cheeks as she closed the door to Isabel Tyger a/k/a Boots's room and walked back down the hall. She finally chose a room whose bedspread was adorned with colorful, quilted tulips. If she was going to stay for even a short time, this would be her room. She'd always loved tulips. What better reason did she need?

Helen sat down on a purple chair, the exact shade of the tulips on the bedspread. She kicked off her sneakers and yanked at her damp socks. She longed for a shower and toothbrush. She knew she didn't dare sit too long, or she would fall asleep. So what if she put her dirty clothes back on. Who would care? Certainly not the two old men down in the kitchen. She was on her feet then, poking in the tiny closet and drawers. She blinked at the contents of the drawers. One set of everything from underwear to outerwear in small, medium, and large. The miniature closet held windbreakers, sweaters and tee shirts on padded hangers in small, medium, and large. On the floor were slippers, sandals, and sneakers ranging in size five through eight. Helen grabbed one of everything in medium before making her way to the bathroom.

Helen's eyeballs snapped to attention the minute she entered the bathroom. She'd never seen a purple toilet seat, much less a purple toilet and vanity. Thick, thirsty, purple towels trimmed in white lace hung from white ceramic hooks. The shower was encased behind sliding Plexiglas doors with sprays of purple pansies painted on each panel.

The toilet tissue was thick and soft and the color of lavender. The cabinet underneath the vanity had an array of talcum powder, scented soaps as well as fragrant liquid soaps, three different kinds of toothpaste and mouthwash along with six toothbrushes still in their plastic bubbles. A blow dryer, curling iron, two combs, two hairbrushes, hand cream, face cream, night cream, and body lotion were lined up neatly. Four different brands of shampoo and conditioner sat next to the body lotions. All new. All unopened. The bottom shelf held a second set of purple towels and a new unopened package of the lavender toilet tissue as well as facial tissues.

"All the comforts of home," Helen murmured.

Helen stripped down and stepped into the steamy shower, where she lathered up, rinsed, and then lathered up a second time. She washed her hair three times before she felt totally clean. She saw the robe hanging on the back of the bathroom door when she stepped from the shower. She grinned when she stretched the belt to the toilet tissue to see if it was a match. It was. She couldn't help but wonder who had color-coordinated this small space. Obviously some pricey decorator, or else Boots had a hidden talent.

The moment she was dressed she felt like a different person.

She had her second wind and would be able to go for another few hours before exhaustion kicked in totally.

In the hallway, Helen stopped to look at the picture she'd given to Boots via Mona at the shelter. The frame, like the one on the ballerina, was rich and costly for such a simple picture. "I'm so sorry, Boots. I wish . . . I wish so many things."

They were waiting for her at the kitchen table. They stared up at her expectantly. "I took a shower. There were clothes in one of the drawers. I hope it was all right to take them."

"They're yours. This house is yours. You can do whatever you wish. We made some sandwiches. I hope you like cheese. It's all there was. Artie and I usually bring something when we come out here. If we had known ahead of time that you were coming, we would have stocked the refrigerator."

"Cheese is fine. Ummm, this coffee is good. I love coffee."

"So did Izz. She liked to dunk her cheese sandwiches in black coffee. We do it, too," Artie said sheepishly.

Helen immediately dunked her sandwich. "Yes, I can see why you would like this. Did Julia Martin call ComStar, Mr. King? Has Sam been in touch with you?"

"No to both questions, Helen. Please, call me Arthur or Artie."

"All right," Helen said.

"How's Lucie? I can't tell you how often I've thought about you two. You really gave me a scare that night."

"I am so grateful to you, Dr. Davis, for saving her life. I wanted to call you so many times to tell you how well she was doing. I couldn't have gone on without that little dog. Most people would never understand something like that."

"Izzie understood only too well. If you're going to call him Artie, then you should call me Gerry. I want us all to be friends. We're going to tell you about Isabel Tyger in the hope you will change your mind about accepting her estate. It's not a very long story. In fact, it's pitifully short. When we finish the story, we're going to take you for a walk."

Helen sat back in the kitchen chair. She listened, her eyes filling with tears from time to time. When Gerry finally got up from the table, he said, "She chose you. Of all the people in the world she could have chosen, she wanted you to carry on for her. Now do you see? Whatever mistakes she made were well-meaning. You owe her forgiveness. If we aren't successful in giving you back your life on paper, I don't think Mr. Tolliver will mind one little bit. He loves you, not your name. We won't give up. We want you to be able to get divorced so you can marry Mr. Tolliver as much as you want it. You must be patient. Now, are you ready for the walk?"

"Daniel will find me here. There are no barricades, no fences. He can drive right up here and knock on the door or shoot the door down. I'm a sitting duck if I stay here."

"Yes, that's true. Artie suggested we hire some personal security for you until we can resolve this matter. Are you comfortable with that?"

"No. Daniel would never let rental cops stop him," Helen snorted. "He found me, didn't he?"

"We could fence in the immediate area in a matter of days. An electrified fence. Guard dogs patrolling the outside are an option as well as the security. It will at least give him pause for thought. The other alternative is to pay him off. You certainly have enough money to do that."

"That's not the answer. If I do that, this was all for nothing. The answer is no. He wants his share of this. The truth is, I think he wants it all. Somewhere along the way, the money aced me out. I don't think he's interested in me anymore since I've been with Sam. I don't know this for a fact. Call it woman's intuition. If something happens to me, he inherits my estate. People have accidents all the time."

"We set up an appointment for tomorrow morning with your attorneys. The other thing Artie and I want you to think about is this. You are now a very rich lady. You could coax your mother to come forward and vouch for you. If she's more interested in your money than she is in you, sad as it may be, the answer lies in your pocketbook. Once you are legally Helen Stanley, your husband doesn't have a prayer of getting anything from you."

"That's what you think," Helen muttered.

"Are we ready to take our walk, Helen?" Artie asked.

"Yes, I'm ready."

Gerry reached into one of the kitchen cabinets. "It's a ritual we observe," he said, holding up a bottle of bourbon. "Izzie loved bourbon."

"I prefer brandy," Helen said.

Gerry turned around and opened the cabinet again and withdrew a bottle of plum brandy. He handed it to Helen. "We just swig from the bottle."

"Sounds good to me," Helen replied.

27

"So, Helen, what do you think?" Artie asked, slurring his words.

Helen tilted the brandy bottle and took a long pull. "What I think is that is the saddest story I ever heard. Your friend Isabel and my friend Boots must have been a very remarkable woman. You two," she said, pointing the brandy bottle in the general direction of the two old men, "are just as remarkable. I can't imagine a friendship enduring all these years. All these little graves. It breaks my heart. How did you manage to do this as often as you did?"

"We loved Izzie," Gerry said simply. "Now do you understand what we meant when we said she chose you because of Lucie?"

"Yes."

"So, will you take over now?" Artie peered over the top of his wire-rimmed glasses. He looked like a wise old owl to Helen.

"How can you ask me something like that when I've had half this bottle of brandy? I can't think straight. My heart feels sore. I'm all choked-up, and my vision is blurry. I can't make a decision like that in this condition."

"We need to know," Gerry said, taking a slug from the bourbon bottle. "Artie needs to know and by God, Izzie is up there wanting to know. Spit it out, girl. Tomorrow you're going to have a hangover, and you won't be able to think then either. You said you would do anything in the world for me for taking care of your dog," he said craftily.

"I did say that. I remember saying that. I meant it, too," Helen said smartly.

"This is the *anything* then. I want you to accept your inheritance. You can't go back on your word or a promise."

Helen took another swig from the brandy bottle. "That wasn't what I meant, and you know it, Gerry."

"See. We're friends already. You're calling me Gerry. Doesn't matter what you meant. You said the words. Isn't that right, Artie?"

The wise old owl nodded solemnly. "If you said the words, then it's a done deal. That's a load off our shoulders, isn't it, Gerry?"

"Yep."

"I have to think about Sam. I love Sam. I'm not giving up my life. Sam won't . . . Sam doesn't want me to be rich. He said he loved me even if I was rich, but he was stuck in a snowbank when he said that. My life will change. Sam's life will change. I don't want Sam to change. I want him just the way he is. He loves teaching kids. My life is full of . . . feathers . . . and belly chains. I'm going to sell belly chains. I can make a fortune on the Internet. I don't need all . . . this," Helen said, waving her arms about.

Overhead a cluster of birds took wing. Helen looked upward and for one brief second she thought she saw Isabel Tyger perched at the top of the tallest tree. She sucked in her breath when the woman she'd known as Boots gave her a thumbs-up salute. Helen blinked, her jaw dropping as she looked at her two companions, who were staring at the same treetop. She almost lost it then when she saw them waving. *This isn't real. I'm hallucinating, and I'm drunk.* She squeezed her eyes shut and reopened them. The vision was still there. Artie and Gerry were still waving, smiles on their faces.

Helen focused on the ten tiny graves in front of her. She looked upward again. Suddenly she was stone-cold sober when the vision atop the trees pointed in the direction of the graves. Clearly the vision was waiting for her response. Helen realized in the whole of her life she'd never been this frightened, this exhilarated. She thought of Lucie and how much she loved the little animal. As much as Boots must have loved the stray dog that had been her only friend. Boots never got a second chance. In the blink of an eye, the thumb of her right hand shot upward. The vision faded.

Helen turned her gaze to the two old men opposite her. Did they see what she'd just seen? Was she supposed to mention it? Were they waiting for her to say something? They were plastered, as Sam liked to say. Maybe she was dreaming and would wake

up any second. She looked toward the ten graves. There seemed
to be a glow around the markers, a strange, golden glow of some
sort. Maybe she was just tired and jet lag was kicking in. Maybe
a lot of things.

"I accept," she said, firmly and clearly. She raised her finger,
"Only if Sam agrees to . . ." Unable to help herself, she looked
upward again. The vision was back on top of the tree. She knew
instinctively no conditions were permitted. She cleared her throat.
"I accept. I will do my best to do what Boots wanted me to do. I
will not give up my life or my own dreams. That's as good as
you're going to get."

"We accept your decision," the wise old owl said solemnly. "So
does she," he said, pointing upward.

"Then I guess we have a done deal," Helen said. "You'll have
to tell me what it is I'm supposed to do in regard to . . . these,"
she said, dropping to her knees by the biggest stone in the row.

"Just come here. Clear the weeds. Sing. Pray. Think. Remember.
Someday you might need to . . . I can't think of a better resting
place for a beloved animal," Gerry said.

"You mean Lucie and Max?" Helen asked in a choked voice.

Helen wrapped her arms around the largest marker and cried
as she'd never cried in her life, deep heart-wrenching sobs that
tore at her body and left her limp and whimpering.

A long while later, Helen struggled to her feet. "Was this my
initiation?" she asked quietly.

"Yes," both men said in unison.

"Did I pass?"

"We weren't sure. But she was," Artie said, pointing to the top
of the tallest tree.

"Is that why you come here?"

"No. We come here because we want to. We've been doing it
for more than sixty years. Old habits are hard to break. She visits
once in a while. Most times when she's ticked off about something
or when things aren't moving fast enough for her." Gerry rolled
his eyes to make his point.

"I don't believe in ghosts," Helen said.

"We don't either."

"We were drunk," Helen said. "Apparitions, ghosts, spirits, smoke, fog, whatever, it's all bunk."

"Yes."

"Then what did we see?"

"What we wanted to see," Gerry said. "Izzie looked out for us all our lives. There's no reason to believe just because she died that she would stop. She always did defy anything that even remotely resembled logic. We'd best be getting back so you can take a nap. You look tuckered out."

"I think I just got my second wind. I'm so wired it would take three sleeping pills to put me to sleep. Let's go back to the house and talk."

"Now that sounds like a plan," Artie said.

Gerry smacked his hands together. "We do make good plans. Your Mr. Tolliver has no faith in us. He called us old codgers and said he was going to strangle us."

"He's part of this deal."

"And that's the way it should be."

"We need to talk about Daniel Ward before we do anything else. I do my best thinking while I'm cooking or baking. What do you say we hang out in the kitchen and get a head start on some of this?"

"Can you make good spaghetti?" Artie asked.

"Sam says it's the best he's ever eaten." Helen grinned.

"Does Sam like Boston cream pie?" Gerry asked.

"Sam loves Boston cream pie."

"So do we," Artie said. "We'll go to the market for you."

"Now that sounds like a plan to me." Helen laughed. "It's a deal."

Daniel Ward tapped furiously on his laptop. Within minutes, by using his mother's Visa card, he would have a rental car, a set of clean clothes, and a hotel room. If he was lucky, she'd never notice the charges. If he was unlucky, she'd call him, warn him, and then press charges. The way he looked at it, the last bill had just gone out which would give him at least twenty-four days till the next billing cycle. Everything was arranged for pickup within the hour. He continued to tap into the computer. His mother certainly did keep a nice healthy balance in her checking account. He would deplete it shortly with a robust withdrawal. Six weeks before, when things were going from bad to worse, he'd gotten the brilliant idea to have duplicate cards made for his mother's accounts. With his expertise it had been a simple matter, and no one was as yet the wiser. He cringed inwardly when he thought about what she would do or say when she found out he was everything she thought he was. He couldn't think about that now. He had to think about his own survival.

When he thought about those rigs on I-95 that kept boxing him in on three sides while Helen got away, he became furious all over again. Only his knowing she would go to the Tyger ranch kept him going.

He'd dumped the rental car he hadn't paid for in Oklahoma and hitched a ride the rest of the way. Let them try and find him. You couldn't get blood out of a stone. What was the worst thing they could do to him? Send him to counseling for credit-card overuse. Yeah, right. The ATM card might be a little more trouble. First they had to find him, and he didn't plan on spending any length of time in one place if he could help it.

You are going to pay for this, Helen. So help me God, when I get my hands on you, you will beg me for mercy. I wish you knew how much I hate you. I'm going to tell you. I'm going to get right in your face and tell you, and then you won't have a face left.

Daniel sat for a moment trying to compose his features. It wouldn't do for him to look like anything other than a weary camper home from a long trip. It was his cover story for the way he looked—unkempt, unshaven, and weary. When he felt confident he had his emotions under control, he turned off the laptop, reminding himself that he would have to charge the battery soon.

Two hours later, Daniel parked his newly rented car in the lot of a Holiday Inn. He registered without a problem and proceeded to his room, where he shaved and showered before donning clean clothes. He was in the Crown Victoria in less than an hour, headed for the nearest steak house, where he ordered a two-pound T-bone steak, a loaded baked potato, salad, and a fifty-dollar bottle of

wine. He consumed it all. He leaned back and lit a cigarette, daring
the waitress to tell him to put it out. He smiled when he thought
of how he'd tricked an old lady into calling the Tyger ranch,
instructing her to ask for Jake Ramos. He'd told her his ears were
blocked from the long cross-country plane ride, and she'd believed
him. She'd said a nice lady answered the phone and said she must
have the wrong number. She'd been so apologetic. He'd thanked
her profusely and said he must have copied the numbers wrong.
Helen was at the Tyger ranch, but then he'd known that's where
she would go. Why not? The place was hers now. His too. They
were still married. Isabel Tyger, stupid bitch that she was, had
screwed up. That screwup was going to net him half of her estate.
Possibly all of it.

In the Crown Victoria that was supposed to be a nonsmoking
car, Daniel lit a second cigarette. His plan was to drive to the ranch,
walk up to the door, and ring the bell. If necessary, he would
shoot off the lock, at which point anything could happen. He was
prepared. For everything and anything. For one split second he
paused in his thinking to wonder if he'd crossed over the edge.

Helen roamed through the empty ranch house. She'd never felt
so alone in her life. Artie and Gerry had gone to Los Angeles and
wouldn't be back until tomorrow night, when she was to return
with them in the Tyger corporate jet. Julia hadn't arrived yet, and
Sam hadn't been in contact with either the vet or Daniel's old boss.
She missed Lucie so much she felt like crying.

She toyed with the idea of going on the computer to check out
her web site to see how her fledgling business was doing.

For five days the story of Boots and the ten tiny graves had
haunted her. She wanted to do something. There were no pictures
of the dog Boots that Isabel had loved so dearly, but Gerry and
Artie had described every hair, every whisker on the dog's body.
The pups as well. Tears blurred her vision when she thought of
their deaths and how it had affected the three old friends. Lucie's
tiny face surfaced in front of her. She had to do something so she
wouldn't think about the meeting she had to attend in Los Angeles
tomorrow afternoon. She was going to take Isabel Tyger's place in

the boardroom. She. Helen Stanley. Artie and Gerry were paving the way, preparing the management team for the arrival of the new owner who would expect . . . what?

Helen flopped down on Isabel's favorite chair and reached for her sketch pad. She was so engrossed in what she was doing and because there was no dog to bark a warning, she had no idea anyone was on the premises until the doorbell rang. With Artie and Gerry in Los Angeles, who would be calling at this hour? Gerry said no one came to the ranch unless they were invited. A shiver of fear ran up and down her arms as she contemplated answering the door. Was it locked? She couldn't remember. Should she turn on the house lights? While sketching, it had grown dark and she'd switched on the reading lamp, but the rest of the house was in total darkness. Better to leave them off, she decided as she made her way to the front door. She saw that the dead bolt was firmly in place.

Sam? Sam would have arrived with his hand on the horn shouting her name every inch of the way up the long driveway. Julia? Lucie would be barking her little head off. That left Daniel. Daniel knew all about this house. He'd been here often enough when ComStar did all Isabel Tyger's work for the foundation.

Helen ran through the dining room and out to the kitchen just as Daniel walked through the door. He looked exactly the way he looked on all those other days when he returned home from work. She looked into his eyes the way she had back then and saw the exact same things. He was in a violent mood.

"Were you waiting for me, Helen?"

"No, Daniel, I was not waiting for you." God, where was the carving knife? The trucker she'd given her gun to had promised to get it to her on his next trip to California. A lot of good that was going to do her now. It had to be behind her somewhere on the counter and too far away to be of any help. She had no weapon of any kind unless she counted the bright red teakettle.

"I'm sick of your bullshit, Helen. It's got to stop once and for all. Why aren't you cooking dinner? I don't see any dishes on the table, and I don't smell anything."

"Because I already ate, that's why. Get out of here, Daniel. You don't belong here. This is my house, not yours."

"What's yours is mine, and don't ever sass me again."

"Or what?" Helen managed to say as she stalled for time. "I'm not afraid of you anymore, Daniel, so don't threaten me. If you do, you'll be sorry."

"That's almost funny coming from you. Let's sit down and talk about how we're going to spend old Isabel's money. With a lot of hard work and ingenuity, I think I can destroy ComStar and Arthur King."

"You aren't getting one cent of the Tyger money. I plan to give it all away. It won't matter to you because you'll be in jail. I'm going to see to it that they lock you up forever. If you don't leave, I'm going to call the police."

"Go to it. Well, what are you waiting for? Call them. You should never make a threat unless you mean to carry it out. Now, sit down! That's a goddamn order, Helen."

"You know what you can do with your orders, Daniel. I told you. I'm not afraid of you anymore."

Helen slowly inched her way around the table until she was directly in front of the butcher-block knife holder. The carving knife was the longest, the one with the biggest handle and sharpest blade. As long as the kitchen chair was in front of her, she could swivel around, grab the knife, and do whatever she had to do.

She saw the gun then. "If you kill me, Daniel, you'll spend your life in jail. You'll never get to spend the money. What will your parents think? Too many people know what you did. They'll all testify against you. Even that nurse Maggie whatever her name was has a story to tell about you. Arthur King told me all about her. Everything is documented. Just go away, Daniel. Leave me alone. Think about your family."

"My mother said you were trailer-park trash. She said it was fitting that I ended up with someone like you. You turned my own mother against me."

"I never even met your mother, Daniel, just like you never met my mother. You said your mother didn't want anything to do with you because you married me. She didn't even know me. Guess what, I don't like her either."

"There you go, lying again. I met your mother yesterday. I told her I was from the insurance company that paid her $25,000. I told her she had to pay it all back now that you're alive. Guess what! She took off. She isn't going to be one bit of help to you. You're just like my mother and sister. You think you're better than anyone else. You think you know everything. I'll show you and them, too."

"By doing what, Daniel?" One more inch and she could safely swing for the knife. She eyed the gun that looked rock-steady in her husband's hands. Maybe she should drop to a crouch, shove the chair toward him, and run through the open door. She might have the element of surprise on her side for a few seconds. As Gerry would say, it was a plan, but would it work?

"I told you to sit down, Helen. I want you to write up a will."

"Not in this lifetime."

"Do it, Helen." She heard the safety on the gun snick back. She could still do it. If she was fast enough, even if he fired, the bullet might go wild. She'd be on the floor, the last place he would expect her to be. She didn't stop to think, didn't stop to worry about a bullet going into her body. She dropped to the ground and shoved the chair across the floor. With one wild kick in the general direction of her husband, a second chair moved, and she hit the open door at a dead run.

The darkness swallowed her up almost immediately.

Behind her she could hear the angry crunch of heavy feet on dry leaves. She could smell her husband's fear, or was it her own?

Don't look back.

Don't think.

Run!

28

She was sitting on the front porch, a small dog cradled in her arms. Even from this distance, Sam could see that it wasn't Helen. He wanted to cry in frustration. Men didn't cry. *Bullshit,* he thought. *If I want to cry, I'll damn well cry.*

Max plopped one massive foot on the button and unhooked his seat belt, then let out a howl that set the fine hairs on the back of Sam's neck on end. "Okay, okay, let me stop the damn car, okay. Yeah, yeah, it's Lucie. Oh, hell, go on and go!" Sam said as he slowed his truck and opened the door. Max flew up the rest of the driveway, where he skidded to a stop. He danced and pawed the ground, finally picking up Lucie by the scruff of the neck and walking over to the car but not before he let out one earsplitting bark of pure joy. He held up the little dog as much as to say, here she is.

"Hey, little lady, where's your mistress?" Sam said, scratching the Yorkie behind her ears.

"I guess you must be Sam. Max and I are acquainted. I'm Julia Martin. I just got here about half an hour ago. Helen doesn't seem to be home, and there are no lights on."

"I'm Sam Tolliver," Sam said, holding out his hand. "Did you go around back?"

"No. Helen must not be home because Lucie would have wanted me to put her down. She just wanted me to hold her. I guess they missed each other," Julia said, pointing to the dogs.

"That's probably the understatement of the year," Sam said. "I just took a chance and came here thinking this was where Helen would come. I've been trying all day to reach those two old coots who seem to be running things and there's been no answer at any of the numbers they gave me. Do you have any idea where Helen might go?"

"Like you, I thought she would come here, so that's why I'm here. I'm too tired to go any farther. I'm going to sleep right here on this front porch. For three whole days."

"Let's check out the back before you get comfortable. I'm assuming this door is locked."

"I did try it and I called Helen's name. Even if she was sleeping, she would have heard me. It's kind of funny, though, Lucie hasn't barked. That tells me Helen isn't here. I am the first to admit I know very little about animals. She's been shaking so badly I had to put her inside my shirt so she could feel my heartbeat. I'm basically a stranger to her. I think I was just too tired to walk around the back. I've been driving with only catnaps the last forty-eight hours."

"Welcome to the club," Sam said, holding out his hand to pull Julia to her feet.

"There's an Avis rental car here. Guess Helen needed some wheels. Oh, oh, what have we here?" Sam said as he walked up the small incline to the back door that was standing wide open. Lucie pawed at his leg to be picked up.

"Something must have happened," Julia said as she picked up one of the kitchen chairs. "This room is too neat and tidy with the exception of these two overturned chairs. You know, dinner's over, you clean up, everything is in its place for morning. The knife rack is out of place, and the big knife is gone. I notice stuff like that," Julia said fearfully. "Furthermore, why would Helen rent a car when Isabel Tyger must have left her some vehicles? There's a big garage right across the way that has four doors, so that must mean there are four cars at Helen's disposal. Guests, unexpected or otherwise, leave their cars in the open. Owners garage their cars. Nobody leaves their door wide open, especially at night. What should we do, Sam?" Her fear was so palpable, Sam cringed.

"I say we call the police. Now!"

"I agree. Then what?"

"We start to look for her. We have an edge here with Max. He'll find her. I hope it is that goddamn husband of hers. I want to kill that son of a bitch with my bare hands," Sam said, as Julia dialed 911. He listened as she rattled off the location and her worry about Helen.

"I'm just as worried as you are, Sam, and you might have to fight me if that bastard surfaces. I want to kill him as much as you do. Let me see if I can find a flashlight. Neither one of us knows this area. Does your dog need something to pick up Helen's scent?"

"No."

Julia opened and closed kitchen drawers until she found a flashlight. "Okay, we're in business. I'll carry Lucie, and you take the flashlight."

"Find Helen, Max. Go, boy!"

Max sprinted off into the darkness, Julia and Sam behind him.

Helen crouched low behind a dense thicket, her breathing ragged, her adrenaline pumping. She prayed that she wouldn't cough or make some noise that would give away her hiding spot. She could hear Daniel stomping through the underbrush ahead of her. She had no way of knowing where she was or how far from the house she'd come. All she knew was she was exhausted.

Overhead, the clouds parted, the three-quarter moon lighting the night. "Damn," she muttered as she waited for a sign that Daniel was far enough ahead of her so she could double back to the house and call the police. The only problem was, she didn't know which direction the house was. There were no pinpoints of light to show her the way. The house could be anywhere.

Helen could feel a cough building in her chest that was going to erupt at any moment. She clamped her hand over her mouth just as a vicious cramp settled in the calf of her leg. She tried to inch her leg forward so she could massage it. The next thing she knew she was flat on her back, and Daniel had both her ankles in his hands.

"You're so fucking predictable, Helen, it's pathetic."

"Let go of me," Helen gasped.

Daniel ignored her as he started to drag her forward. Fallen branches and rocks gouged her neck and back. A branch with sharp ends whipped across her face. She felt something drip down her cheek and neck. Blood. "All right, Daniel. All right. You can have it all. Now, let me go."

Daniel swung around, dropping his viselike grip on Helen's ankles. "I thought you weren't afraid of me."

"I lied. I'm petrified. You aren't stupid, Daniel. If you hurt me, or if you kill me, you'll get nothing. Everything will be tied up for *years*. Years, Daniel. You need me to *give* it all to you. Give. That's the key word here. Not a will. A will would be suspect. You of all people should know that. They'll say you coerced me into signing it. We can go to the attorney's office tomorrow, and I'll sign every-thing over to you. They know I don't want the money. I told them so from the get-go. They won't question my decision."

Helen looked up. Another few minutes and the clouds would sail across the moon. Maybe she could get away. Obviously, Daniel was thinking the same thing. He reached for her to pull her to her feet.

Helen felt the air stir, saw something streak past her, and then she was free and on her knees. "Max!" The Lab barked as he planted himself on Daniel's chest, his huge head almost touching Daniel's face. Even from where she was kneeling she could see the shine to his lustrous coat.

He held out his arms and she ran into them. "Sam."

"It's me. In the flesh. Is that some dog or what?"

"That's some dog all right!"

"Get this mutt off me!" Daniel bellowed.

"I-don't-think-so!" Sam said. "That dog has incredible staying power. He's staying right where he is until the police get here, which should be very shortly. Then again, maybe they won't get here for hours. How does assault with intent to kill sound, Mr. Ward? From where I'm standing, it couldn't happen to a nicer person."

"Fuck you!" Daniel spat.

"Give him a swat for that, Max. You never curse in front of a lady, Mr. Ward."

The big Lab lifted his front paw and pressed down on Daniel's nose. Sam laughed as he squeezed Helen tighter. "Hey, look who's here!"

"Lucie! Oh, God, Lucie, it really is you. Come here, baby. It's okay. Your buddy has things under control. Take a look. Shhh, it's okay. He's never going to hurt either one of us again. I missed you so much." The little dog licked her face, her eyes, her neck as she snuggled against the one person she loved more than anything in the world.

"He is your friend, your partner, your defender, your dog.
You are his life, his love, his leader.
He will be yours, faithful and true, to the last beat of his
*   heart.*
You owe it to him to be worthy of such devotion."

"Cicero said that. Boots sent me that in an e-mail once. I understood it, but I didn't understand it if you know what I mean. Now I know what to do about it. Are the police coming?" she whispered.

"Julia called them. They should be here any minute. What the hell were you thinking of, Helen? There are no words to tell you how worried and scared I've been."

"I don't know, Sam. I thought . . . I wanted to find a way to trap him somehow. I was trying to find my way back to the house to call the police. Ah, I hear the siren now. I hope we can find our way back."

"I'm staying here with this bastard until the police cart him off. You and Julia head back. We made a pretty good path. The cloud cover is easing up."

"I love you, Sam."

"I love you more."

They watched the police car's blue-and-red lights until it was out of sight. "Is this the end of it, Sam?"

"I think so, honey. All you have to do is have your lawyer explain everything tomorrow morning when you go down to the police station to file charges. The paperwork is going to be horrendous, but it will get resolved. He's not going to bother you again. The way he was babbling when they put him in the car tells me he's way over the edge."

"Can I go to bed, Helen?" Julia asked.

"Of course you can go to bed. Take any room you want. I'm going to sit here all night with my fella and tell him how much I love him."

"I'll say good night then. Are you sure you're okay?"

"I'm fine, Julia. Thanks for patching me up. I might look a little beat-up, but I feel fine so I don't want you worrying about me. Sleep tight."

"All night? We're going to talk all night?" Sam said, when the door closed behind Julia.

"Uh-huh, all night. Did you ever make love under the stars, Sam?"

"No."

"Me either. Want to try it? It's exceptionally warm, almost like spring. We can always talk later."

"Yeah, yeah, that sounds like a plan to me."

Helen laughed. "You sound like Artie. With him and Gerry, everything is a plan. Sam, I have so much to tell you. I . . . I told them I would accept the inheritance Boots left me. Tell me right now if it will make a difference to you."

"Helen, rich or poor, I will love you forever and ever. I loved you before I knew you were rich."

"It pretty much means you'll have to move out here. Can you handle that?"

"Whither thou goest . . ."

Helen winced when she lowered herself to the blanket under the stars. "You notice, I came prepared." Sam grinned.

"I noticed. It's so beautiful out. There must be a *zillion* stars out tonight," Helen said as she braced herself for Sam's kiss. His lips were gentle against her brow, slipping into her hairline and descending in a path to the sensitive skin at her ear. She was aware of the spicy scent of his aftershave, of the close stubble of beard on his chin, of the softness of his lips as they traced patterns across her cheeks.

Helen closed her eyes and sighed. Sam was a man who knew how to be tender, to wait for a woman's response, and artfully bring her to full awareness of herself as a woman and of him as a man.

Gently, his hand cupped her face, lifting her chin, raising her lips to his own. Then, just when she thought he would release her, his kiss deepened, the moist tip of his tongue smoothing the satiny underside of her lips and penetrating ever so softly, ever so slowly, into the recesses of her mouth.

A riot of emotions rivered through Helen as she brought up her arms and encircled his back, her fingers smoothing over his shirt, feeling the smooth plane of muscle that bespoke energy, vitality and caring. Prolonging contact between them, she offered herself to his kiss, knowing that this man had kindled her spark of womanhood and she wanted him to bring it to a flame.

Feeling her moist lips soften and part, Sam groaned softly as he moved his mouth hungrily over hers, tasting, savoring the feel of her lips.

Helen could feel her breath coming in ragged little gasps as she kissed him deeply, searchingly. Nothing mattered to her, not Daniel, not Julia, or Boots's inheritance. The only thing that mattered was Sam.

She kissed him as she had never kissed another man. There had been other kisses, other caresses, but none that elicited this response in her.

His gentle fingers caressed her cheek, and when he spoke, his voice was husky with emotion, little more than a whisper wafting through the night. His hand cupped her throat, and he could feel the abandoned rhythmn of her pulses, which sent a streak of fire through him. He'd wanted her from the moment he laid eyes on her. How many times he'd told her that and now he was going to tell her again ... with actions instead of words ...

They were hidden from the eyes of the world, here under the stars. He would take her slowly so as to savor every exquisite moment in the pleasure they would once again share together. Only having her, losing himself within her, would satisfy.

A golden warmth flooded through Helen as Sam brought his mouth to hers. He drew a path from one breast to the other, covering each first with his hands and then with his lips. She clung to the strength of his arms, holding fast as though she were fearful of falling in on herself, never to be found again.

His hands spanned her waist and rounded to her buttocks, lifting her slightly from the blanket. Tortuous, teasing explorations of his tongue made her shudder. Her fingers clutched and pulled at his hair while her body arched into his, feverishly exposing herself to his maddening mouth. He searched for and found the secret places that pushed her to the brink of release, only to have his kiss follow another path before returning again to the first.

A yearning spread through Helen, demanding satisfaction, settling at her core and forcing her to seek relief by writhing and thrashing about restlessly. Sam held her there, forcing her to him, adoring her with his hands and lips until she could no longer deny herself. Her body flamed, her back arched, and her world divided in two parts: her need and his lips. And when the tremors ceased, and his mouth covered hers once again, she tasted herself there. She was satisfied, yet discontented; she had feasted, yet she was famished. There was more she wanted—much, much more. She wanted to share with him the release of his own passion, to participate in bringing him the same wonder.

Moving with him, becoming part of him, Helen fueled his passion and renewed her own. Together they were flung upward; together they found the moon.

Sam's chest heaved, his breathing raspy as Helen settled in the crook of his arm.

"I thought I had lost you," Sam whispered.

"You could never lose me, Sam. I love you too much ever to let that happen. I left because I was afraid ..."

"Shhh," Sam said, placing his index finger on her lips. "We already spent too much of our lives talking about Daniel Ward. He's behind bars where he belongs. That's the end of it. Okay?"

Helen sighed. It was almost too good to be true. "Okay," she whispered in return.

They slept under the stars, their bodies pressed together as one.

The sun peeked over the horizon at the same moment Helen opened her eyes. She lay quietly, staring at the man next to her.

How dear he was. How vulnerable he looked in sleep. Only God knew how much she loved him.

"Do I pass muster?" Sam drawled.

"You faker. You're awake!"

"I've been awake for a long time. I didn't want to move my arm and wake you. Do you think we can get up now?"

"We *have* to get up. I must call Artie and Gerry. I'm supposed to go to a board meeting in Los Angeles. A limo is picking me up, and then I have to go in the private jet. Don'tcha love it, Sam?" She chortled. "We'll be back by six. You can come along if you like."

"I'll wait here for you. What about the police and filing charges?"

"I'll stop on my way to the airport and sign a paper or whatever it is I have to do. You don't think I'll have to see . . ."

"No. I'm going to take a shower and whip us up some breakfast. This man cannot live on love. You need to know that, Helen," Sam said, tweaking her cheek.

"Guess what, this woman can't live on love either. I'll take two eggs over easy, lots of toast, no bacon, too many nitrates. Lots of jam and soft butter. Make a big pot of coffee, too."

"Yes, ma'am. I love you, Helen Stanley."

"I love you, Sam Tolliver. Where are the dogs?"

Sam smiled. "Over there under the tree. Max has Lucie cradled between his paws. Ah, here they come. Man and woman's best friends."

"Sam, you have no idea. I have a story to tell you that will break your heart. Later, though. I just realized something. We have the rest of our lives to talk about things. Kiss me. Tell me how much you love me, Sam."

He did. "I love you more than I loved you yesterday, and tomorrow I will love you even more. Forever and ever and into eternity."

"You're just a smooth-talking dandy, as Artie would say."

"Smooth, eh? I don't think I've ever been called smooth before."

"Trust me. You're smooth. I love smooth. Smooth is good. Boy is it good," Helen said, swatting him on the tush as she sashayed past him on her way to the bathroom.

Sam looked down at the dogs. "And she says I have a way with words."

29

She was nervous. She wished now that she had made arrangements to be seated in the boardroom before the others arrived. Artie and Gerry had said no, she was to walk in like she owned the place. Which she did. She took a deep breath, knowing she looked her best considering the circumstances. If they wanted to pick her apart, let them. She clutched at the manila folder in her hands.

Inside the wood-paneled room, Helen's gaze raked those seated at the long, shiny conference table. All men, and they were all staring at her with sober faces. There didn't appear to be one friendly face in the group. Perhaps they were worried about job security. Her back stiffened as she nodded slightly to show the men they should take their seats. Helen cleared her throat. "Good morning, everyone. I'm Helen Stanley. Why don't we go through the meeting as if Miss Tyger were here? Tell me your names and what it is each of you does at Tyger Toys. When we finish, I'll offer my input. I do have input," she said firmly. She saw grimaces and imagined she could hear suppressed groans.

Helen half listened to the boring minutes as her mind wandered to Sam and the events of the night before. She wasn't going to think about Daniel. Not now, not ever. Daniel was in other hands, and his family would have to deal with whatever was meant to happen to him. He was out of her life for good now. Hopefully, trained professionals would help him, along with his family. Thinking about him was just wasted energy. Thinking about Sam and how much she loved him was going to take up all her time from here on in.

Tonight they were going to sit down and talk about their future and what Boots's legacy was going to mean to both of them. Her hands in her lap, she crossed her fingers. Sam would work with her, support whatever it was she wanted to do. Max and Lucie would be together. She would continue with her business. Sam would continue teaching. What more could she possibly want? Children. Lots and lots of children. Gerry and Artie would make wonderful stand-in grandparents. If they stayed at the ranch, the two old men could continue making the daily pilgrimages they couldn't seem to give up. Everyone would be happy. She smiled. Life was going to be so good.

Helen felt Artie nudge her ankle. It was her turn to speak. She looked around at the expectant faces. Were they worried about their jobs or were they worried about change? The new broom sweeping clean kind of thinking.

"For now, I want to see things continue as before. I'm new to this position, and I haven't had time to fully learn about the toy business. I will learn, though, because Isabel Tyger entrusted this company to me. I won't disappoint her. However, at some point we will be making some changes to move this company forward."

Helen opened the folder in front of her for the sketch she'd made the day before. She unfolded it and held it up. "I want you all to take a look at this picture. It's going to be our new toy. A mascot of sorts. This toy is what's going to move this business forward so that we are in a position to compete with the big guys. I want you all to look at it very carefully. I want this particular toy— family actually—manufactured and ready for next year's Christmas season. The dog's name is . . . *Boots*. The pups need names, all nine of them. Collectibles. Plush, soft, squeezable. A toy for a child to love and snuggle with. I want to see a blow-your-socks-off marketing campaign." She looked at the faces as the picture was passed around the table. She didn't see one iota of genuine interest. When the picture was in her hands again, she spoke softly. "Perhaps you didn't understand what I just said. This is not negotiable. We *will* manufacture this toy. Those of you who disagree or those of you who feel you can't give one hundred percent, leave now. I can have a new team in here in forty-eight hours. We'll meet here again one month from today. I urge you to be creative. I want to see a prototype, and I want a good one. Don't even think about *sloughing* this off with an inferior stuffed animal. I won't tolerate it. For now we can go with a show of hands."

Limp hands waved in the air. She didn't see a single smile, and the lack of enthusiasm rattled her. Artie and Gerry stared at her, wondering what she was going to do next. Obviously, she was supposed to do something. She did. Both hands smacked down on the shiny table surface. "Your lack of enthusiasm bothers me. You cannot hide in a room and look outside once in a while. Your toys are serviceable, stodgy, with no individuality. In short, they're so outdated they are pitiful. Plus," Helen's voice rose to the point of shrillness, "there are no girl toys. I don't care if a Tyger toy lasts for fifty years. It's . . . it's positively un-American for toys not to break. I cannot even begin to imagine why you don't manufacture toys for girls. You need to move forward. You need to find out what children want today. Girls want toys, too. We'll start small with Boots. One month, gentlemen. You are dismissed!" she said coldly.

Helen pushed her chair back and was gathering up her tote bag when she heard a titter and the word feather. She thought she heard the word chain, but she wasn't sure. Her face flamed. She swung around. "Say it to my face, sir."

A portly man with a bald head had the grace to look embarrassed. He stood, shuffled his feet, but stood his ground. "I have to wonder what selling feathers and belly chains has to do with the toy business. This is a family toy business. We make toys for families, families that depend on us for quality."

"One has to wonder, then, what you were doing viewing my web page. Am I to assume that you've all viewed the new owner's site? And am I to assume you all pretty much disapprove? I see. I'll take this under consideration when we meet again, one month from today, at which time we'll review everyone's performance report. Good day, gentlemen."

Helen flopped down on the chair the moment the conference door closed. She looked at Artie and Gerry. "I want to know why Isabel Tyger put up with this. There wasn't one employee in this room under the age of fifty. I have nothing against age. Where are the bright shining lights? Where are the young thinkers? What happened to innovation? Where are the toys of today, tomorrow, and the future?"

"This was the one thing Izzie was afraid to tamper with. Her great-grandfather built this company, then her grandfather ran it, and when he passed it went to her father. She hated it. She associated it with her own childhood. As long as the company made money and she was able to do what she wanted, she was okay with it. She hated these meetings because the employees treated her just the way they treated you. My advice would be to buy out their contracts, give them a good package, and start over with a crackerjack team. Artie and I will be glad to interview, hire, and put together a team who can move this company forward," Gerry said.

"I gave them a month," Helen fretted. "I wouldn't want someone to do that to me without giving me a chance. They are of an age where money is needed for retirement. I have to give them a chance."

Artie hooted with laughter. "Each and every one of the men seated at the conference table is independently wealthy. All they do is come in here for a few hours a day and collect a paycheck at the end of the week. Izz hated the way things ran, but she wouldn't change it. The company runs itself the way it has for the past hundred years. Each year they make X number of wagons, X number of trucks or whatever it is they sell. I was never interested enough to make further inquiries. As I said, the company runs itself. In spite of all that, Tyger Toys shows a tidy profit at the end of each fiscal year. If you fired the lot of them right now, the only thing you would hurt is their pride. The flip side to this is they don't like dealing with women. Izz just couldn't handle it, so she ignored it."

"I guess what you're saying is they won't make the effort to make up a prototype. They'll come in the next time and try to convince me it shouldn't be done, is that it?"

"Yes," Artie and Gerry said in unison.

"Okay. Let's put together a team. Right away."

"Helen, don't let what they said about your other business bother you," Gerry said.

"I won't. One has nothing to do with the other. Sassie Lassie is all mine. Mine and Sam's. I'll never let that go. Who knows, I might even be able to give Victoria what's her name a run for her money." Helen laughed. "Can we leave now? This place is so depressing. All this dark, dismal paneling, all those antiquated toys in the showroom that have six inches of dust on them. Cleaning this all up and using bright paint is my next project. Right now I just want to get back to Sam. Are you coming with me?"

"No, we'll stay here and get started on your new team. You run along and take care of Sam. Give him our regards."

Helen debated a moment before she threw her arms around both men. "I want to thank you for everything. Most of all, I want to thank you for being Boots's friends. She must have loved both of you very much. I'm just sorry I never got to know her the way you did. I'll do my best to live up to her expectations. Call me," she said airily.

"All's well that ends well, eh, Gerry?"

"I'd say so. I'll bet this is going to be some place when our Helen gets done with it. Young blood, bright ideas. Clean white paint. A toy company should look like a toy company. She was right about something else, too. It's downright un-American for toys not to break." Artie rubbed his hands together in anticipation of what was to come.

"This might be a whole new career for us, Artie. All we have to do is sit and talk. Nothing physical unless we get excited. That means no arthritis flare-ups."

"Izz made the right choice. I was worried there for a while. Our Helen is going to do just fine. Once the police and Daniel's doctors see all those picture we took of his apartment, things will straighten out. It all came full circle. I hope *she* knows what we're doing."

"She knows," Gerry said emphatically.

Artie jumped out of the way when one of the dusty wooden wagons slipped from the peg that was holding it to the wall.

"Told you." Gerry laughed.

"You slammed the door. It came loose and fell," Artie said, looking upward.

"Oh yeah."

"Yeah." Artie grinned.

"I love making love to you." Sam sighed happily.

"And I love it when you make love to me," Helen said just as happily. "More wine?"

"Fill that baby to the top," Sam said, holding out a fragile, long-stemmed glass.

"If we're going to stay here, we need to get a bigger bed," Helen said. "We need to talk, Sam."

"Yes, we do. Whatever you want to do is okay with me. I do have to finish out the semester back in Jersey. It's just a few weeks. I can look for a job here. I don't have to worry about furniture. He destroyed it all. I literally have nothing to pack. Are you going to like living in this house, Helen?"

"For now. It would be a great place to bring up kids. The dogs can run to their hearts' content. I can't . . . I won't abandon that little cemetery. Artie and Gerry need a place to visit. For now, Sam. There's so much property. We can build something later on. Are you sure you're okay with this?"

"I'm okay with the part where we live on my salary and bank whatever you make from Sassie Lassie. I'm not okay with the Tyger money. I'll help you with the foundation and any other charitable endeavors you want to explore. I have to pay off my student loans. Me. Not you. Not Isabel Tyger. In case you haven't noticed, I'm a man of integrity."

"Oh, I noticed. There isn't one little thing that I didn't notice about you. I set my cap for you, Sam. Isn't it wonderful that it all worked out?"

"It's a miracle if you ask me. So you're going to do all kinds of good things with that money, huh?"

"You bet."

"I checked your web site while you were in Los Angeles. You're going to be up to your neck in belly chains. You are going to have to hire some help. It's mind-boggling. Whoever would have thought a belly chain would be so popular."

"Sam, do you remember how I told you I used to pass a fancy

lingerie shop on the way home from school? Well, one time there was a mannequin dressed like a Greek goddess in the window. They had it dressed in a silky sheath with a shiny gold chain with a medallion that dropped below the waist. I just thought it was the most beautiful thing I ever saw. I was young and impressionable. I guess it stayed with me. It's a fad for now. Kind of like those spike-heeled shoes.

"Sam, when do you think all the paperwork will be settled, and I can go back to being Helen Stanley?"

"I don't know, Helen. What I do know is, we're getting married the day everything is cleared up. I'll keep tabs on those lawyers and the people who are dealing with Daniel Ward. I don't want you worrying about any of this. All I want you to do is concentrate on me, the dogs, Sassie Lassie, and doing what Isabel Tyger wanted you to do."

"You know what I want to do, Sam?"

"What?" He leered.

"I want to make love to you."

"Best offer today. Is it today or is it tomorrow?"

"Who cares? It's now that's important."

"God, I love you, Helen."

"I love you more," Helen said.

"Always and forever."

"And into eternity." Helen smiled.

Epilogue

~

"By this time tomorrow I will be Mrs. Sam Tolliver. Getting married on Christmas Eve is so special. I want to believe it was meant to happen this way. Best of all, Sam will never be able to forget our anniversary. I am so happy I could just ... bust! Thank you so much, Julia, for agreeing to be my maid of honor."

"You're absolutely giddy, Helen. I've never seen you like this. I hope you will always be this happy. I want to thank you again for ... my lottery winnings. And for the belly chain. You gave me a life I couldn't have had otherwise. And on top of that, I met this wonderful man on that cruise you insisted I take. He's arriving late this afternoon. I told him the whole story about my past. Like Sam, he said whatever came before doesn't matter. You gave me the courage to leave the shelter and go back to my own identity. That was the biggest flaw, Helen. We are who we are. While this bravado may not be for all the people who walk through those doors, it works for some of us. Thanks to you. What in the world am I going to do with a million dollars?"

"I don't have a clue, Julia. You said if you won the lottery you would know what to do with it. That's how much the New Jersey lottery was the week I wrote the check. If that's all you have to worry about in this new life of yours, then you're home free."

"Are you and Sam going to visit me and Tom?"

"Tom is it? You sound like you've made up your mind. Are you going to go back to Montana with him?"

"Yes."

"Then I'm happy for you."

"Is your mother coming to the ceremony, Helen? What about Daniel's sister?"

"I'm not sure about my mother. I invited her. The boys found her for me. That's how I think of Artie, Gerry, and Sam—the boys. I bought her a little house with a nice garden. I took her shopping for new clothes and furniture. I asked her if she could have anything in the world, what would she want. She wanted a face-lift. If the swelling and bruising go down, she might come. I'm not counting on it. I set aside money for her so she never has to work again. We're civil to one another. There's no motherly love there, and I have to accept that. I wish it were different. Isn't it strange, Julia? We always want what we can't have. Daniel's sister never responded to the invitation, so we don't expect her."

"Looks to me like you have it all."

"Oh, God, Julia, I do have it all. All my dreams have come true."

"What about Daniel?"

"That's a long, depressing story. Don't ask me why, but I went to see him. I guess I wanted to see for myself that he wasn't going to be a threat to me any longer. He didn't recognize me. I almost didn't recognize him. He's got a beard and a mustache and he wears those one-piece suits and slippers. He more or less shuffles his way around, if you know what I mean. I found out he was a ward of the state. His mother refuses to have anything to do with him. His father more or less closed up shop. He was paying for him until his money ran out. The foundation is paying now. I know, I know, don't say it, Julia. It was Sam's idea. I balked, but he said it was the humane thing to do, and he was right. I guess he's happy, if that's possible, in his own little world. I'm told he pecks away at a computer all day long. That chapter of my life is gone now. I try not to look back."

"I hope you two are talking about me," Sam said, taking Helen in his arms.

"We were. We said only the nicest things. That's because there wasn't anything bad to say."

"I want to show you ladies something," Sam said, turning the television on for the noon hour news.

"What is it?" Helen asked anxiously.

Sam snorted. "I think it's a last hurrah of some kind. Those are screaming, yelling, fighting-mad mothers who have been waiting in line for Boots and her puppies. This particular store just got a shipment of twenty-five thousand and of those twenty-five thousand, ninety-nine percent of them were rainchecks, which means if there's a mother fighting for one and she doesn't have a raincheck, she isn't going to get it. Boots is the biggest toy seller of all time according to the people who track things like this. How did you know, Helen?"

"I didn't know. I did it as a tribute to Isabel Tyger. That little dog meant the world to her just the way Lucie means the world to me. I guess it will put Tyger Toys on the toy map. I hope she knows."

"I'm sure she does, honey."

"I don't even have one. I was going to keep the prototype, but Artie got the bright idea to auction it off at Thanksgiving for the Leukemia Marathon."

"I'm going to head off for the airport. Can I bring anything back for either of you?" Julia asked.

"Nope. See you at dinner. Julia's going to Montana after the wedding, Sam."

"Good for you, Julia. See you at dinner."

"I'm all yours, Sam."

"Promises, promises."

"I'm so nervous, Julia. Do I look all right? Did I put too much hair spray on? Do these earrings go with my pearls? I think the hem of this dress is an inch too long. What do you think? Something old, something new, something borrowed, something blue. I think I have it all. Do I, Julia? Oh, you look so pretty. Tom is a handsome guy. I like that rugged look. I have too much rouge on. This lipstick isn't the right color. What was I thinking?" Helen babbled.

"Hold it right there. You look perfect. Trust me. I would not let you go to your wedding if one hair was out of place. You're just jittery. All new brides are jittery. We have five minutes. Take a deep breath. I bet Sam is more nervous than you are."

"Sam? Sam could be under fire, and he'd be cool. He doesn't get rattled like I do. Okay, I'm ready."

For one split second Sam thought he swallowed his tongue. She was so beautiful he had a hard time drawing a breath. He wanted to say something but all he could do was stare at his soon-to-be-bride. In just five minutes she would be Mrs. Sam Tolliver. He would have a wife in five minutes. A wave of dizziness threatened to overcome him.

And then she was standing next to him, Artie and Gerry behind them, Julia and Les, Sam's favorite student, to the right of them.

"Dearly beloved, we are . . ."

"Who gives this woman . . ."

"We do," Artie and Gerry chirped in unison.

"Helen, do you take this man, Sam Tolliver, to be your lawfully wedded husband?"

"I do."

"Sam, do you take this woman, Helen Stanley, to be your lawfully wedded wife?"

"I do."

"I now pronounce you man and wife. You may kiss the bride."

When Helen could catch her breath, she turned and gasped. "Mom, you came."

"Well . . . I wasn't sure . . . you look so pretty, Helen. I used to look like you," she said sadly.

"Mrs. Stanley, you're still as pretty as your daughter. I almost can't tell you apart," Sam said gallantly.

"That might be a bit of a fib, young man, but I'll accept the compliment. I brought you a present, Helen. It isn't much. I know you have everything. It's just a little . . . what it is, is your baby bracelet when you were born. I thought you might like to have it and your first baby shoes for your own child."

"Oh, Mom," Helen said, her eyes filling with tears. "Come on, let's have a toast."

"I can't stay, Helen. I . . . I promised to . . . please don't laugh . . . but I promised to sing in the choir for midnight Mass. We're having an early rehearsal."

"Mom, that's great. Will you come for dinner tomorrow?"

"I'd like that, Helen. I'd like that very much. Congratulations to both of you."

"Thanks, Mom."

Tears rolled down Helen's cheeks. Sam kissed them away. "That's the nicest she's ever been to me, Sam."

"Maybe it's the way things will be from now on. This is the season of miracles, isn't it? Look around, Helen. What could be more perfect than this? The Christmas tree is glorious, the house smells heavenly. Our best friends are here. The dogs are happy and healthy and together. I go back to teaching starting next month. We're a couple now. We have a good life and so many tomorrows to look forward to."

"I'm just so happy, Sam."

"Me too, honey."

"We're leaving, too, Helen," Julia said. "Tom wants to go to church before we set out for Montana. I'll say good-bye now. We're going to drop Les off at the airport. He said he doesn't mind hanging out at the airport for an extra hour."

"Promise you'll write and call."

"I promise."

"We'll be on our way, too," Gerry said, his face wistful.

"Oh, no. You two are staying right here with us. We're going to change and take a little walk. All four of us. All six of us if you count the dogs. Then we're going to come back here and open presents. That's some pile," Helen said, pointing to the gifts piled high under the tree. "I spent hours and hours wrapping those presents. I want to be appreciated. Furthermore, you're staying here tonight and we're celebrating Christmas together. In other words, Mr. and Mrs. Sam Tolliver request the honor of your presence for the holiday."

"We accept," Artie said.

"Do we ever," Gerry said.

"This is the first time in all the years of coming here that I don't feel like I've been kicked in the gut," Gerry said.

"I think you made it right, Helen," Artie said.

"I hope so. If I could have any wish in the world right now, it would be that Isabel knows I did my best. Boots and her little family of collectibles will live on forever. Sam said they made toy history."

"She knows," Gerry said.

"Yes, she knows," Artie said.

"It's late, we should be getting back," Sam said, an uneasy feeling settling between his shoulder blades. "It's almost Christmas morning."

The dogs trooped ahead, the others following in single file.

"Egg nog, a chorus of 'Jingle Bells,' and we're off to bed. The presents will have to wait for morning," Artie said.

"I second my friend here," Gerry said.

"I'll pour," Sam said.

"Wait just a minute. Okay, which one of you managed to get me the year's hottest toy and leave it under the tree?" Helen demanded as she picked up the stuffed animal and all the little pups nestled in a wicker basket. "There's kind of a glow to it."

"You can't beg, borrow, or steal one of those," Artie said. "We know, we tried to get you one."

"I did, too, honey. No luck," Sam said.

"Julia didn't leave it, and my mother didn't leave it. It wasn't here when we went down to the cemetery. Why is it glowing like this? Can you see it? Or is it me?"

"I told you she knows," Artie said gruffly.

"You could never keep anything from Izzie. She knew everything," Gerry said.

"I didn't know the lady," Sam said lamely.

"Merry Christmas, Boots," Helen whispered.

And then they were alone.

"Sam?"

"Shhh. It's whatever you want it to be. Let's sit on the couch and enjoy being Mr. and Mrs. Sam Tolliver."

"Sounds like a plan to me." Helen laughed.

"To us," Sam said, clinking his wineglass against Helen's glass.

"To us," Helen said.

Fern Michaels likes to hear from her readers. You can contact her at Fernmic@aol.com.